About the Authors

Kate Hardy has always loved books and could read before she went to school. She discovered Mills & Boon books when she was twelve and decided this was what she wanted to do. When she isn't writing Kate enjoys reading, cinema, ballroom dancing and the gym. You can contact her via her website: katehardy.com

Marion Lennox has written more than a hundred romances and is published in over a hundred countries and thirty languages. Her multiple awards include the prestigious RITA® Award (twice), and the *RT Book Reviews* Career Achievement Award for "a body of work which makes us laugh and teaches us about love." Marion adores her family, her kayak, her dog, and lying on the beach with a book someone else has written. Heaven!

Jessica Matthews's interest in medicine began at a young age, and she nourished it with medical stories and hospital-based television programmes. After a stint as a teenage candy-striper, she pursued a career as a clinical laboratory scientist. When not writing or on duty, she fills her day with countless family and school-related activities. Jessica lives in the central United States, with her husband, daughter and son.

The Forever Family
COLLECTION

July 2019

August 2019

September 2019

October 2019

A Forever Family: Their Christmas Delivery

KATE HARDY

MARION LENNOX

JESSICA MATTHEWS

MILLS & BOON

First Published in Great Britain 2019
By Mills & Boon, an imprint of HarperCollins *Publishers*
1 London Bridge Street, London, SE1 9GF

A FOREVER FAMILY: THEIR CHRISTMAS DELIVERY
© 2019 Harlequin Books S.A.

Her Festive Doorstep Baby © Pamela Brooks 2016
Meant-to-Be Family © Harlequin S.A. 2015
The Child Who Rescued Christmas © Jessica Matthews 2011

ISBN: 978-0-263-27684-8

Special thanks and acknowledgement are given to Marion Lennox for her contribution to the *Midwives On-Call* series

MIX
Paper from
responsible sources
FSC www.fsc.org   **FSC™ C007454**

This book is produced from independently certified FSC™ paper to ensure responsible forest management.

For more information visit: www.harpercollins.co.uk/green

Printed and bound in Spain by CPI, Barcelona

HER FESTIVE
DOORSTEP BABY

KATE HARDY

For Sofia-Grace, the newest baby in our family –
with lots of love on your first Christmas xxx

CHAPTER ONE

Friday 24th December

'HELLO? HELLO?'

There was no answer. It was probably a courier in the middle of a super-frantic shift, Amy thought, needing to deliver as many parcels as humanly possible on Christmas Eve and pressing every single button on the intercom in the hope of finding someone who'd buzz the front door open so they could leave a parcel in the lobby. The silence probably meant they'd stopped waiting for her to answer and were already trying someone else.

She was about to replace the receiver on her intercom system when she heard a noise.

It sounded like a baby crying.

Was it her imagination? Or maybe the courier was listening to something on the radio. An ad, perhaps.

She knew that she was being ridiculous, but something made Amy go out of her own front door and into the main lobby, just to check that everything was all right.

And there, in the corner by the front door, was a cardboard box.

Except she could still hear a baby crying, and this time she was pretty sure it wasn't on a radio.

When she drew closer, she could see that the cardboard box wasn't a parcel at all. The top of the box was open. Inside, wrapped in a soft blanket, was a baby. There were traces of blood on the baby's face and Amy had a moment of panic; but then she thought that the blood might be because the baby was very, very young.

Young enough to be a newborn.

Who on earth would leave a newborn baby in a cardboard box, in the lobby of a block of flats?

She quickly opened the front door and looked outside, but there wasn't anyone in the street who looked as if they'd just left a baby on a doorstep. Nobody running away or huddled in a hoodie, trying to hide their face.

What were you supposed to do when you found an abandoned baby? Should she take the baby straight to hospital to be checked over, or should she ring the police? If she moved the box or picked the baby up to try to soothe it, would she be disturbing forensic evidence that would help the police find the baby's mother?

Yet the baby was so tiny, and the lobby wasn't heated. She could hardly leave the poor little mite to freeze there. She was about to try the other intercoms to see if any of her neighbours was in and could ring the police for her, when the door to the lobby opened and Josh Farnham walked in.

She didn't know Josh very well; he'd moved into one of the flats on her floor about six months ago. They were on smile-and-nod terms, and she occasionally took in a parcel for him, but that was about it.

'Is everything OK?' he asked. And then he frowned as the baby cried again.

'No.' Amy gestured to the cardboard box. 'Someone's just left a baby on our doorstep.'

Josh looked utterly shocked. 'A *baby*? But—who?'

'I have no idea.'

He bent down to touch the baby's hand. Clearly he had the magic touch because the baby immediately stopped crying.

'Someone pressed my intercom but didn't speak,' Amy continued. 'I assumed it was a courier trying to find someone in so they could deliver a parcel to someone in our block, but then I thought I could hear a baby crying.' She spread her hands. 'It could've been on the radio, but something made me come out here to see, just in case. That's when I found the baby.' She bit her lip. 'There's blood on the baby's face, but I think that might be because the baby's a newborn. As in *really* newborn.'

'Have you called the police?' he asked, his blue eyes narrowing.

'I was just about to,' she said, 'but I didn't bring my phone out with me, and I'm not sure if I'm going to mess up the forensics or what have you if I take the baby into my flat.'

'You can hardly wait out here until the police arrive,' Josh said, frowning. 'Both of you would freeze. Look, let me grab some stuff from my flat so I can put up a makeshift barrier round the area where the box is now, to protect any potential evidence, then I'll check the baby over properly while you call the police.' The concern clearly showed in her expression, because he added, 'It's OK. I'm qualified. I'm a doctor in the local emergency department.'

That would explain why she hardly ever saw him. His shifts at the hospital would be very different from her own hours teaching at the local high school. But most of all Amy felt relief that she wasn't going to have to deal with this completely on her own. Where babies were concerned, she was totally clueless, and Josh seemed to know how to deal with them. 'All right. Thanks,' she said.

'I'll be quick,' he promised.

'Should I pick the baby up?' she asked when the crying started again.

'Movement usually helps settle a crying baby. If you walk up and down—obviously avoiding the area where whoever left the baby might've trodden—the baby will probably stop crying.'

That sounded like experience talking. Better and better: because Amy was very used to dealing with teenagers, but her dealings with babies had been minimal.

Especially since Michael had ended their engagement.

She pushed the thought away. *Not now.* She needed to concentrate on helping this abandoned baby, not brood over the wreckage of her past.

'What about supporting the baby's head?' she asked.

'Just hold the baby against you, like this,' Josh said, picking the baby out of the box and then holding the baby close to him to demonstrate, with one hand cradled round the baby's head so it didn't flop back.

'OK.' Carefully, Amy took the baby from him.

His hands brushed briefly against hers and it felt as if she'd been galvanised.

Oh, for pity's sake. Yes, the man was pretty—despite the fact that he needed a shave and she suspected that he'd dragged his fingers rather than a comb through his wavy dark hair—but for all she knew he could be in a serious relationship. This was so inappropriate. Even if he wasn't in a relationship, she didn't want to get involved with anyone. Because then eventually she'd have to admit to her past, and he'd walk away from her—just as Michael had. And then that would make their relationship as neighbours awkward. Amy knew she was better off on her own and keeping all her relationships platonic. Josh Farnham might be one of the most attractive men she'd ever met, but he wasn't for her.

Hoping that he'd mistake her flustered state for nerves about dealing with the baby—which was partially true in any case—Amy murmured something anodyne and started walking up and down the lobby with the baby.

Josh came back what felt like hours later but could only have been five minutes, carrying several tin cans, a pile of bandages, safety pins, a marker pen and a spiral-bound notebook.

'Are you OK to keep holding the baby?' he asked.

No. It was bringing back all kinds of emotions that Amy would much rather suppress. But she wasn't going to burden a near-stranger with her private misery. 'Sure,' she fibbed.

Josh swiftly wrote out some notes saying, *Please do not touch—waiting for police*, then marked off the area where Amy had found the cardboard box. When he'd finished, he held out his arms for the baby. 'My turn, I think,' he said.

'Thanks,' she said, grateful to be relieved of her burden. Though again her hands touched his as they transferred the baby between them, and again she felt that peculiar and inappropriate response to him, that flare of desire. She picked up the box. 'I'd better bring this.'

He nodded. 'Your flat or mine?'

'Mine, I guess,' she said.

She let them into her flat, then called the police and explained what had happened while Josh examined the baby. She couldn't help watching him while she was talking; he was so gentle and yet so sure at the same time. He checked the baby over thoroughly before wrapping the infant in the soft blanket again.

The baby wasn't wearing a nappy and had no clothes. They definitely had a problem here. And what would happen once the baby got hungry? Amy had absolutely nothing in her kitchen that was suitable for a newborn, let alone any way of feeding a baby.

'The police are on their way now. They said they'll contact Social Services and meet them here, too,' she said when she put the phone down. 'How's the baby?'

'Doing fine,' Josh said. 'Our doorstep baby's a little girl. Definitely a newborn. But I'd say she's a couple of weeks early and I'm a bit worried about the mum. She clamped the umbilical cord with one of those clips you use on packaging to keep things fresh, and my guess is she's very young and didn't tell anyone she was having the baby, and she didn't go to hospital so she had the birth somewhere on her own.'

'And then she put the baby in a box and left her in our lobby with no clothes, no nappy, no milk—just the blanket,' Amy said. She winced. 'The poor girl must've really been desperate. Do you see that kind of thing a lot at the hospital?'

'Abandoned babies, improvised cord clamps or complete lack of any baby things?' he asked. 'Not very often to any of them, let alone all three together. Though on the rare occasions the police do bring in an abandoned baby, it usually turns out that the mum's very young and very scared.'

'The police might be able to find this baby's mum and get her to hospital so she can be checked over,' Amy said.

'Let's hope so,' Josh said, sounding very far from convinced.

'I'm sorry. I rather hijacked you when you came into the lobby,' she said. 'I guess now the police are on their way I ought to let you get on.'

Josh didn't know Amy Howes very well—just that she lived in one of the other flats on his floor and she'd taken in a parcel for him a couple of times. He had no idea what she did for a living or even if she had a job.

But what he did know was that her brown eyes were sad behind her smile, and she'd looked slightly panicky at the idea of being responsible for a baby, even for the short time it would take between now and the police arriving. Especially as the baby didn't even have the basics for any kind of care.

He'd only been going to pick up some milk and bread anyway. It wasn't important. The open-all-hours shop round the corner from the hospital would probably still be open when he'd finished his shift, even though it was Christmas Eve.

Not that you'd know it was Christmas, in Amy's flat. There were a couple of cards propped up on the mantelpiece, and a few more stacked in a pile, but there wasn't a tree or any presents. Even when people were going away for Christmas, they usually displayed their cards and had some kind of decorations up. Maybe she didn't celebrate Christmas. Was that because it was too painful for her—like it was for him?

Though it wasn't any of his business.

He shouldn't get involved.

He didn't want to get involved.

And yet he found his mouth opening and the wrong words coming out. 'I'm not due at the hospital until eleven, so I can stay with you until the police get here, if you like.'

'I can't impose on you like that,' she said.

Which was his get-out clause. He ought to agree with her and leave as fast as he could. Though his mouth definitely didn't seem to be with the programme. 'It's not that much of an imposition. If I'd left my flat a couple of minutes earlier, I would've been the one to find the baby,' he said. 'And my medical knowledge might be helpful to the police.'

'True,' she said, looking relieved and grateful. 'Thank you. I have to admit I was a bit worried about looking after the baby on my own.'

'Not used to babies?'

He couldn't quite read the expression on her face before she masked it, but he knew instantly that he'd put his foot in it. Right now he had a pretty good idea that whatever had caused the sadness behind her eyes had involved a baby. A miscarriage, perhaps? Or IVF that hadn't worked and her relationship hadn't survived the strain? And maybe Christmas was the anniversary of everything going wrong for her, just as it was for him?

Not that it was any of his business. And again he reminded himself not to get involved. That pull he felt towards Amy Howes was definitely something he shouldn't act on. If she was recovering from a broken heart, the last thing she needed was to get involved with someone whose track record at relationships was as poor as his.

'I'm more used to dealing with teens,' Amy said. 'I teach maths at the local high school.'

Now that he hadn't expected. 'You don't look like a maths teacher.'

She smiled, then, and Josh's heart felt as if it had turned over. Which was anatomically impossible in the first place; and in the second place Kelly's betrayal had put him off relationships for good. Back off, he reminded himself.

'I'm definitely better at explaining surds and synthetic division than I am at changing nappies,' she said. 'Though that's not the biggest problem. The baby's going to need some nappies and some clothes. I don't know anyone in our block or nearby with a baby who could lend us anything.'

'Me neither,' he said.

'Even if the police arrive in the next five minutes, they're going to be asking questions and what have you—and I have no idea how quickly the baby's going to need a nappy.'

'The average newborn goes through ten to fifteen a day,' Josh said.

'So basically every two to three hours. I could probably make a makeshift nappy out of a towel, but that's not fair on the poor baby.' She shook her head. 'The supermarket on the corner will sell nappies and they might sell some very basic baby clothes. Toss you for it?'

'I'll go,' Josh said. 'I needed to get some bread and milk anyway. I'll pick up nappies, some clothes and some formula milk.'

The panicky look was back on Amy's face. 'What if the baby starts crying again while you're gone?'

'Pick her up and cuddle her. If all else fails, sing to her,' Josh said. 'That usually works.'

'That sounds like experience talking.'

'I'm an uncle of three,' he said. Though he was guiltily aware that he hadn't seen much of his nieces and nephew since his divorce. His family's pity had been hard enough to take, but then he'd become very aware that most of his family saw him as a failure for letting his marriage go down the tubes—and he really couldn't handle that. It had been easier to use work as an excuse to avoid them. Which was precisely why he was working at the hospital over Christmas: it meant he didn't have to spend the holiday with his family and face that peculiar mixture of pity and contempt.

'Any songs in particular?' Amy asked.

'Anything,' he said. 'The baby won't care if you're not word-perfect; she just wants a bit of comfort. I'll see you in a few minutes.' He scribbled his mobile phone number on one of the spare pieces of paper from their makeshift 'crime scene' barrier. 'Here's my number.'

'Thanks. I'll text you in a minute so you've got my number. And I'd better give you some money for the baby stuff.'

'We'll sort it out between us later,' he said. 'Is there anything you need from the supermarket?'

'Thanks, but I did all my shopping yesterday,' she said.

If Josh had done that, too, instead of feeling that he was too tired to move after a hard shift, then he wouldn't have been walking through the lobby when Amy had found the baby, and he wouldn't have been involved with any of this. Though he instantly dismissed the thought as mean. It wasn't the baby's fault that she'd been abandoned, and it wasn't the baby's fault that caring for a baby, even for a few minutes, made it feel as if someone had ripped the top off his scars.

'See you in a bit,' he said, relieved to escape.

Amy looked at the sleeping baby.

A newborn.

Eighteen months ago, this was what she'd wanted most in the world. She and Michael had tried for a baby for a year without success, and they'd been at the point of desperation when they'd walked into the doctor's office after her scan.

And then they'd learned the horrible, horrible truth.

Even though Amy hadn't had a clue and it hadn't actually been her fault that her Fallopian tubes were damaged beyond repair, Michael had blamed her for it—and he'd walked out on her. She'd hoped that maybe once he'd had time to think about it, they could talk it through and get past the shock, but he hadn't been able to do that. All he could see was that Amy had given him an STD, and because of that STD she was infertile and couldn't give him a baby. He wouldn't even consider IVF, let alone adoption or fostering. Even though Amy hadn't had any symptoms, so she'd had no idea that her ex had given her chlamydia, Michael still blamed her for being too stupid to realise it for herself.

The injustice still rankled.

But it wasn't this baby's fault.

Or the fault of the baby's mum.

'Life,' she told the baby, 'is complicated.'

And then she wished she hadn't said a word when the baby started crying.

Pick her up and cuddle her—that was Josh's advice. Except it didn't work and the baby just kept crying.

He'd also suggested singing, as a last resort. But what did you sing to a baby? Every song Amy knew had gone out of her head.

It was Christmas. Sing a carol, she told herself.

'Silent Night' turned out to be a very forlorn hope indeed. It didn't encourage the baby to be quiet in the slightest. 'Hark the Herald Angels Sing' was more like 'Hark the Little Baby Screams'.

This was terrible. She really hoped Josh came back with supplies soon. There was bound to be a massive queue at the checkouts, and what if the supermarket had run out of nappies?

Maybe a Christmas pop song would help. She tried a couple of old classics, but the baby didn't seem to like them, either.

If only Josh had let her toss a coin. As a maths teacher, she knew the probability was fifty-fifty—but she also knew that actually there was a tiny, tiny weighting in favour of heads. She would've called heads and could've been the one to go out for supplies. And Josh, who seemed far better with babies than she was, would've been able to comfort this poor little girl much more easily than Amy could. And how could someone so tiny make so much noise?

'I can't do this,' she said, trying very hard not to burst into tears herself. 'I don't know how to make everything better, baby. I can't even fix my own life, so how can I possibly fix yours?'

The baby was still crying when there was a knock on her door. To her relief, it was Josh.

'Having trouble?' he asked on seeing the red-faced, screaming baby.

'Just a bit,' Amy said dryly. Though it wasn't fair to be sarcastic to him. It wasn't his fault that she was hopelessly inexperienced with babies. 'I tried singing to her. Let's just say she doesn't like Christmas carols. Or Christmas pop songs. And I'm out of ideas.'

'OK. Let me try.' He put the bag on the floor, took the baby from her and started singing 'All I Want for Christmas is You'.

Immediately, the baby stopped crying.

'Clearly you have the knack,' Amy said.

He laughed. 'Maybe she just likes the song.'

Or his voice. He had a gorgeous singing voice, rich and deep. The kind of voice that made your knees feel as if they were melting. To cover her confusion, she asked, 'How did you get on at the supermarket?'

'Ready-mixed formula milk, a couple of bottles, a pack of newborn nappies, some baby bath stuff, three vests and three sleep suits,' he said, indicating the bag. 'Oh, and my milk and bread.'

'Do you want to put the milk in my fridge for now?' she asked.

'Thanks. That'd be good.' Then he grimaced. 'Um.

I think we're going to have to give her a bath sooner rather than later.'

Amy could see the wet patch spreading on the blanket. 'And wash that blanket?'

'Maybe leave the blanket until the police say it's OK to wash it, but we can't leave the baby wet. Is it OK to use your bathroom to clean her up?'

'Sure. I've got plenty of towels.' She found the softest ones in the airing cupboard and placed one on the radiator to keep it warm while Josh ran water into the bath. This felt oddly domestic: and it was almost exactly as she'd imagined her life being with Michael and their baby.

Except, thanks to Gavin, she couldn't have babies. And Michael was no longer part of her life. She'd heard that he'd got married and had a baby on the way, so he'd managed to make his dreams come true—because Amy was no longer holding him back.

She shook herself. This thing with the abandoned baby was only temporary. As soon as the police had taken a statement from her and from Josh, they'd take the baby to some kind of foster home and she probably wouldn't see Josh again for weeks. That frisson of desire she'd felt when his skin had brushed against hers was utterly ridiculous, and she needed to be sensible about this instead of moping for something she couldn't have.

Josh tested the temperature of the water with his elbow. 'OK. Time for your first bath, little one.'

At the first touch of the water, the baby screamed the place down. Even Josh looked fraught by the time he'd finished bathing her, and Amy's teeth were on edge.

The screams abated to grizzling once the baby was out of the bath and wrapped in the warm towel.

'She's hungry, probably,' Josh said.

Amy's heart contracted sharply. 'Poor little mite.' And how desperate the baby's mother must've been to abandon her.

Between them they managed to get the baby into the nappy and sleep suit, and Josh rocked the baby and crooned softly to her while Amy sterilised one of the bottles he'd bought and warmed the formula milk in a jug of hot water. And then it was her turn to cuddle the baby and feed her.

Sitting there, with the baby cradled on her lap, watching her drink greedily from the bottle of milk, really tugged at Amy's heart.

If she'd been less clueless about Gavin's real character—or, better still, hadn't dated him in the first place—her life could have been so different. She could've been sitting here cuddling her own baby, next to the man of her dreams. Instead, here she was, desperately trying to fill her life with work, and right now she was holding a baby she'd have to give back.

She couldn't help glancing at Josh. His expression was unreadable but, before he masked it, she saw definite pain in his eyes. He'd said that he was an uncle of three, but she had a feeling there was a bit more to it than that.

Had he lost a child?

Had someone broken his heart?

Not that it was any of her business. He was her neighbour. They knew next to nothing about each other. And that was the way things were in London. You avoided eye contact as much as you could, smiled and nodded politely if you couldn't avoid eye contact, and you most definitely didn't get involved.

The baby fell asleep almost the second after she'd finished her feed. Amy folded up a towel as a make-shift bed and placed the baby on it, covering her with another towel. She'd just tucked the baby in when her intercom buzzed.

Thankfully the noise didn't wake the baby. 'Hello?'

'It's the police. PC Graham and PC Walters.'

She buzzed them in.

One of them was carrying a sturdy metal case, which she presumed contained forensic equipment, and the other had a notebook.

'I like the scene-of-crime tape improvisation in the lobby,' the first policeman said with a smile. 'I assume you'd like the bandages back when I've finished?'

Josh smiled back. 'No. It's fine to get rid of them. Do you think you'll get anything to help you track down the baby's mother?'

'I'll go and dust the area now,' the first police-man said, 'while my colleague PC Graham here goes through everything with you.'

'Shall I put the kettle on?' Amy asked.

'That'd be lovely. Thank you,' PC Walters said, heading out of the door with his case.

'Mr and Mrs Howes, isn't it?' PC Graham asked.

'Ms Howes and Mr Farnham,' she corrected. 'We're neighbours.'

'I see.' He made a note. 'Would you mind taking me through what happened?'

Between them, Amy and Josh filled in all the de-tails of how they'd found the baby.

'I'm a doctor,' Josh said. 'I've checked the baby

over, and she's fine. I think from all the vernix on her face—that's the white stuff—she's a couple of weeks early, and I have a feeling the mum might be quite young. I'd be a lot happier if you could find the mum and get her checked over, too, because she's at a high risk of infection.'

'It might take a while to find her,' PC Graham said.

'I'm afraid we had to give the baby a bath,' Amy added. 'She didn't have a nappy or any clothes, just the blanket, and the blanket got a bit, um, messy. I haven't washed it yet, in case you need it for forensics, but I've put it in a plastic bag.'

'Thank you. So you didn't recognise the voice over the intercom?' PC Graham asked.

'Nobody spoke,' Amy said. 'I just assumed it was a courier. Then I heard what sounded like a baby's cry. I don't know why, but some instinct made me go out and see for myself.'

'Just as well you did,' the policeman said. 'And you don't know anyone who might have left the baby here?'

'I don't know anyone who's pregnant,' Amy said. Mainly because she'd distanced herself from all her friends and colleagues who'd been trying for a baby, once she'd found out that she could no longer have children herself. It had been too painful being reminded of what she'd lost.

'So what happens now?' Josh asked.

'Once the social worker's here, she'll take the baby to the hospital,' the policeman said.

Josh shook his head. 'I don't really think that's a good idea. Right now, the children's ward is stuffed full of little ones with bronchiolitis.'

'Bronchi-what?' PC Graham asked.

'Bronchiolitis. It's a virus,' Josh explained. 'If adults catch it they get a really stinking cold, but in babies the mucus gums up the tiny airways in the lungs—the bronchioles—and they can't breathe or feed properly. Usually they end up being on oxygen therapy and being tube-fed for a week. And I really wouldn't want a newborn catching it—at that age it's likely to be really serious.'

'What about the general ward?' PC Graham asked. 'Could they look after her there?'

Josh shook his head. 'At this time of year the winter vomiting virus and flu are both doing the rounds in all the wards. As a newborn, she's at high risk of picking up either or both.'

The policeman shrugged and spread his hands. 'Then I don't know. We'll see what the social worker says when she gets here.'

By the time Amy had made mugs of tea, PC Walters was back from his forensic examination of the hallway.

'Did you manage to get anything?' Amy asked.

'A smudged footprint, but no fingerprints. Hopefully we'll get something from the box she left the baby in.' PC Walters looked at Amy's pale beige carpet. 'Though I'm afraid fingerprint powder's a bit messy.'

'It doesn't matter. It won't take that long to vacuum it up afterwards,' Amy said. 'It's more important that you discover something that'll help you find the baby's mum.'

But he didn't manage to get much from the box, either. 'There's a couple of long blonde hairs, but they don't necessarily belong to the mother. Though I found an envelope under the newspaper at the bottom of the box.'

'Newspaper?' Josh asked.

'For insulation against the cold, maybe,' PC Walters said. 'There's a gold chain in there and a note—though there aren't any prints. There are a couple of fibres, so she was probably wearing gloves.'

Amy read the note and then passed it to Josh.

Please look after Hope. I'm sorry.

'So the baby's name is Hope?' Josh asked.

'Seems so.'

Amy shared a glance with Josh. *Hope.* How terribly sad, because hope was clearly the last thing the baby's mother felt right now.

'Do you recognise the handwriting at all?' PC Graham asked.

'No,' Amy said.

'Me neither,' Josh agreed.

'We can take the box back with us—and the blanket—but I don't think it's going to help much,' PC Walters said, accepting a mug of tea.

They went through the whole lot again when Jane Richards, the social worker, arrived ten minutes later.

'So what's going to happen to the baby?' Amy asked.

Jane grimaced. 'At this time of year, everyone's on leave. You're lucky if you can get anyone even to answer a phone. And with Christmas falling partly on a weekend, the chances of getting hold of someone who can offer a foster care placement are practically zero. So I guess the baby's going to have to stay in hospital for a while.'

'The local hospital's on black alert,' Josh said.

'Apart from the fact that beds are in really short supply right now, there's bronchiolitis on the children's ward, and there's flu and the winter vomiting virus in the rest of the hospital. The chances are that Hope would go down with something nasty, so they'll refuse to take her.'

Jane looked at Amy. 'As you're the one who found her, and Christmas is meant to be the season of goodwill… Would you be able to look after her for a few days?'

'Me?' Amy looked at her in shock. 'But don't you have to do all kinds of background checks on me, first?'

'You're a teacher,' Jane said, 'so you'll already have gone through most of the checks. The rest of it is just formalities and, as I'm the senior social worker on duty in this area today, I can use my discretion.'

'I'm more used to dealing with teenagers,' Amy said. 'I've not really had much to do with babies.' Much less the baby she'd so desperately wanted to have with Michael. Something that could never, ever happen for her. 'I'm not sure…' And yet Jane was right. Christmas was the season of goodwill. How could Amy possibly turn away a helpless, defenceless newborn baby?

'I could help out,' Josh said. 'I'm working today and tomorrow, but I could help out between my shifts.'

So she'd have someone to talk things over with, if she was concerned. Someone who had experience of babies—and, better still, was a doctor.

But there was one possible sticking point. Even though she knew it was intrusive, she still had to ask. 'Will your partner mind?' she asked.

'I don't have a partner,' Josh said, and for a moment she saw a flash of pain in his expression.

Did he, too, have an ex who'd let him down badly? Amy wondered. She was pretty sure that, like her, he lived alone.

'I can make decisions without having to check with anyone first,' he said. 'How about yours?'

'Same as you,' she said.

'Which makes it easy.' He turned to Jane. 'OK. We'll look after Hope between us. How long do you need us to look after her?'

She winced. 'Until New Year's Eve, maybe?'

A whole week? 'Just as well it's the school holidays,' Amy said wryly.

'I'm off for a couple of days between Christmas and New Year,' Josh said. 'I'll do as much as I can. But the baby has nothing, Jane. I just went out to get emergency milk, nappies and enough clothes to keep her going until you got here. Her mother left her wrapped in a blanket in the box, and there wasn't anything with her. Well, the police found a note and a gold chain that the mum obviously wanted the baby to have,' he amended, 'but the baby doesn't have any clothes.'

'We don't have anywhere for her to sleep—and, apart from the fact that the police have taken the box, a cardboard box really isn't a suitable bed for a baby,' Amy added.

'I can help there,' Jane said. 'We have things in the office. I can bring you a Moses basket, bedding, nappies and spare clothes, and I can organise milk. Do you have any bottles?'

'Two,' Josh said, 'and I bought a couple of cartons

of ready-mixed formula. We've muddled through with very hot water to sterilise them for now.'

'If you don't mind mixing up your own formula, I can organise more bottles and sterilising equipment,' Jane said. 'What about the baby's mum?'

'We haven't got much on the forensics side,' PC Walters said. 'The best we can do is to put out a press release and ask the local media to tell her to get in touch.'

'If she's as young as I think she might be,' Josh said, 'she'll be worried that she's in trouble—especially if she managed to hide her pregnancy.'

'Strictly speaking, it's a criminal offence to abandon a baby,' PC Graham said, 'but judges are always lenient in the case of newborns and very young, very frightened mums.'

'She really needs to get to hospital or a doctor and let them check her over,' Josh said. 'That's important because, if she's retained any of the placenta or she tore during the delivery, there's a high risk she'll develop an infection—and if it's left untreated she could become really ill.'

'We'll make sure everyone says she won't be in any trouble and we're worried about her health,' PC Graham said.

'And tell her the baby's absolutely fine and being looked after. The poor girl's probably going to be worrying about that, too,' Amy added.

Josh looked at his watch. 'Sorry. I'm going to have to leave you now. I need to be at work.' He scribbled a number on one of the spare sheets of paper. 'You've got my mobile number, Amy, and this is my direct line in the department. You can get a message to me if it's urgent. I'll be back about half-past eight this evening—unless there's a crisis in the department, in which case I'll get a message to you as early as I can.'

Amy really hoped that she wasn't going to have to use that number. 'OK. Thanks.' She paused, knowing that this probably sounded like a come-on, but hoping that he'd take it as the practical suggestion it actually was. 'Look, as you're helping me with the baby, you might as well have dinner here. It's as easy to cook for two as for one.'

'That'd be nice.'

They exchanged a glance, and another frisson of desire ran down her spine—which was completely inappropriate. OK, so they were both single, but this was all about caring for Hope, not having a wild fling with her neighbour.

She fought to keep herself sounding professional. 'Do you have any food allergies, or is there anything you don't eat?'

'No to the allergies.' He smiled. 'As for the rest, I'm a medic in the emergency department, so we tend not to be fussy. We're lucky if we get a chance to grab a chocolate bar. As long as it's food and it's hot, I'm happy.'

She smiled back. 'OK.'

Once Josh had left, PC Graham sorted out the last bits of paperwork and the police left, too.

'I'll be back later this afternoon with supplies,' Jane promised.

'We should have enough milk and nappies to last until then,' Amy said.

'Thanks.' Jane smiled at her. 'You're a life-saver—literally.'

'Not just me. My neighbour helped.' And Amy really had to remind herself that Josh was just her neighbour. They might know each other a bit better and be on friendlier terms after the next few days, but this would be a platonic relationship only.

Amy saw Jane out of the flat, then returned to watch Hope sleeping in her makeshift bed. 'It looks as if it's just you and me, baby,' she said softly. 'For the next week you're going to have complete strangers looking after you and trying to make a family for you.'

But it was Christmas, the season of miracles. With any luck Hope's mum would come forward, Jane would be able to help her, and there would be a happy ending.

CHAPTER TWO

IT WAS HOPE's first Christmas, but Amy's flat looked just like it did on every other day of the year. She hadn't planned to be here for the festive season, so she hadn't bothered putting up a tree. When her plans had fallen through, it had felt like too much effort to get the Christmas decorations out. What was the point when she'd be here on her own?

Now, she had a reason to change that.

Even though she knew the baby wouldn't remember it or even have a clue that it was Christmas, Amy wanted to decorate her flat and make it Christmassy for Hope. Though, between feeds and nappy changes and cuddles to stop the baby crying, it took her four times as long as she'd expected. And she was panicking that she wasn't looking after Hope properly.

'I really have no idea what I'm doing,' she informed the baby, who cried a little bit more, as if agreeing with Amy. 'And I don't know who to ask. If I call Mum, she'll worry and get the next plane home from Canada—and that's not fair, because it's my parents' turn to spend Christmas with my brother Scott and his wife Rae.' Who didn't have children yet, so she couldn't ask her brother or sister-in-law for advice, either. 'Half my colleagues have teenagers, and I'm guessing they're way past remembering what the first couple of days with a newborn are like. And I'm a total cow because I distanced myself from my friends who do have babies. I can hardly ring them and ask for help when I've been so horrible and ignored their babies.'

But it had been too raw, once she'd learned that she was infertile and her dreams of having a baby were never coming true. Although she'd been genuinely pleased for her friends, she just hadn't been able to face watching them bloom through pregnancy or listening to them talk about the latest milestone their babies had reached.

But now she had a baby.

Temporarily.

And walking up and down with Hope like this, holding her close and rocking her in the hope that it would help settle her and stop her crying… This was what Amy's life could've been like, had it not been for Gavin and her own naivety. Why hadn't she even considered that, as he'd been serially unfaithful to her, in the process he might have picked up some kind of STD which didn't have any symptoms and passed it on to her? Why hadn't she got herself checked out just as a precautionary measure?

Maybe because she wasn't the suspicious sort—which was why it had taken her months in the first place to work out that Gavin was seeing other women on the side. A whole string of them. And she'd been stupidly oblivious, thinking everything was just fine between them.

'I'm an idiot,' she said with a sigh. 'But I'll do my

best to give you a decent first few days and first Christmas, Hope.'

This time, the baby gurgled.

And Amy really had to swallow the lump in her throat.

For a second the baby's dark blue eyes seemed to hold all the wisdom in the world.

How different her life could've been. But there was nothing she could do to change it now; all she could do was make the best of her situation. And, with Josh Farnham's help, do her best to make this poor baby's first few days as happy as possible.

When the baby dropped off to sleep again, Amy gently laid her on the makeshift towel bed, covered her up, and tried to work out what she needed to do next.

The intercom buzzed, and Amy rushed to get it before the noise woke the baby. 'Hello, it's Jane Richards again,' a tinny voice informed her.

'Come in,' Amy said, and buzzed her in before putting on the kettle. 'Can I make you tea or coffee?' she asked when the social worker came in laden with a Moses basket and an armful of carrier bags.

'Sorry, I can't stop for more than two minutes,' Jane said. 'I just wanted to drop these off for you, as I promised.' She put down the bags one by one, naming the contents. 'Moses basket, bedding, bottles, sterilising stuff, milk, nappies and newborn-size clothes.'

'Thanks.' The pile looked daunting, Amy thought. How could someone so tiny need so much stuff?

'The thanks are all mine,' Jane said. 'If you hadn't agreed to help out, I would've been really stuck. I did try to see if one of our foster carers could take Hope, but everyone's so busy at this time of year. In reality we're looking at the day after New Year.'

'Right.' Amy took a deep breath. Which meant she was spending the next week with a baby that she'd have to give back. It was a warning not to let herself bond too deeply with Hope.

'So how's it going?' Jane asked.

'It's a lot harder than I thought it would be,' Amy said. 'And I'm supposed to be a well-organised adult. How on earth would a young, inexperienced mum cope on her own?'

'She'd be struggling,' Jane said. 'I don't suppose the police have found Hope's mum, yet?'

'Not that I've heard,' Amy said.

'Right. So what are you struggling with most?' Jane asked. 'Is there anyone you can call on?'

'Only my neighbour,' Amy said. And she had the strongest feeling that Josh might have some issues with looking after a baby, too. Not that she could ask him without either being rude and intrusive, which might make him decide he didn't want to help, or telling him about her past—and the last thing she wanted was for him to start pitying her and seeing her in a different light. 'As for what I'm struggling with, I'm worrying that I'm doing *everything* wrong. I mean, I know I can follow the instructions with the sterilising stuff and the formula milk, and obviously I know to heat the milk in a jug of hot water rather than in the microwave, but am I feeding her enough and is she getting enough sleep?' She grimaced. 'And she cries an awful lot more than I was expecting. I'm not very good at getting her to feel secure and happy.'

'Crash course,' Jane said. 'If the baby's crying, she

either wants feeding, a nappy change or a cuddle. Sing to her, rock her, hold her, dance with her—obviously I mean more like a slow dance than break-dancing.'

That made Amy smile. 'I don't think I can break-dance on my own, let alone with a baby in my arms.'

Jane grinned back. 'I guess. OK. Make the feeds in batches that'll be enough for a day's worth and keep them in the fridge, so all you have to do in the middle of the night is heat up the milk in a jug of hot water. Keep a note of the baby's feed times and how much she takes, and write down when she sleeps and how long. That'll help you see what her routine is. And obviously try to get some sleep when Hope sleeps, or you'll be exhausted by Boxing Day.' She scribbled down a phone number. 'If you're stuck, that's my mobile.'

'You're on duty over Christmas?'

'No,' Jane admitted, 'but without you I wouldn't know what to do with Hope, so I'm happy for you to call me if you need me.'

'Thanks,' Amy said.

'Good luck.'

And then she was on her own with the baby again. She just about had time to make up the Moses basket with the bedding, sterilise the bottles Jane had brought and make up the feeds before Hope woke, crying.

Amy could definitely tell the reason for this one: Hope needed a fresh nappy.

And then the baby was hungry.

And then she wanted a cuddle.

Time was rushing away. Amy knew that Josh would be back soon, and she hadn't even looked at the inside of her fridge, let alone started preparing something to eat.

'I'm supposed to be cooking dinner tonight,' Amy told the baby. Even if the shops hadn't closed early for Christmas Eve, she wouldn't have been able to go out and pick up a pizza in any case because she couldn't leave the baby alone. It was hardly fair to ask Josh to get a takeaway on the way back from his shift. 'We're going to have to go for something that can look after itself in the oven.'

The baby gurgled.

'You have no idea how weird this is,' Amy said. 'Josh and I smile and nod at each other if we pass in the hallway, and that's it. And now he's having dinner with me tonight and helping me look after you.'

No comment from Hope.

'But it's not a date,' Amy added. 'OK, so we're both single. But my past is messy and my future would be problematic for anyone who wants to date me. In fact, I'm just rubbish at picking men. Gavin was a liar and a cheat, and when it came to a crisis Michael walked away because I wasn't enough for him. So I'm better off forgetting all about romantic relationships.'

Though maybe looking after Hope might help her finally come to terms with the fact that she wasn't going to have a child of her own. To the point where she could reconnect with her friends—OK, she'd have a bit of grovelling to do, but she had a feeling that they'd understand when she explained why she'd gone distant on them. She could enjoy babysitting her friends' children and reading stories to them, and hopefully the joy would outweigh the ache in her heart.

'Besides, there's no reason why Josh should be interested in me,' she added. She'd felt that frisson of attraction when they'd accidentally touched while caring for the baby earlier, but she had no idea whether it was mutual. 'We might become friends. Which would be nice. But that's it,' she said firmly.

Hope gurgled then, as if to say, 'How do you know what he thinks?'

She didn't. But she did need his help, so she had no intention of doing or saying anything that might make him back away. 'It's just the way it is,' she said. 'And you, Missy, are going to have to go in the Moses basket for a few minutes, to let me put something together for dinner.'

In the end, Amy had to wait for Hope to fall asleep again. And then she worked at speed to peel and chop the veg, then put them in a casserole dish with a couple of chicken breasts and half a bottle of red wine.

By the time she'd finished, Hope was crying again. Amy suppressed a sigh and went through her mental checklist. Was the baby hungry, wet or just wanted a cuddle? And why was it so hard to work out which cry meant which?

Josh headed back to his flat after his shift. Right now all he wanted to do was to fall onto the sofa and watch something on TV that didn't require him to think too much. He was bone-deep tired, and wished he hadn't offered to help with the baby; but he had a feeling that Amy had only agreed to look after the baby because he'd promised to help. It would be pretty unfair of him to bail out on her now.

And she was cooking dinner for both of them. She hadn't said anything about dessert, but he didn't ex-actly have anything in his fridge that would pass muster. A bottle of wine was the best he could offer as his contribution.

He'd told her he'd be back for half-past eight—and it was twenty-five past now, so he didn't have time for a shower. He was pretty sure he wasn't sweaty and vile, and his hair had a mind of its own anyway, so it would be sticking out at odd angles within five minutes of him putting a comb through it. No point in wasting time.

Besides, this wasn't a date. It wasn't as if he had to dress up, or was trying to impress her by being smooth, suave and charming. Amy was his neighbour and he was simply helping with the baby who'd been abandoned on their doorstep.

At Christmas.

Not that you'd know it was Christmas, looking at his flat. It was even less Christmassy than Amy's was, because he hadn't even bothered putting any cards on the mantelpiece. He wondered if she loathed Christmas as much as he did. For him, Christmas Eve would always be the anniversary of the day his life imploded. When Kelly—who had been so adamant that she wanted to concentrate on her career rather than starting a family—had told him that she was pregnant. That the baby wasn't his. And that she was leaving him for the baby's father.

Josh had been too numb to believe it at first. But while he'd been saving lives and patching up wounds, Kelly had been packing her stuff, ready to leave him. Though in some ways she'd been fair. She'd been scrupulous only to pack things that were hers and to give him first dibs on anything they'd bought together; and she'd actually asked him to divorce her on the grounds of adultery rather than trying to make out that it was his fault or from joint 'irreconcilable differences'. She'd done as much as she could to make it easy on him.

Happy Christmas. Indeed. Every single radio station had been playing Christmas heartbreak songs, and when the third station in a row had been playing a song about a man pleading with his beloved to come home for Christmas, Josh had given up and switched off the radio—because he knew that Kelly wasn't coming home to him. Not for Christmas or at any other time.

He shook himself. It wasn't Amy's fault that his ex had changed her mind about wanting a baby and then decided that she didn't want to have said baby with him.

And it definitely wasn't Amy's fault that his family had reacted in typical Farnham fashion. Josh, the baby of the family, was a big fat failure. He was the only one who hadn't managed to combine a high-flying career with a perfect marriage and family. Obviously they hadn't actually *said* the words to his face, but Josh was aware of it with every look, every raised eyebrow, every whispered aside that was cut short the second he walked into the room.

This year, Kelly would be spending her first Christmas with her new family. Including the new baby.

And Josh genuinely wanted her to be happy. Now he'd got most of the hurt and anger out of his system, he could see that he hadn't been what Kelly had needed. If she'd stayed with him out of a sense of duty, she would've grown to hate him and it would all have grown miserable and messy. As it was, their divorce had been as amicable as possible. They'd sold the house and split the proceeds, and he'd bought the flat here six months ago.

But part of him was still in limbo.

And he really wanted to blot out Christmas Eve.

Except he couldn't. He'd made a promise, and he needed to keep it. He took a deep breath and went down the corridor to Amy's flat, then knocked on the door.

She opened it, looking slightly harassed, with Hope propped up against her shoulder. Clearly looking after the baby on her own had been hard going.

He suppressed the flush of guilt—he'd spent the last nine hours working his shift at the Emergency Department, not down at the pub taking part in several Christmas parties—and handed her the bottle of wine. 'I didn't know if you preferred red or white, so I played it safe.'

'Thank you. It's very nice of you, but you didn't need to.'

'You cooked dinner, so this is my contribution,' he pointed out. 'Something smells nice.'

'It's not very exciting, I'm afraid. Just a casserole and jacket potatoes, and all the veg are mixed in with the casserole.'

But it meant that he hadn't had to cook. 'It sounds lovely.'

'It was the lowest-maintenance thing I could think of,' she admitted wryly. 'Looking after Hope took an awful lot more time and energy than I expected.'

Yes, and if things had been different he would've been celebrating his first Christmas with his daughter—except his ex-wife's baby wasn't actually his daughter. He pushed the thought away. 'So I hear from my colleagues.' And this was his cue to play nice. Amy's brown eyes were so anxious, despite the calm she appeared to radiate. 'Here. My turn to cuddle Hope and keep her happy for a bit.'

And that was definitely gratitude in her eyes as she handed the baby over.

Though her hands brushed against his as they transferred the baby between them, and a frisson of desire flickered down his spine.

Inappropriate. Amy was his neighbour, and he was helping out with a tricky situation. That was it, he reminded himself. He wasn't going to hit on her and he wasn't going to let himself wonder how soft her hair was, or how her skin would feel against his.

'Can I get you a drink?' she asked.

'A glass of wine would be lovely right now,' he admitted. And it might distract him from all the ridiculous thoughts flickering through his head. Thoughts about how Amy's mouth was a perfect Cupid's bow, and wondering what it would feel like if he kissed her.

'Hard shift?'

He shrugged. 'It's always busy this time of year. Ignoring all the viruses and the elderly coming in with breathing problems, there are the falls—especially when it's icy like it has been tonight. And tonight the department will be full of people who drank too much at Christmas Eve parties and either ended up in a fight or fell and hurt themselves.' He gave her a wry smile. 'Tomorrow will be the people who had an accident carving the turkey, and a few more punch-ups because people who really shouldn't be in the same room together for more than ten minutes are forced to play nice for the whole day and it's too much for them, and the day after that will be the people who didn't store the leftover turkey properly and gave themselves food poisoning.'

'That,' she said, 'sounds a tiny bit cynical.'

'Experience,' he said, and grimaced. 'Sorry. I guess I'm a bit tired and not the best company.'

'It's fine.' She handed him a glass of wine. 'Come and sit down. Dinner will be five minutes.'

He went into the living room and blinked in surprise. 'You have a tree.'

She smiled. 'Yes—and you wouldn't believe how long it took me to put it up.'

'But you didn't have a tree this morning.'

'That's because I wasn't intending to be here for Christmas,' she said. 'I was meant to be spending this week in Edinburgh with some of my oldest friends, but they rang yesterday to call it off because they've gone down with the flu.' Amy shrugged. 'There didn't seem much point in putting up a tree when I wasn't going to be here. But now I am, and it's Hope's first Christmas.' Her fair skin flushed. 'It might sound a bit daft, but I wanted to put up a tree for her.'

'No, it's not daft. I get what you mean.' Josh paused. 'So the lack of a tree earlier wasn't because you don't like Christmas?'

'No.' She frowned. 'I take it you don't like Christmas, then?'

'It's not my favourite time of the year,' he admitted, and was relieved when she didn't push it and ask why. Though his mouth didn't seem to want to pay her the same courtesy, because he found himself asking questions. 'So you're not spending Christmas with your family?'

Amy shook her head. 'My brother lives in Canada, so my parents spend alternate Christmases here and over in Canada.'

'And this year is Canada's turn, right?'

'Right,' she agreed.

'So luckily for Hope that means you're here.'

'Yes.' Her expression was sombre when she looked at him. 'Things could have been very different.'

'But you found her in time.' He paused. 'Is there anything I can do to help?'

'I'm about to serve dinner, so if you want to settle Hope in her Moses basket, that'd be good.'

While Amy went to the kitchen, Josh put the baby in the Moses basket. Hope grizzled for a moment and then yawned and fell asleep.

Having dinner with Amy felt weirdly intimate. Like a date—though Josh couldn't even remember the last time he'd dated. He'd had a couple of offers that he'd turned down, and some well-meaning friends had tried to match-make, but he'd taken them to one side and explained that he appreciated their effort but he wasn't ready to date again.

Was he ready now?

And why on earth was he thinking about that?

'The food's very nice,' he said, to cover his awkwardness.

'Thank you.'

He didn't have a clue what to talk about, and it made him feel slightly flustered. He was used to making polite conversation to distract his patients or get more information out of them, or being out with colleagues that he'd known for so long that he didn't have to make small talk. This was definitely outside his comfort zone. Especially as he was becoming more and more aware of how attractive Amy was: not just those huge brown eyes, but the curve of her mouth, her pretty heart-shaped face and the slight curl to her bobbed hair. It made him itch to draw her, and he hadn't felt that urge for a long time either.

'So how long have you lived here?' he asked, trying to get his thoughts back to something much more anodyne and much, much safer.

'Eighteen months. You moved here last summer, didn't you?' she replied.

'Yes. It's convenient for the hospital, just a fifteen-minute walk.'

'It's about that to school, too,' she said. 'Just in the other direction.'

He remembered that she taught maths. 'Did you always want to teach?'

'I didn't want to be an accountant, an engineer or an actuary, so teaching was my best bet for working with maths—and actually it's really rewarding when the kids have been struggling with something and it suddenly clicks for them.' She smiled. 'Did you always want to be a doctor?'

'It was pretty much expected of me—Dad's a surgeon, Mum's a lawyer, my brother Stuart's an astrophysicist and my sisters are both lecturers.' He shrugged. 'One teaches history at Oxford and the other's in London at the LSE.'

'A family of high achievers, then.'

Yes. And he hadn't quite lived up to their expectations. He'd suggested becoming a graphic designer and going to art college instead of studying for his A levels, and the resulting row had left him very aware that he'd been expected to follow in his parents' and siblings' footsteps. In the end he'd settled on medicine; at least there'd been a little bit of drawing involved. And he liked his job. He liked being able to make a difference to people's lives. And he could still sketch if he wanted to.

When he had the time.

Which wasn't often.

Pushing the thought away, he asked, 'Have you heard anything from the police?'

'Not yet. Though Jane the social worker came round with supplies this afternoon.'

'So I notice. That Moses basket looks a little more comfy than a bunch of newspaper and a cardboard box.' His smile faded. 'That poor girl. I hope she's all right.'

'Me, too. And looking after a baby is a lot harder than I expected,' Amy admitted. 'Now I know what they mean about being careful what you wish for.'

He stared at her in surprise. 'You wanted a baby?'

She looked shocked, as if she hadn't meant to admit that, then glanced away. 'It didn't work out.'

That explained some of her wariness this morning. And it was pretty obvious to him that the baby situation not working out was connected with her being single. 'I'm sorry,' he said. 'I didn't mean to bring up bad memories.'

'I know. It's OK.' She shrugged. 'There's nothing anyone can do to change it, so you make the best of the situation, don't you?'

'I guess.' It was what he'd been doing since Kelly had left him. They'd sold their house and he'd bought this flat; it was nearer to work and had no memories to haunt him with their might-have-beens. 'In the circumstances, looking after Hope must be pretty tough for you.'

'It's probably been good for me,' she said. 'And it's kind of helping me to move on.' She bit her lip. 'I've been a bit of a cow and neglected my friends who were pregnant at the time or had small children.'

He liked the fact that she wasn't blaming anyone else for her actions. 'That's understandable if you'd only just found out that option was closed to you. You're human.'

'I guess.'

More than human. What he'd seen so far of Amy Howes told him that she was genuinely nice. 'And you're not a cow. If you were, you would've just told the police and the social worker to sort out the baby between them and pushed everyone out of your flat,' he pointed out. 'So did you ring any of your friends with small children to get some advice?'

'No. I don't want them to think I'm just using them. But I'm going to call them all in the first week of the New Year,' she said, 'and apologise to them properly. Then maybe I can be the honorary auntie they all wanted me to be in the first place and I was too—well, hurting too much to do it back then.'

'That's good,' Josh said. He wondered if helping to look after Hope would help him move on, too. Right now, it didn't feel like it; and if Amy had moved here eighteen months ago, that suggested she'd had a year longer to get used to her new circumstances than he had. Maybe his head would be sorted out by this time next year, then.

He almost told Amy about Kelly and the baby; but,

then again, he didn't want her to pity him, so he knew it would be safer to change the subject. 'What did the social worker have to say?'

'She gave me a very quick crash course in looking after a baby. She said if they cry it means they're hungry, they need a fresh nappy or they just want a cuddle, though I can't actually tell the difference between any of the different cries, yet,' Amy said dryly. 'Jane also told me to write down whenever Hope has milk and how much she takes, and her nap times, so I can work out what her routine is.'

'Sounds good. How's Hope doing so far?'

'She likes a lot of cuddles and she definitely likes you talking to her. Hang on.' She went over to the sideboard and took a notebook from the top, then handed it to him. 'Here. You can see for yourself.'

He looked through the neat columns of handwriting. 'I have to admit, it doesn't mean that much to me,' he said.

'Tsk, and you an uncle of three,' she teased.

'One's in Scotland and two are in Oxford,' he explained. 'I don't see them as much as I should.' It was another failing to chalk up to his list; and he felt guilty about it.

'Hey, you're a doctor. You don't get a lot of spare time,' she reminded him.

'I know, but I ought to make more of an effort.'

'It's not always easy. I don't see much of my brother.'

'He's in Canada, thousands of miles away,' Josh pointed out. 'And I bet you video-call him.'

She nodded.

'Well, then.' Amy was clearly a good sister. Just as Josh wasn't a particularly good brother. When was the last time he'd talked to Stuart, Miranda or Rosemary? He'd used his shifts as an excuse to avoid them.

'I guess,' she said, looking awkward. 'Can I offer you some pudding? It's nothing exciting, just ice cream.'

'Ice cream is the best pudding in the universe,' he said. 'Provided it's chocolate.'

'Oh, *please*,' she said, looking pained. 'Coffee. Every single time.'

He wasn't a fan of coffee ice cream. But he wasn't going to argue with someone who'd been kind enough to make him dinner. 'Coffee's fine,' he fibbed. 'And I'll wash up.'

'That's not fair.'

'You cooked.'

'But you were at work all day.'

He coughed. 'And you've spent hours on your own looking after a baby—that's hard work, even if you're used to it.' Then he flinched, realising what he'd said and how it sounded. 'Sorry. I didn't mean it to come out like that.'

'It's OK,' she said softly. 'I know you didn't mean it like that.'

But the sadness was back in her eyes. Part of him really wanted to give her a hug.

Though that might not be such a good idea. Not when he still felt that pull towards her. He needed to start thinking of her as an extra sister or something. A sister-in-law. Someone off limits. 'Let's share the washing up,' he said instead.

Though being in a small space with her felt even more intimate than eating at her bistro table.

'So what do you usually do on Christmas Eve?' he asked, trying to make small talk.

'Last year, I had my parents staying—and I guess I was busy convincing them that I was absolutely fine and settled here.'

'Were you really absolutely fine?' he asked quietly. Back then she'd been here for six months—exactly the same position that he was in now.

'Not really,' she admitted, 'but I am now.' She paused. 'I heard a couple of months back that my ex got married and he's expecting a baby.'

'The hardest bit is trying to be happy for them when you're feeling miserable yourself.'

Her eyes widened. 'That sounds like experience talking.'

He nodded. And funny how easy it was to talk to her, now he'd started. 'I split up with my wife last Christmas Eve.'

She winced. 'There's never a good time to break up with someone, but Christmas has to be one of the roughest. And the first anniversary's always a difficult one.' She squeezed his hand briefly, but it didn't feel like pity—more like sympathy and as if she'd been there herself, which he knew she had. 'If it helps to know, it does get easier. I know everyone says that time heals. I'm not sure it does that exactly, but it does help you deal with things a bit better.'

'I'm not still in love with Kelly,' he said. 'I want her to be happy. And I'm OK now about the fact it isn't going to be with me.'

'That's good. It's the same way I feel about Michael.'

It felt as if there was some subtext going on, but

Josh didn't trust his emotional intelligence enough to try to work it out.

She shook coffee grounds into a cafetière. 'Milk? Sugar?'

'Black, no sugar, please,' he said.

'Because you're a medic and you're used to grabbing coffee as quickly as you can?' she asked.

'No. It's a hangover from my student days,' he said with a smile. 'I shared a flat with some guys who weren't that good with checking that the milk was in date. The third time you make your coffee with milk that's off, you learn it's safer to drink your coffee black.'

She smiled back. 'I knew a few people like that in my student days, too.'

It was so easy to be with Amy, Josh thought. And it felt natural to curl up on the other end of her sofa, nursing a mug of coffee and listening to music while the baby was napping in the Moses basket.

'So what do you usually do at Christmas?' she asked.

'Work,' he said. 'It feels fairer to let my colleagues who have kids spend Christmas morning with their family.'

'That's nice of you.'

'Ah, but I get to party at New Year while they have to patch up the drunks,' he said with a smile, 'so it works both ways.'

Hope woke then, and started crying softly.

'I'll go and heat the milk,' Amy said.

Josh scooped the baby onto his lap and cuddled her until Amy came back with the milk. 'My turn to feed her,' he said.

When the baby had finished, he wrote the time and millilitres on Amy's chart.

'So at the moment she's feeding every two to three hours,' he said.

'Which means I'm not going to get a lot of sleep tonight.' Amy gave a wry smile. 'It's just as well I'm not going anywhere tomorrow, or I'd be a zombie.'

The sensible bit of his brain told him to back off and keep his mouth shut. The human side said, 'We could take shifts with her.'

'But you've been at work today—and I assume from what you said that you're working tomorrow.'

'And you've been on your own with her today, which pretty much counts as a full-time job,' Josh pointed out. 'If we take turns feeding her, we'll both get a four- or five-hour chunk of sleep.'

'So, what, you take her next door after the next feed and bring her back?'

'Or, if you don't mind me sleeping on your sofa, then we don't have to move her and risk unsettling her.'

Amy frowned. 'You can't possibly sleep on my sofa. It's way too short for you.'

'Student doctors learn to sleep on anything and be fully awake within seconds. I'll be fine,' he said. 'Let me go next door and grab my duvet.'

For a moment, he thought she was going to argue with him. But then she smiled, and he could see the relief in her eyes. 'Thanks. Actually, it'll be good not having the first night with her completely on my own. I'm paranoid I'm doing everything wrong.'

'Hey—she's new at this, too. If you're doing it wrong, she doesn't know any better. And she looks pretty content to me, so I'd say you're doing just fine.'

'Even when she cried non-stop for thirty minutes this afternoon—cried herself to sleep?'

He winced. 'That's tough on you. But don't blame yourself. She would probably have done exactly the same with me.' He smiled at her. 'I'll be back in a tick.'

CHAPTER THREE

WHAT HAVE I DONE? Amy asked herself as Josh went to collect his duvet.

Two years ago, she'd been in what she'd thought was a secure relationship, trying to start a family. A year ago she'd had a broken relationship, broken dreams and a broken heart. This year, she was on an even keel; but it seemed that she was going to be spending the next week with a man she barely knew and a baby who'd been left on their doorstep. It was an odd version of what she'd wished for.

Josh came back carrying a duvet. She wasn't sure if she felt more relieved or awkward that he was still fully dressed; clearly he intended to sleep in his ordinary clothes on her sofa. Though she guessed that went with the territory of his job.

He folded the duvet neatly over the back of her sofa. 'Anything you need me to do?'

'No. Hope's milk is on the top shelf of the fridge. But help yourself to anything you want.'

He smiled. 'Fifteen years ago, that would've guaranteed you an empty fridge.'

'That's what my colleagues at school say.' She smiled back. 'The boys leave crumbs everywhere, and the girls make chocolate mug cakes at three in the morning and leave everything in the sink.'

'Mug cakes?' He looked blank.

'You mix everything together in a mug and then stick it in the microwave. Three minutes later, you have cake,' she explained. 'I haven't actually tried it. But apparently it works perfectly when you really, really want cake at three in the morning.'

'Three minutes. Hmm. You can make a cheese toastie in that,' he said.

She smiled. 'If you get the munchies when it's your turn to feed Hope, feel free to make yourself a cheese toastie.'

He grinned back. 'If I do, I promise I'll clean up the crumbs.'

Almost on cue, Hope woke, wanting milk.

'I'll do the next feed,' Josh said when she'd finished. 'Go and get some sleep, Amy.'

Once Amy had showered and changed into her pyjamas, she lay awake in the dark, thinking that this was the Christmas she'd never expected. It must be just as weird for Josh, too, spending Christmas with an almost complete stranger—and tough for him, because his wife had left him on Christmas Eve last year and the memories had to hurt. But maybe looking after the baby would help distract him from some of the pain.

Part of her wanted to sleep for eternity, she was so tired—which was ridiculous, because she hadn't exactly done much all day. But looking after a newborn baby had been fraught with worry that had unexpectedly worn her out. Was she doing the right thing? How would she know if she was getting it wrong? What if the baby was ill and she hadn't spotted the signs? Or if she made such a mess of changing Hope that the baby ended up with nappy rash—and where would you be able to buy nappy rash cream on Christmas Day, when all the shops were shut?

The worries flickered through her head, stopping her from falling asleep. Part of her wanted to go and check that the baby was OK—but what if she woke Josh? He'd already worked a busy shift today at the hospital. Plus he was used to dealing with babies, and he'd said this was his shift; if he woke and found her checking on the baby, he might think she didn't trust him. And if that upset him enough to make him walk out on her without really discussing anything, the way Michael had walked out on her, how was she going to cope with the baby all on her own for a week?

Be careful what you wish for...

She'd longed for a baby. Now, she had exactly that. A baby to look after. For a week.

And it was terrifying.

Maybe Michael was right about her. She'd been too stupid to guess that Gavin might have given her a symptomless STD, so when she'd finally discovered the truth the treatment had been too late to prevent the damage to her Fallopian tubes. So it was her fault that she was infertile. Maybe she was too clueless to look after a baby, too. Why, why, why had she agreed to help?

She heard the baby start crying, and glanced at the clock. She hadn't even managed to sleep for five minutes. It was Josh's turn to feed the baby, but clearly he was in a deep sleep because the baby's cries grew louder.

Get up and see to the baby, she told herself sharply.

The poor little mite has nobody. Stop being so whiny and self-pitying and *get up*. You can't worry about not coping because you just *have* to. There isn't another option.

She dragged herself out of bed and stumbled into the living room. 'Shh, baby,' she whispered—but the baby just kept screaming.

Just as Amy scooped the baby out of the Moses basket, she heard Josh mumble, 'My turn. I've got this.'

'I'm awake now. I'll do it,' she said.

'We'll do it together,' Josh said. 'Cuddle the baby or do the milk?'

Amy inhaled the sweet, powdery scent of the baby.

A baby she couldn't afford to bond with. So it would be better not to get too close now.

'Milk,' she said, and handed Hope to him.

'Shh, baby,' he crooned.

On autopilot, Amy boiled the kettle and put the baby's bottle in a glass jug to heat the milk. She nearly scalded herself when she poured boiling water into the jug, and it splashed.

'Everything OK?' Josh asked, seeing her jump.

'Yes,' she fibbed. The last thing she wanted was for him to guess how stupid and useless she felt.

'Sorry I didn't wake sooner. I guess my shift took more out of me than I thought,' he said. 'I'm supposed to be helping. I've let you down.'

And then the penny dropped.

She wasn't the only one finding it hard to do this.

'You're fine,' she said. 'We're both new at this. I always tell my class, you learn more if you get it wrong first time.'

'I guess.' He sounded rueful. 'Except a baby is a

hell of a lot tougher than a page of maths problems. And, given how many babies I treat in the course of a month, I should be better at this.'

'There's a big difference between treating a baby and looking after one full time,' she reminded him. 'And didn't you say to me earlier that Hope doesn't know if we're doing it wrong?'

'Yeah. I'm glad I'm not doing this on my own,' he said.

He'd admitted it first, so it made it easier for her to say, 'Me, too. I never expected it to be this hard— you're desperate for sleep, but you're also too scared to sleep because you want to keep an eye on the baby.'

'All the *what ifs*,' he agreed. 'Being a medic is a bad thing, because you know all the worst-case scenarios and your mind goes into overdrive. You start thinking you're seeing symptoms when there aren't any. And then you're not sure if you're being ridiculously paranoid or if you really *are* seeing something.'

'And if you're not a medic, you look up stuff on the Internet and scare yourself stupid,' she said. 'Being a parent—even a stand-in—is way harder than I thought.'

'Especially the first night, when you don't have a clue what to expect,' Josh agreed.

'We're a right pair,' she said ruefully.

'No. We're a team,' Josh said.

And that spooked her even more. It was so long since she'd seen herself in a partnership that she didn't know how to react. Then she shook herself. He meant they were a team, not a couple. She was reading too much into this. To cover how flustered she felt, she shook a couple of drops of milk onto the inside of her wrist to check the temperature. 'I think it's OK for her, now.'

'Thanks. Go back to bed,' he said. 'I've got this.'

'Sure?' she checked.

'Sure.'

'OK.' And this time she felt more relaxed when she snuggled under the duvet—enough to let her drift into sleep.

The next time the baby cried, Amy got up and scooped up the Moses basket. 'Shh, baby,' she whispered. 'Two minutes.'

'OK?' Josh asked from the sofa, sounding wide awake this time.

He hadn't been joking about usually being fully awake in seconds, then.

'It's fine. It's my turn to feed her,' she said quietly. And the way they'd muddled through together earlier had given her confidence. 'Go back to sleep.'

She took the baby into the kitchen and cuddled her as she warmed the milk, then took the baby into her bedroom, kept the light down low, and cuddled the baby as she fed her.

This felt so natural, so right. But she had to remind herself sharply that this was only temporary and she couldn't let herself bond too closely to Hope—or start thinking about Josh as anything more than just a neighbour. By New Year, life would be back to normal again. They'd be back to smiling and nodding in the corridor, maybe exchanging an extra word or two. But that would be it.

Once the baby fell asleep again, Amy laid her gently back in the Moses basket and padded into the living room. Josh was asleep on the sofa, and this time he didn't wake.

* * *

A couple of hours later, when Hope started to grizzle again, Josh was awake in seconds.

'Shh, baby,' he whispered, and jiggled her one-handed against his shoulder as he set about making up a bottle.

When it had been his turn to deal with the baby, he'd made a complete hash of it. Not being used to listening out for a newborn, he'd slept through Hope's cries. But it turned out that Amy had been having the same kind of self-doubts that he had. Given that she'd seemed so cool, calm and collected, he'd been shocked. And then relieved. Because it meant that they were in this *together*.

And they made a good team.

To the point where he actually believed that he could do this—be a stand-in parent to an abandoned baby.

Then he realised he'd been a bit overconfident when he burped Hope and she brought up all the milk she'd just drunk. All over both of them.

He really hoped Amy didn't wake and find them both in this state. 'I dare not give you a bath,' he whispered to the baby. He knew she'd scream the place down, even if he managed to put water in the bath without waking Amy. But when he stripped off her sleep suit and vest, he discovered that luckily the baby wasn't soaked to the skin. Unlike him—but he was the adult and he'd live with it. He changed the baby into clean clothes, gave her more milk, then finally settled her back into the Moses basket.

Which left him cold and wet and smelling disgusting. He could hardly have a shower right now without waking Amy, and he couldn't go back to his own flat because he didn't have a key to Amy's. Grimacing, he stripped off his T-shirt and scrubbed the worst of the milk off his skin with a baby wipe.

Was this what life would've been like if he and Kelly had had a family? Would he have made as much of a mess of being a real dad as he was making of being a stand-in dad? Or maybe Amy was right and he was being too hard on himself. But he was seriously glad he wasn't looking after the baby on his own. It helped to be able to talk to someone else and admit that you didn't know what you were doing, and for them to say the same to you. And he was pretty sure now that he'd be able to get through this week—because Amy was on his team.

The next time Amy heard Hope crying, her eyes felt gritty from lack of sleep. Either the baby had slept a bit longer between feeds this time, or Amy had been too deeply asleep to hear her crying at the last feed.

When she stumbled into the kitchen to put the kettle on and checked the top shelf of the fridge, she realised it was the latter; Josh had done the last feed. He'd left her a note propped against the kettle. His handwriting was hard to read and she smiled to herself. Josh was definitely living up to the cliché of all medics having a terrible scrawl. Eventually she deciphered the note.

On early shift this morning—back for about 5.30 this evening—Merry Christmas, J

Christmas.

Amy hadn't planned to cook the traditional turkey

dinner; she hadn't seen the point of bothering when she was going to be on her own. But now she had unexpected company for dinner. She didn't have a turkey, but she did have the ingredients to make something nice. She could wrap a couple of chicken breasts in bacon, stir fry some tenderstem broccoli with julienned strips of butternut squash and carrot in butter and chilli, and make some baked polenta chips sprinkled with Parmesan.

'I forgot how much I enjoyed cooking,' she told the baby as she fed her. 'I haven't even had people over for dinner since I moved here. I always eat out with my friends. So maybe it's time to move on a bit more and start doing the things I enjoy again.'

The baby simply drank her milk and stared at Amy with those huge dark blue eyes.

'I've spent the last eighteen months living on autopilot,' Amy said. 'Don't you ever make that mistake, Hope. Life's for—well, enjoying.'

Though she was pretty sure that Hope's mum was having a thoroughly miserable Christmas. 'I hope we can find your mum,' she said softly. 'And I really hope we can do something to help her. I really don't know why she left you in our lobby—whether she knew me or Josh from somewhere, or whether it was a completely random choice—but I'm glad she did, because I think you're going to help us as much as we can help you.' And she was glad that Josh had moved in on her floor, because the reason she'd got through that first night with a baby was because of him.

Once she'd showered, washed her hair and dressed, she sent Josh a text.

Hope you're having a good shift. Alternative Christmas dinner this evening. Amy

And whether Hope was responding to her sunny mood and burst of confidence, Amy had no idea, but the baby seemed content, too; she wasn't quite as fractious and unsettled as she'd been the day before. To her relief, there wasn't one of the protracted crying sessions that had left Amy feeling hopeless and frustrated and miserable.

'Merry Christmas, baby,' she said softly. 'It isn't quite the one I think your mum would've liked for you, but hopefully the police are going to find her and reunite you in the next few days.'

Amy ate yoghurt and granola for breakfast, then looked at the small stack of presents beneath the tree. It felt odd, opening her Christmas presents all on her own. But she pushed away the melancholy before it could take hold. She intended to make the best of this Christmas, and she wasn't the only one on her own. It must be much harder for Josh in the circumstances.

Most of the envelopes contained gift vouchers, but one friend had given her the latest crime novel by one of her favourite authors, another had given her some nice Christmassy scented candles and another had bought her posh chocolates.

'That's my table decorations and dessert sorted for this evening,' she told the baby. 'And in the meantime you and I are going to curl up together on the sofa and watch a pile of Christmas movies.'

CHAPTER FOUR

AFTER HIS SHIFT, Josh showered and changed before going down the corridor to Amy's flat.

He felt a bit mean; she was cooking Christmas dinner for him, but he hadn't bought her even a token present. Then again, neither of them had expected this Christmas: for a newborn to be left on their doorstep, and then to be looking after a stranger's baby together when they barely knew each other. A present probably wasn't appropriate in the circumstances. Besides, even if the shops had been open, he didn't have a clue what kind of thing Amy liked—apart from coffee ice cream, and you could hardly wrap that and leave it under a tree. The wine he was carrying came from the rack in his kitchen, and the chocolates were a kind of re-gift. Which definitely made him feel like Scrooge.

'Merry Christmas,' he said when she opened the door in answer to his knock.

'Merry Christmas,' she said. 'I thought we'd eat at about half-past six, if that's OK with you?'

'More than OK. You have no idea how much I appreciate not having to cook for myself, or be forced to munch the leftover sausage rolls people brought in to the department because I'm starving but too tired even to make a cheese toastie,' he said with a smile. He handed her the chocolates and wine. 'This is my contribution for tonight.'

'You really didn't have to, but thank you.'

'And I have to admit that the chocolates are from the Secret Santa at work, which makes me a bit of a Scrooge for kind of re-gifting them,' he confessed.

'No, it just means that you don't usually have chocolate in the house and there aren't any shops open. And they're definitely appreciated,' she said, smiling back. 'How was your shift?'

'Let's just say we've renamed one of the twelve days of Christmas. "Five Turkey Carvers",' he said ruefully. 'I've done quite a bit of stitching up today.'

'Ouch,' she said.

'So how's our little one doing?' Then he realised what he'd said and felt his eyes go wide. 'Um,' he said. 'Sorry. I didn't quite...'

'I know,' she said quietly. 'It kind of feels like being part of a new family.'

'Even though she isn't ours, and we're not...'

'...a couple. Yeah,' she said.

Josh looked at her. Amy wasn't wearing a scrap of make-up, but she was naturally beautiful. He itched to sketch her, and it had been a long while since anyone had made him feel that way.

This was dangerous.

Part of him wanted to run; but part of him was intrigued and wanted more. To cover his confusion, he asked, 'Is there anything I can do to help?'

She shook her head. 'Hope's still asleep and I haven't started cooking dinner yet, so do you want a glass of wine or a cup of tea?'

'As it's Christmas, let's go for the glass of wine,' he said.

'And, as you said you wanted to help, you can open it.'

He followed her into the kitchen. When she handed him the corkscrew, his fingers brushed against her skin and it felt weird, as if he'd been galvanised. He was shockingly aware of her, but he didn't dare look at her because he didn't want her to guess what he was thinking. Had she felt it, too? And, if so, what were they going to do about it?

He shook himself mentally. They weren't going to do anything about it. They were neighbours. Acquaintances. And that was the way it was going to stay.

He opened the wine while she took two glasses from a cupboard; then he poured the wine before lifting his own glass and clinking it against hers. 'Merry Christmas.'

'Merry Christmas,' she echoed.

'I haven't bought you a present,' he said, 'and I feel kind of bad about it.'

'I haven't bought you one, either,' she said. 'I did think about wrapping up a bottle of wine for you or something, but it didn't feel appropriate.'

'Considering we hardly know each other and don't have a clue what each other likes,' he agreed.

'We haven't bought Hope anything, either,' she said, 'but it's fine. Christmas isn't really about the presents, and perhaps what we're actually giving each other is a better Christmas than we were expecting.'

'You know,' he said, 'I think you might be right. You're a wise woman, Amy Howes.'

'It goes with the territory of being a maths teacher,' she said with a smile.

He liked her sense of humour. And, actually, the more he talked to her, the more he liked a lot of other things about her. Which again set his alarm bells ringing. He wasn't supposed to be thinking like that. He was newly divorced. Not in a place to start anything with anyone.

'Maybe,' he said, 'we can make a kind of present for Hope. A book of her days with us. Photographs, that kind of thing.'

'Add in her feed and sleep charts, too?' Amy said. 'That's a really nice idea. And then she's got something to keep.'

'So how has it been with the baby today?' he asked.

'Easier than yesterday. We've been watching Christmas movies,' she said.

'Sounds like a good plan.'

'*Love Actually* is one of my favourite films. And you really can't top the Christmas lobster.'

Then Amy remembered that one of the storylines in the movie involved an affair. Talk about rubbing salt in his wounds. How could she have forgotten that Josh's wife left him for another man, last Christmas Eve? 'Sorry. I just put my foot in it. I didn't mean to make you feel bad.'

'I'm not a fan of romcoms,' Josh said, 'and you haven't put your foot in it—even though I get what you're saying. This is way better than Christmas was last year, believe me.'

Which didn't make her feel any less guilty. Just about anything would be an improvement on his last

Christmas. 'Maybe I should start prepping dinner,' she said awkwardly.

'As the baby's asleep, is there anything I can do?'

'You can keep topping up the wine and chat to me in the kitchen, if you like,' she suggested.

'I'd like that. Funny, two days ago we were almost complete strangers,' he said, 'and now we're spending Christmas together.'

'As a kind of blended family with a baby who's a complete stranger, too,' she said.

'I still don't know anything about you,' he said, 'other than that you're a maths teacher and you have a brother who lives in Canada.'

'And you're an emergency department doctor who's the youngest of four.' She shrugged. 'OK. So what do you want to know? I'm thirty.'

'I'm thirty-two,' he said.

Amy started chopping the carrots into matchsticks.

'And you obviously enjoy cooking—or at least you're good at it,' Josh said.

She smiled. 'Thank you, and I do. Does that mean you don't?'

'I'd rather wash up than cook,' he said. 'Obviously I can cook a few basics—you wouldn't survive as a student unless you knew how to make stuff like spaghetti Bolognese and cheese toasties—but spending all that time making something that people will wolf down in two seconds flat and then forget about...' He smiled. 'Or maybe that's the medic in me talking.'

'So food's fuel rather than a pleasure?'

'At work, yes,' he admitted. 'Shamefully, I eat a chocolate bar on the run for my lunch way more often than I ought to.'

'So what sort of things do you like doing outside work?' Amy grimaced. 'I'm sorry. This sounds like a terrible speed-dating sort of grilling.'

'Speed-dating,' he said, 'is something I've never actually done.'

'Me neither,' she agreed. 'Though I guess, when you get to our age, it's probably about your only option for meeting someone, if you haven't already clicked with someone you met at work or with a friend of a friend at a party.'

'And if you're in a job with unsocial hours, work means that half the time you're not on the same shift and it's hard to find a time when you can actually do something together,' he added. 'Though I think being set up with a friend of a friend is worse than dating someone at work, because then if it doesn't work out it makes things a bit awkward with your friend. You feel a bit guilty and as if you've let your friend down.'

'That sounds like experience talking,' Amy said.

Josh wrinkled his nose. 'I did have a couple of well-meaning friends try to set me up, earlier this year, but I told them I just wasn't ready.'

She nodded. 'I know what you mean. It was a while before I could face dating after I split up with Michael; then, after that, I just didn't meet anyone I could click with.'

Though she had a feeling that she could click with Josh, given the chance. It surprised her how much she liked him and how easy he was to talk to.

'One of my friends tried speed-dating a few months back,' Josh said. 'He tried to talk me into going with him, but it sounded a bit too much like a meat market for me. He did say afterwards that all the women he'd met had had a massive list of questions they'd prepared earlier, and it felt like the worst kind of job interview.'

'I guess asking questions is a quick way of getting to know someone,' she said.

He smiled at her. 'Maybe we should look at one of those lists. It'll save us having to think up our own questions.'

'Good idea,' she said, carefully separating the tenderstem broccoli and adding it to her pile of stir-fry veg before starting on the butternut squash.

Josh took his phone from his pocket and flicked into the Internet. 'Here we go. What you do at work? Well, we already know that about each other. Where are you from?' He frowned. 'That's pretty irrelevant.' He flicked further down the list. 'OK. Let's try this one. What's the one thing about yourself that you'd like me to know?'

'I don't have a clue,' she said.

'Me, neither. Let's skip to the next one.' He grimaced. 'That's all about your last relationship. It's too intrusive. Same as whether you're looking to get married.' He shook his head. 'I can't believe you'd actually ask a complete stranger if they're looking to get married when you're thinking about maybe dating them for the first time. I mean—you might be completely incompatible. Why would you talk about marriage that early on?'

'Maybe that's the point of speed-dating. To speed everything up,' Amy said. 'If you want to settle down but the person you're thinking about dating doesn't, you're both kind of wasting each other's time.'

'That question still feels wrong.' He scrolled down

the page. 'This is a bit more like it. What do you do for fun?'

'Music,' she said promptly. 'Not clubbing—I like live music, whether it's a tiny venue where there's only enough room for a couple of dozen people listening to someone playing an acoustic guitar, or a big stadium with a massive stack of amps and a light show.'

'What kind of music?' he asked.

'All sorts—everything from pop to rock. I'm not so keen on rap,' she said, 'but I love the buzz you get from going to a concert and singing along with the rest of the audience. What about you?'

'I tend to listen to rock music when I'm running,' he said. 'Something with a strong beat that keeps me going.'

'So you're a runner?'

'Strictly outdoor. I like the fresh air, and the views,' he said, 'rather than being cooped up in a gym on a treadmill where you just see the same patch of wall for half an hour or so.'

'Park or river?' she asked.

'If it's wet, river,' he said, 'purely because you're less likely to slide on the mud and rick your ankle. If it's dry, definitely the park because it's lovely to see all that green, especially in spring when all the leaves are new and everything looks fresh. And if I worked regular hours I'd definitely have a dog to run with me.' He shrugged. 'I don't have a dog because my hours aren't regular and it wouldn't be fair to leave the dog alone for so long.'

'You look like a Labrador person,' she said.

He nodded. 'Or a spaniel. Or a Dalmatian—where I lived before, our neighbour had this amazing Dalmatian who used to smile at me. And it really was a friendly greeting rather than baring his teeth, because his tail was wagging so hard the whole time.'

Amy could see the wistfulness on his face. The breakup of his marriage had cost him more than just his relationship.

'How about you?' he asked.

'No to the running. I like spinning classes,' she said, 'because I don't have to worry about riding a bike in traffic and I don't have to drag myself outside when it's wet.'

'That's reasonable—though, actually, running in the rain is great. Dog or cat?'

'Dog,' she said. 'But, like you, I don't want to leave a dog cooped up alone in my flat all day. So I make the most of it when I go to see my parents—they've got Border terriers.'

He continued scrolling through the list of questions. 'Some of these definitely sound more like the sort of thing you'd ask in a job interview. Why would you ask someone if they have a five-year plan?'

'Because you want to know if they're ambitious and would put their career before your relationship; or find out if they're the kind of person who drifts along and gets stuck in a bit of a rut,' she suggested.

'Which in turn probably means your relationship will end up in a rut, too.' He rolled his eyes. 'There have to be easier ways of getting to know what a person's like.'

'In the space of three minutes, or however long it is you have on a speed date? I don't think you have a choice but to ask intrusive questions,' she said.

'I give up on the list. What sort of thing would you ask?'

'About their interests,' she said. 'Dating someone who wanted to spend their whole weekend playing sport or watching sport would be pretty wearing.'

'Yes, because when would you get time to do other things together?' he agreed.

'In the evenings, maybe—something like the cinema?' she suggested.

'I haven't been to the cinema in way too long,' he said. 'I tend to end up waiting for things to come out on DVD, and even then I haven't caught up with all the latest releases, and I've got a pile of stuff I've been meaning to see and haven't had time for.'

'So why don't you go to the cinema?' she asked. 'Because you like the kind of things that nobody else does, so you'd have to go on your own?'

'Art-house movies in a foreign language?' he asked. 'No, it's more that my duty roster tends to get in the way and everyone's already seen the film before I get a chance. I like the big sci-fi blockbusters.'

'Ah. Now I have a question for you. Team Cap or Team Iron Man?' she asked.

'Team Cap,' he said promptly, and she gave him a high five.

'So you like the same kind of films as I do?' he asked.

'Yup. I do like romcoms as well, but I've always been a sci-fi geek. And I bought myself the one that came out last week as an early Christmas present. I know it's not strictly a Christmas movie, but maybe we could watch it tonight.'

'And we can pause it if Hope needs a nappy change or a feed. Great idea.' He smiled at her. 'So we like the same kind of films and music. How about TV?'

'Cop dramas,' she said. 'That's my guilty pleasure. All the Scandinavian noir stuff.'

'Again, I have to watch them on catch-up half the time, but me too,' he said.

'Right. Crosswords or number puzzles?'

He groaned. 'Neither. I'm assuming that you'd go for the maths problems?'

'Absolutely.' She smiled. 'Reading—fiction or non-fiction?'

'Non-fiction,' he said promptly, 'and it's usually medical journals. You?'

'Crime fiction,' she said. 'I guess it's because I like trying to solve the puzzles.'

'Beach holiday or climbing a mountain?' he asked.

'Neither—city break or road trip for me,' she said. 'I like exploring new places and seeing the sights. You?'

'I like the sound of the road trip,' he said. 'I'd love to see New England in the fall. And the hot springs and waterfalls at Yosemite.'

'I'd guessed you'd be bored on a beach, but you strike me as a mountain-climbing type,' she said.

'Not so much mountains,' he said, 'but I did do the coast-to-coast walk for charity, one year, and I loved every second of it—even the blisters.'

'I'm afraid the best I've done in the charity stakes is to make cakes and sponsor friends who do the ten-K runs,' Amy said.

'The main thing is that the money's raised. It doesn't matter who does what,' he said.

Just as Amy finished prepping dinner, Hope woke.

'Well, hello, Munchkin,' he said, and scooped the baby out of her Moses basket. 'So it's Uncle Joshy's turn to feed you.'

'I'll bring the milk in,' Amy said.

When she took the warmed milk in, Josh was sitting on the sofa, talking to the baby in a low voice and letting her wrap her tiny fist round his little finger. The sight put a lump in her throat. Josh was so warm and kind. He'd make a fabulous father one day—but that made him off limits for her, so she'd have to ignore the attraction she felt towards him. If he wanted children, she couldn't take his future away from him like that. And, given the way he was acting with the baby right now, she was pretty sure he'd want a family of his own one day.

Josh took the bottle of milk from Amy. 'Thanks.'

'No problem.'

Hope closed her eyes in bliss as she drank the milk. And it was strange how natural this felt, having a warm little weight in the crook of his arm. In another life, this could've been his baby...

He glanced at Amy. For all his scorn about the speed-dating questions, they had at least established that they had quite a few interests in common. And the more he got to know her, the more he liked her. It had been a while since he'd met someone he felt he could really be himself with.

'Hey. Smile,' she said, and held up her camera.

'For Hope's book?'

'You bet.'

'Then I ought to be sitting with the Christmas tree behind me.' He stood up, without disturbing Hope or stopping her drinking her milk, and moved so Amy could take a more Christmassy photo of them together. 'I'll take one of you with her later, too.'

'Thanks.'

She laid the table while he fed the baby. 'Sorry, it's not going to be a proper Christmas dinner, and I don't have any crackers or party hats—but I do have a Christmas scented candle.'

'Sounds good. Anything I can do to help?'

'You already are,' she said. 'And you've been at work all day. Just chill with the baby.'

This really, really felt like being part of a new little family.

Josh knew he was going to have to keep a tight grip on his imagination, because that so wasn't happening. Yes, he found Amy attractive; but the last thing he wanted to do was to have a fling with her and then for it all to go wrong and make things awkward if he bumped into her in the lobby or the corridor. They needed to keep things strictly platonic, he reminded himself.

And that was what stopped him going to chat to her in the kitchen again when the baby had finished her feed and he'd burped her.

Though sitting there watching the baby fall asleep made his fingers itch to sketch her. When he wrote all the details of the feed down in Amy's notebook, he couldn't resist flicking to the very back of the book. It didn't matter that the paper was lined and he was using a pen rather than a pencil; he gave into the urge and sketched the sleeping baby. And maybe this was something he could add to Hope's book. Something personal.

He was so wrapped up in what he was doing that he didn't notice Amy standing beside him, carrying a glass of wine.

'That's seriously good,' she said. 'Did you ever think about being an artist instead of a doctor?'

His big dream. The one that had been squashed before it had had a chance to grow. For once he answered honestly. 'Not in a family of high achievers,' he said wryly. 'Art wasn't quite academic enough for them.'

'Your parents didn't support you?' She sounded shocked. Clearly her family was the sort to encourage her to follow her dreams rather than insist that she trod the path they'd mapped out for her.

'They didn't like the idea of me going to art school,' Josh admitted. 'They said the world had changed a lot in the last generation and there weren't that many jobs in art.' At least not ones that paid well. Though he ought to be fair about it. 'I guess they had a point.'

'What made you choose medicine instead?' she asked.

'Studying biology meant I could still draw,' he said. 'Besides, art is something I can do for me.'

'Do you do much?'

That was the killer question. He smiled wryly. 'It hasn't quite worked out that way.'

'Make the time, Josh,' she said softly. 'If drawing makes you happy, make the time for it.'

Kelly had never suggested that to him.

But then again, the real him hadn't been enough for her, any more than it had been enough for his family—or Kelly would've had her baby with him instead of with another man.

He pushed the thought away. Now wasn't the time to be maudlin or filled with regrets.

'Dinner's about ready,' she said.

'Perfect timing. Munchkin here's set to sleep for

a couple of hours,' he said. 'Can I bring anything in for you?'

'No, but you can light the candle, if you want. The matches are in the top drawer of the cupboard over there.'

He lit the candle and sat down while she brought in the dishes.

'This is fabulous,' he said after the first taste of the polenta chips sprinkled with parmesan.

'Thanks. It's been a while since I've made these,' she said.

'You told me to make the time for doing something I love—that goes for you, too,' he said gently.

'I guess. I'll make more of an effort in the new year, as long as you promise to do the same.'

'I will,' he agreed. 'I've been thinking—do you reckon the baby's mother picked our block of flats at random?'

'Maybe,' Amy said. 'Are you thinking she didn't?'

'She rang your doorbell. That might've been chance—but supposing you knew her?'

Amy shook her head. 'That's unlikely. I don't know anyone who's pregnant.'

'But we think she's young and scared, right?' he asked, warming to his theory. 'The chances are, she hid her pregnancy from just about everyone. But maybe she knew you from school.'

'I didn't recognise the handwriting, so I don't think she's anyone I teach,' Amy said. She frowned. 'But then again…'

'What if she wrote the note with her non-writing hand?' Josh suggested.

'Or what if,' Amy said slowly, 'she's someone I don't

teach, so I've never really seen her handwriting properly? Now I think about it, there's a girl in my form who's gone very quiet over the last few months. I did have a confidential word with her mum, but she said Freya was being difficult because her new partner had just moved in.'

'It happens,' Josh said. 'How old is she?'

'Fifteen.'

'Then maybe, if she's unhappy at home, she's blotting it out with the help of a boyfriend.'

'I don't think she has a boyfriend,' Amy said. 'At least, not one who's at school. You normally hear the kids talking and work out who's seeing who.'

'Does she look as if she's put on weight?'

Amy thought about it. 'She always wears baggy clothes so it's hard to tell. But, now you mention it, she does look as if she's put on weight. I assumed she was comfort-eating because she was unhappy at home and I didn't want to make her feel any worse by drawing attention to it. Teens are under such pressure when it comes to body image. I didn't want to say something that would make her start starving herself. But I have noticed her dashing off to the loo in the middle of form time over the last term, and I was going to have a quiet word with her next term to check she didn't have an eating disorder.'

'Or maybe,' Josh said, 'she was dashing off to the loo because she was in the last trimester and the baby's weight was putting pressure on her bladder.'

'That's a good point. But why didn't she say anything to me?'

'In the cases I've seen at work,' Josh said, 'where the mum's under age and scared, she's either been in denial about the situation or too scared to tell anyone in case she gets into trouble.'

'That's so sad,' Amy said. 'To be young and scared and not know where to go for help.'

'She didn't say anything to you,' Josh said. 'But it would make sense that she'd leave the baby with someone she knew would help and do the right thing for the baby.'

'Agreed. But this is all speculation,' she said. 'We don't have any proof.'

'And we have to do this through the proper channels,' Josh added. 'If our theory's right, then we could do more harm than good if we go rushing over to see her.'

'Plus we don't have a car seat or anyone to keep an eye on Hope while we go and see her,' she agreed. 'Jane, the social worker, will know the right way to go about this. We can talk to her about it.'

'Tomorrow's Sunday—Boxing Day—and then Monday and Tuesday are bank holidays, so she won't be in the office for a few days,' Josh pointed out.

'She did give me her mobile number, but it was for emergencies—and, because this is a theory and we don't have any real proof, it doesn't really count as an emergency.' Amy frowned. 'I guess it'll have to wait a few days.'

'Or maybe you could text Jane tomorrow?' he suggested. 'Then she'll have the information and she can decide if she wants to take it further any earlier.'

'Good idea,' she said.

'I'm off duty tomorrow.' He gave her a wry smile. 'It would've been nice to take the baby out to the park, but as she doesn't have a coat and we don't have a pram or even a sling, and there's not going to be anywhere open tomorrow where we can buy something for her, I guess we're stuck.'

'It feels a bit like being snowbound,' Amy said, 'but without actually being snowed in.'

'And you haven't left your flat for two days.' Guilt flooded through him. She'd had the majority of the burden of worrying about the baby. 'Sorry, I should've thought of that earlier and suggested you went out to get some fresh air or something.'

'No, it's fine, but probably tomorrow I could do with some fresh air,' she admitted, 'if you don't mind looking after Hope on your own for a few minutes.'

'Sure. That's no problem.'

After dinner, they curled up on the sofa and watched the sci-fi film together. A couple of times, Josh's hand accidentally brushed against Amy's and he seriously considered letting his fingers curl round hers.

But then again, she'd said she wasn't ready for another relationship, and he knew his own head was still in a bit of a mess.

He was definitely attracted to Amy. But how could he trust that love wouldn't go wrong for him again, the way it had with Kelly? It was better to stick to just being friends. That would be safer for all of them.

'I guess it's time to get some sleep,' Amy said when she'd fed Hope and noted everything down. 'I'll do the next feed.'

'Sure?'

'Sure. Feel free to leave the TV on as long as you want, though. You won't be disturbing me.'

'OK. I'll get my duvet,' he said.

'Take my key with you,' she said. 'Merry Christmas, Josh.'

'Merry Christmas, Amy.'

For a moment he thought she was going to rise on tiptoe and kiss him, and his whole body seemed to snap to attention. What would it feel like, her lips against his skin? Would her mouth be as soft and sweet as it looked? And what if he twisted his head to the side so her mouth connected with his instead of with his cheek?

He was shocked to realise how much he wanted it to happen.

And even more shocked to realise how disappointed he was when she simply smiled and headed for the bathroom instead.

Oh, help. He really had to get a grip. He and Amy were neighbours. Maybe they were on the way to being friends. This whole thing of looking after the baby together was seriously messing with his head. He didn't want to risk his heart again. End of. So he was going to be sensible.

Completely sensible.

CHAPTER FIVE

Boxing Day—Sunday

'Josh. *Josh.*'

He was awake instantly, and he could hear the note of panic in Amy's voice. 'What's happened?'

'It's Hope. She feels really hot and she hardly drank any milk just now. I think there's something wrong.'

'Hold on. Where's the light? I'll take a look at her.'

She switched on one of the lamps in the living room.

Josh took the baby from Amy's arms and gently examined her. 'You're right—she does feel hot.'

'I have one of those ear thermometers. Maybe we should take her temperature and see how bad it is?' Amy suggested.

'Unfortunately, those thermometers are too big for a newborn baby's ears,' he said. 'We need a normal digital thermometer. I've got one in my bathroom— I'll go and get it.'

Amy frowned. 'But surely you can't stick a thermometer in a baby's mouth?'

'Nope—you stick it under her armpit,' he said.

'Oh.' Amy looked at him. 'Anything I can do?'

'Strip her down to her nappy and a vest while I get

the thermometer, then hold her for me and talk to her,' he said. 'And if you've got some cooled boiled water, we'll try and get her to drink some.'

When he checked the baby's temperature, he wasn't happy with the reading. 'It's thirty-eight degrees. It's a bit high, but a baby's temperature can go up and down really quickly because at this age their bodies haven't worked out yet how to control their temperature. I'm ninety-five per cent sure this is nothing serious, because the soft spot at the top of her head isn't sunken and she isn't floppy,' he reassured Amy. Though that left a five per cent chance that this was the early stages of something nasty. 'But, given that we don't really know the circumstances of her birth, there's a chance she might have a bacterial infection,' he said. And in that case she would get worse. Quickly, too, though he wasn't going to worry Amy about that now. 'The only way to find out is by a blood test and urine analysis, which I can't do here.'

'So we need to take her to hospital?' Amy asked.

He sighed. 'I'd rather not have to do that, with all the viruses going around, but babies this young can get very unwell quite quickly, so if it *is* an infection I'd want her treated for it as soon as possible. Though, at this time of the morning, the department will be relatively quiet, so we won't have to wait too long.'

'Just take our turn with the drunks who've fallen over after a party or had a punch-up?' she asked wryly.

He smiled. Clearly she'd remembered his grumpy assessment of the seasonal waiting room. 'Yes, but she'll be triaged. We prioritise when we see our patients, depending on their symptoms and how old they are. Hope will get seen really quickly because she's a newborn with a temperature.'

'We don't have a car seat or a pram. How are we going to get her to hospital?' Amy asked.

'We can't risk taking her in the back of the car in her Moses basket,' Josh said. 'Apart from the fact it's illegal and we have departmental guidelines, so we can't let anyone take a child from hospital without an appropriate seat, I also know most accidents take place within a mile of a home. We're going to have to call an ambulance.'

'OK. I'll get Hope dressed again while you call the ambulance, and then I'll throw on some clothes. Give me two minutes.'

She was as good as her word, he noticed, taking only a couple of minutes and not bothering with make-up or anything like that. Practical. He liked that.

'They'll be here in another five minutes,' he said. 'I told them we'd wait in the lobby.'

Between them, they tucked Hope into her Moses basket; Amy grabbed the notebook so they had a record of everything the baby had drunk, and they waited in the lobby until they saw the ambulance pull up outside.

'Josh! You're the last person I expected to see—nobody thought you were even dating anyone, let alone had a new baby,' the paramedic said.

Oh, help. He could really do without any gossip at work. 'The baby's not mine,' he said hastily.

The paramedic looked intrigued. 'So you're helping your...' she glanced at Amy '...friend.'

'The baby's not mine, either,' Amy said. 'We're looking after her temporarily.'

The paramedic's eyes rounded. 'Together?'

'We're neighbours,' Josh added. 'And you might have seen something about the baby in the news.'

'Oh, hang on—is this the Christmas Eve doorstep baby?'

'Yes. Her name's Hope,' Amy said, 'and she's got a temperature.'

'Thirty-eight degrees, axillary,' Josh said, 'and we stripped her off and gave her cooled boiled water, but we don't have any liquid paracetamol. I need blood tests and urine analysis to rule out a bacterial infection. She's not floppy or drowsy so I'm not panicking, but given her age and the fact that we don't know the circumstances of her birth or anything about her medical history...'

The paramedic patted his arm. 'Josh, you're off duty. Stop worrying. We'll handle it. Right now you count as a patient, not staff. Are you coming in with her?'

'We both are,' Josh said.

It was the first time Amy had ever travelled in an ambulance. And even though Josh was able to answer most of the paramedic's questions and she had the notes about Hope's feeds, it was still a worrying experience.

Especially when the paramedic put a tiny oxygen mask on the baby.

'What's wrong?' Amy asked.

'It's a precaution,' Josh said. Clearly he could tell how worried she was, because he took her hand and squeezed it to reassure her. Somehow her fingers ended up curled just as tightly round his.

The drive to hospital was short, but it felt as if it

took for ever. And when Hope was whisked into cubicles the second they arrived, with the doctor acknowledging them but asking them to wait outside, Amy's worries deepened.

'It's routine,' Josh said. 'They'll be taking blood and urine samples to check if she's got an infection.'

'But why can't we stay with her?' Amy asked. 'I mean, I know we're not her actual parents, but...'

'I know.' His fingers tightened round hers. 'As I said, it's routine and we're just going to get in the way. We need to let the team do their job.'

'You work here. Doesn't that make a difference?' Amy asked.

He shook his head.

And then a really nasty thought struck her. He'd said that new babies couldn't regulate their temperatures that well. If Hope had an infection and her temperature shot up... Could she die?

Time felt as if it had just stopped.

'Josh. Tell me she's not going to...' The word stuck in her throat.

He looked at her, and she could see her own fears reflected in his blue eyes.

'We have to wait for the test results,' he said.

The baby wasn't theirs—or at least was only theirs temporarily—but right then Amy felt like a real parent, anxious for news and trying not to think of the worst-case scenarios. Any tiredness she felt vanished under the onslaught of adrenaline. This was the only chance she might have to be a parent. And what if she lost something so precious—the baby she hadn't asked for but was beginning to fall in love with, despite her promises to herself not to let herself get involved?

'Amy,' Josh said softly. 'It's going to be all right. Alison—the doctor who is looking after her—is one of my most experienced juniors. She'll spot any problem and know how to treat it.'

'I guess.'

He must have heard the wobble in her voice, because this time he wrapped his free arm around her and held her close. 'It's going to be OK.'

She leaned back and looked at him. 'You look as worried as I feel.'

'A bit,' he admitted wryly. 'My head knows it's going to be fine. If there was anything really serious going on, Alison would've come out to see us by now.'

'But?'

'But my heart,' he continued quietly, 'is panicking. This must be what it's like to be a parent. Worrying if the baby is OK, or if you're missing something important.'

She nodded. 'I'm glad you're with me. Knowing I'm not the only one feeling like this makes it feel a bit less—well—scary.'

'Agreed.' Though she noticed he was still holding her; clearly he was taking as much comfort from her nearness as she was from his.

And then finally the curtain swished open.

'Hey, Josh. We've done bloods and urine, to rule out bacterial infections,' Alison said. 'And I gave her a proper cord clip. How on earth did you manage to change her nappy round that thing?'

'A mixture of necessity and practice,' Amy said wryly.

'Ouch,' Alison said. 'Well, you know the drill, Josh. We'll have to wait for the test results before we can tell if we need to admit her—and, given all the viruses in the hospital right now, hopefully we won't have to do that. But you can sit with the baby now while we wait for the results to come back, if you like.'

'Yes, please. And no doubt you have potential fractures in the waiting room that need looking at,' Josh said. 'Sure. We won't hold you up any longer.'

When Alison had closed the cubicle curtain behind her, Josh turned to Amy. 'We can't pick her up and hold her,' Josh said, 'because our body warmth will put her temperature up.' Which meant they had to resort to taking turns in letting Hope hold a finger in her left hand, because Hope's right hand was hooked up to a machine.

'So what does this machine do?' Amy asked.

'It's a pulse oximeter. It measures the oxygen levels in her blood,' Josh explained, 'so we know if there's a problem and we need to give her some extra oxygen through a mask, like they did in the ambulance. It's all done by light shining through her skin and it doesn't hurt her.' He was used to explaining the situation, but it felt odd to be on the other side of it, too.

'Right. Are those figures good news or bad?' she asked, gesturing to the screen.

He analysed them swiftly. 'Good. I'm happy with her oxygen sats and her pulse rate.'

Amy bit her lip. 'She's so tiny, Josh, and we're supposed to be looking after her. What if...?'

'If she has an infection, she's in the right place for us to treat it,' Josh reassured her. 'She'll be fine.'

Two hours later, the baby's temperature was down to a more normal level. The results of the blood tests had come back, and to their relief there was no sign of any bacterial infection.

'I'm pleased to say you can take her home. Just keep an eye on her and give her some liquid paracetamol every four to six hours—you know the safe dose for a baby that age,' Alison said to Josh. 'How are you getting home?'

'Ambulance, I guess,' Josh said. 'We don't have a car seat for her. The social worker obviously didn't guess we might have to rush her to hospital.'

'So you've got almost nothing for her?' Alison asked.

'Just the very basics—this Moses basket, some clothes and formula milk,' Amy confirmed.

'Poor little mite. She's lucky you found her,' Alison said. 'And that you could look after her.'

'We're neighbours,' Josh said quickly.

Alison looked at their joined hands and smiled.

Josh prised his fingers free. 'And friends. And worried sick about the baby.'

'She's going to be fine,' Alison said. 'I'll let the ambulance control know that you can go whenever they're ready.'

This time the journey wasn't as terrifying, and Hope slept through the whole thing. Though Amy felt as if she'd never, ever sleep again when she let them back into her flat. 'I'll sit up with her.'

'I'll keep you company,' he said.

'But you—' she began.

'I'm not on duty tomorrow—well, today,' he cut in. 'I'm awake now, too. And we can both catch up on our sleep later when the baby sleeps.'

'Are you sure?'

'Sure. Let's keep the light low for her, so she can sleep and we can see her.'

His duvet was still thrown over her sofa. 'Here—you might as well share the duvet with me,' he said, and tucked it over her. 'Try not to worry. We know it's not a bacterial infection, which is the important thing. Maybe it's the beginnings of a cold. Small babies tend to get temperature spikes when they get a cold. One minute they're fine, the next minute they're ill enough to worry the life out of you, and then they're absolutely fine again.' He took her hand. 'She's going to be perfectly all right, Amy. We're here and we're keeping an eye on her. And, before you say it, I'm used to not getting massive amounts of sleep. It comes with the job.'

'I guess,' she said. He was still holding her hand, and it made her feel better. She didn't pull away.

Amy woke, feeling groggy, to the sound of Hope crying.

When had she fallen asleep? How could she have neglected Hope like that? Guilt flooded through her.

But a crying baby was a good sign, right?

'OK?' Josh asked next to her, sounding much more awake than she felt.

'OK. My turn to sort her out,' she mumbled. Why had she thought it was a good idea to sit up all night on the sofa? She had a crick in her neck and her back ached. Right now she wasn't going to be a lot of use to the baby.

'It ought to be my turn,' he said, 'because she's due some more paracetamol.' He paused. 'They weighed her at hospital. Can you remember how much they said she weighed?'

'I didn't even register it,' she said. 'I was so worried that they were going to find something seriously wrong.'

'It's gone clean out of my head, too.' He blew out a breath. 'I don't want to guess at her weight and estimate the dose of paracetamol, so we're going to have to weigh her.'

'I don't actually own a pair of bathroom scales,' Amy admitted.

'How about kitchen scales, and a tray we can put her on for a moment?' Josh suggested.

She snapped the light on and gave him a wry smile. 'This has to be the strangest Boxing Day morning I've ever spent.'

'Me, too,' he said.

But at the same time it was a morning that filled her with relief—even more than the first night they'd spent with Hope, because now she knew that with Josh by her side she could face anything life threw at her.

'Give her a cuddle and I'll get the scales out,' she said.

She put a soft cloth on a baking tray, then put it on her kitchen scales and set them to zero. 'All righty.'

He set Hope on the tray and Amy peered at the display on the scales. 'Five pounds, ten ounces—or do you need it in metric?'

'Pounds and ounces are fine,' he said. 'I know how much infant paracetamol to give her now.'

He measured a dose of medicine for the baby and gave it to her through the oral syringe while Amy heated the milk.

'Sofa?' he asked.

She nodded and he carried Hope back to the sofa. This time, after he'd transferred the baby into Amy's arms so she could feed the baby, he slid one arm round Amy's shoulder.

It felt too nice for her to protest; right at that moment she felt warm, comforted and safe. After the scare that had taken them to the hospital, this was exactly what she needed. Maybe it was what he needed, too, she thought, and she tried not to overthink it. Or to start hoping that this meant Josh was starting to see her as more than just a neighbour. Yes, they could be friends. But on New Year's Day they'd have to give Hope back to the social worker—and when that part of their lives came to an end, what would happen?

Once the baby had finished drinking her milk—all sixty millilitres of it—Amy put her back in the Moses basket. Without comment, Josh put his arm round her shoulders again. Although part of Amy knew that she ought to put some distance between them, she couldn't help leaning into him, enjoying the feel of his muscular body against hers and his warmth.

They kept watch on the baby with the light turned down low, but finally Amy drifted back to sleep.

The next time Hope woke, it was a more reasonable time. Josh fed the baby while Amy showered and washed her hair, and then she took over baby duties while Josh went next door to shower and change.

She put cereals, yoghurt, jam and butter on the table, placed the bread next to the toaster, and while she waited for the kettle to boil she texted Jane Richards, the social worker.

Hope doing well. Had a bit of a temperature in the middle of the night but we checked her out at hospital and all OK. We have a theory about her mum: might be a girl from my class, but no proof. How do we check it out?

When she'd sent the text, she suddenly realised that she hadn't signed it. From the context, she was pretty sure that Jane would probably be able to work out who the text was from, but she sent a second text anyway.

This is Amy Howes btw. Not enough coffee or sleep! :)

Josh was back in her flat and they'd just finished breakfast when his phone rang.

'Do you mind if I get that?' he asked.

She spread her hands. 'It's fine.'

He returned with a smile. 'Remember Alison, the doctor who saw us last night?'

'Yes.'

'She's bringing us a pram and a snowsuit. She'll call me when she's parked and I'll go and let her in.'

Amy blinked. 'A pram and a snowsuit?'

'I'll let her explain. She's about twenty minutes away.'

True to her word, Alison called him to say that she'd just parked and had all the stuff with her.

'Feel free to ask her up for coffee,' Amy said as he headed for the door. 'It's the least I can do.'

'Thanks.'

He returned with Alison, carrying a pram, and Amy sorted out the hot drinks.

'Thank you so much for lending us the pram and snowsuit,' Amy said.

'No problem.' Alison smiled at her. 'I didn't think about it until after you'd left, but my sister was about to put her pram on eBay—it's one of those with a car seat that clips to the chassis to make a pram. She's happy to lend it to you while you're looking after Hope. And her youngest was tiny, so I've got some tiny baby clothes and a snowsuit as well. At least then you can take her out and all get some fresh air.'

'That's so kind,' Amy said.

'She didn't take much persuading,' Alison said. 'In situations like this, you always think how easily it could have been you or someone close to you. Poor little love. How's she doing?'

'Her temperature's gone down—but, when we had to give her more paracetamol this morning, I forgot how much she weighed,' Josh admitted.

'So poor little Hope had to lie on a towel on a baking tray, so we could weigh her on my kitchen scales,' Amy added.

Alison laughed. 'I can just imagine it. And, tsk, Josh, you being a consultant and forgetting something as important as a baby's weight.'

'I know. I'm totally hanging my head in shame,' Josh said, looking anything but repentant.

Amy suddenly had a very clear idea of what he was like to work with—as nice as he was as a neighbour, kind and good-humoured and compassionate, yet strong when it was necessary. Given his gorgeous blue eyes and the way his hair seemed to be messy again five minutes after he'd combed it, she'd just bet that half the female staff at the hospital had a crush on him. Not that he'd notice. Josh wasn't full of himself and aware of his good looks, the way Gavin and even Michael had been. He was genuine.

And he was off limits, she reminded herself.

Alison peered into the Moses basket. 'She's a little cutie.'

'Pick her up and give her a cuddle, if you like,' Amy said.

Alison smiled, needing no second invitation. 'I love babies. Especially when I can give them back when it comes to nappy changes.'

'Noted,' Josh said dryly.

'So she was just left in the lobby in your flats?' Alison asked.

'Yes.' Amy ran through what had happened. 'And we have a theory that her mum might be in my form group.'

'But if the mum's in your class, Amy, how come you didn't recognise her handwriting?' Alison asked.

'Because she's in my form group, not my class. I don't teach her,' Amy explained. 'It means she's there in the form room for five minutes in the morning for registration, and twenty minutes in the afternoon for registration and whatever other activities we're doing in form time—giving out letters for parents, a chance for any of them to talk to me if they're worried about something, and sometimes we do quizzes and the kind of things that help the kids bond a bit. I never see any of her written work. And it's still only a theory. If we're wrong, then we still have no clue who Hope's mum is.'

'Well, I hope they do find the poor little mite's mum.' Alison looked at Josh. 'So you two are sort of living together this week?'

'As friends,' Josh said swiftly. 'It makes sense, because otherwise we'd have to keep transferring the baby between flats and it'd unsettle her.'

Amy reminded herself that they weren't a couple. Even if they had slept on the sofa together last night and fallen asleep holding hands, and when he'd put his arm round her it had simply been comfort for both of them after their worry about the baby's health.

'It's really nice of you to look after her,' Alison said.

'What else could we do?' Amy asked. 'She's a baby. She didn't ask to be left here. The social worker couldn't get a placement because it was Christmas Eve and nobody was about, and Josh said the hospital's on black alert so the baby couldn't stay there.'

'The winter vomiting virus is everywhere,' Alison confirmed, 'and the children's ward is full of babies with bronchiolitis, something you definitely don't want a newborn to get.' She smiled at them, then handed the baby back to Amy. 'Here you go, cutie. Back to your Aunty Amy. Thanks for the coffee and biscuits. I'm heading home to bed now because I'm working the night shift again tonight and I need some sleep before I face the fractures and the ones who gave themselves food poisoning with the leftovers.'

'Thanks for bringing all this,' Josh said, 'and I owe your sister flowers and some decent chocolate. And you, too.'

Alison waved away the thanks. 'It's good to be able to do something nice for someone at Christmas. It feels as if it's putting the balance back a bit, after all the greed and rampant consumerism.'

When she'd gone, Josh turned to Amy. 'The only time you've been out of the flat since Christmas Eve morning is our middle-of-the-night trip to hospital. Do you want to go and get some fresh air?'

'That'd be good. And I could probably do with picking up something for dinner,' she said. 'I forgot to get something out of the freezer earlier.'

'I ought to be the one buying dinner,' he said. 'You've fed me two days running as it is.'

'It really doesn't matter.' Unable to resist teasing him, she added, 'But if you really want to cook for me...'

'Then you get a choice of spaghetti Bolognese or a cheese toastie,' he said promptly.

'Or maybe I should teach you how to cook something else.' She grabbed her coat and her handbag. 'I'll see you in a bit. I've got my phone with me in case you need me.'

'Great.'

It felt odd, being alone in Amy's flat, Josh thought when she'd gone. Weirdly, it felt like home; yet, at the same time, it wasn't. Everything was neat and tidy and she'd done the washing up while he was seeing Alison out of the flat, so he couldn't do anything practical to help; all he could really do was watch the baby.

He'd texted his parents and his siblings during his break at work on Christmas Day, and hadn't corrected their assumption that he was working today. Not that he really wanted to speak to any of them. If he told them how his Christmas had panned out, he knew they'd try to manage it—which drove him crazy. He was perfectly capable of managing his own life, even if he was the baby of the family and had messed up, in their eyes.

He held the baby and looked at the framed photographs on Amy's mantelpiece. The older couple were clearly her parents, and the man in one of the younger couples looked enough like her to be her brother in Canada. The other couple, he assumed, must be the friends she'd talked about staying with in Edinburgh.

'She really loves her family,' he said to the baby, 'and they clearly love her to bits, too.' He sighed. 'Maybe I should make more of an effort with mine.'

The baby gurgled, as if agreeing.

'They're not bad people. Just they have set views on what I ought to be doing with my life, and right now they feel I'm letting them down. I'm the only one in our family to get divorced. But Kelly didn't love me any more, and I couldn't expect her to stay with me just to keep my family happy. It would have made both of us really miserable, and that's not fair.'

The baby gurgled again.

'Tell you a secret,' he said. 'I think I could like Amy. More than like her.'

The baby cooed, as if to say that she liked Amy, too.

'And I would never have got to know her like this if it wasn't for you, Munchkin. We'd still just be doing the nod-and-smile thing if we saw each other in the corridor or the lobby. But this last couple of days, I've spent more time with her than I have with anyone else in a long, long time.' He paused. 'The question is, what does she think about me?'

The baby was silent.

'I'm not going to risk making things awkward while we're looking after you,' he said. 'But in the New Year I'm going to ask her out properly. Because I'm ready to move on, and I think she might be, too.'

* * *

It felt odd being out of the flat, Amy thought. It was nice to get some fresh air, but at the same time she found she couldn't stop thinking about Hope.

Or about Josh.

But what did she have to offer him?

If he wanted to settle down and have a family, then it couldn't be with her. She knew that there were other ways of having a child as well as biologically, but Michael had refused flat-out even to consider fostering or adoption. She wondered how he would've reacted to Hope; she had a nasty feeling that he would've decided it wasn't his problem and would've left it to the authorities.

Josh, on the other hand, had real compassion. He'd been instantly supportive. Even though he didn't know her well, he'd offered help when it was needed most.

She shook herself. She and Josh were neighbours, making their way towards becoming good friends. Their relationship couldn't be any more than that, so she would have to be sensible about this and damp down her burgeoning feelings towards him.

The supermarket was crowded with people looking for post-Christmas bargains. Amy avoided the clearance shelves and headed for the chiller cabinet. A few minutes later, she paid for her groceries at the checkout, and went back to the flat.

'You're back early,' he said.

'The shops were heaving.' And it hadn't felt right to go to the park without the baby. Which she knew was crazy, because Hope wasn't hers and would only be here for a couple more days. 'I thought we'd have French bread, cheese and chutney for lunch.'

'Sounds perfect. I'll prepare it, if you like, while you give our girl a cuddle.'

Her gaze met his and her heart felt as if it had just done a somersault.

'Temporary girl,' he corrected himself swiftly.

'I know what you meant.' Being with Josh and Hope felt like being part of a new family. It was so tempting, but she mustn't let herself forget that it was only temporary. Clearly Josh felt the same way. If only things were a little different. If only she'd never met Gavin, or had at least been a bit less clueless, so she'd been able to get the chlamydia treated in time…

But things were as they were, and she'd have to make the best of it instead of whining for something she knew wasn't going to happen.

'Did Jane reply to your text?' he asked.

'Not yet. And it wasn't an emergency, so I'm not expecting her to pick it up until at least tomorrow.'

'You're probably right,' he said. 'Hope's temperature has come down a lot, but it's probably too much for her to go out for a stroll in the park.' There was a definite wistfulness in his expression as he glanced at the pram.

'Maybe tomorrow,' she said.

After lunch, they spent the afternoon playing board games. 'I haven't done this for a while, either,' she admitted ruefully. 'I'd forgotten how much fun it is.'

'Remember what you said to me,' he said. 'Make the time for stuff you enjoy.'

Josh sketched Hope again in the back of the notebook after her next feed, and couldn't resist making a sneaky sketch of Amy. Though in a way that was a bad idea, because it made him really aware of the curve of her mouth and the way her hair fell—and it made him want to touch her.

He still couldn't shake how it had felt this morning to draw her into his arms and hold her close. OK, so they'd both been dog-tired and in need of comfort after their worry about Hope and a very broken night—but it had felt so right to hold her like that and fall asleep with her on the sofa.

For Hope's sake, he needed to rein himself back a bit.

'While Madam's asleep,' Amy said, thankfully oblivious to what he'd been thinking, 'maybe I can teach you how to cook something really simple and really impressive.'

'Which is?' he asked.

'Baked salmon with sweet chilli sauce, served with mangetout and crushed new potatoes.'

It sounded complicated. But clearly Amy was good at her day job, because she gave him really clear instructions and talked him through making dinner.

'I can't believe I made this,' he said, looking at the plates. After the first mouthful, he amended that to, 'I *really* can't believe I made this.'

'Healthy and impressive,' she said. 'And it's easy. Josh, what you do at work every day is way harder than cooking dinner.'

'Maybe.' But cooking for one was no fun. Which was the main reason why he lived on toasted sandwiches and takeaways.

They spent the evening curled up on the sofa, watching films. Josh was careful this time not to give in to the temptation of holding Amy's hand or drawing her into his arms.

But, after Hope's last feed of the evening, he could see the worry on Amy's face.

'Maybe we should both sleep on the sofa again tonight,' he said. 'We can still take turns at getting up for her, but it also means if you're worried you can wake me more quickly.'

She took a deep breath. 'Don't take this the wrong way,' she said, 'but I was thinking along the same lines. My bed's a double and it'll be a lot more comfortable than the sofa. We're adults and we can share a bed without…'

His mouth went dry as he finished the sentence mentally. *Without making love.*

Which was what he really wanted to do with Amy. Kiss her, discover where she liked being touched and what made her eyes go dark with pleasure.

'Fully dressed,' he said. Because lying in bed with her, with them both wearing pyjamas, might be a little too much temptation for him to resist. And he hoped she couldn't hear the slight huskiness in his voice.

'Of course.'

Her bedroom was exactly as he'd expected, all soft creams and feminine, yet without being frilly or fussy and over the top. There was a framed picture of a seascape on the wall, the curtains were floral chintz, and the whole room was restful and peaceful.

Though when he lay next to her in bed with the light off—with both of them fully dressed—he was far from feeling restful and peaceful. He was too aware of the last time he'd shared a bed with someone, just over a year ago. OK, so he'd finally got to the stage where he could move on with his life... But could it be with Amy? He definitely had feelings for her, and he was fairly sure that it was mutual; but was it because they'd had this intense sharing of space over the last few days, while they'd been looking after Hope, or was it something real? Would he be enough for her, the way he hadn't been for Kelly? Or would everything between them change again at New Year, once the baby had gone?

When Hope cried, Amy got out of bed on autopilot and scooped the baby from the Moses basket. As she padded into the kitchen with the baby in her arms, she woke up fully. Was it her imagination, or did Hope feel hot again?

And then Hope only took half her usual amount of milk.

Panic welled through her, and she switched on her bedside light on its lowest setting. 'Josh.'

He woke immediately and sat up. 'What's wrong?'

'I might be being paranoid, but she didn't take that much milk just now, and I think she's hot again.'

He checked the baby over, then grabbed the thermometer and took her temperature. 'Her temperature's normal.'

'So I'm just being ridiculous.'

He settled the baby back into the Moses basket. 'No. You're being completely normal. I'd worry, too.' He wrapped his arms round her. 'You're doing just fine, Amy.'

For someone who was never going to be a mum?

She wasn't sure what made her lean into him—the worry that had made her knees sag, or just the fact that he was there, holding her and seeming to infuse his strength into her as he kept his arms round her.

And was that his mouth against her cheek, in a reassuring kiss?

Something made her tip her head back.

The next thing she knew, his mouth was against hers. Soft, reassuring, gentle.

And then it wasn't like that any more, because somehow her mouth had opened beneath his and her arms were wrapped round his neck, and he was holding her much more tightly. And the warmth turned to heat, to sheer molten desire.

Then he pulled back.

Oh, God. How embarrassing was she? Throwing herself at her neighbour. Pathetic.

'Sorry,' she mumbled, hanging her head and unable to meet his eyes. Hot shame bubbled through her. What the hell had she just done?

'I should be the one apologising to you.'

Because he'd been kind? Because he'd stopped before she'd *really* made a fool of herself?

'No,' she muttered, still not wanting to look at him and see the pity in his face.

'Maybe I should sleep on your sofa again,' he said.

And then things would be even more awkward between them in the morning. 'No, it's fine. We're neighbours—*friends*—and we're adults; and we both need to be here for Hope.' She took a deep breath. 'We can both pretend that just now didn't happen.'

'Good idea,' he said.

But she still couldn't face him when she climbed into bed and switched off the light. And she noticed that there was a very large gap in the bed between them, as if he felt as uncomfortable and embarrassed about the situation as she did.

If only she'd kept that iron control she'd prided herself on so much before today. If only she hadn't kissed him. If only she hadn't given in to temptation.

She'd just have to hope that the broken night would affect his memory and he'd forget everything about what had just happened.

And she'd really have to put out of her mind how good it had felt in those moments when he'd kissed her back.

CHAPTER SIX

Bank Holiday Monday

AMY WAS WARM and deeply, deeply comfortable.

And then she realised why.

Somehow, during the night, the large gap in the bed between her and Josh had closed. Now her head was pillowed on his shoulder, his arm was round her shoulders, her arm was wrapped round his waist, and her fingers were twined with his.

They were sleeping like lovers.

Oh, help. This was a seriously bad idea. She couldn't offer Josh a future and it wasn't fair to lead him on.

Gently, she disentangled her fingers from his. She'd just started to wriggle quietly out of his arms, hoping she wouldn't wake him, when he said, 'Good morning.'

No running away from the situation, then. They were going to have to face this head on.

'Good morning,' she muttered. 'I—um—sorry about this.'

'Me, too.' Though he didn't sound concerned or embarrassed.

'I—um—we're both tired and sleep-deprived,' she said. 'And I guess this was bound to happen as we're sharing a bed. Propinquity and all that. It doesn't mean we have…' She paused, looking for the right word. 'Intentions.'

'Absolutely,' he agreed.

Was he smiling?

She didn't dare look.

'I'll go and make us a cup of tea before Hope wakes,' she said, and wriggled out of his arms properly.

She splashed her face with cold water in the bathroom, in the hope that it would bring back her common sense. It didn't. She could still feel the warmth of Josh's arms around her, and she wanted more. So much more.

How selfish could she get?

Cross with her own stupidity, she filled the kettle with water and rummaged in the cupboard for the tea bags.

Waking with Amy in his arms was just what Josh had been dreaming about. It had taken him a moment to realise that he was awake, and she really *was* in his arms.

She'd blamed it on them both being tired and sleep-deprived, and the fact that they'd slept in the same bed. But she'd sounded distinctly flustered.

So did she feel the same way about him that he was starting to feel about her?

He'd promised himself that he'd hold back from starting a relationship with her until after the baby was settled—either with her birth mother, or with long-term foster parents. But they'd kissed, last night. They'd woken in each other's arms, as if they were meant to be there. He'd been awake before Amy and she'd stayed in his arms for a few moments after she'd woken—which she wouldn't have done if she hadn't wanted to be there.

So maybe he needed to be brave and tell her what was in his head, and see if she felt the same way.

He climbed out of bed, checked that Hope was still asleep and not overheated, and then walked into the kitchen. Amy was making the tea, dressed in rumpled clothes and with her hair all over the place—and she'd never looked more beautiful to him or more natural.

'Hey.' He walked over to her and wrapped his arms round her. 'I know I probably shouldn't be doing this, and we don't know each other very well, but we've spent a lot of time together over the last couple of days and I really like you.' He paused. 'And I think you might like me too.'

This was the moment where either she would push him away in utter shock and he'd have to avoid her for the next six months until things were back on an even keel between them, or she would tell him that she felt the same.

He really hoped it was going to be the latter.

But then an expression of pure misery crossed her face and she stepped back out of his embrace. 'I do like you,' she admitted, 'but we can't do this.'

'Because of the baby?'

She took a deep breath. 'No, not because of her.'

'Then why?' Josh asked, not understanding.

'I need to tell you something about myself.' She finished making the mugs of tea, and handed one to him. 'Let's go and sit down.'

'This sounds serious.'

'It is,' she said grimly, 'and there isn't an easy way to say it, so I'm not going to sugar-coat it.'

He followed her into the living room. She sat down at one end of the sofa; he sat next to her, wondering just what kind of bombshell she was about to drop. Was she still married to her ex? No, she couldn't be—hadn't she said something about him getting married to someone else and expecting a baby now? So what kind of thing would hold her back from starting a new relationship?

He could see her eyes fill with tears. Whatever it was, it was something really serious. Something that hurt her. And he ached for her.

Finally, she said, her voice sounding broken, 'I can't have children.'

Josh wanted to reach out and take her hand and tell her that it didn't change the way he felt, but he could see the 'hands off' signals written all over her. And as a doctor he knew the value of silence. If he let her talk, tell him exactly what was holding her back, then he might have more of a chance of being able to counter her arguments.

'That's why Michael—my ex—broke off our engagement and left,' she continued.

Josh was horrified. It must've been hard enough for Amy, finding out that she couldn't have children, but then for the man who was supposed to love her and want to marry her to walk out on her over the issue… That shocked him to the core. How could Michael have been so selfish? Why hadn't he put Amy first? And how it must've hurt her when she'd learned that his new wife was expecting a baby.

'We'd been trying for a baby for a year or so without success, so we went for investigations to find out why we couldn't conceive.' She looked away. 'I knew that the guy I'd dated before Michael had cheated on me. I found it had been more than once and with more than one other woman, and that's why I left him. I didn't want to stay with someone who didn't love me or respect me enough to be faithful. But what I didn't realise was that he'd given me chlamydia.'

Josh knew then exactly what had happened to her. 'You didn't have any symptoms?'

She shook her head. 'And obviously, because I didn't know I had it, that meant I was still infected when I started seeing Michael and we moved in together. I infected Michael. He didn't have symptoms, either.'

Quite a high percentage of people who'd been infected with chlamydia didn't have symptoms. Not that it would comfort her to know that. 'Amy, it wasn't your fault.'

She shook her head. 'I should've been more careful. Used condoms with Gavin—the one who cheated on me—instead of the Pill.'

How could she possibly blame herself? 'Before you found out that he'd cheated on you, you trusted him. How long were you together?'

'Two years.'

'So of course you'd think the Pill was a safe form of contraception. Any woman in your shoes would.' Josh shook his head, angry on her behalf. 'Gavin cheated on you, and he was the one who infected you. How could anyone possibly think it was your fault?'

'Because I should've got myself checked out. I should've realised that, because Gavin had been sleeping around, there could be consequences.'

'But you didn't have symptoms. Actually, around two thirds of women and about fifty per cent of men don't have symptoms if they're infected with chlamydia. And, if you don't have symptoms, how are you supposed to know there's a problem? It's *not* your fault,' he said again. 'I'm probably speaking out of turn, but it was totally unfair of Michael to blame you.'

'It happened. And you can't change the past, just learn from it.' She shrugged. 'So now you know. As a doctor, you've probably already guessed what the problem is, but I'll spell it out for you. The chlamydia gave me pelvic inflammatory disease and the scar tissue blocked my Fallopian tubes, so I can't have children. If you're looking to have a family in the future, then I'm not the one for you and we need to call a halt to this right now.'

And that was really what was holding her back? This time, he did reach over and take her hand. 'First of all, having children isn't the be-all and end-all of a relationship. Lots of couples can't have children or choose not to. It doesn't make their relationship and how they feel about each other any less valid. And if this thing between us works out the way I hope it might, then if we do decide in the future that we want children then we still have options. Did your specialist not mention IVF?'

She swallowed. 'Yes, but Michael didn't want to do that.'

Josh wasn't surprised. And he'd just bet the other man's reasoning was purely to do with himself, not to do with how tough the IVF process could be for a woman.

'It's not an easy option and there are no cast-iron guarantees,' he said, 'but it's still an option for tubal infertility. One of the doctors I trained with had severe endometriosis which blocked her Fallopian tubes, and she had a baby through IVF last year.'

Was that hope he saw flickering in her eyes, just then?

'And if that's not a route you want to go down—because the treatment cycle is pretty gruelling and it isn't for everyone—there's fostering or adoption.'

She blinked, as if not expecting him to have reacted that way. 'Michael wasn't prepared to even consider that.'

Because Michael was a selfish toad. Not that it was Josh's place to say so. 'I'm not Michael,' he said.

'I know.' She took a deep breath. 'But I wanted you to know the situation upfront. So, if it's a problem for you, you can walk away now and there's no damage to either of us.'

Even though they'd only got close to each other over the last couple of days, Josh had the strongest feeling that walking away from her would definitely cause damage to both of them.

'I like you,' he said again, 'and I think you might just like me back. And that's what's important here. Everything else is just details and we can work them out. Together.'

She looked at him as if she didn't quite believe him.

'If you want to work them out, that is,' he said. 'Your infertility doesn't make any difference to the way I feel about you. I still want to start dating you properly. Get to know you.'

'And it's really that easy?'

'It is for me.' He paused. 'Though, since you told me about your ex, I guess you need to know about mine.'

* * *

The woman who'd left him last Christmas Eve, pregnant with another man's child.

Amy really couldn't understand why on earth anyone would dump a man like Josh—a man who was kind and caring as well as easy on the eye. In the intense couple of days they'd spent together, she hadn't found a deal-breaking flaw in him.

'Kelly worked in advertising—so maybe if I'd gone to art college instead of med school we would've ended up working together.' He shrugged. 'But we met at a party, where we were both a friend of a friend. We fell for each other, moved in together a couple of weeks later and got married within three months.'

Alarm bells rang in the back of Amy's head. Wasn't this exactly what she and Josh were doing? Falling in love with each other a little too quickly and not thinking things through? A whirlwind romance had gone badly wrong for him before. Then again, her last two relationships had both lasted for a couple of years, so taking things slowly hadn't exactly worked for her, either.

'I assumed Kelly would want a family at some point in the future, the way I did, and she assumed that we were both ambitious and were going to put our careers first,' he said. 'We probably should have talked about that a lot more before we got married.'

He wanted a family.

Amy's heart sank.

OK, he'd said to her that her infertility didn't make a difference. But it did. As he'd said, IVF treatment could be gruelling and there were no guarantees that it would work. She'd looked into it, in the days when she'd still hoped that Michael might change his mind, and the chances of having a baby were roughly one in four. Odds which might not be good enough for Josh. Right now, they were looking after a baby together. What would happen in New Year, when life went back to normal? Would he realise then what a mistake he was making, trying to make a go of things with her?

'Kelly was working really long hours on the promise of getting a promotion. Obviously I supported her,' Josh continued, 'but then she fell in love with one of her colleagues. She said they tried to fight the attraction; but, on one project they were working on together, they went to visit a client and it meant an overnight stay. They were in rooms next to each other in the hotel; they'd had dinner out with the client and too much wine; and one thing led to another. That's when the affair started.'

Clearly Josh hadn't had a clue about it. Amy reached over and squeezed his hand. 'That's hard.'

'Yeah.' He sighed. 'She got the promotion, but she was still working crazy hours. I assumed it was because of the pressure of work in her new job, but it was actually because she was seeing the other guy.' He gave her a wry smile. 'Then she told me she was pregnant.'

'And you thought it was yours?'

'I knew it wasn't,' he said softly, 'because we'd both been working mad hours and were too tired to do anything more than fall into bed and go straight to sleep when we got home at night. We hadn't had sex for a couple of months, so there was no way the baby could possibly be mine. Though Kelly never lied to me about it. She told me it was his and she was sorry— she'd fallen in love with him and was leaving me.' He looked away. 'Funny, she ended up with the family she said she didn't want, but maybe it was really that she just didn't want to have a family with me. I wasn't enough for her.'

How could Josh possibly not be enough for someone? Amy squeezed his hand again. 'Josh, you didn't do anything wrong. It wasn't your fault.' She gave him an awkward smile. 'I guess you can't help who you fall in love with.' Hadn't she made that same mistake, falling for Mr Wrong?

'And Kelly was fair about it. She didn't try to heap the blame on me for the divorce.'

'Even when the split's amicable, it's still tough,' Amy said. 'I'm sorry you got hurt like that.'

'But?' he asked, clearly sensing that she had doubts.

'But,' she said softly, 'you said you wanted to have a family with Kelly. Even if we put IVF into the equation, there's still a very strong chance I won't be able to give you a family. So I'll understand if you want us to stay just friends.'

He shook his head. 'I want more than that from you, Amy. And in any relationship you have to make a compromise.'

'But this is one hell of a compromise. It means giving up on your plans to have a family.'

'Right now, it's still early days between you and me, and we're not making any promises to each other of happy ever after,' he said. 'But I really like you, Amy, and if it's a choice of being with you and looking at alternatives for having a family, or not being with you, then I'm on the side of alternatives.' He smiled at her. 'And we're not doing so badly with Hope. I'm beginning to think that her mum gave her exactly the right name, and also that you were right because the baby's giving us the Christmas we both need. She's brought us together and she's giving us a chance to find happiness again—together.'

Amy thought about it. 'Yes,' she said.

'So, you and me. No pressure. We'll see where things take us.'

'Sounds good to me,' Amy said. And it felt as if spring flowers had just pushed through the ground to brighten up the days after a long, long winter.

Just before lunch, Jane the social worker rang. 'How's the baby doing?' she asked.

'Fine,' Amy said. 'She's still got a bit of a temperature, but it's going down.'

'Good. So what's this theory you've got about the baby's mum?'

'Hang on—let me put you on speaker phone so Josh can hear as well and chip in,' Amy said. 'We think she might be a girl in my form. I didn't recognise the handwriting on the note because I don't actually teach her, so there's no reason for me ever to see her work or her writing.'

'We did think about maybe going round to see her for a chat,' Josh said.

'No—it's better to leave this to the authorities,' Jane said, 'especially if you don't have any proof that it's definitely her. What makes you think it's her, Amy?'

'She's gone very quiet, lately. I did bring it up with her mum, who said it was because her new partner had moved in and Freya was having trouble adjusting to the idea of someone she saw trying to take her dad's place.' She paused. 'Freya wears quite baggy clothes, not skinny trousers or anything. And because it's winter it's easier to hide a pregnancy under a baggy sweater.'

'Does she look as if she's put on weight?'

'A little bit, but body image is a really sensitive area for teens, and I guessed she might be comfort-eating if she wasn't happy at home,' Amy said. 'Drawing attention to it would only have made her feel worse, and the last thing I wanted was for her to start starving herself or taking diet pills. I was going to have a chat with her in the New Year.' She paused. 'I thought that might be why she kept rushing to the loo.'

'But that's also a symptom of late pregnancy,' Josh said.

'So how do we tackle this?' Amy asked.

'You don't. I do it,' Jane said. 'Under the safeguarding rules, Amy, I know you can give me the contact information of a student you're worried about, so can you tell me her name and address?'

Amy had accessed Freya's school records earlier, and gave Jane the relevant details.

'Thanks. I'll liaise with the police, then do a preliminary visit and see if I can get any information,' Jane said. 'And thank you.'

'Will you let me know how you get on?' Amy asked.

'I'm afraid any conversations I have will be confidential, unless I have Freya's permission to talk to you,' Jane said, sounding regretful.

'We understand. But please tell her from us that the baby's doing just fine and we'd be happy to send her a picture, or for her to come and visit Hope,' Josh said. 'And if she does turn out to be our missing mum, please persuade her to see a doctor to get checked over.

She won't be in trouble, but we need to be sure that she's all right.'

'I will,' Jane promised.

Amy looked at Josh when she'd ended the call. 'I really hope we've done the right thing.'

'We have,' he said. 'Jane's in a neutral position so, if our theory's wrong, then Freya won't be too embarrassed to walk into your form room next term. If it's right, then Jane knows all the procedures and can get Freya the help she needs.'

'I'd still rather go and see her myself,' Amy said. 'As you say, Jane's neutral and she's really nice, but she's still a stranger. Surely Freya's more likely to open up to me because she knows me?'

'If our theory's right, Freya left Hope with you because she trusted you to do the right thing and talk to the right people for her. Which you've done,' Josh pointed out.

'I guess.'

Hope woke; as soon as Amy picked her up, she could tell what the problem was. 'Nappy. Super-bad nappy,' she said.

'Oh, great,' Josh said with a sigh. 'And it's my turn to change her.'

'I'm not arguing.' Amy smiled and handed the baby over. Josh carried Hope to the bathroom. 'Come on, Munchkin. Let's sort you out.'

Josh was gone a very long time. And Amy could hear screaming, interspersed with him singing snatches of what sounded like every song that came into his head. Each one sounded slightly more desperate.

She was just about to go and see if she could do

anything to help when he came back into the kitchen carrying a red-faced, still grizzly baby.

'I was just about to come and see if you needed anything. Do I take it that it was really bad?' she asked.

'Let's just say she needed a bath,' he said grimly. 'And she doesn't like baths yet.'

'Hence the screaming and the singing?'

'Yeah.' He blew out a breath. 'I'm glad I'm not a teenager. After that nightmare in the bathroom just now, I'd be paranoid that my face was all it took to make any girl scream and run away.'

Amy couldn't help laughing. 'Hardly. You're quite pretty.'

'Pretty?' He gave her a speaking look.

'If you were a supply teacher at my school,' she said, 'you'd have gaggles of teenage girls hanging around the staff room every lunchtime in the hope of catching a glimpse of you.'

'That,' he said, 'sounds scary. I think I'd rather deal with—wait for it…' He adopted a pose and warbled to the tune of 'The Twelve Days of Christmas'. 'Five turkey carvers! Four black eyes, three throwing up, two broken ankles and a bead up a toddler's nose.'

'I ought to introduce you to our head of music,' she said, laughing. 'Between you, I can imagine you writing a panto about *The Twelve Days of ED*.'

'Better believe it.'

'So, what do you want to do this afternoon?'

'It's wet and miserable out there, and although Hope's on the mend I'd rather not take her out, even though we've got the pram and snowsuit,' Josh said.

'Festive films on the sofa, then,' she said.

He wrinkled his nose. 'I feel a bit guilty, just slob-bing around on the sofa.'

'As you said, it's not the weather for going out,' she reminded him. 'And you've had tough enough shifts to justify doing nothing for a day or so. Well, nothing but alternate feeds, changing the odd really vile nappy and singing songs to stop Hope crying.'

'Well, if you put it that way...' He stole a kiss. 'Bring on the films.'

Snuggled up on the sofa with Josh and the baby, Amy had never felt more at peace. What had started off as a miserable Christmas was rapidly turning into one of the best Christmases ever.

'Do you want me to take the sofa tonight?' he asked when Hope had had her late evening feed.

'I think we go for the same deal as last night,' Amy said. 'Except maybe this time we could change into pyjamas instead of sleeping in our clothes?'

'Give me two minutes next door,' he said.

And she burst out laughing when he returned in a pair of pyjamas covered in Christmas puddings. 'That's priceless. I'm almost tempted to take a snap of you wearing them and put it in Hope's book.'

'Absolutely not. These were my best friend's wife's idea of a joke,' he said. 'I don't usually wear pyjamas. When they stayed at my flat after my housewarm-ing, I ended up wearing a ratty old T-shirt and a pair of boxer shorts so I'd be decent, and she said I needed proper pyjamas for when I had guests. This is the only pair I own. And this is the first time I've worn them.'

Amy went hot all over at the thought of Josh, in bed with her, naked. All the words flew out of her head and she just said, flustered, 'I, um...'

He took her hand and kissed the back of each finger in turn, then turned her hand over and pressed a kiss into the palm. 'Don't be flustered. There's no pressure,' he said, his voice low and husky and sexy as anything. 'Let's go to bed. Platonically.'

And he was as good as his word. No pressure. He simply curled his body round hers, wrapped his arm round her waist, and rested his cheek against her shoulder. And, as she fell asleep, Amy felt happier than she'd been in a long, long while.

CHAPTER SEVEN

Tuesday

ON TUESDAY MORNING, Josh woke to find his arms wrapped round Amy and hers wrapped round him. And suddenly the whole world felt full of promise. He couldn't resist kissing her awake. To his relief, she didn't back away from him the way she had the previous morning; this time, she smiled and kissed him back.

'Well, happy Tuesday,' he said.

She stroked his face. 'Absolutely.'

'My turn to bring you a cup of tea in bed,' he said, kissed her lingeringly and climbed out of bed.

'Wonderful,' she said, smiling back at him.

Funny, being in her kitchen was so much better than being in his own. Even though they had similar decor, all in neutral tones, her place felt like *home*. Josh even found himself humming a happy song as he made tea.

He could hear Hope crying, and called through, 'I'll heat up some milk for Munchkin.'

'Thanks,' Amy called back.

He took the two mugs of tea and bottle of milk through to Amy's bedroom, where he found Amy cuddling the baby and crooning to her. He set the tea on her bedside table and climbed back in next to them. 'Want me to feed her?'

'Sure.' Amy transferred the baby into his arms.

Feeding the baby, cuddled up next to Amy in bed... It made Josh realise exactly what he wanted out of life—what he wanted to happen in the New Year.

To be part of a family, just like this, with Amy. Domestic bliss.

Given her fertility issues, it wasn't going to be easy. But he thought it was going to be worth the effort. The only thing was: after they gave Hope back at New Year, would Amy change her mind about him?

Amy sipped her tea and watched Josh feeding the baby. This was exactly what she wanted. To be a family, with Josh. Although part of her was still worried that her infertility was going to be an issue, he'd been very clear about being happy to look at the options of IVF treatment, adoption or fostering. So maybe it wouldn't be an issue after all.

'She's drunk a bit more than usual, this morning,' Josh said. 'That's a good sign. Maybe we can take her out this morning.'

Amy went over to the window and peeked through the curtain. 'The sun's shining.'

'How about we go for lunch in the park?' he suggested.

'And we can try out Alison's sister's pram. Great idea.' She paused. 'How often are you supposed to weigh babies?'

'I don't know.' He smiled. 'Time for the baking tray again?'

'Hey. It was being inventive,' she protested, laughing. 'And it worked, didn't it?'

Once they'd showered and dressed, Amy changed Hope's nappy and they weighed her. 'Five pounds, twelve ounces.'

'We need to write that in her book,' Josh said, and did so while Amy got the baby dressed. Between them, they got her into the snowsuit.

'It dwarfs her,' he said ruefully.

'Better too big than too small,' Amy said.

'I guess.' Josh tucked the baby into the pram underneath a blanket, and then put the apron on the pram. 'Just in case it's a bit breezy out there,' he said.

'Good idea,' Amy agreed.

Once they'd got their own coats on, they negotiated the pram out of the flat.

'This is where I'm really glad we're on the ground floor,' Amy said.

'Me, too,' Josh said. 'Even though this pram's really light, it wouldn't be much fun carrying it up or down a flight of stairs—especially if you're doing it on your own.'

They exchanged a glance, and Amy knew that he too was thinking of Hope's mum. If she was given a flat in a high-rise block, it could be tough for her to cope.

'Let's go to the park,' she said firmly. 'This is your first official trip out, Hope.'

'We ought to commemorate that for Hope's book,' Josh said. 'Time for a selfie.'

'In the lobby?'

'With the pram. You bet.' He looked at her. 'Ready?'

They crouched either side of the pram, and Josh angled his phone so he could take the snap of the three of them together.

Hope slept all the way to the park. Meanwhile Josh slid his arm round Amy's shoulders, and they both had one hand on the handle of the pram, pushing it together.

This felt like being part of the family Amy had always wanted. She knew it was just a fantasy, and if the police couldn't find Hope's mother then the baby would go formally into care, but for now she was going to enjoy feeling this way.

The sun seemed to have brought out all the other new parents, Josh thought. People happily strolling along the paths, pushing prams, sometimes with a toddler in tow as well. Slightly older children were playing on the swings, slides and climbing frames in the park, while their parents chatted and kept an eye on them from benches placed around the perimeter of the play area.

Just for a moment he could imagine the three of them here in three years' time: himself pushing Hope on the swings as she laughed and begged to be pushed higher, while Amy stood watching them, her face radiant and her belly swollen with their new baby.

Except there were no guarantees that the IVF treatment would work, and the chances of them actually being able to keep Hope were minimal.

He knew he was being ridiculous. Right from the start, this had been a temporary arrangement; the baby was theirs only for a week, and that was simply because they were the neighbours who'd found her abandoned on their doorstep on a day where none of the official services were able to help. They couldn't be a family with Hope.

But maybe they could help another child, through fostering or adoption.

And he knew without doubt that Amy was the one he wanted to share that family with. Thanks to Hope, he'd found that he was finally ready to move on from the wreckage of his marriage to Kelly; and because he'd been cooped up with Amy for several days he'd had the chance to get to know her properly. He could actually be himself with Amy, and it was a long time since he'd felt that.

When they stopped for a coffee and a toasted sandwich in the café in the park, the pictures were still in his head, and he found himself sketching the scene on the back of a napkin.

If only this wasn't temporary.

But for now he was going to enjoy the Christmas break he'd expected to hate.

Later that afternoon, Amy was in the middle of feeding Hope when her intercom buzzed.

'Would you mind getting that?' she asked Josh.

'Sure.' He picked up the handset. 'Hello?'

'Is that Josh? It's Jane Richards.'

'Come in,' he said, and buzzed her in. 'It's Jane,' he said to Amy as he replaced the handset. 'I'll put the kettle on.'

Had Jane talked to Freya? And was their theory right? Or was Jane just checking up on them in their role as temporary foster parents?

Josh answered the door when Jane knocked. 'The kettle's just about to boil. Tea or coffee?'

'Tea would be wonderful, thanks,' she said.

'How do you like your tea?'

'Reasonably strong, with a dash of milk and no sugar, please.' And then Jane did a double take as she saw the pram in the corner of the living room. 'Have you two been shopping or something?'

'No—it's a loan from the sister of one of my colleagues,' he said. 'She lent us a snowsuit as well, so we took Hope for a walk in the park across the road today. I think she enjoyed her first trip out.'

'And her temperature's normal again?' Jane asked.

'Yes. We wouldn't have taken her out if we'd been in the slightest bit worried about her—that's why we left it until today,' Amy said. 'She's doing fine. We weighed her this morning and she's put on two ounces.'

'You've borrowed baby scales?' Jane asked.

'Not exactly.' Josh and Amy shared a glance and grinned.

'What am I missing?' Jane asked.

'We improvised,' Josh said. 'It involved Amy's kitchen scales, a towel and a baking tray.'

Jane laughed. 'Well, clearly it worked. And you both look very comfortable with her.'

'We've had our moments,' Josh said wryly. 'She really hates having baths. You have to sing her through them.'

'But I can show you her sleep and feed charts,' Amy said. 'And we're doing a book of her first days, either for her mum or for Hope herself. We're including photos and what have you, so Hope—and her mum—don't feel they've missed anything in the future.'

'That's really sweet of you,' Jane said, accepting the mug of tea gratefully from Josh.

'Do you have any news for us?' Josh asked.

'About Freya?' She grimaced. 'I'm telling you this unofficially, because strictly speaking this should all be confidential, but I need some help—and, because it's your theory, I think you're the best ones to give me advice.'

'Why do you need help?' Amy asked, confused.

'I went to the house, but Freya's mum refused to let me in,' Jane said. 'She was quite difficult with me, so my gut feeling tells me that she has something to hide. If Freya definitely hadn't had a baby, all she had to do was call the girl down and let me see her, and I could've ticked whatever box on a form and gone away again.'

'Unless she didn't actually know that Freya had had the baby. Amy, you said she was wearing baggy clothes at school?' Josh asked.

Amy nodded.

'So she might have done the same at home. Freya could have hidden the pregnancy from her mum, had the baby—well, wherever—then gone straight home again after she'd left the baby on our doorstep. If she told her mum that she was having a really bad period, that would explain why she was bleeding so much after the birth. She's at the age where periods are still all over the place, and some girls get quite severe period pains,' Josh said thoughtfully.

'And Freya's mum did say that there were problems with the stepfather. Maybe there had been a huge row or something,' Amy suggested, 'and one of the neighbours had tried to intervene, and Freya's mum thought that someone had called you to complain about the way she was treating her daughter.'

'I still think she's hiding something. She wouldn't look me in the eye,' Jane said. 'Does Freya have a close friend she might have confided in?'

'Her best friend Alice is the most likely person,' Amy said.

'Do you have her details? And this comes under the safeguarding stuff for Freya, if you're worrying about data protection,' Jane added quickly.

Amy powered up her laptop, logged into the school system and wrote Alice's details down for Jane.

'I could have an unofficial word with her, maybe,' Amy suggested.

Jane shook her head. 'No, you need to leave this to official channels. If Alice tells me something helpful then I can do something to help Freya.' She sighed. 'Poor kid. I kind of hope your theory's wrong.'

'So do I,' Josh said, 'but I have a nasty feeling that we're right.'

'I'll be in touch, then,' Jane said. 'And thank you for everything you're doing. Obviously we'll get you financial recompense for—'

'No,' Amy cut in. 'It's nice to be able to do something practical to help. Call it a Christmas gift to Hope and her mum.'

'Seconded,' Josh said firmly. 'We're not doing this for the money.'

'OK. Well, thank you,' Jane said. 'I'll go and have a word with Alice.'

When the social worker had gone, Josh looked at Amy. 'Are you all right?'

She nodded. 'Just thinking about Freya.'

'Hopefully Jane can intervene and get her the help she needs,' Josh said. 'Hey. I could cook us dinner tonight.'

'Seriously?'

'Seriously. You've made me rethink about my cooking skills, since you taught me how to make that salmon thing.'

'OK. That'd be lovely.'

'I'll just go and get some supplies,' he said. 'I can't keep raiding your fridge.'

'You mean, I don't have anything in my kitchen that you can actually cook,' she teased.

He grinned. 'Busted.'

'I'll print out the photos we've taken of Hope and stick them in her book while you're gone,' she said.

'And label them,' he said, 'because your handwriting's a lot neater than mine.'

'Agreed.'

'Anything you need from the shops?'

'No, it's fine.' She kissed him lingeringly. 'See you later.'

In the supermarket, Josh bought ingredients for spaghetti Bolognese. Pudding would definitely have to be shop-bought, he thought, and was delighted to discover a tiramisu cheesecake in the chiller cabinet. He knew Amy liked coffee ice cream, so this looked like a safe bet.

And then he walked through the healthcare aisle and saw the condoms.

He didn't have any, and he guessed that she didn't either. It wasn't quite making an assumption; tonight wasn't going to be the night. But at some point in the future he was pretty sure that they were going to make love, and it would be sensible for them to have protection available. And he had a feeling Amy would be a lot more comfortable using condoms than any other kind of contraception, given her history.

Putting the packet of condoms in his basket felt weird. He hadn't even had to think about this for a long time; during most of their relationship, Kelly had been on the Pill. Or so he'd thought. He couldn't even remember the last time he'd bought condoms. But this made him feel like a teenager, nervous and excited all at the same time.

He shook himself and added a bottle of Pinot Grigio to his basket. And then, by the checkouts, he saw the stand of flowers. He couldn't resist buying a bunch for Amy—nothing flashy and over-the-top that would make her feel awkward and embarrassed, but some pretty gerberas and roses in shades of dark red and pink.

When he got back to the flat, she greeted him with a kiss.

'For you,' he said, handing her the flowers with a flourish.

She looked delighted. 'They're gorgeous. Thank you. That's so sweet—you didn't have to.'

'Apart from the fact that men are supposed to buy their girlfriends flowers, and you're officially my girlfriend,' he pointed out, 'I wanted to.'

She hugged him. 'And I love them. Gerberas are my favourite flowers.'

'More luck than judgement,' he said. 'And I've cheated on the pudding.'

'Need me to do anything to help after I've put these in water?'

'Nope. Though I'd better run the pudding by you, in case you hate it.'

'Oh, nice choice, Dr Farnham,' she said when he showed her the box. 'Tiramisu and cheesecake—there isn't a more perfect combination.'

He laughed. 'Just don't look at the nutritional label, OK?'

'Would that be doctor's orders?' she teased.

'It would.' He smiled at her. 'Go and sit down and carry on with whatever you were doing.'

'Reading a gory crime novel.'

'Go and sit down and I'll make dinner.'

She looked intrigued. 'So is it going to be a cheese toastie or the famous spaghetti Bolognese?'

'Wait and see.'

Except it went disastrously wrong. Not only did he burn the sauce badly enough to ruin the meal, he actually set off the smoke alarm.

And Hope took great exception to the smoke alarm. She even managed to drown it out with her screams.

Amy walked into the kitchen, jiggling the screaming baby in an attempt to calm her. 'Open the windows and flap a damp tea-towel underneath the smoke alarm,' she said. 'I set it off when I first moved in and my toaster decided not to pop the toast out again after it was done.'

It didn't make him feel any better, but he followed her instructions and eventually the smoke alarm stopped shrieking.

Hope, on the other hand, took a fair bit longer to

stop shrieking, and he'd completely run out of songs by the time Amy had warmed some milk and given the baby an unscheduled feed in an attempt to stop her screaming.

'Sorry. I don't *think* I've ruined your saucepan. But it's a close-run thing.' He grimaced. 'And there's no way I can serve up dinner.'

But Amy didn't seem fazed in the slightest. She just laughed. 'These things happen. Stick the saucepan in water and we'll soak it for a while. I'm sure it will have survived. And we'll get a takeaway for dinner. Do you fancy Indian, Chinese or pizza?'

'Pizza. And I'm buying, because dinner was supposed to be my treat tonight,' he said ruefully.

'We'll go halves,' she said, 'and you do the washing up.'

'Including the burned saucepan. Deal.' He sighed. 'It's the last time I try to impress you,' he grumbled.

She kissed him. 'Don't try to impress me. Just be yourself.'

Being himself instead of being who other people wanted him to be was what had led to a rift between himself and his family, and he was pretty sure it had also contributed a fair bit to the breakdown of his marriage.

But then again, Amy wasn't anything like Kelly or his family. Maybe it would be different with her. Maybe he'd be enough for her.

He hoped.

After the pizza—and after, to Josh's relief, he'd managed to get her saucepan perfectly clean—they spent another evening of what really felt like domestic bliss. Amy switched on her stereo and played music by some gentle singer-songwriters that had Hope snoozing comfortably, while the two of them played cards for a while and then stretched out on the sofa together, spooned together with his arms wrapped round her waist and his cheek against hers.

He couldn't remember feeling this chilled-out and happy for a long, long time. They didn't even need to talk: it was enough just to be together, relaxing and enjoying each other's warmth.

Later that evening, when Hope had had her last feed of the evening and they'd gone to bed, he found their goodnight kisses turning hotter, to the point where they were both uncovering bare skin.

He stopped. 'I don't want to rush you.'

Her skin heated. 'Sorry. You're right. We shouldn't take this too fast.'

Though he wanted to. And the expression in her gorgeous brown eyes told him that she might want to, too. He stroked her face. 'I, um, bought stuff today in the supermarket. Just in case. Not because I expect it, but… Well. Later. When we're both ready.'

She kissed him. 'We have kind of known each other for months.'

'Just not very well,' he added in fairness.

Was it his imagination, or had her pupils just gone wider?

'Maybe it's time we remedied that.'

He went very still. 'Are you sure?'

She kissed him. 'Very sure. Because the way you make me feel… I haven't felt that in a long, long time.'

'Same here,' he said.

'Then maybe we ought to seize the day.'

'Carpe diem,' he agreed.

He fetched the condoms, and checked that the baby was OK. And then there was nothing left to hold them back.

CHAPTER EIGHT

Wednesday

'SO ARE YOU back on duty today?' Amy asked.

'I'm afraid so,' Josh said. 'But I'm on a late shift, so I thought maybe we could take Hope out for a walk this morning and make the most of the sunshine.'

'Sounds good to me,' she said, smiling.

How much things had changed since Christmas Eve. Just five short days: and in that time Amy had grown much more confident with the baby.

She'd grown much more confident in herself, too. For the last eighteen months, she'd felt as if she wasn't good enough to be anyone's partner, because she couldn't offer them a family and a future. Josh had shown her just how mistaken she was. And last night, when they'd made love, he'd been so gentle with her, so tender.

Even catching his eye right now made her feel hot all over, remembering how his hands had felt against her skin, how his mouth had coaxed a response she hadn't even known she was capable of.

And Josh seemed different, too. Even though he'd told her everything about his past, she'd sensed a kind of barrier still there: as if he didn't trust anyone enough to let them see who he really was. After last night, that barrier was gone.

Walking along the riverside, hand in hand with Josh and pushing the pram, made Amy feel as if the world was full of sunshine.

And then her mobile phone rang.

'Amy Howes,' she said.

'Amy, it's Jane Richards. Where are you?'

'With Hope and Josh, by the river.' Amy went cold. The deal was that they'd be looking after Hope until New Year's Eve. There could only be two reasons why Jane was calling: either she'd found Hope's mother, or she'd found a permanent foster carer. 'Is something wrong?' she asked, knowing that the answer would be 'yes'—at least from her perspective.

'I need to see you, I'm afraid. Can I meet you at your flat?'

She took a deep breath. 'OK. We can be back in fifteen minutes.'

'Great. I'll be there,' Jane said.

Amy hung up and turned to Josh. 'You've probably already worked out that that was Jane.'

'She's found Hope's mum?'

'She didn't say. But it's either that or she's found a more permanent set of foster parents.' She held her breath for a moment in the hope that it would stop her bursting into tears.

This was ridiculous.

She'd always known that this was a temporary situation. That they'd be looking after Hope until New Year's Eve at the latest, and then they'd have to give her back.

But she'd already bonded with the baby. She'd learned the difference between a cry to say Hope was hungry, a cry to say she needed a fresh nappy, and a cry to say she wanted a cuddle. Josh, too.

Without the baby bonding them together, was this thing between them too new and too fragile to survive? Would she lose Josh as well as the baby?

'Hey. We always knew we'd have to give her back,' Josh said softly.

'I know. But I'll…' To her horror, Amy felt a tear sliding down her face.

Josh drew her into his arms and held her close. 'Miss her,' he finished. 'Me, too. It's going to be strange without Munchkin around.'

And they'd go back to living in their separate flats. Next week, term would start again and Josh would be working very different hours from hers. Would she manage to keep seeing each other? Josh himself had said how difficult it was to find time to date someone when you worked shifts.

'Amy. I take it she wants to see us?'

Amy nodded.

'When?'

'Now.' It felt as if she was forcing the word past a massive lump in her throat.

His arms tightened round her. 'Then we need to go back.'

To face the beginning of the end?

'I know,' she said softly, and made the effort to pull herself together.

Jane was waiting in the lobby by the time they got back to their block.

'I'll make tea,' Josh said. 'Strong, a dash of milk, no sugar, right?'

'Thank you,' Jane said.

Back in her flat, Amy took Hope out of the pram and her snowsuit. So this was the last time she was going to hold her. The baby Amy had promised herself she wouldn't bond with—and yet she had. This was the last cuddle. The last time she'd smell that soft powdery baby scent. The last time she'd see those beautiful dark blue eyes.

She couldn't say a word. All she could do was cuddle the baby and wish that things were different.

Jane waited until Josh was back with them and sitting next to Amy before she told them what had happened.

'This is in strictest confidence,' the social worker warned. 'I shouldn't even be telling you any of this—but without you we wouldn't have found out the full story, so I think you have a right to know. Just…' She grimaced.

'We know. And we'll keep it to ourselves,' Josh said.

'I went to see Alice, first thing this morning.' Jane bit her lip. 'She told me everything.'

'So were we right and Freya is Hope's mother?' Amy asked.

'Yes. But she doesn't have a boyfriend.' Jane took a deep breath. 'It's pretty nasty. You know you said she wasn't getting on with her mum's new partner?'

'Oh, no.' Amy felt her eyes widen as she guessed at the horrible truth. 'Please tell me he didn't interfere with her.'

Jane grimaced. 'Unfortunately, he did a lot more

than that. Freya told her mum what was happening, but she wouldn't believe the girl.'

'Surely she must've known what was going on?' Josh asked.

'Not necessarily,' Amy said. 'When I talked to her, she said that Freya was jealous and being difficult. Maybe she thought that Freya was lying about the guy to break them up and get her mother's full attention back—or even make the space to get her father back with her mother again.'

'It's easy to judge when you're outside the situation,' Jane agreed. 'She might not have known what was happening—or she might have refused to see it because she didn't want to face the truth.'

'So then Freya became pregnant?' Josh asked.

Jane nodded. 'She said she didn't know what to do when she found out.'

'I wish she'd come to me,' Amy said.

'That's what Alice's mum said, too. Between the two of you, I think you would've helped the poor child,' Jane said. 'Freya said she thought about talking to you, but she was scared you wouldn't believe her, either.'

'Poor girl. I would've listened. Why didn't Alice come and see me? She's in my form, too.'

'Freya swore Alice to secrecy,' Jane said. 'Alice agreed, but only on condition Freya promised to have the baby in hospital. She told me she thought that if Freya had the baby in hospital, someone there would get her to tell the truth and they'd help her.'

'But obviously she didn't go to hospital when she started having contractions. There's no way they would have discharged her from the ward, even with the virus situation at the hospital,' Josh said. 'Plus the baby had one of those freezer clips as a cord clamp. It looked to me as if the mum had read up about birth and was doing the best she possibly could.'

'The baby was a couple of weeks early. I guess it took her by surprise,' Jane said. 'She had the baby in the shed at home.'

Amy winced. 'In the middle of winter, all on her own, with no support. That poor child. Has she gone to hospital now?'

Jane nodded. 'I took her there myself. She's being checked over properly.'

'What about the stepfather?' Josh asked.

'I spoke to the police on the way to Freya's. They have him in custody.'

'I sincerely hope they throw the book at him and make sure he can never, ever do that to another girl,' Amy said.

'They will,' Jane reassured her.

Amy knew she had to be brave and ask the question. 'So what happens to Hope?'

'She's going to stay with Freya for a day or two, until Freya decides what she wants to do—whether she wants to keep the baby or give her up for adoption,' Jane said. 'I've got an infant seat in the car, so I can take her with me now.'

'Where are they going to stay?' Josh asked.

'Probably at the hospital—though I know there are the virus problems still, so maybe they'll go back to her mother's,' Jane said.

Amy frowned. 'Is that really a good idea? Especially if the stepfather gets out on bail?'

'Or we'll find her a safe place,' Jane said. 'It depends on what Freya wants to do.'

'I'm glad you're taking what she wants into account,' Josh said. 'It sounds to me as if the poor girl hasn't really had anyone on her side for a long time.' He looked at Amy. 'Though obviously you would've been there for her, if she'd given you the chance.'

'Yeah.' And now Freya wanted her baby back. 'I guess I'd better get Hope's stuff together,' Amy said. Keeping busy was the best way to get through this. She handed the baby to Josh, then went to bag up the sleep suits that Jane had brought, the Moses basket and bedding and bottles and sterilising equipment.

Funny, all that extra stuff should've made her flat feel cluttered. It hadn't. And, without the baby, the place was going to feel so empty.

Stupid of her to fall in love with the baby.

And equally stupid of her to fall in love with Josh.

Because there wasn't going to be a happy ending. Didn't they say be careful what you wish for? What they didn't say was that you might get what you really wanted but then have to give it back.

'I need to wash the stuff that Alison's sister lent us,' she said. 'And we've got the necklace that Freya left with Hope—she needs that. And the book we did, with her sleep chart and feed chart and weight, and pictures of her first few days and—' Her voice caught.

'I'm sorry,' Jane said. 'You've both been brilliant.'

'We're just going to miss her, that's all,' Josh said. 'We've got used to her being around.'

'Of course you have.'

Josh kissed the baby's forehead. 'Well, Munchkin, look after yourself.'

The baby grizzled, as if picking up on the dark mood in the room.

'Goodbye, Hope,' Amy whispered, unable to bear holding the baby again because she knew just how hard it would be to hand her over to the social worker.

'I'll be in touch,' Jane said.

'I'll walk you down to your car. Carry the stuff,' Josh offered.

'And I'd better start washing the things that Alison lent us,' Amy said. She didn't think she could handle watching Jane drive away with the baby.

She half expected Josh not to come back, but he knocked on her door when he'd seen Jane into her car.

'Are you OK?' he asked.

What was the point in lying? 'Not really.'

'I'll ring work and see if I can swap shifts with someone,' he said.

'No. They need you at the hospital,' Amy said.

Meaning that you don't? Josh wondered, but didn't dare to ask. Just in case that was what she said. Right now, he could see that she was hurting. He knew that when people were hurt they often said things they didn't mean but the words still caused an awful lot of damage. It would be better to back off now and regroup.

He glanced at his watch. 'Actually, I do have to go, if you're sure you don't want me to try and change my shift.'

When she said nothing, he sighed inwardly. 'I'll be home as soon as I can,' he promised.

Amy turned away. 'Sorry. I think I just need some time on my own.'

Did that mean she didn't want him to come over after work?

As if he'd spoken out loud, she said, 'I'll see you tomorrow, maybe.'

Josh went cold.

He hadn't been enough for Kelly.

And, now the baby wasn't here, Amy didn't need his help any more. She didn't need him. So he wasn't enough for her, either. What kind of delusional fool was he, to think this was going to work out?

'OK. Call me if you need me,' he said, but he knew she wouldn't.

And it was pointless trying to put his arms round her and kiss her, or tell her that everything was going to be all right. He'd seen that closed-off look with Kelly, too, and he knew what it meant.

The end.

So it was over almost as soon as it had started, Amy thought as Josh closed her front door behind him.

This morning, she'd been so happy. She'd had everything she ever wanted. A baby, and a partner who cared about her—a partner who was a decent man, one who wouldn't lie or cheat or let her down.

Except, now the baby had gone, Josh had walked away from her just as easily as Michael had. No doubt he'd been relieved when she'd said she wanted some time on her own. It meant he hadn't had to do the 'it's not you, it's me' speech.

Well, she'd pick herself up, dust herself down, and remember not to let people too close again in future.

Josh was too busy at work to get a chance to pop up to the maternity ward to see if Freya and Hope were there. When he'd finished his shift, it was too late to visit; if Freya was still on the ward, he thought, the poor girl would probably be asleep.

He walked home, and paused outside Amy's door. Should he knock and see how she was doing?

Then again, she'd said she wanted space. And she hadn't texted him, even though she knew he'd pick up any messages as soon as he'd finished his shift.

Well, he wasn't going to give up on her that easily. He knocked on the door. 'Amy? Are you there?'

She didn't answer.

He tried her mobile. A recorded voice informed him that the phone was switched off and he should leave a message or send a text.

Right.

He was pretty sure she wouldn't reply to those, either.

With a heavy heart, he carried on down the corridor to his own flat. Funny how empty the place seemed. And was it his imagination or did the place smell musty?

At least cleaning everything kept him too busy to think for a little while. He didn't bother making himself a sandwich because he just wasn't hungry. But when it came to bedtime... His double bed felt way too wide. It was worse than when he'd first moved in to the flat, because now he knew what it would feel like if the place was really home rather than simply a place to sleep and store his clothes.

But he wasn't enough for Amy, just as he hadn't been enough for Kelly. He'd just have to get used to that. And he was never going to risk his heart again.

CHAPTER NINE

Thursday

JOSH ACTUALLY TOOK his break at lunchtime, the next day, and paid a quiet visit to the maternity ward rather than heading for the canteen.

'Hey, Josh—are you coming up to see us, for a change? Usually you call us down to the Emergency Department to see a patient,' one of the obstetricians teased.

'Actually, I haven't come to see you—I've come to visit a friend of a friend during my lunch break,' he said. And that was sort of true. If you could count a week-old baby as a friend.

'Who?'

'Freya. If she's still here. I know she and the baby came in yesterday.'

His colleague frowned. 'Oh, our young missing mum? Yes, she's here. She's—' He stopped.

'Patient confidentiality,' Josh said with a sigh. 'I know. Does it help if you know I looked after the baby?'

'Downstairs?'

'Yes.' It wasn't a total stretch of the truth—he and

Amy *had* brought Hope in to the Emergency Department, and he had indeed been looking after Hope... Albeit as a stand-in parent, rather than as a doctor.

'Ah. Well, if we're talking as fellow clinicians, the baby's doing fine. Freya does have an infection, but we've put her on antibiotics and it should clear up in a couple of days. We're keeping her in for the moment to keep an eye on her.'

'Great.' Josh gave his sweetest smile. 'Can I put my head round the door for two seconds and say hello?'

'Actually, it might do the poor kid good to have a visitor,' the obstetrician said. 'Sure.'

'Thanks. Where do I find her?'

'She's in room six.'

Even better: Freya was in a room on her own, so she wouldn't be embarrassed about their conversation being overheard. 'Great. Thanks.'

He knocked on the door of room six, then went in when he heard Freya call, 'Yes?'

'Hello,' he said with a smile. 'Freya, isn't it?'

She looked at him, her eyes wide and suddenly full of fear. 'Have you come to take the baby? Are you from the police?'

'No and no,' he reassured her. The poor kid was really upset, and she could do with a bit of handholding, he thought. He knew the perfect person to do that, but right now he had a feeling that Amy's head might not be in the right place. 'And you're not in trouble. My name's Josh and I'm a doctor,' he said, indicating his white coat and his hospital identity card.

'I haven't seen you before. Are you from the maternity ward?' she asked.

'No, I'm from the Emergency Department.'

She frowned. 'But I haven't been in an accident or anything. Why do you need to see me?'

'Actually,' he said, 'I came to say hello to you and to see how Munchkin's doing.'

'Munchkin?' Freya looked confused.

'Hope,' he explained.

She frowned again. 'Why do you call her Munchkin?'

'Because she's tiny—you know, like the people in *The Wizard of Oz*.'

'Oh. And how do you know her name's Hope?'

He could understand why the poor girl was so suspicious. She'd been through a lot. Right then, he really wanted to give her a hug and tell her everything was going to work out just fine, but it wouldn't be appropriate. Plus, given what had happened to her, the contact from a strange man would probably worry her even more. 'Because,' he said quietly, 'I'm Miss Howes's neighbour and I've been helping her look after the baby for the last week.'

'Oh.' Freya bit her lip. 'Sorry. I ruined your Christmas.'

'On the contrary,' he said. 'I was planning to have a really lousy Christmas on my own, doing my shift downstairs and then eating my body weight in leftover sausage rolls that hadn't been stored properly and probably ending up with food poisoning—and because of you I had a decent Christmas dinner cooked for me and I got to spend Christmas with someone really nice.'

There was the hint of a smile, just for a moment, and then her expression switched back to gloom again.

'So can I give her a cuddle?' he asked.

'I guess.'

He picked the baby up, and settled down with her on the chair next to Freya's bed. 'Hey, Munchkin. I know you're asleep so you're not going to answer, but have you missed Uncle Joshy's terrible singing?'

Freya blinked in surprise. 'You sing to her?'

'Yup. Little tip from me—you'll need to do that a lot when she has a bath,' he said. 'She absolutely hates baths. She screams the place down.'

'What do you sing to her?'

'Anything. She doesn't care what it is, as long as you sing,' he said with a smile. And he was relieved that finally Freya seemed to be responding to him. 'So how are *you* doing?' he asked, trying to keep his voice as gentle and non-threatening as possible.

She shrugged. 'OK, I suppose.'

Well, it was probably a stupid question. He went back to safer ground. 'Hope's a really beautiful baby, you know. And her name fits her perfectly.'

A tear slid down her cheek. 'And I'm going to have to give her away.'

'Why?'

'I'm fifteen. I'm supposed to be at school.' She shook her head, looking anguished. 'I can't go to school with a baby, can I?'

'Won't your mum help?'

'No chance.' Freya gave a snort of disgust. 'She hates me—and I hate her, too.'

'Hate's a very strong word,' he said softly. 'Families can be complicated, and sometimes they can make you feel as if you've let them down. And sometimes you feel that they're the ones who let you down.'

'She thinks it's all my fault. The baby.'

He waited, giving Freya the space to find the words.

'She thinks I led him on. But I didn't.'

'I know,' he said gently.

She looked shocked. 'You believe me?'

'Yes.'

'*She* doesn't.'

'Maybe your mum just needs a bit of time to think about it,' he suggested.

'She won't change her mind.' Freya dragged in a breath. 'And I know she wants him back.'

He could understand exactly why Freya didn't want to live with her stepfather again. He didn't want the girl having to live with the man again, either. He'd quite like to rearrange the man's body parts, except he knew that violence didn't solve anything and locking the man away for a long time was a better option. 'Maybe there's another way,' he said. 'Jane, the social worker, is really nice. She might be able to find you a foster family who'll look after you and the baby.'

Freya's expression was filled with disbelief. 'Who's going to take on a fifteen-year-old and a baby? I'm going to end up in a children's home, and everyone's going to despise me.'

'There are nice people out there. People who are kind. People who help others.' He paused. 'That's why you rang Miss Howes's doorbell, isn't it?'

Freya nodded. 'She's my form teacher. Everyone loves her, because she's kind and funny.'

Yeah. And Amy had been his, for just a little while. Being without her made his heart ache.

'I knew she'd look after the baby and know what to do,' Freya continued.

'Maybe you could've talked to her when you found out you were pregnant,' he said.

'I wanted to—Alice, she's my best friend, she said I ought to, but I made her promise she wouldn't tell anyone, not even her mum.' Freya bit her lip. 'I would've told Miss Howes about *him*, but I was scared. He said if I told anyone he'd make sure nobody believed me and I'd get taken into care.'

Being taken into care probably would've been the best thing for her, Josh thought. It would have got her away from the man who'd been systematically abusing her. 'Miss Howes would've believed you. Luckily Alice did tell her mum in the end,' he said, 'because you needed antibiotics and you could've been very ill without them.' He paused. 'Would Alice's mum let you stay with them, maybe?'

Freya shook her head. 'They don't have enough room. There isn't a spare bedroom, and Alice's bedroom is too small for more than one bed, let alone another bed and a cot. So I don't know what's going to happen to me.'

'There are nice people in the world, Freya,' he said again, 'and Jane will make sure someone really nice looks after you and Hope, if you want to keep her.'

'I do.' Freya glanced down at the baby. 'Even though she's his—well, she's a girl, so she won't look like him and she won't remind me of him.'

'She's gorgeous. She's definitely got your nose and chin,' he said.

'Thank you,' she said, 'for looking after Hope for me.'

'It was a pleasure,' he said, meaning it. 'We did a notebook for her first few days—we wrote down when she slept and when she had some milk, and took some photographs.'

'I know—Miss Richards gave it to me. Thank you.'

'You've probably already worked it out for yourself, but mine's the terrible handwriting,' he said.

'Who did the drawings in the back?' she asked.

'Me,' he said.

'You're good.'

He inclined his head in acknowledgement. 'Thank you.'

'Why aren't you an artist instead of a doctor?' she asked.

'It's how things worked out,' he said. 'Sometimes, your plans don't work out quite as you thought they would, but you can still find a chance to be happy.'

'I guess,' she said, sounding unconvinced, but he hoped that she'd think about what he'd said and realise that he was telling the truth. 'Would you tell Miss Howes thanks for me?'

'Sure,' he said. Though he might have to do it by text, if she was avoiding him.

'And sorry. She's really kind. I know I shouldn't have just dumped Hope in that blanket in a cardboard box, but I just didn't know what to do.'

'Hey.' He patted her hand. 'You were having a tough time. And you knew Amy—Miss Howes—would make sure Hope was all right, so that was one thing less you had to worry about.'

'Yeah.' She sniffed.

'I've got to go back to work, now,' he said. 'But maybe I can come and see you and Hope again tomorrow?'

'I'd like that,' she said.

'And I'll bring my sketchbook. Do you a proper picture of you both together.' He stroked the baby's face. 'Nice to see you, Munchkin. Even if you weren't going to wake up and say hello.' Gently, he transferred the baby back to Freya's arms. 'If you need anything, get them to call me. Josh Farnham in Emergency. They know me up here anyway,' he said.

Freya's eyes filled with tears. 'That's so kind. Thank you.'

And not enough people had been kind to the girl, he thought savagely. He'd quite like a little chat with Freya's mother about how to treat a child properly—and she'd be squirming so much by the time he'd finished, she'd treat the girl decently for ever after. 'No worries, Freya,' he said. 'Take care.'

He thought about it through the rest of the day. Freya's assessment of Amy: *Everyone loves her, because she's kind and funny.*

Amy was more than that. Much more.

She made him feel as if the sun had come out after a week of pouring rain.

And the week they'd just shared... Yes, it had been intense, almost like being snowbound but without the snow: but it hadn't just been the baby holding them together. What they had was real.

She'd definitely pushed him away, yesterday. And, now he thought about it, he realised why. She was kind and funny and nice—and she was trying to do what she thought was best for him. Setting him free to find someone who could give him the family he wanted without any complications.

Except if she'd actually said that to him, he would've had the chance to tell her that it wasn't what he wanted. Yes, he wanted a family; but he wanted her more. He needed to convince her that it didn't matter if they couldn't have children. And maybe he needed to prove to her that he could be enough for her, the way he hadn't been enough for Kelly. What they had was too good to throw away.

He actually ran home, after his shift.

And this time he didn't knock on Amy's door; instead, he rang her buzzer on the intercom.

When she didn't answer, he wondered for a moment if she'd gone out. But something told him she was home alone, feeling as miserable as he did without her. There was only one way he could think of to make her talk to him: to lean on the buzzer, and not stop until she answered.

'Yes?' She sounded cross and miserable at the same time.

'Amy, it's Josh. We need to talk.'

'I—'

'No excuses and no refusals,' he said. 'We really do need to talk, Amy. Just give me five minutes. Please.'

She sighed. 'You didn't have to lean on the buzzer. You could've just knocked on my door.'

'And you would've ignored me, like you did last night,' he pointed out. 'Can I come in?'

She sighed again. 'I don't have any choice, do I?'

'Nope,' he said. 'We need to talk.' If she said no after she'd listened to what he had to say, then fair enough—he'd accept that. But he needed to tell her how he felt, and she needed to know what was going on in his head. The only way that was going to happen was if they talked instead of avoiding the issues.

'See you in a second,' she said.

It took him more like twenty seconds to get to her door, but at least this time she opened it when he knocked.

And she looked as if she hadn't slept. There were dark hollows under her eyes and her face was lined with misery.

'How are you doing?' he asked.

'Not brilliant,' she admitted.

Even though he'd meant to keep at arm's length until they'd talked, he couldn't just stand there and let her feel awful. He wrapped his arms round her and held her close. 'I know. Me, too. And I've missed you even more than I miss Hope.'

'Josh, I—'

'Please, just let me talk,' he said. 'If you say no when you've heard me out, I won't push you. But don't say no before you've heard what I have to say.'

'OK.' She wriggled out of his arms. 'Let's sit down. Coffee?'

'No, thanks.' He knew it was a delaying tactic, and he didn't want to wait any more. He wanted to get this sorted out right now. He followed her in to the living room and sat next to her on the sofa. 'I went to see Freya and Hope today.'

Her eyes widened. 'How are they?'

'Doing OK,' he said. 'Freya wants to keep the baby, but she doesn't want to go back to live with her mum—and she's worried about how school's going to work, with a baby.'

'We can support her,' Amy said. 'We can do a lot to help, now we know about the situation.'

He smiled. 'I knew you'd say that. And she also said she rang your doorbell because she knew you'd look after the baby and you'd know what to do.' He paused. 'She says everyone loves you, because you're kind and funny.'

Amy blinked, and he had the strongest impression that she was close to tears. 'That's nice.'

'You're more than that,' he said. 'And that's why I want to talk to you.' This time, he reached over to take her hand. 'I know this is fast and I know we both have issues from the past we'll still have to work through. But I like you—no, I more than like you, Amy.' He might as well tell her the whole lot. 'Over the last week, I've fallen in love with you. Not because of the baby, but because you're bright and you're funny and you're warm, and you have this whole aura about you that makes me feel as if the sun's just come out after a week of rain. And I know that sounds flowery and cheesy and maybe even a bit smarmy, but it's not meant to be like that.' He threw his free hand up into the air in exasperation. 'I just don't have any better words to describe it.'

'Oh, Josh.'

The expression on her face gave him hope, so he pushed on.

'I know Michael left you because you couldn't have children, but he was an idiot. He was missing the point. And I'm not Michael. Yes, I always thought I wanted a family, and spending this last week looking after Hope with you made me realise that I do still want that. But it doesn't matter that you can't have children. We did a great job as foster parents for Hope, this week, and we could do that again for another child.'

'But it's still a massive compromise,' Amy said. 'I wasn't enough for Michael.'

'And I wasn't enough for Kelly. But you're not Kelly, and I'm not Michael.' He paused. 'You're enough for me. You're everything I want. And I want you with or without a family, Amy.'

'I'm not brilliant at relationships. Not long-term,' she said. 'There was Gavin.'

'Who cheated on you. He was a snake.'

'And Michael.'

'Who was a selfish toad. I don't think your problem's with relationships, Amy—it's that you pick amphibians.'

She winced. 'Don't pull your punches.'

'There's no point in trying to sugar-coat things. You and me, we're about honesty. So we know we can trust each other. I've got my faults, just like everyone else, but I'm most definitely not a reptile,' he said. 'So do something different, this time, to make it work. Pick a man who's not a snake or a toad. Pick me.'

Could she really believe this?

Would she be enough for Josh?

Then again, she knew he had a similar issue, feeling that he hadn't been enough for his ex-wife. They were coming from the same sort of place and wanted the same sort of things.

'Pick me, Amy,' he said again, his voice soft. 'Because I choose you, too.'

'We haven't even gone out on a date together,' she said.

'Yeah—our relationship has been a bit backwards, so far. Baby first, then...' He smiled. 'Well.'

Sex. Amy's skin heated at the memories.

'Let's go out on a date tonight,' he said. 'I need a shower, but whatever I do to my hair it's going to look like this within five minutes, so I hope you'll forgive the fact that it looks a mess.'

'There's nothing wrong with your hair. It's cute.' And then, just because he looked a little bit worried and she thought he needed a bit of reassurance, she ran her fingers through his hair to smooth it slightly. 'Sexy,' she said.

'You think I'm sexy?'

'I think you're a lot of things.' And because he'd said it all first, she had the courage to say it back to him. 'You're kind and you're caring and you're reliable. You're calm in a crisis. And it scares the hell out of me that we've been on nod-and-smile terms for six months, but we've just spent a week together like a real family, and somewhere along the way I fell in love with you and I never expected anything like that to happen.'

'And you're still scared it's going to go wrong,' he said.

She nodded.

'Me, too. But we can work on that,' he said. 'Together. How long's it going to take you to get ready?'

'How dressy are we talking?'

'I know a bistro not too far from here where they do live music,' he said. 'And I patched up the chef six months ago, so I'm pretty sure they'll be able to find us a table for two.'

'Little black dress and lipstick, and do something with my hair—that'll be about twenty minutes,' she calculated swiftly.

'Deal.' He looked at her. 'And we're supposed to seal a deal, aren't we?'

In answer, she leaned forward and kissed him.

And he kissed her back until her knees went weak.

'Twenty minutes,' he said, and headed for the door. Then he leaned back round the doorframe. 'I love you,' he said, blew her another kiss, and left.

Yesterday, when Amy had had to give Hope back— even though she'd known it was going to happen—had been one of the hardest days of her life. A real emotional roller coaster that had left her miserable and lonely and aching.

Today, it felt as if she'd climbed all the way back to the top. Except this time there wasn't a sharp descent back into the shadows.

A bistro with live music. Dressy but not *too* dressy, then.

The little black dress, tights and lipstick took a couple of minutes. Her hair took slightly longer, pulled into a loose up-do with a few strands left to frame her face and soften the effect.

And then Josh rang the doorbell.

How long was it since she'd gone on a proper date? Nerves throbbed through her, but she lifted her chin and strode over to answer the door.

In a dark suit with a white shirt buttoned to the neck but without a tie, and his hair sticking up all over the place, Josh looked sexy as hell. He took her breath away.

Clearly he was just as nervous as she was, because he opened his mouth to speak and nothing came out.

Crazy. They'd spent most of the last week together, talking about practically everything in the universe.

As if he was thinking exactly the same thing, he said, 'Um, this is insane. We talked all week. But now it's our first date and I don't know what to say to you.'

'Me, too,' she said. 'You look nice.'

'You look amazing,' he said. Then he grinned. 'But actually you still look amazing when your hair's all over the place and you've slept in your clothes, so I'm not being shallow.'

'Neither was I. But thank you for the compliment.' She inclined her head in acknowledgement.

'I feel like a teenager,' he said.

'Me, too.'

'But,' he said, 'I did definitely get us a table. So hopefully this won't be the date from hell.'

'Unless the heel of my shoe gets stuck in a grate and falls off, and I knock a glass of red wine across the table and ruin your shirt.'

'Or the chef does a body swap with me and I burn the spaghetti Bolognese again…'

She laughed and took his hand. 'I think we'll be all right.'

The restaurant turned out to have a wonderful menu, and the musician that night was a singer-song-writer who alternated between the guitar and the piano. And once the food and wine had relaxed them enough that they were at ease with each other again, it turned out to be the perfect date. They didn't stop talking through the meal, and then Josh held her hand as they enjoyed the music together.

They walked home along the riverside, their arms wrapped round each other, and Josh kissed Amy under every single lamp-post. Although it had turned cold, Amy didn't care; she was simply enjoying Josh's near-ness.

He paused outside her front door. 'I guess, as this is our first date, this is where I kiss you goodnight and wish you sweet dreams?'

'And I ask you in for coffee?' She spread her hands. 'Or there's the alternative version.'

His eyes darkened. 'Which is?'

'Sweet dreams, Josh.' She kissed him.

'And now I invite you in for coffee?' he asked.

She nodded.

Josh caught his breath as he realised exactly what she meant. 'And you stay?' he asked very softly.

'You've already seen my bedroom,' she said. 'And, if this is going to be an equal relationship...'

He didn't need a second invitation. He took her hand and led her to his flat.

He made coffee, as promised; but they didn't get to drink it because he ended up carrying her to his bed instead.

Afterwards, she fell asleep in his arms. This time neither of them wore pyjamas and there were no barriers between them. And Josh thought that maybe the future was going to work.

There was just one more thing that would make life perfect—and he'd suggest that to her in the morning.

CHAPTER TEN

Friday—New Year's Eve

THE NEXT MORNING, Josh woke, warm and comfortable.

Best of all, Amy was lying asleep in his arms.

And today was New Year's Eve. A time for new beginnings. A time, he hoped, for them to make a decision together that might just change everything for both of them.

He gently moved his arm from under her shoulder, and climbed out of bed without waking her. It took just a couple of minutes to throw on some clothes and brush his teeth, and he paused to write her a note just in case she woke while he was gone.

Gone to get breakfast.
Back in five minutes. x

He stuck the note to the inside of his front door, where she couldn't possibly miss it, and headed for the bakery just down the street.

When he returned, he peeked into his bedroom and Amy was just stirring.

'Well, good morning, sleepyhead,' he teased.

She squinted at him. 'Why are you dressed? Have you got to go to work?'

'Nope. I worked Christmas, so I get New Year's off,' he said. 'I'm dressed because I just went out to get us some breakfast.' He smiled. 'I did leave you a note on the front door in case you woke while I was away, but clearly you didn't. Stay where you are and I'll bring in the goodies.'

He came back two minutes later with a tray, a plate of warm croissants, jam and butter, and two mugs of coffee.

'You made coffee that fast?' she asked.

'No. I bought it from the bakery and I just poured it out of the paper cups into mugs,' he admitted. 'I didn't want to spend any more time away from you than I had to.'

'Croissants and proper coffee. The perfect breakfast in bed. Very decadent, Dr Farnham,' she said with a smile.

'I have a much better idea for being decadent, Miss Howes,' he said. 'How about Valentine's Day in Paris—proper Parisian croissants?'

'I really like the sound of that,' she said. 'But, if it's in term-time, I won't be able to take the day off. We might have to have an unofficial Valentine's Day instead.'

'Works for me,' he said.

Once they'd finished breakfast, he asked, 'What would you like to do today?'

'I really don't mind, as long as it's with you—or is that being greedy?'

'It's what I had in mind, too,' he said. 'Maybe we can go for a walk somewhere.'

'Sounds good to me,' she said, and kissed him. 'But I can hardly go out in last night's little black dress. I need to go next door and shower and change.'

'Thirty minutes?' he asked.

'That'd be great. Though I'll do the washing up first.'

'No. I'll do that while you get ready.' He kissed her again. 'Knock for me when you're done.'

Half an hour later, Amy knocked on Josh's door—having showered, washed her hair, dried it quickly and changed into jeans, a sweater and comfortable mid-heeled boots.

'You look beautiful,' he said, and kissed her.

'So do you.' She kissed him back. 'So where are we going?' she asked.

'I was thinking, maybe we can start by visiting Freya and Hope in hospital.'

'Are you sure they haven't been discharged?' she asked.

He nodded. 'I rang the ward and checked this morning.'

'Are we actually allowed to do this?'

He shrugged. 'Give me a good reason why you can't visit one of your pupils in hospital?'

'Because we've spent most of the past week looking after her baby?' Amy suggested.

'Then you're not visiting as her form tutor. You're visiting as a friend,' he pointed out.

'I'd like to see them,' Amy said. 'But we're not going empty-handed.'

'Good idea,' Josh said. 'They told me on the ward yesterday that she hadn't had any visitors.'

Amy looked shocked. 'Not even her mum, or her best friend?'

'Nope. That's why I said I'd pop in to see her today. And I promised I'd do a sketch of her and the baby together.' He indicated his sketchbook and pencils. 'Maybe I can get it framed for her.'

'That's a really lovely idea. And I agree, we should definitely make a fuss of her,' Amy said. 'Shops, first?'

'Absolutely.'

Between them, they found a couple of cute outfits for Hope in tiny baby size, the cutest and softest little polar bear, and a board book. 'And we need to take something for Freya, too.'

'Not flowers or balloons,' Josh said. 'They're the first things that get banned as part of virus control regulations.'

'Nice smellies, then,' Amy said, and dragged him off to a small shop that specialised in cruelty-free beauty products. 'They're really popular with her year group,' Amy explained, when Josh looked mystified.

'You really do notice things, don't you?' he asked.

'I'm supposed to notice things. I'm a form tutor. And I missed Freya's pregnancy completely,' Amy said, 'so I let her down.'

He gave her a hug. 'I don't think you're the one who let her down, honey.'

She bought wrapping paper, tape, ribbon and a 'congratulations on your baby girl' card, and they stopped for a very brief coffee so Amy could wrap the presents.

'How do you do that?' Josh asked when he saw the beautifully wrapped parcels and curled ribbons. 'I wrap something and—well, I think a five-year-old could do a better job than I do.'

'It's all about angles,' she said.

'Maths teacher stuff.' He rolled his eyes.

'You got it.' She winked at him. 'But, given that you have to stitch people up without leaving scars, surely you can wrap things?'

'Wrapping,' he said, 'is way harder than suturing. Trust me on that.' He grinned. 'Let's go and see the girls.'

They learned from the midwife at the reception desk that Freya was still in room six, and Josh rapped softly on the door. 'Freya? Hello? Can we come in?'

'Josh! You said you'd come back,' she said, looking pleased to see him.

'I promised you a sketch. And I'm off duty today, so I thought now would work nicely.'

'It's so nice to see you. Thank you ever so much. It was getting a bit—well...'

'Boring, on your own?' he asked.

'A bit.' She beamed at him. 'Hope, we've got a visitor.' But then she bit her lip when she saw Amy walk into the room behind Josh. 'Oh—Miss Howes! I'm so sorry for what I did.'

'We're out of school, so you can call me Amy, and there's absolutely no need for you to apologise because you've really had a hard time,' Amy said, and gave the girl a hug. 'How are you doing?'

'I'm getting better.' A tear slid down Freya's face. 'But I ruined your Christmas.'

'No, you fixed it,' Amy said, 'because I was meant to be spending it in Edinburgh with my oldest friends—but they got the flu, so I was going to be all alone and miserable at home. Instead, I got to spend Christmas with Josh and Hope.'

'That's what he said when he came yesterday.'

Amy smiled. 'I promise we didn't confer before-hand—and how's your gorgeous baby?'

Freya indicated the crib to the side of the bed. 'She's asleep right now. Thank you for looking after her.'

'I enjoyed it,' Amy said. 'Though it was a bit of a steep learning curve—I'm more used to dealing with teenagers.' She paused and took Freya's hand. 'You could've come to talk to me, Freya, and you still can. Any time. And if you want to come back to school and do your exams, we can support you and make sure you have everything you need.'

'Really?'

'Really,' Amy said firmly.

Another tear slid down Freya's cheek. 'I wish my mum would be like you.'

'She's not been to see you yet?' Amy asked.

Freya shook her head. 'And I'm kind of glad, because I don't want to see her.'

'But you've just had a baby—surely you want your mum.'

Freya nodded, and this time she burst into tears.

Amy held her until she stopped crying.

'I don't want to give Hope away,' Freya said, 'but she'll make me. And there's nothing I can do, because who's going to let a fifteen-year-old with a baby live with them?'

Amy glanced at Josh. She could think of a solution that might work for all of them. But she couldn't say anything to Freya until she'd discussed it with Josh. Saying that you'd consider fostering someone and actually doing it were two very different things.

'Things will get better with your mum,' Amy said. 'Sometimes when you're very lonely you make wrong decisions.'

Josh looked worried, as if he thought that was a coded message to him—that she'd been lonely and agreeing to a relationship with him had been a wrong decision. She caught his eye and gave the tiniest shake of her head to reassure him, then blew him a secret kiss, and saw the tension in his shoulders relax again.

'Maybe giving each other a bit of space will help your mum make a different decision,' Amy said gently.

'She'll still choose him over me.'

Amy thought that was probably true, but it wouldn't help anything to agree with Freya right at that moment. 'It's always difficult to second-guess what someone else is going to do and right now I think you need to concentrate on yourself and the baby,' she said. 'Josh tells me you had an infection.'

Freya nodded. 'They're giving me antibiotics. And I feel a bit better than I did.'

'That's good,' Amy said.

'And we brought you both a little something,' Josh said, handing Freya the parcels and the card.

Freya opened the parcel with the sleep suits and the tiny dungarees and sweater. 'Oh, they're gorgeous,' she said. 'Look, Hope. Your first present.' She was in tears again by the time she'd unwrapped the polar bear, and sobbing openly when she opened the gift for her.

'Hey.' This time Josh was the one to give her a hug.

'It's just…'

'It's all a bit overwhelming,' Josh said, 'and you've just had a baby. Do you want me to leave the sketch until another day?'

'When my face isn't all blotchy and stuff? Yes, please.' Freya looked forlorn. 'Or is that being vain and greedy?'

'Of course it's not,' Josh reassured her.

Amy took her hand and squeezed it. 'Has Alice come to visit you yet?'

'No, even though I texted her to let her know I'm here.' Freya bit her lip. 'She probably thinks I don't want to see her because she told her mum everything when she promised me she'd keep it secret.'

'I wouldn't normally act as a go-between,' Amy said, 'but I think this is a special case. Do you want me to have a word with her?'

'Would you?'

'Of course I will.' Amy smiled at her. 'Tell you what—how about I take a photo of you and Hope on my phone to show her?'

'Even though my face is all blotchy?'

'Sweetie, you look just fine. And it's not going to be plastered all over social media, I promise. It's just so I can show Alice.'

Freya brightened, and Amy took the photograph.

She and Josh had a brief cuddle with the baby. 'We'd better let you get some rest,' Amy said, 'but we can come back and see you tomorrow, if you like?'

Freya's eyes filled with tears again, and she scrubbed them away. 'Sorry. I'm being pathetic. That'd be really nice. We'd like that, wouldn't we, Hope?'

The baby gurgled, as if in agreement.

Amy and Josh went from the hospital to Alice's house. Alice's mother opened the door to them. 'Oh, Miss Howes! Is there…?'

Amy smiled at her. 'I just wanted to say thank you for persuading Alice to talk to Jane Richards about Freya. This is my friend, Josh Farnham. And I wondered if we could see Alice for about two minutes?'

'Yes, that's fine. Come in.'

Alice's mother called the teenager down from her room.

'Miss Howes!' Alice stopped dead in the doorway.

'Hello, Alice. This is my friend, Josh,' Amy introduced him swiftly. 'We came to show you something.' Amy opened the photograph on her phone and handed it to Alice.

'Oh—Freya and her baby! But she's so tiny!' Alice said on seeing the baby. 'But how did you...?'

'Freya left the baby on our doorstep on Christmas Eve,' Amy said. 'We kind of worked out that Freya was the mum—but, without your help in confirming that so we could help her, Freya would be very ill right now. So well done for being so brave.'

'But isn't Freya angry with me for telling?' Alice asked, looking worried. 'I mean, she hasn't texted me or anything, and she hasn't been on any of the usual social media. I thought her mum had confiscated her phone and laptop but, after Miss Richards talked to me about the baby, I thought maybe Freya just didn't want to speak to me.'

'I think she's relieved you did tell, actually. She said she'd texted you to say she was in hospital,' Josh said.

'Oh, no! But I didn't get her text,' Alice said biting her lip.

'Josh and I have been her only visitors. She'd really love it if you came to see her,' Amy said gently.

'I think she's worried that you don't want anything to do with her any more.'

'But that's daft. She's my best friend. Of course I want to see her—and the baby. Can we, Mum?' Alice asked.

Alice's mum nodded. 'Of course. We'll go and buy her something nice for the baby too—I assume she's keeping the baby, Miss Howes?'

'She wants to, yes. Her little girl's called Hope.'

'That's nice.'

Amy smiled in agreement, 'And, Alice, I hope you know you can always talk to me in confidence,' she said. 'Sometimes I might have to act on what you tell me—like the social worker did, to keep Freya safe— but that's why I'm your form tutor. I'm there if you need me.'

Alice blushed, clearly not quite sure what to say. 'Thank you.'

'Anyway—we'd better go,' Amy said. 'But thanks for all your help. You did the right thing.'

Alice's mum showed them out. 'I feel better knowing there's someone like you at school keeping an eye out for the kids,' she said.

'Me? I'm just ordinary,' Amy said.

And Josh thought, no, you're not ordinary. You're really special.

Once they'd left Alice's house, Josh steered them towards the nearest coffee shop. 'I think we need to talk,' he said.

'Agreed.'

He ordered them both coffee and found a quiet table. 'Poor Freya's really been through the mill.'

'And she clearly doesn't want to go back to her

mum's, as you said yesterday. She wants to keep the baby. And she thinks she's not going to be able to do that.'

'She told me yesterday she was scared she'd end up in a children's home and everyone there would despise her.'

'Poor kid.' Amy winced. 'You know what you were saying about considering fostering?'

'Yes.' Even though he knew he was probably rushing it, Josh was pretty sure that Amy was thinking along exactly the same lines as he was. 'I think we've just found two kids who need us to be their family.'

'It's a lot to ask, Josh. Teenagers aren't easy, and neither are babies. Plus this thing between you and me—this is all really new.'

He took her hand. 'But it's also really *right*. With you, I feel as if I've found the place where I fit.'

'Me, too.' She tightened her fingers round his. 'There are probably regulations against me fostering her because I'm her form tutor.'

'There's probably a way to cut through the red tape. And we know someone who'll help,' Josh pointed out. 'Because this is a solution where we're all going to win. We all get a family. You're right in that it's not going to be plain sailing, but we can work on it together.' He paused. 'So. Your flat or mine?'

'That's a problem. Both our flats have only one bedroom, and we're going to need at least two—if not three,' Amy said.

'So either we rent out our flats and then take out a lease on a bigger place,' he said. 'Or we could sell the flats, pool our resources and buy a bigger place together.'

She took a sip of coffee. 'You know, a week ago, I was on my own and focused on my career. If someone had told me that just one week later I'd find someone who feels like my missing half and we'd be talking about house-hunting together, I would never have believed them.'

'Yeah, it's fast. Scarily fast.' He took a deep breath. 'And it was fast for me with Kelly, too, and you know that went wrong, so I'm not surprised you're having doubts. Though, just so you know, I'm not having doubts.'

'I'm not having doubts, either. Doing things fast went wrong for you last time; but doing things slowly went wrong for me the last two times. So maybe we just need to forget about the past. We're both older and wiser, and we're not going to repeat our mistakes,' she said. 'We're looking to the future. Together.'

'You, me, and a ready-made family of a teen and a baby. Works for me,' he said. 'It's not going to be perfect, and we're going to have downs as well as ups, but I'm sure this is the right thing.'

'Me, too,' Amy agreed.

'Now we just need to sort out the red tape.'

'Do you want to call Jane, or shall I?' Amy asked.

'We'll do it together,' he said. 'Just as we're going to tackle everything else.'

She took out her phone, switching it to speaker mode so Josh could hear as well, and called Jane.

'Jane? It's Amy and Josh. We were wondering—can we see you today, please?'

'Sorry, no can do. I'm afraid I'm stacked up with meetings,' Jane said.

'But you have to have a lunch break, right?' Josh asked.

'Right.' Jane sounded wary.

'If we meet you with sandwiches and coffee,' Josh said, 'can we steal the ten minutes it would've taken you to queue up to get your coffee?'

Jane gave a wry laugh. 'You obviously both really want to talk to me.'

'We do,' they said in unison.

'All right. One o'clock in the picnic bit in the park opposite my office—not because I'm trying to wriggle out of anything but, if I meet you in the office, someone's bound to drag me off into another meeting,' she said.

'The park's perfect,' Amy said.

She gave them the details; at one o'clock, Josh and Amy were waiting in the park with sandwiches, cake and coffee.

Five minutes later, Jane rushed over. 'Sorry. I couldn't get off the phone.' Her eyes widened at the array of food. 'Wow. I should let you hijack my lunch break more often.'

'We forgot to ask you what you like, so there's a variety,' Josh said.

'Fabulous. Thank you. Right. So what do you want to talk to me about?' she asked, gratefully accepting the paper cup of coffee that Amy handed to her.

'We've been to see Freya,' Amy said.

'Which is *not* what I would've advised,' Jane said.

Josh spread his hands. 'We happened to be in the area.'

Jane scoffed. 'Right.'

'She told us she doesn't want to go back to live with her mum,' Amy said.

'I don't particularly want her doing that, either,' Jane said grimly.

'But she's worried about who's going to take in a fifteen-year-old with a baby,' Josh said.

'And we have a solution,' Amy added with a smile. 'Something that means everyone wins.'

'I have no idea how you get accepted as a foster parent,' Josh said, 'but we were hoping you'd know how to cut through all the red tape and fast-track it for us.'

Jane blinked. 'Hang on. Are you telling me that you'd be prepared to foster both Freya and Hope?'

'Together,' Amy said. 'Yes.'

'But...' Jane looked confused. 'Last week, when I first met you and you agreed to look after Hope, you said you were just neighbours and barely knew each other.'

'That,' Josh said, 'was before the Christmas that changed everything. We want to be a family. And we want Freya and Hope included in that family.'

'Which is a really good start. Though you'll both have to go through an assessment process,' Jane said, 'and, if you pass—though I'm pretty sure you will—then you'll need training.'

'That's fine. School holidays won't be a problem,' Amy said, 'given that I'm a teacher.'

'You'll need a spare room,' Jane warned. 'And, with you both being in separate flats, probably one of you will have to be named as the main foster carer.'

'We've already talked about that,' Josh said, 'and we plan to go house-hunting for a place big enough for all of us.'

'It's a new year and new beginning,' Amy said. 'For all of us.'

'Then in that case,' Jane said, 'I'll do everything I can to help make this work.'

Amy and Josh lifted their paper cups of coffee in a toast. 'We'll drink to that. Our new family.'

EPILOGUE

A year later—Christmas Eve

'YOU LOOK AMAZING,' Amy's father, George, said outside the hospital chapel.

'Utterly gorgeous.' Amy's mother, Patricia, tweaked Amy's headdress and veil. 'And so do you two,' she added to Freya, who was carrying Hope in one arm and a bouquet in her free hand. 'My three girls. Look at you. And our little Hope looks so cute in that dress.'

Amy blinked back the tears. Her parents had taken Freya and Hope straight to their hearts and insisted that they were part of the family, even before the fostering had become official.

'We need a picture, George,' Patricia said.

'All four of you together. *My* girls,' he added proudly.

They posed for the photograph, and then Patricia went to sit in the front row at the chapel.

'Ready for this?' George asked softly.

'Absolutely ready,' Amy said. 'How about you, Freya?'

'Bring it on,' the teenager said with a smile.

* * *

Josh looked back down the aisle. The hospital chapel was packed with their family and friends; and his brother was standing beside him as his best man. Since Amy had been in his life, his relationship with his family had been a lot less prickly; although his family had been unnerved at first by his unconventional ready-made family, Amy had made them see that it worked and Josh was actually happy.

Amy's brother Scott was sitting at the piano; when Patricia sat down in the front row of the chapel, Scott took his cue to begin playing the largo from 'Winter' from Vivaldi's *Four Seasons*.

And then the door opened and Amy walked down the aisle towards him on her father's arm. Her short veil was held in place by a narrow crown of deep red roses, to match the ones in her bouquet, and she wore a very simple cream ankle-length dress. Behind them walked Freya as the bridesmaid, wearing a dark red version of Amy's dress, holding Hope in her arms, also wearing a dark red version of Amy's dress, but with the addition of a cream fluffy bolero to keep her warm.

My family, Josh thought.

And from today it would be that little bit more official, with Amy becoming Mrs Farnham.

Christmas Eve was the perfect day for their wedding day. A year since they'd first got to know each other properly. The anniversary of the beginning of the happiest days of their lives—and it would only get better.

'I love you, Mrs-Farnham-to-be,' he mouthed as Amy joined him at the altar.

'I love you, too,' she mouthed back.

They'd chosen to sing carols rather than hymns, picking the happiest ones that everyone knew—'Silent Night', 'Hark the Herald Angels Sing' and 'O Little Town of Bethlehem'.

And, after the ceremony, everyone in the congregation sang 'All You Need Is Love', accompanied by Scott on the piano, as Amy and Josh walked down the aisle for the first time as a married couple.

They'd booked the reception at the hotel across the road from the hospital, with a simple sit-down meal for their family and closest friends; but they'd also invited Jane the social worker and Freya's mum.

After the meal, Amy's father stood up. 'I'd like to thank everyone for coming today. Patricia and I are absolutely delighted to welcome Josh into our family—he's a lovely man, a great doctor and a fantastic artist. But, most of all, he makes my daughter happy, and as parents that's all that Patricia and I want. And I'm also delighted that we have Freya and Hope as well. So I'd like everyone to raise their glasses: I give you Josh, Amy, Freya and Hope.'

Once everyone had echoed the toast, Josh stood up. 'I'd like to thank George, Patricia, Scott and Rae for making me feel like part of their family from the first moment they met me. Today's a special day for me—it's the first Christmas Eve since my graduation where I haven't been on duty in the Emergency Department. That means this is my first real family Christmas, and I'm loving every second of it so far. Today's the first anniversary of the beginning of the happiest time in my life. So I'd like you to raise a glass to my beautiful bride, Amy, who's made me the happiest man alive, and to our beautiful bridesmaid and ring-bearer, Freya and Hope, who bring joy to our lives every day.'

'Amy, Freya and Hope,' everyone chorused.

Josh's brother Stuart stood up next. 'It's really good to see my brother so happy. And I couldn't be more thrilled to welcome Amy, Freya and Hope to our family. Because of them, my son and my two nieces are getting to see much more of their uncle. They're living proof that no matter how unconventional a family might seem, if they love each other, it'll all work out.' He smiled. 'I have a feeling the rest of the speeches aren't going to be very conventional, either. So, instead of telling you stories about Josh, I'm going to hand you over to his colleagues and Amy's to tell you what their life is like.'

The head of the music department at Amy's school stood up. 'Most of the time I get my classes to sing this as a cumulative song, but today we're doing just the last verse for you, because we'd like you to know what Christmas Eve is usually like for a maths teacher and an emergency department doctor.'

Josh took Amy's hand and squeezed it.

'Did you know about this?' she asked.

He grinned. 'Just a little bit.'

The head of music was joined by five more of Amy's colleagues and six of Josh's. Together, they sang the first line: 'On the twelfth day of Christmas, for Josh and Amy…'

Then each sang a line in turn and sat down again.

Twelve lesson-plannings,
Eleven past papers,
Ten simultaneous equations,

Nine books to mark,
Eight probabilities,
Seven bits of algebra,
Six Colles' fractures,
Five turkey carvers!
Four black eyes,
Three throwing up,
Two broken ankles,
And a bead up a toddler's nose.

Everyone applauded, and the singers all stood up again to take a bow.

Then it was Amy's turn to speak. 'I'd like to thank the Farnhams for taking us all to their hearts and making us part of their family. Thank you very much to our colleagues for their revue—absolutely spot on. And I'm afraid there's a little bit more singing now, because it's a very special person's first birthday. Without her, Josh and I might never have met properly, so please join with us in singing a very special song for Hope.'

At her signal, one of the waitresses brought out a chocolate cake in the shape of a figure one, with a single candle, and placed it on the table in front of Freya and the toddler.

Everyone sang happy birthday to Hope; Freya helped her daughter blow out the candle. When everyone cheered, Hope clapped her hands and looked thoroughly pleased with herself.

Then Freya stood up. 'I know it's not usual for the bridesmaid to make a speech, and I'm not very good at talking in public, but there's something I really want to say. Last Christmas was the worst of my life, and…' She paused, her face turning bright red, and then took a deep breath. 'And I thought I'd never see my baby again. This Christmas, life couldn't be any better. I'm thrilled to be celebrating Josh and Amy getting married, as well as Hope's first birthday. Amy's taught me so much and Josh has inspired me to become a nurse. They've both been really fantastic foster parents—and they've helped make things better with my mum, too. And Mum helped me to make something special for them.'

Freya's mother quietly took a parcel from beneath the table and handed it to Freya, who walked over to Amy and Josh and hugged them both before giving the parcel to them.

Together, they opened it to find the most beautiful frame containing a photograph of the four of them from the summer, on their first day in their new house.

Everyone clapped; Freya's face turned bright red again and she sat down again very quickly.

Josh and Amy stood up together, then. 'Thank you, Freya. It's the perfect present,' Josh said.

'And we're so glad that everyone's here today to share our special day with us,' Amy added.

'We'll cut the cake in a second,' Josh said.

'But before we start the dancing we want everyone to just chill out, relax and have a good time,' Amy finished. 'Because we really want to come and say hello to everyone and have a chat. Just have a drink while you're waiting for cake.'

Everyone clapped, and they posed for photographs before they cut the cake.

Freya's mum hugged both of them when they got to her. 'Thank you both so much. It's because of you that I'm starting to rebuild my relationship with Freya. I know it's not going to be easy, but your support means a lot to both of us. Thank you for doing for her what I was...' She grimaced. 'Well, too stupid to see. And I still can't believe you actually invited me to your wedding.'

'You're Freya's mum. That makes you part of our family,' Amy said, and hugged her.

'Everyone makes mistakes,' Josh said quietly, 'and everyone deserves a second chance. I'm really glad you came, because I think you need to be here on your granddaughter's first birthday—and it means a lot to Freya and Hope that you're here.'

Freya's mum swallowed hard. 'Thank you.'

Everyone seemed to be happy for them, Amy thought. And Jane also greeted them both with a hug. 'You two are my big success story,' she said. 'I remember last Christmas. And seeing you with Freya and Hope—well, you really make me feel my job's worthwhile. On the days when everything's going wrong, I think of you two and it makes everything a lot better.'

When they'd finally managed to have a word with everyone and were back in their seats at the top table, Josh's brother Stuart stood up.

'Ladies and gentlemen—it's time for the first dance,' he said. 'I have it on very reliable information that our Josh sings this to stop babies crying, and it actually works, so see me later if you want to hire him.'

Everyone laughed.

'But, seriously, this is the perfect song for the perfect couple at a perfect Christmas wedding. I give you Josh and Amy,' he said, and the DJ began to play 'All I Want for Christmas is You'.

Josh took his bride in his arms and danced her round

the floor. 'I love you,' he said, 'and this is the best Christmas ever.'

'I love you, too,' Amy said. 'And you're right. Today, I have everything I've ever wanted: you and our new family.'

'You and our new family,' he echoed, and kissed her.

* * * * *

MEANT-TO-BE
FAMILY

MARION LENNOX

With thanks to my fellow authors who've helped
make this *Midwives On-Call* series fabulous.
A special thank you to Alison Roberts for her
friendship, her knowledge and her generosity in
sharing, and to Fiona McArthur whose midwife
skills leave me awed.

CHAPTER ONE

LATE. LATE, LATE, LATE. This was the third morning this week. Her boss would have kittens.

Not that Isla was in the mood to be angry, Em thought, as she swiped her pass at the car-park entry. The head midwife for Melbourne's Victoria Hospital had hardly stopped smiling since becoming engaged. She and her fiancé had been wafting around the hospital in a rosy glow that made Em wince.

Marriage. 'Who needs it?' she demanded out loud, as she swung her family wagon through the boom gates and headed for her parking spot on the fifth floor. She should apply for a lower spot—she always seemed to be running late—but her family wagon needed more space than the normal bays. One of the Victoria's obstetricians rode a bike. He was happy to park his Harley to one side of his bay, so this was the perfect arrangement.

Except it was on the fifth floor—and she was late again.

The car in front of her was slow going up the ramp. *Come on...* She should have been on the wards fifteen minutes ago. But Gretta had been sick. Again.

Things were moving too fast. She needed to take the little girl back to the cardiologist, but the last time she'd taken her, he'd said...

No. Don't go there. *There* was unthinkable. She raked

her fingers through her unruly curls, trying for distraction. She'd need to pin her hair up before she got to the ward. Had she remembered pins?

It didn't work. Her mind refused to be distracted, and the cardiologist's warning was still ringing in her ears.

'Emily, I'm sorry, but we're running out of time.'

Was Gretta's heart condition worsening, or was this just a tummy bug? The little girl had hugged her tight as she'd left, and it had been all she could do to leave her. If her mum hadn't been there... But Adrianna adored being a gran. 'Get into work, girl, and leave Gretta to me. Toby and I will watch *Play School* while Gretta has a nap. I'll ring you if she's not better by lunchtime. Meanwhile, go!'

She'd practically shoved her out the door.

But there *was* something wrong—and she knew what it was. The cardiologist had been blunt and she remembered his assessment word for word.

It was all very well, hearing it, she thought bleakly, but seeing it... At the weekend she'd taken both kids to their favourite place in the world, the children's playground at the Botanic Gardens. There was a water rill there that Gretta adored. She'd crawled over it as soon as she could crawl, and then she'd toddled and walked.

Six months ago she'd stood upright on the rill and laughed with delight as the water had splashed over her toes. At the weekend she hadn't even been able to crawl. Em had sat on the rill with her, trying to make her smile, but the little girl had sobbed. She knew what she was losing.

Don't! Don't think about it! Move on. Or she'd move on if she could.

'Come on.' She was inwardly yelling at the car in front. The car turned the corner ponderously then—praise be!—turned into a park on Level Four. Em sighed with relief, zoomed up the last ramp and hauled the steering wheel left, as she'd done hundreds of times in the past to turn into her parking space.

And…um…stopped.

There was a car where Harry's bike should be. A vintage sports car, burgundy, gleaming with care and polish.

Wider than a bike.

Instead of a seamless, silent transition to park, there was the appalling sound of metal on metal.

Her wagon had a bull bar on the front, designed to deflect stray bulls—or other cars during minor bingles. It meant her wagon was as tough as old boots. It'd withstand anything short of a road train.

The thing she'd hit wasn't quite as tough.

She'd ripped the side off the sports car.

Oliver Evans, gynaecologist, obstetrician and in-utero surgeon, was gathering his briefcase and his suit jacket from the passenger seat. He'd be meeting the hospital bigwigs today so he needed to be formal. He was also taking a moment to glance through the notes he had on who he had to meet, who he needed to see.

He vaguely heard the sound of a car behind him. He heard it turning from the ramp…

The next moment the passenger side of his car was practically ripped from the rest.

It was a measure of Em's fiercely practised calm that she didn't scream. She didn't burst into tears. She didn't even swear.

She simply stared straight ahead. Count to ten, she told herself. When that didn't work, she tried twenty.

She figured it out, quite quickly. Her parking spot was supposed to be wider but that was because she shared the two parking bays with Harry the obstetrician's bike and Harry had left. Of course. She'd even dropped in on his farewell party last Friday night, even though it had only been for five minutes because the kids had been waiting.

So Harry had left. This car, then, would belong to the doctor who'd taken his place.

She'd just welcomed him by trashing his car.

'I have insurance. I have insurance. I have insurance.' It was supposed to be her mantra. Saying things three times helped, only it didn't help enough. She put her head on the steering wheel and felt a wash of exhaustion so profound she felt like she was about to melt.

His car was trashed.

He climbed from the driver's seat and stared at his beloved Morgan in disbelief. The Morgan was low slung, gorgeous—and fragile. He'd parked her right in the centre of the bay to avoid the normal perils of parking lots—people opening doors and scratching his paintwork.

But the offending wagon had a bull bar attached and it hadn't just scratched his paintwork. While the wagon looked to be almost unscathed, the passenger-side panels of the Morgan had been sheared off completely.

He loved this baby. He'd bought her five years ago, a post-marriage toy to make him feel better about the world. He'd cherished her, spent a small fortune on her and then put her into very expensive storage while he'd been overseas.

His qualms about returning to Australia had been tempered by his joy on being reunited with Betsy. But now... some idiot with a huge lump of a wagon—and a bull bar...

'What the hell did you think you were doing?' He couldn't see the driver of the wagon yet, but he was venting his spleen on the wagon itself. Of all the ugly, lumbering excuses for a car...

And it was intact. Yeah, it'd have a few extra scratches

but there were scratches all over it already. It was a battered, dilapidated brute and the driver'd be able to keep driving like the crash had never happened.

He wanted to kick it. Of all the stupid, careless…

Um…why hadn't the driver moved?

And suddenly medical mode kicked in, overriding rage. Maybe the driver had had a heart attack. A faint. Maybe this was a medical incident rather than sheer stupidity. He took a deep breath, switching roles in an instant. Infuriated driver became doctor. The wagon's driver's door was jammed hard against where his passenger door used to be, so he headed for its passenger side.

The wagon's engine died. Someone was alive in there, then. Good. Or sort of good.

He hauled the door open and he hadn't quite managed the transition. Rage was still paramount.

'You'd better be having a heart attack.' It was impossible to keep the fury from his voice. 'You'd better have a really good excuse as to why you ploughed this heap of scrap metal into my car! You want to get out and explain?'

No!

Things were already appalling—but things just got a whole lot worse.

This was a voice she knew. A voice from her past.

Surely not.

She *had* to be imagining it, she decided, but she wasn't opening her eyes. If it really was…

It couldn't be. She was tired, she was frantically worried about Gretta, she was late and she'd just crashed her car. No wonder she was hearing things.

'You're going to have to open your eyes and face things.' She said it to herself, under her breath. Then she repeated it in her head twice more but her three-times mantra still didn't seem to be working.

The silence outside the car was ominous. Toe-tappingly threatening.

Maybe it'd go away if she just stayed…

'Hey, are you okay?' The gravelly voice, angry at first, was now concerned.

But it was the same voice and this wasn't her imagination. This was horrendously, appallingly real.

Voices could be the same, she told herself, feeling herself veering towards hysteria. There had to be more than one voice in the world that sounded like his.

She'd stay just one moment longer with her eyes closed.

Her passenger door opened and someone slid inside. Large. Male.

Him.

His hand landed on hers on the steering wheel. 'Miss? Are you hurt? Can I help?' And as the anger in his voice gave way to caring she knew, unmistakably, who this was.

Oliver. The man she'd loved with all her heart. The man who'd walked away five years ago to give her the chance of a new life.

So many emotions were slamming through her head… anger, bewilderment, grief… She'd had five years to move on but, crazy or not, this man still felt a part of her.

She'd crashed his car. He was right here.

There was no help for it. She took a deep, deep breath. She braced herself.

She raised her head, and she turned to face her husband.

Emily.

He was seeing her but his mind wasn't taking her in. Emily!

For one wild moment he thought he must be mistaken. This was a different woman, older, a bit…worn round the edges. Weary? Faded jeans and stained windcheater. Unkempt curls.

But still Emily.

His wife? She still was, he thought stupidly. His Em.

But she wasn't his Em. He'd walked away five years ago. He'd left her to her new life, and she had nothing to do with him.

Except she was here. She was staring up at him, her eyes reflecting his disbelief. Horror?

Shock held him rigid.

She'd wrecked his car. He loved this car. He should be feeling…

No. There was no *should*, or if there was he hadn't read that particular handbook.

Should he feel grief? Should he feel guilt?

He felt neither. All he felt was numb.

She'd had a minute's warning. He'd had none.

'Em?' He looked…incredulous. He looked more shocked than she was—bewildered beyond words.

What were you supposed to say to a husband you hadn't seen or spoken to for five years? There was no handbook for this.

'H-hi?' she managed.

'You've just crashed my car,' he said, stupidly.

'You were supposed to be a bike.' Okay, maybe that was just as stupid. This conversation was going exactly nowhere. They'd established, what, that he wasn't a bike?

He was her husband—and he was right beside her. Looking completely dumbfounded.

'You have a milk stain on your shoulder.'

That would be the first thing he'd notice, she thought. Her uniform was in her bag. She never put it on at home— her chances of getting out of the house clean were about zero—so she was still wearing jeans and the baggy wind-cheater she'd worn at breakfast.

Gretta had had a milky drink before being ill. Em had picked her up and cuddled her before she'd left.

Strangely, the stain left her feeling exposed. She didn't want this man to see…her.

'There are child seats in your wagon.'

He still sounded incredulous. Milk stains? Family wagon? He'd be seeing a very different woman from the one he'd seen five years ago.

But he looked…just the same. Same tall, lean, gorgeous. Same deep brown eyes that crinkled at the edges when he smiled, and Oliver smiled a lot. Same wide mouth and strong bone structure. Same dark, wavy hair, close cropped to try and get rid of the curl, only that never worked. It was so thick. She remembered running her fingers through that hair…

Um, no. Not appropriate. Regardless of formalities, this was her husband. Or ex-husband? They hadn't bothered with divorce yet but she'd moved on.

She'd just crashed his car.

'You're using Harry's car park,' she said, pointing accusingly at…um…one slightly bent sports car. It was beautiful—at least some of it still was. An open sports car. Vintage. It wasn't the sort of car that you might be able to pop down to the car parts place in your lunch hour and buy a new panel.

He'd always loved cars. She remembered the day they'd sold his last sports car.

His last? No. Who knew how many cars he'd been through since? Anyway, she remembered the day they'd sold the sleek little roadster both of them had loved, trading it in for a family wagon. Smaller than this but just as sensible. They'd gone straight from the car showroom to the nursery suppliers, and had had the baby seat fitted there and then.

She'd been six months pregnant. They'd driven home with identical smug looks on their faces.

He'd wanted a family as much as she had. Or she'd thought he did. What had happened then had proved she hadn't known him at all.

'I've been allocated this car park,' he was saying, and she had to force herself back to here, to now. 'Level Five, Bay Eleven. That's mine.'

'You're visiting?'

'I'm employed here, as of today.'

'You can't be.'

He didn't reply. He climbed out of the wagon, dug his hands deep in his pockets, glanced back at his wreck of a car and looked at her again.

'Why can't I, Em?' The wreck of the car faded to secondary importance. This was suddenly all about them.

'Because I work here.'

'It's the most specialised neonatal service in Melbourne. You know that's what I do.'

'You went to the States.' She felt numb. Stupid. Out of control. She'd been sure her ex-husband had been on the other side of world. She didn't want him to be here.

'I did specialist training in in-utero surgery in the States.' This was a dumb conversation. He was out of the car, leaning back on one of the concrete columns, watching her as she clung to the steering wheel like she was drowning. 'I've accepted a job back here. And before you say anything, no, I didn't know you were working here. I thought you were still at Hemmingway Private. I knew when I came back that there was a chance we might meet, but Melbourne's a big place. I'm not stalking you.'

'I never meant...'

'No?'

'No,' she managed. 'And I'm sorry I crashed into your car.'

Finally things were starting to return to normal. Like

her heart rate. Her pulse had gone through the roof when the cars had hit. She'd been subconsciously trying to get it down, practising the deep-breathing techniques she used when she was pacing the floor with Gretta, frightened for herself, frightened for the future. The techniques came to her aid instinctively now when she was frightened. Or discombobulated.

Discombobulated was how she felt, she conceded. Stalking? That sounded as if he thought she might be frightened of him, and she'd never been frightened of Oliver.

'Can we exchange details?' she managed, trying desperately to sound normal. Like this was a chance meeting of old acquaintances, but they needed to talk about car insurance. 'Oliver, it's really nice to see you again...' Was it? Um, no, but it sounded the right thing to say. 'But I'm late as it is.'

'Which was why you crashed.'

'Okay, it was my fault,' she snapped. 'But, believe it or not, there are extenuating circumstances. That's not your business.' She clambered out of the car and dug for her licence in her shabby holdall. She pulled out two disposable diapers and a packet of baby wipes before she found her purse, and she was so flustered she dropped them. Oliver gathered them without a word, and handed them back. She flushed and handed him her licence instead.

He took it wordlessly, and studied it.

'You still call yourself Emily Evans?'

'You know we haven't divorced. That's irrelevant. You're supposed to take down my address.'

'You're living at your mother's house?'

'I am.' She grabbed her licence back. 'Finished?'

'Aren't you supposed to take mine?'

'You can sue me. I can't sue you. We both know the fault was mine. If you're working here then I'll send you my insurance details via interdepartmental memo. I don't carry them with me.'

'You seem to carry everything else.' Once more he was looking into the car, taking in the jumble of kids' paraphernalia that filled it.

'I do, don't I?' she said, as cordially as she could manage. 'Oliver, it's good to see you again. I'm sorry I wrecked your car but I'm running really, really late.'

'You never run late.' He was right: punctuality used to be her god.

'I'm not the Emily you used to know,' she managed. 'I'm a whole lot different but this isn't the time or the place to discuss it.' She looked again at his car and winced. She really had made an appalling mess. 'You want me to organise some sort of tow?'

'Your car's hardly dented. I'll handle mine.'

'I'm…sorry.' She took a deep breath. 'Oliver, I really am sorry but I really do need to go. If there's nothing I can do…'

He was peering into her wagon. 'I doubt your lock's still working,' he told her. 'Once my car's towed free…'

'Locks are the least of my worries.' She slung her bag over her shoulder, knowing she had to move. She knew Isla was short-staffed this morning and the night staff would be aching to leave. 'Look at the stains,' she told him. 'No villain in their right mind would steal my wagon and, right now, I don't have time to care. I'm sorry to leave you with this mess, Oliver, but I need to go. Welcome to Victoria Hospital. See you around.'

CHAPTER TWO

RUBY DOWELL WAS seventeen years old, twenty-two weeks pregnant and terrified. She was Oliver's first patient at the Victoria.

She was also the reason he'd started so soon. He'd been recruited to replace Harry Eichmann, an obstetrician with an interest in in-utero procedures. Oliver had started the same way, but for him in-utero surgery was more than a side interest. For the last five years he'd been based in the States but he'd travelled the world learning the latest techniques.

The phone call he'd had from Charles Delamere, Victoria's CEO, had been persuasive, to say the least. 'Harry's following a girlfriend to Europe. There's no one here with your expertise and there's more and more demand.

'It's time you came home. Oliver, right now we have a kid here with a twenty-one-week foetus, and her scans are showing spina bifida. Heinz Zigler, our paediatric neurologist, says the operation has to be done now. He can do the spinal stuff but he doesn't have the skills to stop the foetus aborting. Oliver, there are more and more of these cases, and we're offering you a full-time job. If you get here fast, we might save this kid shunts, possible brain damage, a life with limited movement below the waist. Short term, I want you to fight to give this kid a happy ending. Long term we're happy to fund your research. We'll cover the costs of whatever extra training you want, any staff you need. We want the best, Oliver, and we're prepared to pay, but we want you now.'

The offer had been great, but he'd had serious reservations about returning to Melbourne. He'd walked away from his marriage five years ago, and he'd thought he'd stay away. Em had deserved a new life, a chance to start again with someone who'd give her what she needed.

And it seemed his decision had been justified. Seeing her this morning, driving a family wagon, with milk stains on her shoulder, with every sign of being a frazzled young working mum, he'd thought...

Actually, he hadn't thought. The sight had knocked him sideways and he was still knocked sideways. But he needed to focus on something other than his marriage. After a brief introduction with Charles, he was in the examination room with Ruby Dowell. Teenage mother, pregnant with a baby with spina bifida.

'At twenty-two weeks we need to get on with this fast,' Charles had told him. 'There's such a short window for meaningful intervention.'

Ruby was lying on the examination couch in a cubicle in the antenatal clinic and, as with all his patients, he took a moment at the start to assess the whole package. Her notes said she was seventeen. She'd been attending clinics in the Victoria's Teenage Mums-To-Be programme. When the spina bifida had been detected on the scans she'd been offered termination but had declined, although the notes said she intended to give the baby up for adoption after birth. Right now she was dressed in shorts and an oversized T-shirt. Her mouse-blonde, shoulder-length hair was in need of a wash and a good cut. Apart from the bump of her pregnancy she was waif thin, and her eyes were red-rimmed and wide with fear.

She looked like a wild creature trapped in a cage, he thought. Hell, why was she alone? Her notes said she was a single mum, but she should have her mother with her, or a sister, or at least a friend.

It was unthinkable that such a kid was alone. Charles had said that Isla, his daughter and also the Victoria's head midwife, was in charge of the Teenage Mums-To-Be programme. Why hadn't she organised to be here, or at least sent a midwife in her place?

But now wasn't the time to head to the nurses' station and blast the powers that be for leaving her like this. Now was the time for reassurance.

'Hey,' he said, walking into the cubicle but deliberately leaving the screens open. He didn't need to do a physical examination yet, and he didn't want that trapped look to stay a moment longer. 'I'm the baby surgeon, Oliver Evans. I'm an obstetrician who's specially trained in operating on babies when they're still needing to stay inside their mums. And you're Ruby Dowell?'

He hauled a chair up to the bedside and summoned his best reassuring manner. 'Ruby, I'm here to get to know you, that's all. Nothing's happening right now. I'm just here to talk.'

But the terrified look stayed. She actually cringed back on the bed, fear radiating off her in waves. 'I'm... I'm scared of operations,' she stuttered. 'I don't want to be here.'

But then the screen was pulled back still further. A woman in nursing uniform, baggy tunic over loose pants, was fastening the screen so Ruby could see the nurses' station at the end of the corridor.

Emily. His wife.

His ex-wife? She'd never asked for a divorce but it had been simply a matter of signing the papers, any time these last five years.

'I'm scared of operations, too,' Em said, matter-of-factly, as if she'd been involved in the conversation from the start. 'I think everyone is. But Dr Evans here is the best baby surgeon in the known universe, I promise. I've known him for ever. If it was my baby there'd be no one else I'd want. Dr Evans is great, Ruby. He's kind, he's skilled and he'll give your baby the best chance of survival she can possibly have.'

'But I told you…I don't want her.' Ruby was sobbing now, swiping away tears with the back of her hand. 'My mum said I should have had an abortion. She would have paid. I don't know why I didn't. And now you're operating on a baby I don't even want. I just want you all to go away.'

In-utero surgery was fraught at the best of times. It was full of potential dangers for both mother and baby. To operate on a mother who didn't want her baby to survive…

He didn't know where to start—but he didn't need to, because Em simply walked forward, tugged the girl into her arms and held her.

Ruby stiffened. She held herself rigid, but Em's fingers stroked her hair.

'Hey, it's okay, Ruby. We all know how hard this is. Pregnancy's the pits. You feel so on your own, and you're especially on your own. You decided not to go ahead with an abortion, going against what your family wanted you to do. That took courage, but there's only so much courage a girl can be expected to show. That's why Isla's been helping you and it's why I'm here now. I'm *your* midwife, Ruby. I'll be with you every step of the way. All the decisions will be yours but I'm right with you. Right now, if you want Dr Evans to go away and come back later, he will. Just say the word.'

She met Oliver's gaze over Ruby's shoulder and her message was unmistakable. Back me up.

So Em was this girl's midwife? Then where the hell had she been when he'd walked in?

Coping with her crashed car, that's where, and then changing out of her mum clothes into nursing gear. Still, surely she could have made it earlier.

'We've had a drama with a prem birth I had to help with,' she said, as if he'd voiced his question out loud. She was still holding, still hugging, as Ruby's sobs went on. 'That's why I'm late, Ruby, and I'm sorry. I wanted to be here when you arrived. But I'm here now, and if you decide to proceed with this operation then you're my number one priority. Do you need some tissues? Dr Evans, hand me some tissues.'

'You helped with an earlier birth?' he asked, before he could help himself, and she had the temerity to glare at him.

'Yep. I had to step in and help the moment I hit the wards. Plus I crashed my car this morning. I crashed my wagon, Ruby, and guess whose gorgeous car I drove into? None other than Dr Evans. It's his first day on the job and I hit him. It's a wonder he hasn't tossed me out of the room already.'

And Ruby's sobs hiccupped to a halt. She pulled back and looked at Em, then turned and stared at Oliver.

'She hit your car?'

'Yes,' he said. He wouldn't normally impart personal information to a patient but he guessed what Em was doing, and he could only agree. What Ruby needed was space to settle. He could help with that—even though he had to get personal to give it to her.

'I have a sixty-four Morgan Plus-4 sports car,' he said, mournfully, like the end of the world was nigh, which was about how he'd felt when he'd seen the damage—before he'd realised the driver of the other car had been Em. 'It's two-tone burgundy with black interior, a gorgeous two-seater. It's fitted with super sports upgrades, including twin Weber carbs, a Derrington header and a bonnet scoop. It also has chrome wire wheels, a badge bar with twin Lucas fog lamps and a tonneau cover. Oh, and it's retrofitted with overdrive transmission. Now it's also fitted with one smashed side—courtesy of your midwife.'

'Yikes,' Em said, but she didn't sound in the least subdued. 'Twin Weber carbs and a Derrington header, hey? Did I damage all that?'

'And if you knew how long it took to get those fog lamps…'

'Whoops. Sorry. But you scratched my car, too.' But Em was talking at Ruby rather than at him and she still sounded cheerful. Chirpy even.

'Scratched…' he muttered, and she grinned.

'That's okay. I forgive you. And they're cars. They're just things. That's what insurance is for. Whereas babies aren't things at all,' Em continued, leading seamlessly back to the reason they were all there. 'Ruby, your little girl is a person, not a thing, and she's far, far more precious. You made the decision to go ahead with this pregnancy. You made the decision early not to choose abortion and you chose it again when the scan showed spina bifida. But you've been telling me you think you might have her adopted when she's born…'

'I can't…deal with it.'

'You don't have to deal with it,' Em said soundly. 'There are lots of parents out there who'll give their eye teeth to have a baby like yours to love. That's right, isn't it, Dr Evans?'

'I… Yes.' But her words were like a punch in the gut. That last night… He'd tried to make her see one last time. *'Em, I can't. I know adoption's the only way, but I can't do it. I can't guarantee to love a child who's not our own.'*

'It will be our own.'

'Em, no.'

It had been their last conversation. He'd turned and walked away from the only woman he'd ever loved and it had nearly killed him. But she'd deserved the family she'd wanted so much. He'd had to give her that chance, and from the evidence he'd seen today, she'd taken it.

But now wasn't about him. It was all about Ruby. The kid's terror had been put aside. He had to take advantage of it.

Which meant putting thoughts of Em aside. Putting aside the knowledge that his wife, his ex-wife, presumably—did you need to formally sign papers to accept a marriage was over?—was in the same room.

'Ruby, you created this little girl,' he said, as Em continued to hold her. 'You can have her adopted at birth, but until then you need to look after her. And the staff here have already explained to you—to look after her means an operation now.'

'But why?' Ruby demanded, suddenly belligerent. 'I don't understand. The kid's got spina bifida—Dr Zigler showed me on the scans. What difference does it make whether you operate now or operate when it's born?'

There was fear behind the question. Oliver recognised it. He'd done many in-utero procedures by now, and sometimes one of the hardest things was having the mum understand that the tiny child inside her was an independent being already. Something totally separate from her. This was a child who could be shifted in her uterus, who even at twenty-two weeks could cope with complex surgery and then be resettled, because, no matter how amazing the technology, the womb was still the safest place for her to be.

'Ruby, you know your baby has spina bifida,' he said now, gently. Em still had her arm around the girl. He was talking to them both, as he'd normally talk to a woman and her partner, or a woman and her mum or support person. Em had slid naturally into that role. A good midwife sometimes had to, he thought, and Em had always been brilliant at her job. Efficient, kind, skilled and empathic. He'd worked with her once and he'd loved it.

It was totally disconcerting to be working with her again, but he needed to focus on Ruby.

'You know we've picked up the spina bifida on the ultrasound,' Oliver said matter-of-factly, trying to take the emotion out of the situation. 'You've seen it?'

'It just looked blurry. I couldn't figure it out.'

So she didn't understand. 'Heinz Zigler's a great paediatric neurologist,' Charles had told him. 'He's technically brilliant, but communication's not his strong suit. He'll do the spinal surgery but everything else—including explanations to the mum—we're leaving to you.'

So now he needed to explain from the ground up. 'The scans do look blurry,' he admitted. 'I have trouble reading them myself. Fine detail like the nerve exposure around vertebrae needs incredibly specialised knowledge to see, but the radiologists here are superb. They've double-checked each other's work, and Dr Zigler agrees. Everyone's sure. But would you like me to explain what I think is happening? I don't talk in fine detail, Ruby. I just see the overview. That's actually what I do, total patient care, looking after you as well as your baby. I'm an obstetrician and a surgeon who specialises in looking after mums and bubs if bub needs an operation before it's time for her to be born.'

Silence. Ruby cast him a scared look and subsided. He waited, while Ruby pulled herself together a bit more, while Em handed her a wad of tissues, while both women readied themselves to front what was coming.

'Heinz says he told you the fine detail,' he said at last, when he thought Ruby was as ready as she was going to be. 'But here's the broad outline. The bones of your baby's spine—the vertebrae—haven't formed properly to protect your baby's spinal cord. The spinal cord holds the nerves that control your baby's movements. Because those nerves run right through the body, if the cord gets damaged then long term, your baby might not be able to walk. She might not have control of her bladder and bowel. If she has a severe problem she can also end up with a build-up of fluid in her brain. Then she'll need a shunt, all her life, to drain the excess fluid and relieve pressure.'

Ruby was crying again now, but not sobbing. Em's arm was around her, holding her close, but Ruby's attention was held. Her distress was taking second place to her need to know, and she seemed to be taking it in.

'So,' she whispered. 'So?'

'So the good thing is,' he said, still gently, 'that many problems of spina bifida aren't directly caused by the spina bifida itself. Doctors cleverer than me, like Heinz—did you know he's top in his field in research?—have worked out that the exposure of the spinal cord to the normal fluid in your womb, the amniotic fluid, is what progressively destroys the exposed nerves during pregnancy. If we can operate now, really early, and cover the exposed cord, then we prevent much of the damage. Your baby's much more likely to be able to live a normal, happy life.'

'But not with me,' Ruby whispered.

That was another issue altogether. Adoption. This was a single mum, a teenager, facing a life apart from the baby she was carrying.

'You haven't decided definitely on adoption,' Em murmured, and the girl shook her head.

'I can't think...'

'And you don't need to think.' Em's hold on her tightened. 'There's too much happening now for you to think past what you need to face right now. But, Ruby, regardless of what you decide to do when your baby's born, regardless of whether you decide you can care for her yourself or if you want to give her to parents who need a baby to love, she'll still be your daughter. You have the choice now to make a huge difference in your daughter's life.'

'You're…sure she has to have this operation?' Ruby whispered. 'I mean…really sure?'

'We're sure,' Oliver told her, suddenly immensely grateful for Em's presence. Without Em he doubted whether he'd have been able to get past the fear. 'But the operation's not without risks.' He had to say that. There was no way he could let this kid agree to surgery without warning her. 'Ruby, there are risks to you and risks to your baby. I believe those risks are small but they're still there.'

'But…I will make a difference.'

'Heinz tells me that because the spinal cord exposure is relatively high and very obvious on the ultrasound, then if we leave the operation undone, your daughter will probably spend her life in a wheelchair,' he said bluntly. 'And with the amount of exposure…there will be fluid build-up in the brain. She'll need a shunt and there may even be brain damage.'

'That's why Dr Evans has arrived here so fast,' Em went on smoothly. 'We haven't had a specialist in-utero surgeon on staff, but when we saw your ultrasound Dr Zigler knew we had to get the best obstetrician here as fast as we could. That's who Dr Evans is. The best. So now it's up to you, Ruby, love. Will you let us operate on your baby?'

'Heinz and I can close the gap over the cord,' Oliver told her. 'There's probably already a little damage done, but it's so early that damage should be minimal. What we'll do is put you to sleep, cut the smallest incision in your tummy as possible—you'll be left with a scar but I'm very neat.' He grinned at the girl, knowing a bit of pseudo modesty often worked, and he got a shaky smile in return. 'Then we'll gently turn your baby over where she's lying—with luck we won't have to take her out. Once her back is exposed Heinz will check everything, tweak things to where they should be, then we'll close the gap over her spinal cord. We'll settle her back down again and tuck her in, stitch you up and leave you both to get on with your pregnancy. You'll need to stay in hospital for about a week, maybe a bit longer, until we're sure we haven't pressured bub into coming early, but then everything should proceed as normal.'

'And she won't have to be in a wheelchair?'

'Ruby, we can't make any promises.' He caught her hand and held it. Em was still hugging her, and Oliver thought, not for the first time, Em was a wonderful midwife. She knew when to intervene and she knew when to shut up. She also exuded a quiet calm that was a tranquilliser all by itself.

He'd met her ten years ago. He'd been a barely qualified doctor, she'd been a student nurse, but already the confidence she'd engendered in the patients he'd worked with had been impressive. He'd seen her with some terrified teenage mums.

There was no nurse he'd rather have by his side and by the time they'd dated twice he'd known there was no woman he'd rather have with him for ever. Their attraction had been instant, their marriage inevitable.

It was only babies…or lack of babies…that had driven them apart.

The night their son had been stillborn had been the worst night of his life. He'd watched Em's face contort with an anguish so deep it had seemed endless, and there had been nothing he could do to stop it. He'd been unable to help her. He'd been unable to reach her.

But it was hardly the time to be thinking of that now. It was hardly the time to be thinking of it ever. After five years, they'd moved on.

'I can't make any promises,' he repeated, hauling himself back to the here and now, to the needs of the teenage kid in front of him. 'The procedure Heinz and I are trained to perform usually has an excellent outcome but there are exceptions. I won't hide that from you, Ruby. There are risks. There's a chance of infection, for you as well as your baby. We'll take every care in the world…'

'But no guarantees.'

'No guarantees,' he agreed. 'So it's up to you. This is your daughter, Ruby. It's up to you to make the choice.'

'I'm too young to have a daughter.' It was a wail and Em's arm tightened around her.

'That's where I come in,' she said solidly, a blanket of comfort and reassurance. 'You want advice, I'm full of advice. You want a hug, that's what I'm here for, too.'

'You can't be here with me all the time.'

'I can't,' Em agreed. 'I have my own son and daughter to look after. But I'm here every day during the week, and if I'm needed, I can come in at other times. My mum lives with me so I can usually drop everything and come. I don't do that for all my mums, but I'll try for you.'

'Why?' Ruby demanded, suspicious.

'Because you're special,' she said soundly. 'Isn't that right, Dr Evans? You're one special woman, and you're about to have one special daughter.'

But Oliver was hardly listening. Somehow he managed to make a grunt of acquiescence but his mind felt like it was exploding.

I have my own son and daughter to look after.

Somehow…a part of his brain had hoped—assumed?— that she'd stayed…as Em. The Em he'd left five years ago.

She hadn't. She'd moved on. She was a different woman.

I have my own son and daughter to look after…

'What do you think, Ruby?' Em was saying gently. 'Do

you want to go ahead with the operation? Do you want time to think about it?'

'I don't have a choice,' Ruby whispered. 'My baby… It's the best thing…'

It was. Oliver watched Ruby's hand drop to cover the faint bulge of her tummy, the instinctive gesture of protection that was as old as time itself.

And the gesture brought back the wedge that had been driven so deep within his marriage that it had finished it. Em had wanted to adopt, and he'd known he couldn't love like parents were supposed to love. He was right, he thought bleakly. He'd always been right. What was between Ruby and her baby was what her baby needed. Ruby was this baby's mum. Adoption was great if there was no choice, but how could an adoptive parent ever love a child as much as this?

He knew he couldn't and that knowledge had torn his marriage apart.

But Em was watching him now, with those eyes he'd once thought he could drown in. He'd loved her so much, and yet he'd walked away.

And she'd walked, as well.

I have my own son and daughter to look after.

It was nothing to do with him. He'd made his choice five years ago, and Em had obviously made choices, too.

He needed to know what those choices had been.

But now wasn't the time or the place to ask. All he could do was turn his attention back to Ruby, reassure her as much as possible and then set about working out times and details of the forthcoming surgery.

As they finished, a woman who introduced herself as one of the hospital social workers arrived. It seemed Ruby needed help with housing—as well as everything else, she'd been kicked out of her parents' house. She was stay-

ing in a boarding house near the hospital but she wouldn't
be able to stay there when the baby was born.

There'd be more talk of adoption. More talk of options.

Ruby's surgery was scheduled for the day after tomorrow, but for now he was redundant. He was free to head
to the next mum Charles had asked him to see.

He left, but his head was spinning.

Em was still sitting on the bed, still hugging Ruby. *I
have my own son and daughter to look after.*

Whatever she'd done, it had been her choice. He'd
walked away so she'd have that choice.

Why did it hurt so much that she'd taken it?

CHAPTER THREE

EM GOT ON with her day, too.

One of the wonderful things about being a midwife was that it took all her care, all her attention. She had little head-space for anything else. What was the saying? Find a job you love and you'll never have to work again? She'd felt that the first time she'd helped deliver a baby and she'd never looked back.

She sometimes…okay, she often…felt guilty about working when her mum was home with the kids, but the decision to foster had been a shared one. Her mum loved Gretta and Toby as much as she did. They had the big old house, but they needed Em's salary to keep them going.

Sometimes when Em got home her mother was more tired than she was, but whenever she protested she was cut off at the pass.

'So which baby are we giving back? Don't be ridiculous, Em. We can do this.'

They could, and knowing the kids were at home, waiting…it felt great, Em thought as she hauled off her uniform at the end of her shift and tugged on her civvies. Right, supermarket, pharmacy—Gretta's medications were running low—then home. She'd rung her mum at lunchtime and Adrianna had been reassuring. 'She's looking much better.' But, still, there was no way she was risking running out of Gretta's drugs.

'Big day?' Sophia Toulson, one of the more recent arrivals to the Victoria's midwifery staff, was hauling her uniform off, too, but instead of pulling on sensible clothes like Em's—yikes, where had that milk stain come from?—she was putting on clothes that said she was heading out clubbing or to a bar—to a life Em had left behind years ago.

Not that she missed it—much. Though there were times…

'It has been a big day,' she agreed, thinking of the night to come. Em had had three sleepless nights in a row. Gretta needed to be checked all the time. What she'd give for a solid eight-hour sleep…

'But have you met the new obstetrician? You must have—he's been fast-tracked here to operate on your Ruby. Em, he's gorgeous. No wedding ring, either. Not that that tells you anything with surgeons—they hardly ever wear them. It's not fair. Just because rings can hold infection it gives them carte blanche to disguise their marital state. But he's come from the States and fast, so that hints at single status. Em, you'll be working with him. How about giving it a shot?'

Yeah, right. Propositioning Oliver? If Sophia only knew… But somehow she managed to grimace as if this conversation were completely normal, an anonymous, gorgeous obstetrician arriving in the midst of midwives whose first love was their job, and whose second love was dissecting the love lives of those around them.

She turned to face the full-length mirror at the end of the change room. What she saw there made her grimace. Faded jeans, with a rip at the knee. Trainers with odd shoelaces. A windcheater with a milk stain running down the shoulder—why hadn't she noticed that before she'd left the house?

Her hair needed a cut. Oliver had loved her hair. She'd had it longer then and the dull brown had been shiny. It had bounced—she'd spent time with decent shampoo and conditioner, and she'd used a curling wand to give it body.

Now she bought her shampoo and conditioner in bulk at the discount store and her curling wand was rusting under the sink.

Oliver had never seen her like this—until today.

Sophia was suggesting she make a play for him?

'Can you see Oliver Evans with someone like me?' she asked incredulously. 'Sophia, get real.'

'You could try,' Sophia said, coming up behind her friend and staring over her shoulder at the reflection. 'Em, you're really pretty. With a bit of effort...'

'All my effort goes into the kids.'

'You're burying yourself.'

'I'm giving them a chance.' She glanced at her watch and grimaced again. 'Ouch. I need to go. Have a great time tonight.'

'I wish I could say the same for you. Home with your mum and two kids...' She bit her lip and Em knew why. Sophia had the same problem she did—she'd barely worked with her for a month before she'd winkled out of her the reason for the gravity behind what somehow seemed a forced gaiety.

Did all women who couldn't have children feel like this? Maybe they did, but Em's solution horrified Sophia.

'I love it,' she said soundly, even defiantly, because she did. Of course she did. 'And you have fun at... Where are you going?'

'The Rooftop Bar. Madeleine just happened to mention to your Dr Evans that we might be there.' She grinned and started searching her bag for her lipstick. 'If you're not interested...'

'He's all yours,' Em said tightly. 'Best of luck. The

supermarket's waiting for me. Whoo-hoo, a fabulous night for both of us.'

'Right,' Sophia said dryly. 'Em, I wish…'

'Well, don't wish,' Em said, more sharply than she'd intended. 'Don't even think about it. This is the life I chose for myself, and I'm happy. Dr Oliver Evans might be at the bar and I guess that's the life he's chosen, too. We're all where we want to be, and we can't ask for more than that.'

Oliver's day wasn't supposed to be frantic. Weren't new staff supposed to have an orientation day, a shift where they spent the time acquainting themselves with ward and theatre staff, meeting everyone in the canteen, arranging stuff in their office? Not so much. Harry, it seemed, had left in a hurry. His lady had been enticing; he'd left without giving proper notice and the work had backed up.

Apart from that, Harry hadn't had specialist in-utero surgical training. It seemed that word of Oliver's arrival had flown around Melbourne before he arrived. He had three consultations lined up for the afternoon and more for the next day.

Ruby's case was probably the most complex. No, it *was* the most complex, he thought, mostly because the scans showing the extent of the problem had made him wince.

Plus she was alone. His next mum, Lucy, arrived with a support cast, husband, parents, an entourage of six. Her baby had a congenital heart malfunction. The little boy in utero was a twenty-four-weeker. He needed an aortic valvuloplasty—opening the aortic foetal heart valves to allow blood flow. It was one of the most common reasons for in-utero surgery, the one that Oliver was most comfortable with—as long as he had the backup of decent cardiac surgeons.

Oliver had already met Tristan Hamilton, the Victoria's neonatal cardiothoracic surgeon—in fact, they'd gone to university together. Tristan had backed up Charles's calls, pressuring him to come, and he had been one of the inducements. Tristan was incredibly skilled, and if he could work side by side with him, for this mum, things were likely to be fine.

But what seemed wrong was that Lucy and her little boy had huge family backup—and Ruby had no one.

But Ruby had Em.

That had to be compensation. Em would be terrific.

If indeed she was with her. She'd been running late that morning. She'd looked harassed, like she had one too many balls in the air.

She'd come flying into Ruby's room half an hour after she'd hit his car, burbling about an early delivery. Really? Or had she spent the half hour on the phone to her insurance people?

It was none of his business.

Still, it was a niggle…

Isla Delamere was the Victoria's head midwife—plus she was the daughter of the CEO. Apparently she'd also just become engaged to the hospital's neonatal intensive care specialist. Isla was not a person to mess with, he'd decided. He'd been introduced to her by Charles, and as he was about to leave he saw her again.

'You have how many in-utero procedures lined up for me?' he said, half joking. 'You guys believe in throwing me in at the deep end.'

'You just do the surgery,' she said, smiling. 'My midwives will keep everything running smoothly. I have the best team…'

'My midwife this morning was running late.' He shouldn't have said it. He knew it the moment he'd opened his mouth. The last thing he wanted was to get Em into trouble and this woman had power at her fingertips, but Isla didn't seem bothered.

'I'm sorry about that. We had three births within fifteen minutes of each other just as Em came on duty. I know her care of Ruby's a priority, but one of the births was prem, the mum was out of her tree, and there's no one better at calming a frantic mum than Em. I only used her for the final fifteen minutes but it made a difference. You did cope by yourself until then?'

She raised her beautifully formed eyebrows quizzically…head midwife wondering if surgeon could cope without a little assistance…

Right. He'd got his answer but now Isla thought he was a wimp. Great start.

'Some of the staff are going to the Rooftop Bar after work,' Isla told him. 'Have you been invited? You're welcome to join us.'

'Thanks but I have a problem to sort.'

'Your car?' She was still smiling and, he thought, that was just the sort of thing that hospital staff the world over enjoyed. Specialist's car being trashed, especially since most staff here could never afford to run a car like Betsy.

He loved that car and now she was a mess. But…

'Em's promised to sort it,' Isla told him. 'She's not the sort of woman to let her insurance lapse.'

'It's not the insurance…'

'And she's really sorry. She was stricken when she first came in this morning. She's been so busy all day I suspect she hadn't had time to apologise but—'

'Will she be at the bar now?'

'Em? Heavens, no. She has two kids waiting for her at home.'

'Two?'

'Gretta's four and Toby's two. They're special kids but, wow, they're demanding.'

'I guess…' And then he asked because he couldn't help himself. Had a miracle happened? *Gretta's four*…She must have moved like the wind. 'Her partner...' He knew there couldn't have been a marriage because there'd never been a divorce but...there must be someone. 'Is he a medic? Does she have help?'

But Isla's eyebrows hit her hairline. Her face closed, midwife protecting her own. 'I guess that's for you to ask Em if it's important for you to know,' she said shortly, clearing her desk, making signals she was out of there. Off to the Rooftop Bar to join her colleagues? 'She doesn't talk about her private life. Is there anything else you need?'

More information, he thought, and he'd bet Isla knew everything he wanted to know. But he couldn't push without opening a can of worms. Evans was a common name. Em had clearly not told anyone there was a connection.

Better to leave it that way, maybe.

'Thanks, no.'

'Goodnight, then. And good luck with the car. You might let Em know when you have it sorted. She's beating herself up over it. She's a great midwife and I don't like my midwives stressed. I'd appreciate it if you could fix it.'

'I'll try,' he said, but it was too late. Isla had gone.

He headed down to the car park. He hadn't been back to assess the damage during the day—he hadn't had time.

The park next to his was empty. Em was gone.

Her wagon had still been drivable. Her doors had been bent, but the wheels were still okay, whereas his... One of the wheels was far from okay and he wasn't driving anywhere. He stooped and examined it and thought of the hassle it had been to find the right parts for his little beauty. Where was he going to find another wheel rim? And the panels were a mess.

Strangely, it didn't upset him as much as he'd thought it might. He checked the damage elsewhere and knew he'd have to get her towed—actually, carried, as there was no way she could be towed like this. And then he'd go searching for the parts he needed.

He kind of liked searching the internet for car parts. It was something to do at three in the morning when he couldn't sleep.

Which was often.

He rounded the front of the car and there he saw a note in his windshield. Em?

Oliver, I really am sorry about this. I've put my hand up, it was all my fault, and I've told my insurance company to pay without arguing. I photocopied my driver's licence and my insurance company details— they're attached. One of the girls on the ward knows of a great repair place that specialises in vintage cars—the details are here, too. See you when you next see Ruby.
Em

It was all about the car. There was nothing personal at all.

Well, what did he expect? A *mea culpa* with extras? This was more than generous, admitting total culpability. Her insurance company would hate her. As well as that, she'd probably have to pay the first few hundred dollars, plus she'd lose her no-claim bonus.

He could afford it. Could she?

He re-read the note. What was he hoping for? Personal details?

Her driver's licence told him all he was going to get. Emily Louise Evans. She was still using his name, then. So…single mother? How? Had she gone ahead and adopted by herself? He checked again, making sure he was right—she was living at her mother's address.

He liked Adrianna. Or he had liked her. He hadn't seen his mother-in-law for years.

He could drop in…

Why?

'Because she shouldn't accept full responsibility,' he said out loud. 'If she's supporting kids…'

She'd said she'd already phoned her insurance company and confessed, but maybe he could reverse it. Maybe he could take some of the load.

The independent Em of five years ago would tell him to shove it.

Yeah? He thought back to the Em of five years ago, shattered, gutted, looking towards the future with a bleakness that broke his heart.

'If you won't do it with me then I'll do it alone. If you think I can go back to the life we led… I'm over nightclubs, Oliver. I'm over living just for me.'

'Isn't there an us in there?'

'I thought there was, but I thought we wanted a family. I hadn't realised it came with conditions.'

'Em, I can't.'

'So you're leaving?'

'You're not giving me any choice.'

'I guess I'm not. I'm sorry, Oliver.'

Five years…

Okay, their marriage was long over but somehow she still seemed…partly his responsibility. And the cost of this repair would make her insurance company's eyes water.

It behoved him…

'Just to see,' he told himself. He'd thought he'd drop in to visit Adrianna when he'd come to Melbourne anyway, to see how she was.

And talk to Adrianna about Em?

Yeah, but he was over it. He'd had a couple of relationships in the last five years, even if they had been fleeting. He'd moved on.

'So let's be practical,' he told himself, and hit his phone and organised a tow truck, and a hire car, and half an hour later he was on the freeway, heading to the suburb where his ex-mother-in-law lived. With his wife and her two children, and her new life without him.

'You hit who?'

'Oliver.' Em was feeding Toby, which was a messy joy. Toby was two years old and loved his dinner. Adrianna had made his favourite animal noodles in a tomato sauce. Toby was torn between inspecting every animal on his spoon and hoovering in the next three spoonfuls as if there was no tomorrow.

Adrianna was sitting by the big old fire stove, cuddling Gretta. The little girl's breathing was very laboured.

Soon...

No. It hurt like hot knives to have to think about it. Much better to concentrate on distractions, and Oliver was surely a distraction.

'He's working at the Victoria?'

'Yep. Starting today.'

'Oh, Em... Can you stay there?'

'I can't walk away. We need the money. Besides, it's the best midwifery job in Melbourne. I love working with Isla and her team.'

'So tell him to leave. You were there first.'

'I don't think you can tell a man like Oliver Evans to leave. Besides, the hospital needs him. I read his CV on the internet during lunch break. His credentials are even more awesome than when I knew him. He's operating on Ruby's baby and there's no one better to do it.'

And that had Adrianna distracted. 'How is Ruby?'

Em wasn't supposed to bring work home. She wasn't

supposed to talk about patients outside work, but Adrianna spent her days minding the kids so Em could work. Adrianna had to feel like she was a part of it, and in a way she was. If it wasn't for her mum, she'd never be able to do this.

This. Chaos. Animal noodles. Mess on the kitchen floor. Fuzzy, a dopey half-poodle, half something no one could guess at, was currently lurking under Toby's highchair on the off-chance the odd giraffe or elephant would drop from on high.

'Hey, it's all done.' There was a triumphant bang from the laundry and Mike appeared in the doorway, waving his spanner. 'That's that mother fixed. I'd defy any drop to leak anywhere now. Anything else I can do for you ladies?'

'Oh, Mike, that's fabulous. But I wish you'd let us pay—'

'You've got free plumbing for life,' Mike said fiercely. Mike was their big, burly, almost scary-looking next-door neighbour. His ginger hair was cropped to almost nothing. He wore his jeans a bit too low, he routinely ripped the sleeves out of his T-shirts because sleeves annoyed him, and in his spare time he built his body. If you met Mike on a dark night you might turn the other way. Fast.

Em had met Mike on a dark night. He'd crashed into their kitchen, banging the back door so hard it had broken. 'Em, the wife… My Katy… The baby… There's blood, oh, my God, there's blood… You're a midwife. Please…'

Katy had had a fast, fierce delivery of their third child, and she'd haemorrhaged. Mike had got home to find her in the laundry, her baby safely delivered, but she'd been bleeding out.

She'd stopped breathing twice before the ambulance had arrived. Em had got her back.

Mike and Katy were now the parents of three boys who promised to grow up looking just like their dad, and Mike was Em's slave for ever. He'd taken Em and her household under his wing, and a powerful wing it was. There were usually motorbikes parked outside Mike and Katy's place—multiple bikes—but no matter what the pressure of his family, his job or his biker mates, Mike dropped in every night—just to check.

Now, as Toby finished the last mouthful of his noodles, Mike hefted him out of his highchair and whirled him round and hugged him in a manner that made Em worry the noodles might come back up again. But Toby crowed in glee.

'Can I take him next door for a few minutes?' he asked. 'We've got a new swing, a double-seater. My boys'll be outside and Henry and Tobes'll look a treat on it. Give you a bit of peace with Gretta, like.'

He glanced at Gretta but he didn't say any more. What was happening was obvious. Gretta was more and more dependent on oxygen, but more and more it wasn't enough.

If Mike took Toby, Em could sit by the fire and cuddle Gretta while Adrianna put her feet up and watched the telly. Toby was already lighting up with excitement.

'That'd be great, Mike, thank you,' Em told him. 'I'll pop over and pick him up in an hour.'

'Bring Gretta with you,' Mike said. 'Give her a go on the swing. If she's up for it.'

But she wasn't up for it. They all knew it, and that knowledge hung over the house, a shadow edging closer.

Today Oliver's presence had pushed that shadow back a little, made Em's thoughts fly sideways, but, Oliver or not, the shadows were there to stay.

CHAPTER FOUR

THE LAST TIME Oliver had visited his ex-mother-in-law, her house had looked immaculate. Adrianna was devoted to her garden. At this time of year her roses had always looked glorious, her herbaceous borders had been clipped to perfect symmetry and her lawns had always been lush and green, courtesy of the tanks she'd installed specifically so she could be proud of her garden the year round.

Not now.

The grass on the lawn was a bit long and there were bare patches, spots where things had been left for a while. Where once an elegant table setting had stood under the shade of a Manchurian pear, there was now a sandpit and a paddling pool.

A beach ball lay on the front path. He had to push it aside to reach the front door.

It took him less than a minute to reach the door but by the time he had, the last conversation he'd had with Em had played itself out more than a dozen times in his head.

'Em, I can't adopt. I'm sorry, but I can't guarantee I can love kids who aren't my own.'

'They would be your own,' she'd said. She'd been emotional, distraught, but underneath she'd been sure. *'I want kids, Oliver. I want a family. There are children out there*

who need us. If we can't have our own...to not take them is selfish.'

'To take them when we can't love them is selfish.'

'I can love them. I will.'

'But I can't.' He'd said it gently but inexorably, a truth he'd learned by fire.

'You're saying I need to do it alone?'

'Em, think about it,' he'd said fiercely. *'We love each other. We've gone through so much...'*

'I want a family.'

'Then I can't give it to you. If this is the route you're determined to take, then you'll need to find someone who can.'

He'd walked away, sure that when she'd settled she'd agree with him. After all, their love was absolute. But she'd never contacted him. She hadn't answered his calls.

Adrianna had spoken to him. 'Oliver, she's gutted. She knows your position. Please, leave her be to work things out for herself.'

It had gutted him, too, that she'd walked away from their marriage without a backward glance. And here was evidence that she'd moved on. She'd found herself the life she wanted—without him.

He reached the door, lifted his hand to the bell but as he did the door swung inwards.

The guy opening the door was about the same age as Oliver. Oliver was tall, but this guy was taller and he was big in every sense of the word. He was wearing jeans, a ripped T-shirt and big working boots. His hands were clean but there was grease on his forearms. And on his tatts.

He was holding a child, a little boy of about two. The child was African, Oliver guessed, Somalian maybe, as dark as night, with huge eyes. One side of his face was badly scarred. He was cradled in the guy's arms, but he was looking outwards, brightly interested in this new arrival into his world.

Another kid came flying through the gate behind Oliver, hurtling up the path towards them. Another little boy. Four? Ginger-haired. He looked like the guy in front of him.

'Daddy, Daddy, it's my turn on the swing,' he yelled. 'Come and make them give me a turn.'

The guy scooped him up, as well, then stood, a kid tucked under each arm. He looked Oliver up and down, like a pit bull, bristling, assessing whether to attack.

'Life insurance?' he drawled. 'Funeral-home plans? Not interested, mate.'

'I'm here to see Emily.'

'She's not interested, either.'

He was still wearing his suit. Maybe he should have changed. Maybe a tatt or two was necessary to get into this new version of his mother-in-law's home.

'I'm a friend of Em's from the hospital.' Who was this guy? 'Can you tell her I'm here, please?'

'She's stuffed. She doesn't need visitors.' He was blocking the doorway, a great, belligerent bull of a man.

'Can you ask her?'

'She only has an hour at most with Gretta before the kid goes to sleep. You want to intrude on that?'

Who was Gretta? Who was this guy?

'Mike?' Thankfully it was Em, calling from inside the house. 'Who is it?'

'Guy who says he's a friend of yours.' Mike didn't take his eyes off Oliver. His meaning was clear—he didn't trust him an inch. 'Says he's from the hospital. Looks like an undertaker.'

'Mike?'

'Yeah?'

'It'll be Oliver,' she called, and Mike might be right

about the 'stuffed' adjective, Oliver conceded. Her voice sounded past weariness.

'Oliver?'

'He's the guy I was married to.' *Was?*

'Your ex is an undertaker? Sheesh, Em…'

'He's not an undertaker. He's a surgeon.'

'That's one step before the undertaker.'

'Mike?'

'Yeah?'

'Let him in.'

Why didn't Em come to the door? But Mike gave him a last long stare and stepped aside.

'Right,' he called back to Em. 'But we're on the swings. One yell and I'll be here in seconds. Watch it, mate,' he growled at Oliver, as he pushed past him and headed down the veranda with his load of kids. 'You upset Em and you upset me—and you wouldn't want to do that. You upset Em and you'll be very, very sorry.'

He knew this house. He'd been here often with Em. He'd stayed here for weeks on end when, just after they were married, Em's dad had been diagnosed with inoperable lung cancer.

It had taken the combined skill of all of them—his medical input, Em's nursing skill and Adrianna's unfailing devotion—to keep Kev comfortable until the end, but at the funeral, as well as sadness there had also been a feeling that it had been the best death Kev could have asked for. Surrounded by his family, no pain, knowing he was loved…

'This is how I want us to go out when we have to,' Em had whispered to him at the graveside. 'Thank you for being here.'

Yeah, well, that was years ago and he hadn't been with her for a long time now. She was a different woman.

He walked into the kitchen and stopped dead.

Different woman? What an understatement.

She was sitting by Adrianna's old kitchen range, settled in a faded rocker. Her hair was once more loose, her curls cascading to her shoulders. She had on that baggy wind-cheater and jeans and her feet were bare.

She was cuddling a child. A three- or four-year-old?

A sick child. There was an oxygen concentrator humming on the floor beside them. The child's face was buried in Em's shoulder, but Oliver could see the thin tube connected to the nasal cannula.

A child this small, needing oxygen… His heart lurched. This was no ordinary domestic scene. A child this sick…

The expression on Em's face…

Already he was focusing forward. Already he was feeling gutted for Em. She gave her heart…

Once upon a time she'd given it to him, and he'd hurt her. That she be hurt again…

This surely couldn't be her child.

And who was Mike?

He'd paused in the doorway and for some reason it took courage to step forward. He had no place in this tableau. He'd walked away five years ago so this woman could have the life she wanted, and he had no right to walk back into her life now.

But he wasn't walking into her life. He was here to talk to her about paying for the crash.

Right. His head could tell him that all it liked, but his gut was telling him something else entirely. Em… He'd loved her with all his heart.

He looked at her now, tired, vulnerable, holding a child who must be desperately ill, and all he wanted was to pick her up and carry her away from hurt.

From loving a child who wasn't hers?

Maybe she was hers. Maybe the in-vitro procedures had finally produced a successful outcome. But if this was her child...

His gut was still churning, and when she turned and gave him a tiny half-smile, a tired acknowledgement that he was there, a sort of welcome, the lurch became almost sickening.

'Ollie.'

No one had called him Ollie for five years. No one dared. He'd hated the diminutive—Brett, his sort of brother, had mocked him with it. *'Get out of our lives, Pond Scum Ollie. You're a cuckoo. You don't belong here.'*

Only Em had whispered it to him in the night, in his arms, when their loving had wrapped them in their own cocoon of bliss. Only Em's tongue had made it a blessing.

'Hey,' he said softly, crossing to where she sat, and, because he couldn't help himself, he touched her hair. Just lightly. He had no right, but he had to...touch.

It was probably a mistake. It hauled him into the intimate tableau. Em looked up at him and smiled, and it was no longer a half-smile. It was a smile of welcome. Acceptance.

A welcome home? It was no such thing. But it was a welcome to *her* home, to the home she'd created. Without him.

'Gretta, we have a visitor,' she murmured, and she turned slightly so the child in her arms could see if she wanted.

And she did. The little girl stirred and opened her eyes and Oliver's gut lurched all over again.

Isla had said Em had a two- and a four-year-old. This little one was older than two, but if she was four she was tiny. She was dressed in a fuzzy pink dressing gown that almost enveloped her.

She was a poppet of a child, with a mop of dark, straight hair, and with huge eyes, almost black.

Her lips were tinged blue. The oxygen wasn't enough, then.

She had Down's syndrome.

Oh, Em… What have you got yourself into?

But he couldn't say it. He hauled a kitchen chair up beside them both, and took Gretta's little hand in his.

'I'm pleased to meet you, Gretta.' He smiled at the little girl, giving her all his attention. 'I'm Oliver. I'm a friend of your…' And he couldn't go on.

'He's Mummy's friend,' Em finished for him, and there was that lurch again. 'He's the man in the picture next to Grandma and Grandpa.'

'Ollie,' the little girl whispered, and there was no outsider implication in that word. She was simply accepting him as part of whatever this household was.

There was a sudden woof from under the table, a scramble, another woof and a dog's head appeared on his knee. It was a great, boofy, curly brown head, attached to a body that was disproportionally small. It woofed again but its tail wagged like a flag in a gale.

'This is Fuzzy,' Em said, still smiling at him. His presence here didn't seem to be disconcerting her. It was as if he was simply an old friend, dropping by. To be welcomed and then given a farewell? 'Mike gave us Fuzzy to act as a watchdog. He sort of does, but he's always a bit late on the scene.'

'Oliver!' And here was the last part of the tableau. Adrianna was standing in the door through to the lounge and her eyes weren't welcoming at all. 'What are you doing here?'

Here was the welcome he'd expected. Coldness and accusation…

'Mum…' Em said warningly, but Adrianna was never one who could be put off with a mere warning.

'You hit Em's car.'

'Mum, I told you. I hit his.'

'Then he shouldn't have been parked where you could hit him. What are you doing here?'

'Offering to pay for the damage.'

Her eyes narrowed. 'Really?'

'Really.'

'Mum, it was my fault,' Em protested, but Adrianna shook her head.

'It's your no-claim bonus that's at risk. Oliver's a specialist obstetric surgeon, and I'm betting he has no mortgage and no kids. He can afford it.'

'Mum, it's my debt.'

'You take on the world,' her mother muttered. 'Oliver owes you, big time. My advice is to take his money and run. Or rather take his money and say goodbye. Oliver, you broke my daughter's heart. I won't have you upsetting her all over again. Raking up old wounds…'

'He's not,' Em said, still gently, and Oliver was aware that her biggest priority was not Em or the emotions his presence must be causing, but rather on not upsetting the little girl in her arms. 'Mum, he's welcome. He's a friend and a colleague and he's here to do the honourable thing. Even if I won't let him. I can afford to pay, Oliver.'

'I won't let you,' he told her.

'I'll make you a cup of tea, then,' Adrianna said, slightly mollified. She humphed across to the kettle, made tea—and, yep, she remembered how he liked it. She plonked two mugs on the table, one for Em, one for him. Then she hoisted Fuzzy into one arm, took her own mug in the other hand and headed back to the sitting room. 'Semi-final of *Boss of My Kitchen*,' she said briefly over her shoulder. 'Shall the croquembouche disintegrate into a puddle? The tension's a killer. Nice to see you, Oliver—sort of—but don't you dare upset Em. Goodbye.'

And she disappeared, using a foot to shove the door closed behind her.

Her message couldn't be clearer. *My daughter wants me to be polite so I will be, but not one inch more than I must.*

He was left with Em, and the little girl in her arms. Sitting in Adrianna's kitchen.

It was a great kitchen.

He'd always loved this house, he thought, inconsequentially. Kevin and Adrianna had built it forty years ago, hoping for a huge family. They'd had four boys, and then the tail-ender, Emily. Adrianna's parents had moved in, as well, into a bungalow out the back. Em had said her childhood had been filled with her brothers and their mates, visiting relations, cousins, friends, anyone Adrianna's famous hospitality could drag in.

Oliver and Em had built a house closer to the hospital they both worked in. They'd built four bedrooms, as well, furnishing them with hope.

Hope hadn't happened. The IVF procedures had worn them down and Josh's death had been the final nail in the coffin of their marriage. He'd walked out and left it to her.

'You're not living in our house?' He'd signed it over to her before going overseas, asking their lawyer to let her know.

'It's better here,' she said simply. 'My brothers are all overseas or interstate now, but I have Mum, and Mike and Katy nearby. The kids are happy here. I've leased our house out. When I emailed you, you said I could do what I like. I use half the rent to help with expenses here. The other half is in an interest-bearing deposit for you. I told you that in the email. You didn't answer.'

He hadn't. He'd blocked it out. The idea of strangers living in the gorgeous house he and Em had had built with such hopes...

'I couldn't live there,' Em said, conversationally. 'It doesn't have heart. Not like here. Not like home.'

Yeah, well, that was another kick in the guts, but he was over it by now. Or almost over it. He concentrated on his tea for a bit, while Em juggled Gretta and cannula and her mug of tea. He could offer to help but he knew he'd be knocked back.

She no longer needed him. This was her life now.

Gretta was watching him, her great brown eyes carefully assessing. Judging? Who knew? The IQs of kids with Down's syndrome covered an amazingly broad spectrum.

He touched the cannula lightly. 'Hey, Gretta,' he said softly. 'Why do you need this?'

'For breeving,' she lisped, but it was as if even saying the words was too much for her. She sank back against Em and her eyes half closed.

'Gretta has an atrioventricular septal defect,' Em said matter-of-factly, as if it was a perfectly normal thing for a kid to have. No problem at all.

But those three words told Oliver all he needed to know about the little girl's condition.

An atrioventricular septal defect... Common term— hole in the heart.

A large percentage of babies with Down's syndrome were born with congenital heart defects. The most common problem was atrioventricular septal defects, or holes in the heart. That this little one was at home with oxygen, with a cannula helping her breathe, told Oliver there was more than one hole. It must be inoperable.

And he had to ask.

'Em, is she yours?'

The words echoed around the kitchen, and as soon as they came out he knew it was the wrong thing to ask.

The arms holding Gretta tightened, and so did the look on Em's face.

'Of course she's mine,' she whispered, but the friendliness was gone. 'Gretta's my daughter. Oliver, I think you should leave.'

'I meant—'

'You meant is she adopted?' Her face was still bleak. 'No, she's not adopted. I'm Gretta's foster-mum, but her birth mother has given all responsibility to me. That means I can love her as much as I want, and that's what I do. I love her and love her and love her. Gretta's my daughter, Oliver, in every sense of the word.'

'You have another…son?'

'You'll have met Toby on the way out with Mike, and he's my foster-child, too. He has spinal kyphoscoliosis. He's the bravest kid. I'm so proud of my kids. Mum's so proud of her grandkids.'

He got it. Or sort of. These were fostered kids. That's what Em had wanted him to share.

But that's what he'd been, he thought bleakly. Someone else's reject. Much as he approved of the idea in theory, in practice he knew it didn't work.

But what Em did was no longer his business, he reminded himself. This was what she'd decided to do with her life. He had no business asking…

How could he not?

'Who's Mike?' he asked, and he hadn't known he was going to ask until he did.

'My lover?' Her lips twitched a little at the expression on his face. 'Can you see it? Nope, Mike's our next-door neighbour, our friend, our man about the house. He and Katy have three kids, we have two, and they mix and mingle at will. You like going to Katy's, don't you, Gretta?'

There was a faint nod from Gretta, and a smile.

And the medical part of Oliver was caught. If Gretta

was responding now, as ill as she was, her IQ must be at the higher end of the Down's spectrum.

He watched Em hold her tight, and he thought, She's given her heart...

And he never could have. He'd never doubted Em's ability to adopt; it was only his reluctance...his fear...

'Is there anything I can do to help?' he found himself saying. 'Now that I'm here?'

'But you don't want to be here.' Em shifted a little, making herself more comfortable. 'You've moved on. At least, I hope you have. I'd have thought you'd have asked for a divorce, found a new partner and had kids by now. You wanted kids. What's stopping you?'

And there was a facer. He had wanted children, they both had, but after a stillbirth and so many attempts at IVF it had worn them—and their marriage—into the ground. Em had told him to leave.

No. She hadn't. She'd simply said she wanted to adopt a child, and that was a deal-breaker.

'I haven't found the right person,' he said, trying to make it sound flippant, but there was no way he could make anything about what had happened to them flippant. The last year or so of their marriage had been unswervingly grey. He looked at Em now and he thought some of the grey remained.

A lot of the grey?

He glanced around the kitchen, once sparkling and ordered, if a bit cluttered with Adrianna's bits and pieces from the past. But now it was all about the present. It was filled with the detritus of a day with kids—or a life with kids.

But this was what Em wanted. And he hadn't?

No, he thought fiercely. It had been what he'd wanted more than anything, and that's why he'd walked away.

So why hadn't he found it?

There was the sound of feet pounding up the veranda, a perfunctory thump on the door and two little boys of about six and four burst in. They were followed by Mike, carrying the toddlers. The six-year-old was carrying a bunch of tattered kangaroo paws, flowers Oliver had seen in the next-door front garden. Tough as nails, Australian perennials, they hardly made good cut flowers but these were tied with a gaudy red bow and presented with pride.

'These are for Gran Adrianna,' the urchin said. And when she obviously wasn't in the kitchen, he headed through the living-room door and yelled for her. 'Gran? Gran Adrianna, we've got you a present. Mum says happy birthday. She was coming over to say it but she's got a cold and she says she wants to give you flowers for your birthday and not a cold.'

And Em turned white.

CHAPTER FIVE

EVERYONE ELSE WAS looking at the kid with the flowers, and then at Adrianna, who reappeared and stooped to give the kids a hug. Only Oliver saw the absolute mortification that crossed Em's face.

She'd forgotten, he thought. Of course she had. Even if she'd remembered this morning, after crashing her car, doing a huge day on the wards, then coming home to such a sick kid, forgetting was almost inevitable.

Think. Think! he told himself. He used to live in this town. Cake. St Kilda. Ackland Street. Cake heaven. It wasn't so far, and the shops there stayed open late.

'Are you guys staying for the cake?' he asked, glancing at his watch, his voice not rising, speaking like this was a pre-ordained plan. 'It'll be here in about twenty minutes. Em asked me to order it but it's running a bit late. Adrianna, is it okay if I stay for the celebration? Em thought it might be okay, but if you'd rather I didn't… Mike, can you and the kids show me the swing while we wait? I'm good at pushing.'

'Em asked you to order a cake?' Adrianna demanded, puzzled, and Oliver spread his hands.

'I crashed into her car this morning. She's been run off her legs all day and I asked if there was anything I could do. Therefore, in twenty minutes there'll be cake. Swing? Kids?'

'Oliver…' Em started, but Oliver put up his hand as if to stop her in mid-sentence. Which was exactly what he intended.

'She always wants to pay,' he told his ex-mother-in-law, grinning. 'She's stubborn as an ox, your Em, but you'd know that, Adrianna. We seem to have been arguing about money all day. I told you, Em, I'm doing the cake, you're on the balloons. Sorry I've mistimed it, though. I'll pay ten percent of the balloons to compensate. Any questions?'

'N-no,' Em said weakly, and his grin widened.

'How about that? No problems at all. Prepare for cake, Adrianna, and prepare for Birthday.'

And suddenly he was being towed outside by kids who realised bedtime was being set back and birthday cake was in the offing. Leaving an open-mouthed Em and Adrianna in the kitchen.

Two minutes later, Mike was onside. They were pushing kids on swings and Oliver was on the phone. And it worked. His backup plan had been a fast trip to the supermarket for an off-the-shelf cake and blow-them-up-yourself balloons but, yes, the shop he remembered had decorated ice cream cakes. They were usually pre-ordered but if he was prepared to pay more… How fast could they pipe Adrianna's name on top? Candles included? Could they order a taxi to deliver it and charge his card? Did they do balloons? Next door did? Was it still open? How much to bung some of those in the taxi as well? He'd pay twice the price for their trouble.

'You're a fast mover,' Mike said, assessing him with a long, slow look as they pushed the double swing together. And then he said, not quite casually, 'Should I worry? If Em gets hurt I might just be tempted to do a damage.'

So Em had a protector. Good. Unless that protector

was threatening to pick him up by the collar and hurl him off the property. He sighed and raked his hair and tried to figure how to respond.

'Mate, I'm not a fast mover,' he said at last. 'For five years I haven't moved at all. I'm not sure even what's happening here, but I'm sure as hell not moving fast.'

'Oh, Em, you remembered.' The moment the boys were out of the house Adrianna stooped and enveloped Em— and Gretta—in a bear hug. 'I've been thinking all day that no one's remembered and… Oh, sweetheart, I'm sorry.'

'You're sorry!' Em struggled to her feet, still cradling Gretta. She should confess, she thought, but as she looked at her mum's face she thought, no. Confession might make her feel better, but right now Adrianna was happy because her daughter had remembered. Oliver had given her that gift and she'd accept, because to do anything else would be cruel. Her mum did so much…

Oliver had rescued her. It'd be dumb to spoil his efforts with more than Adrianna had to know.

But she wasn't going to be dishonest. Not entirely. 'Mum, I remembered when I woke up this morning,' she said. 'But when Gretta was sick I forgot to say it. It was such a rush all day and there's been nothing I could do. But when I met Oliver—'

'You knew he was coming?'

'He ordered the cake. And you know he's always loved you.' And that at least was the truth.

'Oh, Em…'

'And I've bought you a half-day spa voucher.' Yeah, she was lying about that but she could order and get it printed tonight. 'And if we can, I'll do it with you.' That's what Adrianna would like most in the world, she knew, but how would she manage that? But she looked at her mum's tired face and thought she had to do it. It might have to wait until Gretta was better, but she would do it.

If Gretta got better.

'Oh, but, Em…Gretta…'

'It can't be all about Gretta,' Em said gently, and that, too, was true. No matter how much attention Gretta needed, there were others who needed her, as well. It'd be a wrench to spend one of her precious free days…

But, no. This was her mum.

Oliver had saved the situation for now. The least she could do was take it forward.

The cake was amazing, an over-the-top confection that made the kids gasp with wonder. The taxi driver brought it in with a flourish then directed the kids to bring in the balloons. Whatever Oliver had paid, Em thought numbly, it must have been well and truly over the top, as the balloons were already filled, multi-coloured balls of floating air, bursting from the cab as soon as the doors were open, secured only by ribbons tied to the cab doors.

The kids brought them in, bunch upon bunch, and the kitchen was an instant party.

Katy arrived from next door, summoned by her kids. She wouldn't come right in—her flushed face verified her self-diagnosis of a streaming head cold and she declared there was no way she was risking Gretta catching anything—but she stood in the doorway and sang 'Happy Birthday' with the rest of them and watched while Adrianna blew out the candles and sliced the creamy caramel and chocolate and strawberry confection into slices that were almost cake-sized each.

'I can't believe it,' Adrianna said mistily, between mouthfuls of cake. 'Thank you all so much.'

And Em looked across at Oliver, who was sitting with Toby on his knee, one spoonful for Oliver, one spoonful for Toby, and she caught his gaze and tried to smile. But it didn't come off.

This was how it could have been, she thought. This was what she'd dreamed of.

But she'd pushed too hard, too fast. Josh's death had gutted her. She remembered sobbing, 'I can't do IVF any more, I'm too tired. There are babies out there who need us. We'll adopt. You're adopted, Oliver, you know it can work.'

But: 'It doesn't work,' he'd said, not angrily, just flatly, dully, stating immutable facts. 'It's second best and you know it.'

His reaction had shocked her. She'd been in no mood to compromise, and suddenly everything had escalated. The tension of five years of trying for a family had suddenly exploded. Leaving them with nothing.

What had he been doing for five years? Building his career, by the look of his CV. Turning into a wonderful doctor.

A caring doctor... His patience with two-year-old Toby, not the easiest kid to feed, was wonderful. The way he responded to the kids around the table, the mess, the laughter...

The way he smiled up at Adrianna and told her he was so sorry he'd missed her last five birthdays, she'd have to have five slices of cake to make up for it...

He was wonderful.

She wanted to weep.

She wanted to set Gretta down, walk around the table and hug him. Hold him.

Claim him again as her husband?

Right, like that was about to happen. The past was the past. They'd made their decisions and they'd moved on.

'Em's given me an afternoon at the day spa,' Adrianna said happily, cutting across her thoughts. Or almost. Her thoughts were pretty intense right now, pretty much centred on the gorgeous guy with the toddler, right across the table from her. She was watching his hands. She'd loved those hands—surgeon's hands. She remembered what those hands had been able to do.

She remembered…

'That's gorgeous,' Katy was saying from the doorway. 'But, Em, you still haven't had that colour and cut Mike and I gave you for Christmas. Right, Adrianna, this time it's going to work. As soon as I get over my snuffles I'm taking all five kids and you two are having your Christmas and birthday treats combined. This weekend?'

Once again, right. As if. Em gave her a smile, and then went to hug Adrianna, but she thought Katy would still be recovering by this weekend and her boys would probably catch her cold after her and Gretta was still so weak…

Adrianna should—and would—have her day spa but there'd be no day spas or colour and cuts for Em until… until…

The *until* was unthinkable. She hugged Gretta and her mind closed.

'What about this Saturday and using me?' Oliver asked, and she blinked. Had she misheard?

'You?'

'Anyone can see you've got the cold from hell,' he told Katy. 'Even if you're not still contagious you'll be wiped out, and you have three of your own to look after. Whereas I've just moved to Melbourne and my job hasn't geared up yet. There's nothing to stop me coming by and taking care of a couple of kids for a few hours.' He spooned chocolate ice-cream cake into Toby's waiting mouth and grinned at the little boy. 'Piece of cake, really. We'll have fun.' And then he smiled across at Gretta, focusing entirely on the little girl. 'How about it, Gretta? Will you let me take care of you and Toby?'

Gretta gazed back at him, clearly not understanding

what was happening, but Oliver was smiling and she responded to the smile. She tried a tentative one of her own.

She was one brave kid, Oliver thought. But she looked so vulnerable... Her colour... Oxygen wasn't getting through.

'That'd be fantastic,' Adrianna breathed. 'Em worries about Gretta's breathing, but with you being a doctor...'

'Is he a doctor?' Katy demanded.

'He's Em's ex,' Mike growled, throwing a suspicious, hard stare at Oliver.

'But I'm still reliable,' Oliver said—hopefully—and Katy laughed.

'Hey, I hooked with some weirdos in my time,' she told the still-glowering Mike. 'But a couple of them turned into your mates. Just because they didn't come up to my high standards doesn't mean they're total failures as human beings. What do you say, Em? Trust your kids for a few hours with your ex? And him a doctor and all. It sounds an offer too good to refuse to me.'

And they were all looking at her. From what had started as a quiet night she was suddenly surrounded by birthday, kids, mess, chaos, and here was Oliver, threatening to walk into her life again.

No. Not threatening. Offering.

She'd been feeling like she was being bulldozed. Now... She looked at Oliver and he returned her gaze, calmly, placidly, like he was no threat at all. Whatever he'd been doing for the last five years it was nothing to do with her, but she knew one thing. He was a good man. She might not know him any more, but she could trust him, and if a specialist obstetrician and surgeon couldn't look after her Gretta, who could?

Her mind was racing. Gretta and Toby were both accustomed to strangers minding them—too many stays in hospital had seen to that. Oliver was currently feeding Toby like a pro.

She *could* take Adrianna for an afternoon out. She glanced again at her mum and saw the telltale flicker of hope in her eyes. She was so good… Without Adrianna, Em couldn't have these kids.

The fact that she'd once hoped to have them with Oliver…

No. Don't go there. She hauled herself back from the brink, from the emotions of five years ago, and she managed a smile at Oliver.

'Thank you, then,' she said simply. 'Thank you for offering. Mum and I would love it. Two p.m. on Saturday? We'll be back by five.'

'I'll be here at one.'

Four hours… Did she trust him that long?

Of course she did, she told herself. She did trust him. It was only… She needed to trust herself, as well. She needed to figure out the new way of the world, where Oliver Evans was no longer a lover or a husband.

It seemed Oliver Evans was offering to be a friend.

An hour later she was walking him out to his car. Amazingly, he'd helped put the kids to bed. 'If I'm to care for them on Saturday, they should see me as familiar.' The children had responded to his inherent gentleness, his teasing, his smile, and Em was struggling not to respond, as well.

But she was responding. Of course she was. How could she not? She'd fallen in love with this man a decade ago and the traces of that love remained. Life had battered them, pushed them apart, but it was impossible to think of him other than a friend.

Just a friend? He had to be. She'd made the decision five years ago—Oliver or children. She'd wanted children so much that she'd made her choice but it had been like chopping a part of herself out. Even now... The decision had been made in the aftermath of a stillbirth, when her emotions had been all over the place. If she was asked to make such a decision again...

She'd make it, she thought, thinking of the children in the house behind her. Gretta and Toby. Where would they be without her?

Someone else might have helped them, she thought, but now they were hers, and she loved them so fiercely it hurt.

If she'd stayed with Oliver she would have had...nothing.

'Tell me about the kids,' he said, politely almost, leaning back on the driver's door of his car. His rental car.

It had been a lovely car she'd destroyed. That's what Oliver must have decided, she thought. He'd have a gorgeous car instead of kids—and now she'd smashed it.

'I'm sorry about your car,' she managed.

He made an exasperated gesture—leave it, not important. But it was important. She'd seen his face when he'd looked at the damage.

'Tell me about the kids,' he said again. 'You're fostering?'

'Mum and I decided...when you left...'

'To have kids?'

'You know I can't,' she said, evenly now, getting herself back together. 'For the year after you left I wasn't... very happy. I had my work as a midwife. I love my work, but you know that was never enough. And then one of my mums had Gretta.'

'One of your mums.'

'I know... Not very professional, is it, to get so personally involved? But Gretta was Miriam's third child. Miriam's a single mum who hadn't bothered to have any prenatal checks so missed the scans. From the moment the doctors told her Gretta had Down's she hadn't wanted anything to do with her. Normally, Social Services can find adoptive parents for a newborn, even if it has Down's, but Miriam simply checked herself out of hospital and disappeared. We think she's in Western Australia with a new partner.'

'So you've taken her baby...'

'I didn't take her baby,' she said, thinking suddenly of the way he'd reacted to her suggestion of adoption all those years ago. It had been like adoption was a dirty word.

'I wasn't accusing...'

'No,' she said and stared down at her feet. She needed new shoes, she thought inconsequentially. She wore lace-up trainers—they were the most practical for the running she had to do—and a hole was starting to appear at her left big toe. Not this pay, she thought. Maybe next? Or maybe she could stick a plaster over the toe and pretend it was a new fashion. One of the kids' plasters with frogs on.

'What do you know about Miriam?' Oliver asked, and she hauled her attention back to him. Actually, it had never really strayed. But distractions were good. Distractions were necessary.

'We...we don't hear from Miriam,' she told him. 'But it's not for want of trying. Her two older children are in foster care together on a farm up near Kyneton—they're great kids and Harold and Eve are a wonderful foster-mum and dad—but Gretta couldn't go with them. Her heart problems have meant constant hospitalisation. We knew from the start that her life would be short. We knew it'd be a fight to keep her alive, so there was a choice. She could stay in hospital, institutionalised until she died, or I could take her home. She stayed in hospital for two months and then I couldn't bear it. Mum and I reorganised our lives and brought her home.'

'But she will die.' He said it gently, as if he was making sure she knew, and she flushed.

'You think we don't know that? But look at her tonight. She loved it. She loves...us.'

'I guess...'

'And don't you dare bring out your "Well, if she's adopted you can't possibly love her like your own" argument to say when she dies it won't hurt,' she snapped, suddenly unable to prevent the well of bitterness left from an appalling scene five years ago. 'We couldn't possibly love her more.'

'I never said that you couldn't love an adopted child.'

'Yes, you did.'

'I just said it's different and I hold by that. It's not the same love as from birth parents and you know it.'

'As Miriam's love? No, it's not and isn't Gretta lucky that it's not?'

'Em...'

'What?' She had her hands on her hips now, glaring. He'd shocked her so much, all those years ago. She'd been totally gutted when Josh had been stillborn, devastated beyond belief. She'd curled into a tight ball of misery, she'd hardly been able to function, but when finally daylight had begun to filter through the blackness, she'd clung to what had seemed her only hope.

'Oliver, let's stop with the in-vitro stuff. It's tearing me apart—it's tearing us apart. Let's try instead for adoption.'

But his reaction had stunned her.

'Em, no.' He'd said it gently but the words had been implacable. *'I can't guarantee to love a child who's not my own. I won't do that to a child.'*

It had been a divide neither of them could cross. She had been so desperate for a child that she couldn't accept his refusal to consider adoption—and Oliver had walked away rather than concede.

'I love Gretta and so does Adrianna,' she said now, forcing herself to stay calm. Forcing herself to put the hurt of years ago on the back burner. 'So, moving on…'

'Toby?'

And mentioning her son's name was a sure way to defuse anger. Even saying his name made her smile.

'Adrianna found Toby,' she told him. 'Or rather Adrianna helped Toby find us.'

'Would you like to tell me about him?'

She'd prefer not to, actually. She was finding it disturbing on all sorts of levels to stand outside in the dusk with this man who'd once been her husband. But he had offered to take the children on Saturday, and she did need help. These last few months, with Gretta's health deteriorating, had been taking their toll on Adrianna. This Saturday would be gold for both of them, she knew, and Oliver had offered.

Therefore she had to be courteous. She had to share.

She had to stand outside with him a moment longer, even though a part of her wanted to turn around and run.

Why?

It was how he made her feel. It was the way her body was responding. He'd been her husband. She'd thought she knew this man at the deepest, most primeval level—yet here he was, standing in the dusk asking polite questions about children he knew nothing about.

Her children.

'Toby has multiple problems.' Somehow she'd pulled herself together…sort of. 'He's African, as you can probably guess. He has scoliosis of the spine; his spine was so bent he looked deformed even when he was born, and his family abandoned him. One of the poorest families in the village took him in. His pseudo-mum did the best she could for him but he hadn't been fed properly and he was already suffering from noma—a facial bacterial infection.

She walked for three days to the nearest hospital to get him help—can you imagine that? But then, of course, she had to go back to her own family. But she'd fought for him first. One of the international aid agencies took on his case and brought him over here for facial reconstruction. So far he's been through six operations. He's doing great but...'

'But you can't keep him.'

She stilled. 'Why not? The hospital social worker in charge of his case knew Adrianna and I were already fostering Gretta, and she took a chance, asking us if we'd be willing to take him on. Adrianna did all the paperwork. Mum drove this, but we both want it. Theoretically he's supposed to go home when he's been treated. We're still in touch with his African foster-mum but she's so poor and she's very happy that he stays here. So in practice we're fighting tooth and nail to keep him.'

'Em, for heaven's sake...' He sounded appalled. 'You can't look after the world's waifs and strays. There are too many.'

'I can look after the ones I love,' she threw back at him, and tilted her chin. Defiant. She knew this argument—and here it came.

'You can't love him.'

'Why not?'

'He's not your kid.'

'Then whose kid is he? The woman who bore him? The woman who walked for three days to save him but can't afford to feed him? Or Mum and me, who'll do our damnedest to keep him healthy and safe?'

'Em...' He raked his hair, a gesture she knew all too well. 'To take two kids like Gretta and Toby... A kid who'll die and a kid you might lose. They'll break your heart.'

'You just said I can't love them. You can't have it both ways, Oliver.'

'Is this what you wanted me to do? Adopt the kids the world's abandoned?'

'I don't think I expected anything of you,' she managed, and was inordinately proud of how calm she sounded. 'At the end of our marriage all I could see was what I needed. I know that sounds selfish, and maybe it is, but it's what I desperately wanted. Despite loving you I couldn't stop that wanting. You always knew I wanted a family. I'm a midwife, and I'm a midwife because watching babies come into the world is what I love most. I'd dreamed we could have our own family...'

'And when that didn't happen you walked away.'

'As I remember it, you walked.'

'Because it's not fair for me to adopt. These kids need their own parents.'

'They don't have them. Are you saying second best is worse than nothing?'

'They'll know...that they're second best.'

'Oliver, just because that happened to you...'

And she watched his face close, just like that.

He didn't talk about it, she thought. He'd never talked about it but she'd guessed.

She thought, fleetingly, of her in-laws, of Oliver's adoptive parents. But she had to think fleetingly because thinking any more made her so angry she could spit.

She only knew the bare bones but it was enough. She could infer the rest. They'd had trouble conceiving so they'd adopted Oliver. Then, five years later, they'd conceived naturally and their own son had been born.

Oliver never talked about it—never would talk about it—but she'd seen the family in action. Brett was five years younger than Oliver, a spoiled brat when Em had first met him and now an obnoxious, conceited young man who thought the world owed him a living.

But his parents thought the sun shone from him, and

it seemed to Em that they'd spent their lives comparing their two sons, finding fault with Oliver and setting Brett on a pedestal.

Even at their wedding…

'He's done very well for himself,' Em had overheard his adoptive mother tell an aunt. *'Considering where he comes from. We've done what we could, but still… I know he's managed to get himself qualified as a doctor but… His mother was a whore, you know, and we can never forget that. Thank God we have Brett.'*

It had been as much as Em could do not to front the woman and slap her. It wouldn't have been a good look on her wedding day—bride smacks mother-in-law—but she'd come awfully close. But Oliver had never talked of it.

It was only when the adoption thing had come up when Josh had died that the ghosts had come from nowhere. And she couldn't fight them, for Oliver wouldn't speak of them.

'Oliver, we're doing our best,' she told him now, gentling, reminding herself that it was his ghosts talking, not him. She knew it was his ghosts, but she'd never been allowed close enough to fight them. 'Mum and I are loving these kids to bits. We're doing all we possibly can…'

'It won't be enough.'

'Maybe it won't.' She was suddenly bone weary again. Understanding could only go so far. 'But we're trying the best that we can. We'll give these kids our hearts, and if that's not enough to let them thrive then we'll be incredibly sad but we won't be regretful. We have love to give and we're giving it. We're trying, whereas you… You lacked courage to even think about it. "No adoptions," you said, end of story. I know your background. I know how hard it was for you to be raised with Brett but your parents were dumb and cruel. The whole world doesn't have to be like that.'

'And if you ever had a child of your own?'

'You're saying I shouldn't go near Gretta or Toby because I might, conceivably, still have a child biologically?'

'I didn't mean that.' He raked his hair again, in that gesture she'd known and loved. She had a sudden urge to rake it herself, settle it, touch his face, take away the pain.

Because there was pain. She could see it. This man was torn.

But she couldn't help him if he wouldn't talk about it. To be helped you had to admit you needed help. He'd simply closed off, shut her out, and there was nothing she could do about it.

She'd moved on, but he was still hurting. She couldn't help him.

'Go home,' she said, gently again. 'I'm sorry, Oliver, I have no right to bring up the past, but neither do you have a right to question what I'm doing. Our marriage is over and we need to remember it. We need to finalise our divorce. Meanwhile, thank you for tonight, for Adrianna's birthday. I'm deeply appreciative, but if you want to pull out of Saturday's childminding, I understand.'

'I'll be here.'

'You don't need to…'

'I will be here.'

'Fine, then,' she said, and took a step back in the face of his sudden blaze of anger. 'That's good. That's great. I'll see you then.'

'I'll see you at the hospital tomorrow,' he said. 'With Ruby.'

And her heart sank. Of course. She was going to see this man, often. She needed to work with him.

She needed to ignore the pain she still saw in his eyes. She needed to tell herself, over and over, that it had nothing to do with her.

The problem was, that wasn't Em's skill. Ignoring pain.

But he didn't want her interference. He never had.

He didn't want her.

Moving on…

'Goodnight, then,' she managed, and she couldn't help herself. She touched his face with her hand and then stood on tiptoe and lightly kissed him—a feather touch, the faintest brush of lips against lips. 'Goodnight, Oliver. I'm sorry for your demons but your demons aren't mine. I give my heart for always, non-negotiable, adoption, fostering, marriage… Ollie, I can no more change myself than fly. I'm just sorry you can't share.'

And she couldn't say another word. She was suddenly so close to tears that she pushed away and would have stumbled.

Oliver's hand came out to catch her. She steadied and then brushed him off. She did it more roughly than she'd intended but she was out of her depth.

'Thank you,' she whispered, and turned away. 'Goodnight.' And she turned and fled into the house.

Oliver was left standing in the shadows, watching the lights inside the house, knowing he should leave, knowing he had to.

'I give my heart for always.'

What sort of statement was that?

She'd been talking about the kids, he told himself, but still…

She'd included marriage in the statement, and it was a statement to give a man pause.

CHAPTER SIX

EM HARDLY SAW Oliver the next day. The maternity ward was busy, and when she wasn't wanted in the birthing suites, she mostly stayed with Ruby.

The kid was so alone. Today was full of fill-in-the-blanks medical forms and last-minute checks, ready for surgery the next day. The ultrasounds, the visit and check by the anaesthetist, the constant checking and rechecking that the baby hadn't moved, that the scans that had shown the problem a week ago were correct, that they had little choice but to operate... Everything was necessary but by the end of the day Ruby was ready to get up and run.

She needed her mum, a sister, a mate, anyone, Em thought. That she was so alone was frightening. Isla dropped in for a while. Ruby was part of Isla's teen mums programme and Ruby relaxed with her, but she was Ruby's only visitor.

'Isn't there anyone I can call?' Em asked as the day wore on and Ruby grew more and more tense.

'No one'll come near me,' Ruby said tersely. 'Mum said if I didn't have an abortion she'd wash her hands of me. She said if I stayed near her I'd expect her to keep the kid and she wasn't having a thing to do with it. And she told my sisters they could stay away, too.'

'And your baby's father?'

'I told you before, the minute I told him about it, he was off. Couldn't see him for dust.'

'Oh, Ruby, there must be someone.'

'I'll be okay,' Ruby said with bravado that was patently false. 'I'll get this kid adopted and then I'll get a job in a shop or something. I just wish it was over now.'

'We all wish that.'

And it was Oliver again. He moved around the wards like a great prowling cat, Em thought crossly. He should wear a bell.

'What?' he demanded, as she turned towards him, and she thought she really had to learn to stop showing her feelings on her face.

'Knock!'

'Sorry. If I'm intruding I'll go away.'

'You might as well come in and poke me, too,' Ruby sighed. 'Everyone else has. I'm still here. Bub's still here. Why is everyone acting like we're about to go up in smoke before tomorrow? Why do I need to stay in bed?'

'Because we need your baby to stay exactly where she is,' Oliver told her, coming further into the room. He had a bag under his arm and Ruby eyed it with suspicion. 'Right now she's in the perfect position to operate on her spine, and, no, Ruby, there's not a single thing in this bag that will prod, poke or pry. But I would like to feel your baby for myself.'

Ruby sighed with a theatrical flourish and tugged up her nightie.

'Go ahead. Half the world already has.'

'Has she moved?'

'Nah.' She gave a sheepish grin. 'I feel her myself. I'm not stupid, you know.' And she popped her hand on her tummy and cradled it.

There was that gesture again. Protective. *Mine.*

Oliver sat down on the bed and felt the rounded bump

himself, and Em looked at the way he was examining the baby and thought this was a skill. Ruby had been poked and prodded until she was tired of it. Oliver was doing the same thing but very gently, as if he was cradling Ruby's unborn child.

'She's perfect,' he said at last, tugging Ruby's nightie back down. 'Like her mother.'

'She's not perfect. That's why I'm here.'

'She's pretty much perfect. Would you like to see a slide show of what we're about to do?' He grinned at Ruby's scared expression. 'There's not many gory bits and I can fast-forward through them.'

'I'll shut my eyes,' Ruby said, but he'd caught her, Em thought. She wasn't dissociated from this baby. Once again she saw Ruby's hand move surreptitiously to her tummy.

He flicked open his laptop. Fascinated, Em perched on the far side of the bed and watched, too.

'This is one we prepared earlier,' Oliver said, in the tone TV cooks used as they pulled a perfect bake from the oven. 'This is Rufus. He's six months old now, a lovely, healthy baby, but at the start of this he was still inside his mum, a twenty-two-weeker. This is the procedure your little one will have.'

The screen opened to an operating theatre, the patient's face hidden, the film obviously taken for teaching purposes as identities weren't shown. But the sound was on, and Em could hear Oliver's voice, calmly directive, and she knew that it was Oliver who was in charge.

She was fascinated—and so was Ruby. Squeamishness was forgotten. They watched in awe as the scalpel carefully, carefully negotiated the layers between the outside world and the baby within. It would be an intricate balance, Em knew, trying to give the baby minimal exposure to the outside world, keeping infection out, disturbing the baby as little as possible yet giving the surgeons space to work.

There were many doctors present—she could hear their voices. This was cutting-edge surgery.

'I can see its back,' Ruby breathed. 'Oh…is that the same as my baby?'

'They're all different,' Oliver said. 'Your daughter is tilted at a better angle.'

'Oh…' Ruby's eyes weren't leaving the screen.

They could definitely see the baby now, and they could see how the baby was slightly tilted to the side. Carefully, carefully Oliver manoeuvred him within the uterus, making no sudden movements, making sure the move was no more dramatic than if the baby himself had wriggled.

And now they could see the spine exposed. The telltale bulge…

'Is that the problem? The same as mine?' Ruby whispered, and Oliver nodded.

'Rufus's problem was slightly lower, but it's very similar.'

Silence again. They were totally focused, all of them. Oliver must have seen this many times before, Em thought—and he'd been there in person—but he was still watching it as if it was a miracle.

It was a miracle.

'This is where I step back and let the neurosurgeon take over,' Oliver said. 'My job is to take care of the whole package, you and your baby, but Dr Zigler will be doing this bit. He's the best, Ruby. You're in the best of hands.'

They watched on. The surgery was painstaking. It was like microsurgery, Em thought, where fingers were reattached, where surgeons fought hard to save nerves. And in a way it was. They were carefully working around and then through the bulge. There'd be so many things to work around. The spinal cord was so fragile, so tiny. The task was to repair the damage already done, as far as possible, and then close, protecting the cord and peripheral nerves from the amniotic fluid until the baby was born.

'Is…is it hurting?' Ruby breathed, as the first incision was made into the tiny back.

'Is *he* hurting? No. Rufus is anaesthetised, as well as his mum. Did you see the anaesthetist working as soon as we had exposure? The jury's out on whether unborn babies can feel pain. There are those who say they're in a state similar to an induced coma, but they certainly react to a painful touch. It makes the procedure a little more risky—balancing anaesthetic with what he's receiving via his mum's blood supply—but the last thing we want is to stress him. Luckily the Victoria has some of the best anaesthetists in the world. Vera Harty will be doing your anaesthetic and your daughter's. I'd trust her with a baby of my own.'

Ruby was satisfied. She went back to watching the screen.

Em watched, too, but Oliver's last statement kept reverberating.

I'd trust her with a baby of my own.

The sadness was flooding back. Oliver had been unable to have a baby of his own—because of her. She had fertility problems, not Oliver.

He'd left her years ago. He could have found someone by now.

Maybe he had. Maybe he just wasn't saying.

But he hadn't. She knew him well, this man.

There'd been an undercurrent of longing in the statement.

They'd both wanted children. She'd released him so he could have them. Why hadn't he moved on?

Watch the screen, she told herself. Some things were none of her business. Oliver was none of her business—except he was the obstetrician treating her patient.

She went back to being professional—sort of. She went back to watching Rufus, as Oliver and Ruby were doing.

The procedure was delicate and it took time but it seemed Oliver was in no hurry to finish watching, and neither was Ruby. Em couldn't be, either. Her job was to keep Ruby calm for tomorrow's operation, and that's what was happening now. The more familiar the girl was about what lay ahead, the more relaxed she'd be.

And not for the first time, Em blessed this place, this job. The Victoria considered its midwives some of the most important members of its staff. The mothers' needs came first and if a mum needed her midwife then Isla would somehow juggle the rest of her staff to cover.

Unless there was major drama Em wouldn't be interrupted now, she thought, and she wasn't. They made an intimate trio, midwife and doctor, with Ruby sandwiched between. Protected? That's what it felt like to Em, and she suspected that's how Ruby felt. Had Oliver set this up with just this goal? She glanced at him and knew her suspicion was right.

The first time she'd met him she'd been awed by his medical skills. Right now, watching him operate on screen, feeling Ruby's trust growing by the second, that awe was escalating into the stratosphere.

He might not make it as a husband, but he surely made it as a surgeon.

Back on screen, the neurosurgeon was suturing, using careful, painstakingly applied, tiny stitches, while Oliver was carefully monitoring the levels of amniotic fluid. This baby would be born already scarred, Em thought. He'd have a scar running down his lower back—but with luck that was all he'd have. Please…

'It worked a treat,' Oliver said, sounding as pleased as if the operation had happened yesterday, and on screen the neurosurgeon stood back and Oliver took over. The final stitches went in, closing the mum's uterus, making the incision across the mum's tummy as neat as the baby's. 'Rufus was born by Caesarean section at thirty-three weeks,' Oliver told them. 'He spent four weeks in hospital as a prem baby but would you like to see him now?'

'I… Yes.' Ruby sounded as if she could scarcely breathe.

'We have his parents' permission to show him to other parents facing the same procedure,' Oliver told her. 'Here goes.'

He fiddled with the computer and suddenly they were transported to a suburban backyard, to a rug thrown on a lawn, to a baby, about six months old, lying on his back in the sun, kicking his legs, admiring his toes.

There was a dog at the edge of the frame, a dopey-looking cocker spaniel. As they watched, the dog edged forward and licked the baby's toes. Rufus crowed with laughter and his toes went wild.

'He doesn't…he doesn't look like there's anything wrong with him,' Ruby breathed.

'He still has some issues he needs help with.' Oliver was matter-of-fact now, surgeon telling it like it was. 'He'll need physiotherapy to help him walk, and he might need professional help to learn how to control his bladder and bowels, but the early signs are that he'll be able to lead a perfectly normal life.'

'He looks…perfect already.' Ruby was riveted and so was Em. She was watching Ruby's face. She was watching Ruby's hand, cradling her bump. 'My little one…my little girl…she could be perfect, too?'

'I think she already is.' Oliver was smiling down at her. 'She has a great mum who's taking the best care of her. And you have the best midwife…'

Em flashed him a look of surprise. There was no need to make this personal.

But for Ruby, this was nothing but personal. 'Em says

she'll stay with me,' Ruby told him. 'At the operation and again when my baby's born. There's a chance that she can't—she says no one's ever totally sure because babies are unpredictable—but she's promised to try. I hope she can, but if she's not then she's introduced me to Sophia, or Isla will take over. But you'll look after...' Her hand cradled the bump again as she looked anxiously at Oliver. 'You'll look after us both?'

'I will.' And it was a vow.

'Tell me again why I need a Caesarean later—when my baby's born properly?'

He nodded, closed his laptop and sat back in a visitor's chair, to all appearances prepared to chat for as long as Ruby wanted. He was busy, Em knew. As well as the promises he'd made her to childmind on Saturday, she knew he already had a full caseload of patients. But right now Ruby was being given the impression that he had all the time in the world, and that time was Ruby's.

He was...gorgeous. She knew it, she'd always known it, but suddenly the thought almost blindsided her.

And it was more than him being gorgeous, she thought, feeling dazed. She was remembering why she'd loved this man.

And she was thinking—idiotically—that she loved him still.

Concentrate on medicine, on your patient, on anything other than Oliver, she told herself fiercely. Concentrating on Oliver was just too scary.

What had Ruby asked? Why she needed a Caesarean?

'You see the incision we just cut in Rufus's mum's uterus?' Oliver was saying, flicking back to the screen, where they could see the now closed incision in the abdomen. 'I've stitched it with care, as I'll stitch you with care, but when your bub comes out, she'll push. You have no idea how hard a baby can push. She wants to get out to meet you, and nothing's going to stop her. So maybe she'll push against that scar, and if she pushes hard enough on very new scar tissue she might cause you to bleed. I have two people I care about, Ruby. I care about your daughter but my absolute priority is to keep you safe. That means a Caesarean birth, because, much as I want to meet your baby, we'll need to deliver her before she even thinks about pushing.'

'But if you wanted to keep me really safe you wouldn't operate in the first place,' Ruby muttered, a trace of the old resentment resurfacing. But it didn't mess with Oliver's composure.

'That's right,' he agreed, his tone not changing. 'I believe we *will* keep you safe but there are risks. They're minor but they're real. That's why it's your choice. You can still pull out. Right up to the time we give you the anaesthetic, you can pull out, and no one will think the worse of you. That's your right.'

The room fell silent. It was such a hard decision to make, Em thought, and once again she thought, Where was this kid's mum?

But, surprisingly, when Ruby spoke again it seemed that worry about the operation was being supplanted by something deeper.

'If I had her...' Ruby said, and then amended her statement. '*When* I have her...after she's born, she'll have a scar, too.'

'She will,' Oliver told her, as watchful as Em, waiting to know where Ruby was going with this.

'And she'll have it for ever?'

'Yes.'

'She might hate it—as a teenager,' Ruby whispered. 'I know I would.'

'I'll do my best to make it as inconspicuous as possible—and cosmetic touch-ups when she's older might help even more. It shouldn't be obvious.'

'But teenagers freak out about stuff like that. I know I would,' Ruby whispered. 'And she won't have a mum to tell her it's okay.'

'If she's adopted, she'll have a mum,' Em ventured. 'Ruby, we've gone through what happens. Adoption is your choice all the way. You'll get to meet the adoptive parents. You'll know she goes to parents who'll love her.'

'But...I'll love her more. She's *my* baby.'

And suddenly Ruby was crying, great fat tears slipping down her face, and Em shifted so she could take her into her arms. And as she did so, Oliver's laptop slid off the bed and landed with a crash on the floor.

Uh-oh. But Em didn't move. For now she couldn't afford to think of computers. For now holding this girl was the most important thing in the world.

But still... A car and then a laptop...

She was starting to be an expensive ex-wife, she thought ruefully, and she almost smiled—but, of course, she didn't. She simply held Ruby until the sobs receded, until Ruby tugged away and grabbed a handful of tissues. That was a bit late. Em's shoulder was soaked, but who cared? How many times had Em ever finished a shift clean? She could count them on one hand. She always got her hands dirty, one way or another.

And it seemed, so did Oliver, for he was still there. Most consultants would have fled at the first sign of tears, Em thought. As a breed, surgeons weren't known for their empathy.

He'd risen, but he was standing by the door, watching, and there was definitely sympathy. Definitely caring.

He was holding the two halves of his laptop. The screen had completely split from the keyboard. And the screen itself...smashed.

'Whoops,' she said, as Ruby blew her nose.

He glanced down at the ruined machine. 'As you say, whoops.'

And as Ruby realised what he was holding, the teenager choked on something that was almost a laugh. 'Em's smashed your computer,' she said, awed. 'Do you mind?'

'I can't afford to mind.'

'Why not?' She was caught, pulled out of her misery by a smashed computer.

'Priorities,' he said. 'You. Baby. Computer. In that order.'

'What about Em?' she asked, a touch of cheekiness emerging. 'Is she a priority?'

'Don't you dare answer,' Em told him. 'Not until you've checked that your computer is covered by insurance. Ruby, if you're rethinking your plans to adopt…'

'I think…I might be.'

'Then let's not make any decisions yet,' she said, hurriedly. Surely now wasn't the time to make such an emotional decision? 'Let's get this operation over with first.'

Ruby took a deep breath and looked from Oliver to Emily and back again. 'Maybe I do need a bit of time,' she conceded. 'Maybe a sleep…time to think.'

'Of course you do.' She pulled up her covers and tucked her in. 'Ruby, nothing's urgent. No decisions need to be made now. Just sleep.'

'Thank you. And, Dr Evans…'

'Mmm?' Oliver was about to leave but turned back.

'I hope your computer's all right.'

'It will be,' he said. But it wouldn't. Em could see the smashed screen from where she stood. 'But even if it's not, it's not your problem,' he said, gently now, almost as a blessing. 'From here on, Ruby, we don't want you to worry about a thing. You've put yourself in our hands and we'll keep you safe. Em and I are a great team. You and your baby are safe with us.'

His lovely, gentle bedside manner lasted until they were ten feet from Ruby's door. Em closed the door behind her, looked ahead—and Oliver was staring straight at her. Vibrating with anger.

'You're planning on talking her out of keeping her baby?'

The turnabout from empathy to anger was shocking. The gentleness had completely gone from his voice. What she saw now was fury.

She faced him directly, puzzled. 'What are you saying? I didn't. I'm not.'

'You are. She'd decided on adoption but now she's changing her mind. But you stopped her.'

'I didn't stop her. I'd never do that.' She thought back to the scene she'd just left, trying to replay her words. 'I just said she had time…'

'You told her not to make a decision now. Why not? Right now she's thinking of keeping her baby. You don't think it's important to encourage her?'

'I don't think it's my right to direct her one way or another.' She felt herself getting angry in response. 'All I saw in there was a frightened, tired kid who's facing major surgery tomorrow. Who needs to stay calm and focused. Who doesn't need to be making life-changing decisions right now. She's already decided enough.'

'But maybe when you're emotional, that's the time to make the decision. When she knows she loves her baby.'

'She'll always love her baby.' Em was struggling to stay calm in the face of his anger—in the face of his accusation? 'Ruby is a seventeen-year-old, terrified kid with no family support at all. If she decides to keep this baby, it'll change her life for ever. As it will if she gives it up for adoption. What I did in there—and, yes, I interceded—was give her space. If she wants to keep her baby, she'll need every ounce of strength and then some.'

'She'll get support.'

'And she can never be a kid again. But, then, after this, maybe being a kid is no longer an option. But I agree, that's none of my business. Oliver, is this discussion going anywhere? I've been away from the birthing suites for over an hour and I don't know what's going on. I may well be needed.'

'You won't influence her?'

'Why would I influence her?'

'Because you believe in adoption.'

'And you don't? Because of what happened to you when you were a kid?' Anger was washing over her now. Yes, she should get back to the birthing suites but what was it he was accusing her of? 'Get over it, Oliver. Move on. Not every adoptive mother is like yours, and not every birth mother is capable of loving. There's a whole lot of grey in between the black and white, and it's about time you saw it.'

'So you won't encourage her to adopt?'

'What are you expecting me to do?' She was confused now, as well as angry. She put her hands on her hips and glared. 'Are you thinking I might pop in there, offer to adopt it myself and get myself another baby? Is that what you're thinking?'

'I would never—'

'You'd better not. A midwife influencing a mother's decision is totally unethical. How much more so is a midwife offering to adopt? I'll do neither. I have my kids, Oliver, and I love them to bits. I have no wish for more.'

'But Gretta's going to die.'

Why had he said it? It had just come out, and he could

have bitten his tongue from his head. Em's face bleached white and she leaned back against the wall for support.

Dear heaven… What sort of emotional drop kick was he? Suggesting one kid was going to die so she was lining up for another? Where had the thought come from?

It was confusion, he thought. Maybe it was even anger that she'd got on with her life without him.

Or maybe it was sheer power of testosterone washing through him—because the woman who should be his wife was looking at him as if he was a piece of dirt.

Where to start with apologies? He'd better haul himself back under control, and fast. 'Hell, Em, I'm sorry. I didn't mean that the way it came out, truly.' He reached out and touched her stricken face, and the way he felt… sick didn't begin to describe it. 'Can you forget I said it? Of all the insensitive oafs…I know Gretta's health has nothing to do with…anything. I'm so sorry. Can you wipe it? I know you love Gretta…'

'Are you talking about Emily's little girl?'

They both turned to face the newcomer, and it was a relief to turn away from each other. The tension between them was so tight it was threatening to break, to fly back and hit both of them.

Oliver recognised the young man heading towards them. Oliver had been introduced to Noah Jackson earlier in the week. He was a surgical registrar, almost at the end of his training. 'Technically brilliant,' Tristan, the paediatric cardiologist, had told him. 'But his people skills leave a whole lot to be desired.'

And now he proceeded to display just that.

'Hi, Em,' he called, walking up to them with breezy insouciance. 'Are you discussing Gretta's progress? How's she going?'

'She's…okay,' Em said, and by the way she said it Oliver knew there was baggage behind the question.

'You ought to meet Gretta,' Noah told Oliver, seemingly oblivious to the way Em's face had shuttered. 'She's worth a look. She has Down's, with atrioventricular septal defects, massive heart problems, so much deformity that even Tristan felt he couldn't treat her. Yet she's survived. I've collated her case notes from birth as part of my final-year research work. I'd love to write her up for the med journals. It'd give me a great publication. Em's care has been nothing short of heroic.'

'I've met her,' Oliver said shortly, glancing again at Em. Gretta—a research project? He could see Em's distress. 'Now's not...' he started.

But the young almost-surgeon wouldn't be stopped. 'Gretta wasn't expected to live for more than a year,' he said, with enthusiasm that wouldn't be interrupted. 'It'll make a brilliant article—the extent of the damage, the moral dilemma facing her birth mother, her decision to walk away—Em's decision to intervene and now the medical resources and the effort to keep her alive this far. Em, please agree to publication. You still haven't signed. But Tristan says she's pretty close to the end. If I could examine her one last time...'

And Oliver saw the wash of anger and revulsion on Em's face—and finally he moved.

He put his body between the registrar and Em. Noah was tall but right now Oliver felt a good foot taller. Anger did that. Of all the insensitive...

'You come near Em again with your requests for information about her daughter—her *daughter*, Noah, not her patient—and I'll ram every page of your case notes down your throat. Don't you realise that Em loves Gretta? Don't you realize she's breaking in two, and you're treating her daughter like a bug under a microscope?'

'Hey, Em's a medical colleague,' Noah said, still not

getting it. 'She knows the score—she knew it when she took Gretta home. She can be professional.'

'Is that what you're being—professional?'

'If we can learn anything from this, then, yes...'

Enough. Em looked close to fainting.

The lift was open behind them. Oliver grabbed Noah by the collar of his white jacket, twisted him round and practically kicked him into the lift.

'What...?' Noah seemed speechless. 'What did I say?'

'You might be nearing the end of your surgical training,' Oliver snapped. 'But you sure aren't at the end of your training to be a decent doctor. You need to learn some people skills, fast. I assume you did a term in family medicine during your general training, but whether you did or not, you're about to do another. And another after that if you still don't get it. I want you hands-on, treating people at the coal face, before you're ever in charge of patients in a surgical setting.'

'You don't have that authority.' The young doctor even had the temerity to sound smug.

'You can believe that,' Oliver growled. 'You're welcome—for all the good it'll do you. Now get out of here while I see if I can fix the mess you've made.'

'I haven't made a mess.'

'Oh, yes, you have,' Oliver snapped, hitting the 'Close' button on the lift with as much force as he'd like to use on Noah. 'And you've messed with someone who spends her life trying to fix messes. Get out of my sight.'

The lift closed. Oliver turned back to Em. She hadn't moved. She was still slumped on the wall, her face devoid of colour. A couple of tears were tracking down her face.

'It's okay,' she managed. 'Oliver, it's okay. He's just saying it like it is.'

'He has no right to say anything at all,' Oliver snapped,

and he couldn't help himself. She was so bereft. She was so gutted.

She was…his wife?

She wasn't. Their long separation to all intents and purposes constituted a divorce, but right now that was irrelevant.

His Em was in trouble. *His Em.*

He walked forward and took her into his arms.

She shouldn't let him hold her. She had no right to be in his arms.

She had no right to want to be in his arms.

Besides, his words had upset her as much as Noah's had. His implication that she could replace Gretta…

But she knew this man. She'd figured it out—the hurt he'd gone through as a kid, the rejection, the knowledge that he'd been replaced by his adoptive parents' 'real' son.

Noah was just plain insensitive. He was arrogant and intelligent but he was lacking emotional depth. Oliver's comments came from a deep, long-ago hurt that had never been resolved.

And even if it hadn't, she thought helplessly, even if he was as insensitive as Noah, even if she shouldn't have anything to do with him, for now she wanted to be here.

To be held. By her husband.

For he still felt like her husband. They'd been married for five years. They'd lain in each other's arms for five years.

For five years she'd thought she had the perfect marriage.

But she hadn't. Of course she hadn't. There had been ghosts she'd been unable to expunge, and those ghosts were with him still. He couldn't see…

Stop thinking, she told herself fiercely, almost desperately. Stop thinking and just be. Just let his arms hold me. Just feel his heart beat against mine. Just pretend…

'Em, I'm sorry,' he whispered into her hair.

'For?'

'For what I said. Even before Noah, you were hurt. I can't begin to think how I could have said such a thing.'

'It doesn't matter.' But it did. It was the crux of what had driven them apart. For Oliver, adoption was simply a transaction. Hearts couldn't be held…

As theirs hadn't. Their marriage was over.

But still she held. Still she took comfort, where she had no right to take comfort. They'd been separated for five years!

So why did he still feel like…home? Why did everything about him feel as if here was her place in the world?

'Hey!' A hospital corridor was hardly the place to hold one's ex-husband—to hold anyone. It was busy and bustling and their sliver of intimacy couldn't last.

It was Isla, hurrying along the corridor, smiling—as Isla mostly smiled right now. The sapphire on her finger seemed to have changed Em's boss's personality. 'You know I'm all for romance,' she said as she approached. 'But the corridor's not the place.' She glanced down at the sapphire on her finger and her smile widened. 'Alessi and I find the tea room's useful. No one's in there right now…'

'Oh, Isla…' Em broke away, flushing. 'Sorry. It's not… Dr Evans was just…just…'

But Isla had reached them now and was seeing Em's distress for herself. 'Nothing's wrong with Ruby, is there?' she asked sharply.

'No.' Oliver didn't break his composure. 'But you have a problem with Dr Noah Jackson. He seems to think Em's Gretta is a research experiment.'

'Noah's been upsetting my midwife?' Isla's concern switched to anger, just like that. 'Let me at him.'

'I don't think there's any need,' Em managed. 'Oliver practically threw him into the lift.'

'Well, good for you,' Isla said, smiling again. 'I do like an obstetrician who knows when to act, and one who knows the value of a good cuddle is worth his weight in gold.' She glanced again at her ring. 'I should know. But, Em, love, if you've finished being cuddled, I would like you back in the birthing suite.'

'Of course,' Em said, and fled.

There was a moment's silence. Then…

'Don't you mess with my midwives,' Isla said, and Oliver looked at her and thought she saw a whole lot more than she let on.

'I won't.'

She eyed him some more. 'You two have baggage? Your name's the same.'

'We don't have…baggage.'

'I don't believe it.' She was still thoughtful. 'But I'll let it lie. All I'll say is to repeat—don't mess with my midwives.'

Thursday night was blessedly uneventful. Gretta seemed to have settled. Em should have had a good night's sleep.

She didn't but the fact that she stared into the dark and thought of Oliver was no fault of…anyone.

Oliver was no business of hers.

But he'd held her and he felt all her business.

Oliver…

Why had he come here to work? Of all the unlucky coincidences…

But it wasn't a simple coincidence, she conceded. The Victoria had one of Australia's busiest birthing units. It was also right near her mother's home so it had made sense that she get a job here after the loss of Josh.

And after the loss of Oliver.

Don't go there, she told herself. Think of practicalities.

It made sense that Oliver was back here, she told herself. Charles Delamere head-hunted the best, and he'd have known Oliver had links to Melbourne.

So she should leave?

Leave the Victoria? Because Oliver had…cuddled her?

It's not going to happen again, she told herself fiercely. And I won't leave because of him. There's no need to leave.

He could be a friend. Like Isla. Like Sophia.

Yeah, right, she told herself, punching her pillow in frustration. Oliver Evans, just a friend?

Not in a million years.

But she had no choice. She could do this. Bring on tomorrow, she told herself.

Bring on a way she could treat Oliver as a medical colleague and nothing else.

CHAPTER SEVEN

FRIDAY. EM'S DAY was cleared so she could focus on Ruby. Isla was aware of the situation. 'If she really has no one, then you'd better be with her all the way.'

So she stayed with Ruby in the hour before she was taken to Theatre. She spent their time discussing—of all things—Ruby's passion for sewing. Ruby had shyly shown her her handiwork the day before, so Em had brought in one of Toby's sweaters. Ruby was showing her how to darn a hole in the elbow.

'Darning's a dying art,' she'd told Em, so Em had found the sweater and brought a darning mushroom—Adrianna had one her grandmother had used!—and needle and thread and asked for help.

Ruby took exquisite care with the intricate patch. When she was finished Em could scarcely see where the hole had been, and darning and the concentration involved worked a charm. When the orderlies came to take Ruby to Theatre, Ruby was shocked that the time had already arrived.

She squeezed Em's hand. 'Th-thank you. Will I see you later?'

'I'm coming with you,' Em declared, packing up the darning equipment. 'Isla's told me if I'm to help deliver your baby at term then I should introduce myself to her now. So I'm to stay in the background, not faint, and admire Dr Evans's handiwork.'

'You'd never faint.'

'Don't you believe it,' Em told her, and proceeded to give her some fairly gross examples. She kept right up with the narrative while Ruby was pushed through to Theatre, while pre-meds were given, while they waited for the theatre to be readied. Finally, as Ruby was wheeled into Theatre, they were both giggling.

Oliver was waiting, gowned and ready. So, it seemed, was a cast of thousands. This was surgery at its most cutting edge. They were operating on two patients, not one, but one of those patients was a foetus that was not yet viable outside her mother. The logistics were mind-bending and it would take the combined skills of the Victoria's finest to see it succeed.

Shock to the foetus could cause abortion. Therefore the anaesthetic had to be just right—they had not only the Victoria's top anaesthetist, but also the anaesthetic registrar. Heinz Zigler was gowned and ready. Tristan Hamilton, paediatric cardiologist, was there to check on the baby's heart every step of the way. There were so many possible complications.

The surgery itself was demanding but everything else had to be perfect, as well. If amniotic fluid was lost it had to be replaced. If the baby bled, that blood had to be replaced, swiftly but so smoothly the loss couldn't be noticed. Everything had to be done with an eye to keeping the trauma to the baby at the absolute minimum.

'Hey, Ruby.' Oliver welcomed the girl warmly as she was wheeled in, and if he was tense he certainly wasn't showing it. 'What's funny?'

'Em's been telling me—' Ruby was almost asleep from the pre-meds but she was still smiling '—about muddles. About her work.'

'Did she tell you about the time she helped deliver twins and the team messed up their bracelets?' Oliver was smiling with his patient, but he found a chance to glance—and smile—at Em. 'So Mathew Riley was wrapped in a pink rug and Amanda Riley was wrapped in a blue rug. It could have scarred them for life.'

Em thought back all those years. She'd just qualified, and it had been one of the first prem births where she'd been midwife in charge. Twins, a complex delivery, and the number of people in the birthing room had made her flustered. Afterwards Oliver had come to the prem nursery to check on his handiwork. The nurse in charge—a dragon of a woman who shot first and asked questions later— had been in the background, as Oliver had unwrapped the blue bundle.

Em had been by his side. She'd gasped and lost colour but Oliver hadn't said a word; hadn't given away by the slightest intake of breath that he'd become aware she'd made a blunder that could have put her job at risk. But the mistake was obvious—the incubators had been brought straight from the birthing suite and were side by side. There was no question who each baby was. Without saying a word, somehow Oliver helped her swap blankets and wristbands and the charge nurse was unaware to this day.

That one action had left her…smitten.

But it hadn't just been his action, she conceded. It had also been the way he'd smiled at her, and then as she'd tried to thank him afterwards, it had been the way he'd laughed it off and told her about dumb things he'd done as a student…and then asked her to have dinner with him…

'I reckon I might like to be a nurse,' Ruby said sleepily. 'You reckon I might?'

'I reckon you're awesome,' Oliver told her. 'I reckon you can do anything you want.'

And then Ruby's eyes flickered closed. The chief

anaesthetist gave Oliver a nod—and the operation was under way.

Lightness was put aside.

Oliver had outlined the risks to Ruby—and there were risks. Exposing this tiny baby to the outside world when she was nowhere near ready for birth was so dangerous. Em had no idea how many times it had been done in the past, how successful it had been, but all she knew as she watched was that if it was her baby there was no one she'd rather have behind the scalpel than Oliver.

He was working side by side with Heinz. They were talking through the procedure together, glancing up every so often at the scans on the screens above their heads, checking positions. They wanted no more of the baby exposed than absolutely necessary.

Another screen showed what they were doing. To Em in the background she could see little of the procedural site but this was being recorded—to be used as Rufus's operation had been—to reassure another frantic mum?

Please let it have the same result, she pleaded. She was acting as gofer, moving equipment back and forth within reach of the theatre nurse as needed, but she still had plenty of time to watch the screen.

And then the final incision was made. Gently, gently, the baby was rotated within the uterus—and she could see the bulge that was the unsealed spine.

There was a momentary pause as everyone saw it. A collective intake of breath.

'The poor little tacker,' Tristan breathed. 'To be born like that…she'd have had no chance of living a normal life.'

'Then let's see if we can fix it,' Oliver said in a voice Em had never heard before. And she knew that every nerve was on edge, every last ounce of his skill and Heinz's were at play here.

Please…

The complexity, the minuscule size, the need for accuracy, it was astounding.

Oliver was sweating. Not only was the intensity of his work mind-blowing, but the theatre itself had to be set at a high enough temperature to stop foetal shock.

'Em.' Chris, the chief theatre nurse, called back to her. 'Take over the swabs.'

All hands were needed. Em saw where she, too, was needed. She moved seamlessly into position and acted to stop Oliver's sweat obscuring his vision.

He wasn't aware of her. He wasn't aware of anything.

They were using cameras to blow up the images of the area he and Heinz were working on. Every person there was totally focused on the job or on the screens. Two people at once—two hearts, two lives...

She forgot to breathe. She forgot everything but keeping Oliver's vision clear so he could do what had to be a miracle.

And finally they were closing. Oliver was stitching—maybe his hands were steadier than Heinz's because he was working under instruction. He was inserting what seemed almost microstitches, carefully, carefully manoeuvring the spinal wound closed. Covering the spinal cord and the peripheral nerves. Stopping future damage.

The spine was closed. They were replacing the amniotic fluid. Oliver was closing the uterus, conferring with Heinz, seemingly relaxing a little.

The outer wound was being closed.

The thing was done.

Emily felt like sagging.

She wouldn't. She wiped Oliver's forehead for the final time and at last he had space to turn and give her a smile. To give the whole team a smile. But his smile ended with Em.

'We've done it,' he said with quiet triumph. 'As long as

we can keep her on board for another few weeks, we've saved your baby.'

'Your baby'...

Where had that come from?

And then she thought back to the teasing he'd given her when they'd first met, when they'd been working together, she as a brand-new nurse, he as a paediatric surgeon still in training.

'Em, the way you expose your heart... You seem to greet every baby you help deliver as if it's your own,' he'd told her. 'By the end of your career, you'll be like Old Mother Hubbard—or the Pied Piper of Hamelin. Kids everywhere.'

And wouldn't she just love that! She thought fleetingly of the two she was allowed to love. Gretta and Toby.

She did love them, fiercely, wonderfully, but she looked down at Ruby now and she knew that she had love to spare. Heart on her sleeve or not, she loved this teenage mum, and she loved the little life that was now securely tucked back inside her.

The heart swelled to fit all comers...

She thought back to Oliver's appalling adoptive mother and she thought he'd never known that.

He still didn't know it and they'd gone their separate ways because of it.

She stood back from the table. Her work there was done. She'd wait for Ruby in the recovery ward.

The team had another patient waiting for surgery. Oliver was moving on.

Em already had moved on. She just had to keep moving.

'Well done.' Out at the sinks the mood was one of quiet but deep satisfaction. There'd be no high fives, not yet—everyone knew the next few days would be critical—but the procedure had gone so smoothly surely they'd avoided embryo shock.

Tristan hitched himself up on the sinks and regarded his friend with satisfaction. He and Oliver had done their general surgical training together. They'd split as Oliver had headed into specialist surgical obstetrics and Tristan into paediatric cardiology, but their friendship was deep and longstanding.

Tristan alone knew the association between Em and Oliver. They'd had one heated discussion about it already...

'The hospital grapevine will find out. Why keep it secret?'

'It's not a secret. It's just a long time ago. Moving on...'

But now...

'Are you telling me you and Em have really moved on?' Tristan demanded as he watched his friend ditch his theatre garb. 'Because, sure, Em's your patient's midwife and she was in Theatre as an observer in that capacity, but the contact you and she had... You might not have been aware how often you flicked her a glance but every time you were about to start something risky, it was like you were looking to her for strength.'

'What the...?' Where had this come from? As if he needed Em for strength? He'd been operating without Em for years.

He'd never depended on her.

'You might say it's in the past,' Tristan went on, inexorably. 'But she's still using your name, and as of today, as an onlooker, it seems to me that the marriage isn't completely over.'

'Will you keep your voice down?' There were nurses and orderlies everywhere.

'You think you can keep this to yourself?'

'It's not obvious.'

'It's obvious,' Tristan said, grinning. 'Midwife Evans and Surgeon Evans. Sparks. The grapevine will go nuts.'

'You're not helping.'

'I'm just observing.' Tristan pushed down from the bench. He and Oliver both had patients waiting. Always there were patients waiting.

'All I'm saying is that I'm interested,' Tristan said, heading for the door. 'Me and the rest of staff of the Victoria. And some of us are even more interested than others.'

Trained theatre staff were rostered to watch over patients in Recovery, but Isla had cleared the way for Em to stay with Ruby. With no family support, the need to keep Ruby calm was paramount. So Em sat by her bedside and watched. Ruby was drifting lightly towards consciousness, seeming to ease from sedation to natural sleep.

Which might have something to do with the way Em was holding her hand and talking to her.

'It's great, Ruby. You were awesome. Your baby was awesome. It's done, all fixed. Your baby will have the best of chances because of your decision.'

She doubted Ruby could hear her but she said it anyway, over and over, until she was interrupted.

'Hey.' She looked up and Sophia was watching her. Sophia was a partnering midwife, a friend, a woman who had the same fertility issues she did. If there was anyone in this huge staff she was close to, it was Sophia. 'Isla sent me down to see how the op went,' she said, pulling up a chair to sit beside Em. 'All's quiet on the Western Front. We had three nice, normal babies in quick succession this morning and not a sniff of a contraction this arvo. Isla says you can stay here as needed; take as long as you want.'

'We're happy, aren't we, Ruby?' Em said gently, squeezing Ruby's hand, but there was no response. Ruby's natural sleep had grown deeper. 'The operation went brilliantly.'

And then, because she couldn't help herself, she added a rider. 'Oliver was brilliant.'

'Yeah, I'd like to talk to you about that,' Sophia said, diffidently now, assessing Ruby as she spoke and realising, as Em had, that there was little chance of Ruby taking in anything she said. 'Rumours are flying. Someone heard Tristan and Oliver talking at the sinks. Evans and Evans. No one's put them together until now. It's a common name. But…Evans isn't your maiden name, is it? Evans is your married name. And according to the rumours, that marriage would be between you and Oliver.'

Whoa. Em flinched. But then…it had to come out sooner or later, she thought. She might as well grit her teeth and confess.

'It was a long time ago,' she murmured. 'We split five years ago but changing my name didn't seem worth the complications. I was Emily Green before. I kind of like Emily Evans better.' She didn't want to say that going to a lawyer, asking for a divorce, had seemed…impossibly final.

'As you kind of like Oliver Evans?' Sophia wiggled down further in her chair, her eyes alight with interest. 'The theatre staff say there were all sorts of sparks between you during the op.'

'Ruby's in my care. Oliver was…keeping me reassured.' But she'd said it too fast, too defensively, and Sophia's eyebrows were hiking.

Drat hospitals and their grapevines, she thought. Actually, they were more than grapevines—they were like Jack's beanstalk. Let one tiny bean out of the can and it exploded to the heavens.

What had Oliver and Tristan been talking about to start this?

And…how was she to stop Sophia's eyebrows hitting the roof?

'You going to tell Aunty Sophia?' she demanded, settling down further in a manner that suggested she was going nowhere until Em did.

'You knew I was married.'

'Yeah, but not to Oliver. Oliver! Em, he's a hunk. And he's already getting a reputation for being one of those rarest of species—a surgeon who can talk to his patients. Honest, Em, he smiled at one of my mums on the ward this morning and my heart flipped. Why on earth…?'

'A smile doesn't make a marriage.' But it did, Em thought miserably. She'd loved that smile. What they'd had…

'So will you tell Aunty Sophia why you split?'

'Kids,' she said brusquely. She'd told Sophia she was infertile but only when Sophia had told her of her own problems. She hadn't elaborated.

'He left you because you couldn't have babies?'

'We…well, I already told you we went through IVF. Cycle upon cycle. What I didn't tell you was that finally I got pregnant. Josh was delivered stillborn at twenty-eight weeks.'

'Oh, Em…' Sophia stared at her in horror. 'You've kept that to yourself, all this time?'

'I don't…talk about it. It hurts.'

'Yeah, well, I can see that,' Sophia said, hopping up to give her friend a resounding hug. 'They say IVF can destroy a marriage—it's so hard. It split you up?'

'The IVF didn't.' Em was remembering the weeks after she'd lost Josh, how close she and Oliver had been, a couple gutted but totally united in their grief. If it hadn't been for Oliver then, she might have gone crazy.

Which had made what had come next even more devastating.

'So what…?'

'I couldn't…do IVF any more,' Em whispered.

Silence.

Ruby seemed soundly asleep. She was still holding the girl's hand. She could feel the strength of Ruby's heartbeat, and the monitors around her told her Ruby's baby was doing fine, as well. The world went on, she thought bleakly, remembering coming out of hospital after losing Josh, seeing all those mums, all those babies...

'Earth to Em,' Sophia said gently at last, and Em hauled herself together and gave her a bleak little smile.

'I wanted a family,' she whispered. 'I think...I was a bit manic after the loss but I was suddenly desperate. Maybe it was an obsession, I don't know, but I told Oliver I wanted to adopt, whatever the cost. And in the end, the cost was him.'

'He didn't want to adopt?'

'He's adopted himself. It wasn't happy, and he wouldn't concede there was another side. He wouldn't risk adoption because he didn't think he could love an adopted kid. And I wasn't prepared to give, either. We were two implacable forces, and there was nowhere to go but to turn away from each other. So there you have it, Sophia. No baby, no marriage. Can I ask you not to talk about it?'

'You don't have to ask,' Sophia said roundly. 'Of course I won't. But this hospital...the walls have ears and what it doesn't know it makes up. Now everyone knows you were married...'

'It'll be a one-day wonder,' Em told her, and then Ruby stirred faintly and her eyes flickered open.

'Well, hi,' Em said, her attention totally now on Ruby. 'Welcome to the other side, Ruby, love. The operation was a complete success. Now all we need to do is let you sleep and let your baby sleep until we're sure you're settled into nice, normal pregnancy again.'

CHAPTER EIGHT

SATURDAY.

Oliver did a morning ward round, walked into Ruby's room—and found Em there.

According to his calculations—and he'd made a few—Em should be off duty. Why was she sitting by Ruby's bedside?

She was darning…a sock?

Both women looked up as he walked in and both women smiled.

'Hey,' Ruby said. 'Is it true? Were you two married?'

'How…?' Em gasped.

'I just heard,' Ruby said blithely. 'It's true, isn't it?'

Em bundled up her needlework and rose—fast. 'Yes,' she managed. 'But it was a long time ago. Sorry, Oliver, I'll be out of your way.'

'Why are you here?' Damn, that had sounded accusatory and he hadn't meant to be.

'I'm off duty but Ruby's teaching me how to darn.'

'That's…important?'

'It is, as a matter of fact,' she said, tossing him a look that might well be described as a glower. And also a warning to keep things light. 'The whole world seems to toss socks away as soon as they get holes. Ruby and I are doing our bit to prevent landfill.'

'Good for you.' He still sounded stiff but he couldn't help it. 'Are you going home now?'

'Yes.'

'So why did you two split?' Ruby was under orders for complete bed rest but she was recovering fast, the bed rest was more for her baby's sake than for hers, and she was obviously aching for diversion.

'Incompatibility,' Em said, trying for lightness, stooping to give Ruby a swift kiss. 'He used to pinch all the bed-covers. He's a huncher—you know the type? He hunches all the covers round him and then rolls in his sleep. I even tried pinning the covers to my side of the bed but I was left with ripped covers and a doomed marriage. I'll pop in to-morrow, Ruby, but meanwhile is there anything you need?'

'More socks?' Ruby said shyly, and Em grinned.

'Ask Dr Evans. I'll bet he has a drawer full. I need to go, Ruby, love. Byee.'

And she was gone.

It had been an informal visit. She'd been wearing jeans and a colourful shirt and her hair was down. She had so much to do at home—he knew she did.

Why was she here on a day off?

Because she cared?

She couldn't stop caring. That had been one of the things he'd loved about her.

He still loved?

'You're still dotty about her,' Ruby said, and he realised he'd been staring at the corridor where she'd disappeared.

'Um…no. Just thinking I've never walked in on a darn-ing lesson before. How's bub?'

'Still kicking.'

'Not too hard?'

'N-no.' And once again he copped that zing of fear.

This was why Em had 'popped in', he thought. This kid was far too alone.

That was Em. She carried her heart on her sleeve.

If it was up to Em they would have adopted, he thought, and, despite the things he'd said to her after Josh had died, he was beginning to accept she was capable of it. *It?* Of loving a child who wasn't her own. The way she'd held Gretta... The way she'd laughed at Toby... Okay, Em was as different from his adoptive mother as it was possible to be, and it had been cruel of him to suggest otherwise.

It had taken him a huge leap of faith to accept that he'd loved Em. Even though he'd supported her through IVF, even though he'd been overjoyed when she'd finally conceived, when Josh had died...

Had a small part of him been relieved? Had a part of him thought he could never extend his heart to all comers?

He would have loved Josh. He did. The morning when they'd sat looking down at the promise that had been their little son had been one of the worst of his life. But the pain that had gone with it...the pain of watching Em's face...

And then for Em to say let's adopt, let's put ourselves up for this kind of pain again for a child he didn't know...

'Let's check your tummy,' he told Ruby, but she was still watching him.

'You are still sweet on her.'

'She's an amazing woman. But as she said, I'm a huncher.'

'Is it because you couldn't have children?'

How...? 'No!'

'It's just, one of the nurses told me Em's got two foster-kids she looks after with her mum. If you and she were married, why didn't you have your own?'

'Ruby, I think you have quite enough to think about with your own baby, without worrying about other people's,' he said, mock sternly.

'You're saying butt out?'

'And let me examine you. Yes.'

'Yes, Doctor,' she said, mock meekly, but she managed the beginnings of a cheeky grin. 'But you can't tell me to butt out completely. It seemed no one in this hospital knew you guys have been married. So now everyone in this hospital is really, really interested. Me, too.'

After that he was really ambivalent about the babysitting he'd promised. Actually, he'd been pretty ambivalent in the first place. Work was zooming to speed with an intensity that was staggering. He could easily ring and say he was needed at the hospital and it wouldn't have been a lie.

But he'd promised, so he put his head down and worked and by a quarter to one he was pulling up outside the place Em called home.

Em was in the front yard, holding Toby on a push-along tricycle. When she saw him she swung Toby up into her arms and waved.

Toby hesitated a moment—and then waved, too.

The sight took him aback. He paused before getting out of the car. He knew Em was waiting for him, but he needed a pause to catch his breath.

This was the dream. They'd gone into their marriage expecting this—love, togetherness, family.

He'd walked away so that Em could still have it. The fact that she'd chosen to do it alone…

But she wasn't alone. She had her mum. She had Mike next door and his brood. She had great friends at the hospital.

The only one missing from the picture was him, and the decision to walk away had been his.

If he'd stayed, though, they wouldn't have had any of this. They'd be a professional couple, absorbed in their work and their social life.

How selfish was that? The certainties of five years ago were starting to seem just a little bit wobbly.

'Hey, are you stuck to the seat?' Em was carrying Toby towards him, laughing at him. She looked younger today, he thought. Maybe it was the idea that she was about to have some free time. An afternoon with her mum.

She was about to have some time off from kids who weren't her own.

But they were her own. Toby had his arms wrapped around her, snuggling into her shoulder.

He had bare feet. Em was tickling his toes as she walked, making him giggle.

She loved these kids.

He'd thought… Okay, he'd thought he was being self-less, walking away five years ago. He'd been giving up his marriage so Em could have what she wanted. Now… Why was he now feeling the opposite? Completely, ut-terly selfish?

Get a grip, he told himself. He was here to work.

'Your babysitter's here, ma'am,' he said, finally climb-ing from the car. 'All present and correct.'

She was looking ruefully at the car. 'Still the hire car? Can't you get parts?'

'They're hard to come by.' He'd spent hours on the in-ternet tracking down the parts he needed.

'Oh, Ollie…'

No one called him Ollie.

Em did.

She put her hand on his arm and he thought, She's com-forting me because of a wrecked car. And she's coping with kids with wrecked lives…

How to make a rat feel an even bigger rat.

But her sympathy was real. Everything about her was real, he thought. Em… He'd loved this woman.

He loved this woman?

'Hey, will you go with Uncle Ollie?' Em was saying,

moving on, prising Toby away from his neck-hugging. 'I bet he knows how to tickle toes, too.'

'I can tickle toes.' He was a paediatric surgeon. He could keep a kid entertained.

But Toby caught him unawares. He twisted in Em's arms and launched himself across, so fast Oliver almost didn't catch him. Em grabbed, Oliver grabbed and suddenly they were in a sandwich hug, with Toby sandwiched in the middle.

Toby gave a muffled chortle, like things had gone exactly to plan. Which, maybe in Toby's world, they had.

But he had so much wrong with him. His tiny spine was bent; he'd have operation after operation in front of him, years in a brace...

He'd have Em.

He should pull away, but Em wasn't pulling away. For this moment she was holding, hugging, as if she needed it. As if his hug was giving her something...

Something that, as his wife, had once been her right?

'Em...'

But the sound of his voice broke the moment. She tugged away, flipped an errant curl behind her ear, tried to smile.

'Sorry. I should expect him to do that—he does it all the time with Mike. He has an absolute conviction that the grown-ups in his life are to be trusted never, ever to drop him, and so far it's paid off. One day, though, Toby, lad, you'll find out what the real world's like.'

'But you'll shield him as long as you can.'

'With every ounce of power I possess,' she said simply. 'But, meanwhile, Mum's ready to go. She's so excited she didn't sleep last night. Gretta's fed. Everything's ready, all I need to do is put on clean jeans and comb my hair.'

'Why don't you put on a dress?' he asked, feeling... weird. Out of kilter. This was none of his business, but he was starting to realise just how important this afternoon was to Em and her mum. And how rare. 'Make it a special occasion.'

'Goodness, Oliver, I don't think I've worn a dress for five years,' she flung at him over her shoulder as she headed into the house. 'Why would the likes of me need a dress?'

And he thought of the social life they'd once had. Did she miss it? he wondered, but he tickled Toby's toes, the little boy giggled and he knew that she didn't.

They left fifteen minutes later, like a pair of jail escapees, except that they were escapees making sure all home bases were covered. Their 'jail' was precious.

'Mike might come over later to collect Toby,' Em told him. 'Toby loves Mike, so if he does that's fine by us. That'll mean you only have Gretta so you should cope easily. You have both our cellphone numbers? You know where everything is? And Gretta needs Kanga…if she gets upset, Kanga can fix her. But don't let her get tired. If she has trouble breathing you can raise her oxygen…'

'Em, trust me, I'm a doctor,' he said, almost pushing them out the door.

'And you have how much experience with kids?'

'I'm an obstetrician and a surgeon.'

'My point exactly. Here they're outside their mum, not inside, and you don't have an anaesthetist to put them to sleep. There's a stack of movies ready to play. You can use the sandpit, too. Gretta loves it, but you need to keep her equipment sand-free…'

'Em, go,' he said, exasperated. 'Adrianna, take Em's arm and pull. Em, trust me. You can, you know.'

'I do know that,' Em told him, and suddenly she darted back across the kitchen and gave him a swift kiss on the cheek. It was a thank-you kiss, a perfunctory kiss, and why it had the power to burn... 'I always have,' she said simply. 'You're a very nice man, Oliver Evans. I would have trusted you to be a great dad, even if you couldn't trust yourself. That's water under the bridge now, but I still trust you, even if it's only for an afternoon.'

And she blinked a couple of times—surely they weren't tears?—then ducked back and kissed Gretta once again—and she was gone.

And Oliver was left with two kids.

And silence.

The kids were watching him. Toby was in his arms, leaning back to gaze into his eyes. Cautiously assessing? Gretta was sitting in an oversized pushchair, surrounded by cushions.

To trust or not to trust?

Toby's eyes were suddenly tear-filled. A couple of fat tears tracked down his face.

Gretta just stared at him, her face expressionless. Waiting to see what happened next?

Both were silent.

These were damaged kids, he thought. Rejects. They'd be used to a life where they were left. They'd come from parents who couldn't or wouldn't care for them and they had significant medical problems. They'd be used to a life where hospital stays were the norm. They weren't kids who opened their mouths and screamed whenever they were left.

Could you be stoic at two and at four? That's how they seemed. Stoic.

It was a bit...gut-wrenching.

Kanga—it must be Kanga: a chewed, bedraggled, once blue stuffed thing with long back paws and a huge tail—was lying on the table. He picked it—him?—up and handed him to Toby. Gretta watched with huge eyes. This wasn't what was supposed to happen, her eyes said. This was *her* Kanga.

He lifted Gretta out of her chair with his spare arm and carried both kids out into the yard, under the spreading oak at the bottom of the garden where the lawn was a bit too long, lushly green.

He set both kids down on the grass. Fuzzy the dog flopped down beside them. He, too, seemed wary.

Toby was still holding Kanga. Warily.

He tugged Gretta's shoes off so both kids had bare feet. Em had made the tickling thing work. Maybe it'd work for him.

He took Kanga from Toby, wriggled him slowly towards Gretta's toes—and ticked Gretta's toes with Kanga's tail.

Then, as both kids looked astonished, he bounced Kanga across to Toby and tickled his.

Toby looked more astonished. He reached out to grab Kanga, but Oliver was too fast. The tickling tail went back to Gretta's toes—and then, as Toby reached further, Kanga bounced sideways and tickled Fuzzy on the nose.

Fuzzy opened his mouth to grab but Kanga boinged back to Gretta, this time going from one foot to the other.

And then, as Gretta finally reacted, Kanga boinged up and touched her nose—and then bounced back to Toby.

Toby stared down in amazement at his toes being tickled and his eyes creased, the corners of his mouth twitched—and he chuckled.

It was a lovely sound but it wasn't enough. Kanga bounced back to Gretta, kissed her nose again, then bounced right on top of Fuzzy's head.

Fuzzy leaped to his feet and barked.

Kanga went back to Toby's toes.

And finally, finally, and it was like a minor miracle all by itself, Gretta's serious little face relaxed. She smiled and reached out her hand.

'Kanga,' she said, and Kanga flew to her hand. She grabbed him and held, gazing dotingly at her beloved blue thing.

'Kanga,' she said again, and she opened her fingers—and held Kanga back out to Oliver.

Her meaning was clear. He's mine but it's okay to play. In fact, she wanted to play.

But that one word had left her breathless. What the…? He'd seen the levels of oxygen she was receiving and she was still breathless? But she was still game.

She was trusting.

He wanted to hug her.

She was four years old. He'd met her twice. He was feeling…feeling…

'Hey!' It was Mike, and thank heaven for Mike. He was getting emotional and how was a man to keep tickling when he was thinking of what was in store for this little girl? He looked across at the gate and smiled at Mike with gratitude.

'Hey, yourself.'

'We're going to the beach,' Mike called. 'You want to come?'

'I'm sitting the kids,' he said, and Mike looked at him like he was a moron.

'Yeah. Kid-sitting. Beach. It's possible to combine them—and your two love the beach. Katy and Drew are staying home—Katy's still under the weather but her mum's here and Drew has a mate over. But we have four kid seats in the wagon—we always seem to have a spare kid—and why not?'

Why not? Because he'd like to stay lying under the tree, tickling toes?

It wouldn't last. His child entertainment range was limited, to say the least, and both kids were looking eager.

But, Gretta… Sand… Maybe he could sort it.

'What if we put one of the car seats into your car,' Mike said, eyeing the rental car parked at the kerb. 'Rental cars always have bolts to hold 'em. That way you can follow me and if Gretta gets tired you can bring her straight home. And we have beach shelters for shade. We have so much beach gear I feel like a pack mule going up and down the access track. Katy's mum's packed afternoon tea. Coming?'

'Yeah,' he said, because there was nothing else he could say. But there was part of him that was thinking as he packed up and prepared to take his charges beachwards, *I wouldn't have minded caring for them myself. I wouldn't have minded proving that I could be a…*

A father? By minding them for a couple of hours? Would that make him a hero? Could it even disprove what he'd always felt—that you couldn't love a kid who wasn't your own? Of course it couldn't.

It was just that, as the kids had chuckled, he'd felt, for one sliver of a crazy moment, that he could have been completely wrong. That maybe his judgement five years ago had been clouded, distorted by his own miserable childhood.

And an afternoon alone with these kids would prove what? Nothing. He'd made a choice five years ago. It had been the only honest option, and nothing had changed.

Except the way Gretta was smiling at the thought of the beach seemed to be changing things, like it or not. And the knowledge that Em would think giving Gretta an afternoon at the beach was great.

Would it make Em smile?

'You coming, mate, or are you planning on writing a thesis on the pros and cons?' Mike demanded, and he caught himself and took Kanga from Toby and handed him to Gretta.

'We're coming,' he told him. He looked at the muscled

hulk of a tattooed biker standing at the gate and Oliver Evans, specialist obstetric surgeon, admitted his failings. 'But you might need to help me plan what to take. I'm a great obstetrician but as a father I'm the pits.'

'You reckon he'll be okay? You reckon he'll manage?'

'If you're worried, ring Mike.'

Em and her mum were lying on adjoining massage tables. They had five minutes' 'down' time before the massage was to begin. The soft, cushioned tables were gently warmed, the lights were dim, the sound of the sea washed through the high windows and a faint but lovely perfume was floating from the candles in the high-set sconces.

They should almost be asleep already but Em couldn't stop fretting.

'Ring Mike and ask him to check,' Adrianna said again. 'We all want you to enjoy this. I want to enjoy this. Check.'

So she rang. She lay on her gorgeous table and listened to Mike's growl.

'You're not supposed to be worrying. Get back to doing nothing.'

'You've got Toby?'

'Me and Oliver—that's one hell of a name, isn't it?— we're gunna have to think of something shorter—have Toby—and my kids and Gretta. We're at the beach. Want to see? I'm sending a video. Watch it and then shut up, Em. Quit it with your worrying. Me and your Ollie have things in hand.'

He disconnected. She stared at the phone, feeling disconcerted. Strange. That her kids were somewhere else without her... With Oliver. Ollie...

No one called him Ollie except her, but now Mike was doing the same. It was like two parts of her life were merging.

The old and the new?

It was her imagination. Oliver…Ollie?…would do this afternoon of childminding and move on.

A ping announced the arrival of a message. She clicked and sure enough there was a video, filmed on Mike's phone and sent straight through.

There was Toby with Mike's two littlies. They were building a sandcastle—sort of. It was a huge mound of sand, covered with seaweed and shells. Fuzzy was digging a hole on the far side and Mike's bitser dog was barking in excitement.

As Em watched, Toby picked up a bucket of water and spilt it over the castle—and chuckled. Mike laughed off camera.

'If you think I don't have anything better to do than fill buckets for you, young Toby—you're right…'

And then the camera panned away, down to the shoreline—and Em drew in her breath.

For there was Oliver—and Gretta.

They were sitting on the wet sand, where the low, gentle waves were washing in, washing out.

Oliver had rigged a beach chair beside them, wedging it secure with something that looked like sandbags. Wet towels filled with sand?

Gretta's oxygen cylinder was high on the seat, safe from the shallow inrushes of water, but Ollie and Gretta were sitting on the wet sand.

He had Gretta on his knee. They were facing the incoming waves, waiting for one to reach them.

'Here it comes,' Oliver called, watching as a wave broke far out. 'Here it comes, Gretta, ready or not. One, two, three…'

And he swung Gretta back against his chest, hugging her as the water surrounded them, washing Gretta's legs, swishing around his body.

He was wearing board shorts. He was naked from the waist up.

She'd forgotten his body...

No, she hadn't. Her heart couldn't clench like this if she'd forgotten.

'More,' Gretta whispered, wriggling her toes in the water, twisting so she could see the wave recede. Her eyes were sparkling with delight. She was so close to the other side, this little one, and yet for now she was just a kid having fun.

A kid secure with her... Her what?

Her friend. With Oliver, who couldn't give his heart.

Silently Em handed her phone to her mum and waited until Adrianna had seen the video.

Adrianna sniffed. 'Oh, Em...'

'Yeah.'

'Do you think...?'

'No.'

'It's such a shame.'

'It's the way it is,' Em said bleakly. 'But...but for now, he's making Gretta happy.'

'He's lovely,' Adrianna said stoutly.

'Don't I know it?' Em whispered. 'Don't I wish I didn't?'

'Em...'

The door opened. Their massage ladies entered, silently, expecting their clients to be well on the way on their journey to complete indulgence.

'Are you ready?' the woman due to massage Em asked. 'Can you clear your mind of everything past, of everything future and just let yourself be. For now there should be nothing outside this room.'

But there was, Em thought as skilful hands started their skin-tingling work. There was a vision of her ex-husband holding her little girl. Making Gretta happy.

Massages were wonderful, she decided as her body responded to the skill of the woman working on her.

They might be wonderful but thinking about Oliver was...better?

He sat in the waves and watched—and felt—Gretta enjoy herself. She was a wraith of a child, a fragile imp, dependent on the oxygen that sustained her, totally dependent on the adults who cared for her.

She trusted him. She faced the incoming waves with joy because she was absolutely sure Oliver would lift her just in time, protect the breathing tube, hug her against his body, protect her from all harm.

But harm was coming to this little one, and there was nothing anyone could do about it. He'd mentioned Gretta to Tristan and Tristan had spelt out the prognosis. With so much deformity of the heart, it was a matter of time...

Not very much time.

That he had this time with her today was precious. He didn't know her, she wasn't his kid, but, regardless, it was gold.

If he could somehow take the pain away...

He couldn't. He couldn't protect Gretta.

He couldn't protect Em.

Hell, but he wanted to. And not just for Em, he conceded. For this little one. This little girl who laughed and twisted and buried her face in his shoulder and then turned to face the world again.

Em loved her. *Loved her.*

An adopted child.

He'd thought... Yeah, okay, he knew. If Em was able to have her own child it'd all change. Gretta would take second place.

But did he know? Five years ago he'd been sure. He'd

been totally judgmental and his marriage was over because of it.

Now the sands were shifting. He was shifting.

'More,' Gretta ordered, and he realised two small waves had washed over her feet and he hadn't done the lift and squeal routine. Bad.

'Em wouldn't forget,' he told Gretta as he lifted and she squealed. 'Em loves you.'

But Gretta's face was buried in his shoulder, and that question was surfacing—again. Over and over.

Had he made the mistake of his life?

Could he…?

Focus on Gretta, he told himself. Anything else was far too hard.

Anything else was far too soon.

Or five years too late?

CHAPTER NINE

BY THE TIME Em and Adrianna arrived home, Oliver had the kids squeaky clean. He'd bathed them, dressed them in their PJs, tidied the place as best he could and was feeling extraordinarily smug about his child-minding prowess.

The kids were tired but happy. All Em and Adrianna had to do was feed them and tuck them into bed. He could leave. Job done.

They walked in looking glowing. They both had beautifully styled, shiny hair. They both looked as squeaky clean as the kids—scrubbed? They'd obviously shopped a little.

Em was wearing a new scarf in bright pink and muted greens. It made her look...how Em used to look, he thought. Like a woman who had time to think about her appearance. Free?

And impressed.

'Wow.' Both women were gazing around the kitchen in astonishment. The kids were in their chairs at the table. Oliver had just started making toast to keep them going until dinner. 'Wow,' Adrianna breathed again. 'There's not even a mess.'

'Mike took them all to the beach,' Em reminded her, but she was smiling at Oliver, her eyes thanking him.

'Hey, I had to clean the bathroom,' Oliver said, mock wounded. 'I've had to do some work.'

'Of course you have.' Adrianna flopped onto the nearest chair. 'Hey, if we make some eggs we could turn that toast into soldiers, and the kids' dinner is done. Kids, how about if I eat egg and toast soldiers too, and then I'll flop into bed, as well. I'm pooped.' But then she turned thoughtful. 'But, Em, you aren't ready for bed yet. You look fabulous, the night's still young, the kids are good and Oliver's still here. Why don't you two go out to dinner?'

Em stared at her like she'd lost her mind. 'Dinner…'

'You know, that thing you eat at a restaurant. Or maybe it could be fish and chips overlooking the bay. It's a gorgeous night. Oliver, do you have anything else on?'

'No, but—'

'Then go on, the two of you. You know you want to.'

'Mum, we don't want to.'

'Really?' Adrianna demanded. 'Honestly? Look at me, Em, and say you really don't want to go out to dinner with Oliver. Oliver, you do the same.'

Silence.

'There you go, then,' she said, satisfied. 'Off you go. Shoo.'

What else could they do but follow instructions? The night was warm and still, a combination unusual for Melbourne, where four seasons were often famously represented in one day. But this night the gods were smiling. Even the fish-and-chip kiosk didn't have too long a queue. Oliver ordered, then he and Em walked a block back from the beach to buy a bottle of wine, and returned just as their order was ready.

They used to do this often, Em thought. Once upon a time…

'I still have our picnic rug,' Oliver said ruefully, as they collected their feast. 'But it's in the back of the Morgan.'

'I'm sorry.'

'Don't be. Just be glad your wagon only got scratches—
you're the one who's dependent on it. Moving on... Hey,
how about this?' A family was just leaving an outside
table and it was pretty much in the best position on the
beachfront. Oliver swooped on it before a bunch of teenagers reached it, spread his parcels over it and signalled
her to come. Fast.

'You're worse than the seagulls,' she retorted, smiling
at his smug expression. 'Talk about swoop for the kill...'

'Table-swooping's one of my splinter skills,' he told her.
'Surely you remember.'

'I try...not to.'

'Does that help? Trying not to?'

Silence. She couldn't think of an answer. They unwrapped their fish and chips and ate a few. They watched
a couple of windsurfers trying to guide their kites across
the bay with not enough breeze, but the question still hung.

How soon could you forget a marriage? Never? It was
never for her.

'I... How was America?' she asked at last, because she
had to say something, the silence was becoming oppres-
sive.

'Great. I learned so much.'

'You went away an obstetrician and came back...'

'I'm still first and foremost an obstetrician.'

'But you have the skills to save Ruby's baby—and
countless others. You must feel it's worth it.'

'Em...'

'And you wouldn't have done that if we'd stayed together.' She was determined to get this onto some sort of
normal basis, where they could talk about their marriage
as if it was just a blip in their past. It was nothing that
could affect their future. 'But I'm surprised you haven't

met anyone else.' She hesitated but then ploughed on. She needed to say this. Somehow.

'You ached to be a dad,' she whispered, because somehow saying it aloud seemed wrong. 'I thought... There's nothing wrong with you. It's me who has the fertility problems. I thought you'd have met someone else by now and organised our divorce. Isn't that why we split? I sort of...I sort of wanted to think of you married with a couple of kids.'

'Did you really want that?' His curt response startled her into splashing her wine. She didn't want it anyway, she decided. She put down her glass with care and met his look head-on.

Say it like it is.

'That's what you wanted. That's why I agreed to separate.'

'I thought ending the marriage was all about you needing a partner so you could adopt.'

'It's true I wanted kids,' she managed, and her voice would hardly work for her. It was hard even to whisper. 'But I never wanted another husband than you.'

'You didn't want me.'

'Your terms were too hard, Oliver. Maybe now...maybe given some space it might be different. But we'd lost Josh and I was so raw, so needy. All I wanted was a child to hold...I think maybe I was a little crazy. I demanded too much of you. I hadn't realised quite how badly you'd been wounded.'

'I hadn't been wounded.'

'I've met your adoptive parents, remember? I've met your appalling brother.'

'I'm well over that.'

'Do you ever get over being not wanted? You were adopted, seemingly adored, and then suddenly supplanted by your parents' "real" son. I can't imagine how much that must have hurt.'

'It's past history.'

'It's not,' she said simply. 'Because it affects who you are. It always will. Maybe…' She hesitated but this had been drifting in and out of her mind for five years now. Was it better left unsaid? Maybe it was, but she'd say it anyway. 'Maybe it will affect any child you have, adopted or not. Maybe that's why you haven't moved on. Would you have loved Josh, Oliver, or would you have resented him because he'd have had the love you never had?'

'That's nuts.'

'Yeah? So why not organise a divorce? Why not re-marry?'

'Because of you,' he said, before he could stop himself. 'Because I still love you.'

She stilled. The whole night seemed to still.

There were people on the foreshore, people on the beach. The queue to the fish-and-chip shop was right behind them. Kids were flying by on their skateboards. Mums and dads were pushing strollers.

Because I still love you…

He reached out and touched her hand lightly, his lovely surgeon's fingers tracing her work-worn skin. She spent too much time washing, she thought absently. She should use more moisturiser. She should…

Stop blathering. This was too important.

Five years ago they'd walked away from each other. Had it all been some ghastly mistake? Could they just… start again?

'Em…' He rose and came round to her side of the table. His voice was urgent now. Pressing home a point? He sat down beside her, took both her hands in his and twisted her to face him. 'Do you feel it, too?'

Did she feel it? How could she not? She'd married this

man. She'd loved him with all her heart. She'd borne him a son.

He was holding her, and his hold was strong and compelling. His gaze was on her, and on her alone.

A couple of seagulls, sensing distraction, landed on the far side of the table and edged towards the fish-and-chip parcel. They could take what they liked, she thought. This moment was too important.

Oliver... Her husband...

'Em,' he said again, and his hold turned to a tug. He tugged her as he'd tugged her a thousand times before, as she'd tugged him, as their mutual need meant an almost instinctive coming together of two bodies.

Her face lifted to his—once again instinctively, because this was her husband. She was a part of him, and part of her had never let go. Never thought of letting go.

And his mouth was on hers and he was kissing her and the jolty, nervy, pressurised, outside world faded to absolutely nothing.

There was only Oliver. There was only this moment.

There was only this kiss.

She melted into him—of course she did. Her body had spent five years loving this man and it responded now as if it had once again found its true north. Warmth flooded through her—no, make that heat. Desire, strength and surety.

This man was her home.

This man was her heart.

Except he wasn't. The reasons they'd split were still there, practical, definite, and even though she was surrendering herself to the kiss—how could she not?—there was still a part of her brain that refused to shut down. Even though her body was all his, even though she was returning his kiss with a passion that matched his, even though her hands were holding him as if she still had the right to hold, that tiny part was saying this was make-believe.

This was a memory of times past.

This would hurt even more when it was over. Tug away now.

But she couldn't. He was holding her as if she was truly loved. He was kissing her regardless of the surroundings, regardless of the wolf whistles coming from the teenagers at the next table, regardless of…what was true.

It didn't matter. She needed this kiss. She needed this man.

And then the noise surrounding them suddenly grew. The whistles stopped and became hoots of laughter. There were a couple of warning cries and finally, finally, they broke apart to see…

Their fish…

While they had been otherwise…engaged, seagulls had sneaked forward, grabbing chips from the edge of their unwrapped parcel. Now a couple of braver ones had gone further.

They'd somehow seized the edge of one of their pieces of fish, and dragged it free of the packaging. They'd hauled it out…and up.

There were now five gulls…no, make that six…each holding an edge of the fish fillet. The fish was hovering in the air six feet above them while the gulls fought for ownership. They'd got it, but now they all wanted to go in different directions.

The rest of the flock had risen, too, squawking around them, waiting for the inevitable catastrophe and broken pieces.

Almost every person around them had stopped to look, and laugh, at the flying fish and at the two lovers who'd been so preoccupied that they hadn't even defended their meal.

A couple more gulls moved in for the kill and the fish almost spontaneously exploded. Bits of fish went everywhere.

Oliver grabbed the remaining parcel, scooping it up before the scraps of flying fish hit, and shooed the gulls away. They were now down to half their chips and only one piece of fish, but he'd saved the day. The crowd hooted their delight, and Oliver grinned, but Em wasn't thinking about fish and chips, no matter how funny the drama.

How had that happened? It was like they'd been teenagers again, young lovers, so caught up in each other that the world hadn't existed.

But the world did exist.

'I believe I've saved most of our feast,' Oliver said ruefully, and she smiled, but her smile was forced. The world was steady again, her real world. For just a moment she'd let herself be drawn into history, into fantasy. Time to move on...

'We need to concentrate on what's happening now,' she said.

'We do.' He was watching her, his lovely brown eyes questioning. He always could read her, Em thought, suddenly resentful. He could see things about her she didn't know herself.

But he'd kept himself to himself. She'd been married to him for five years and she hadn't known the depth of feeling he'd had about his childhood until the question of adoption had come up. She'd met his adoptive parents, she'd known they were awful, but Oliver had treated them—and his childhood—with light dismissal.

'They raised me, they gave me a decent start, I got to be a doctor and I'm grateful.'

But he wasn't. In those awful few weeks after losing Josh, when she'd finally raised adoption as an option, his anger and his grief had shocked them both. It had resonated with such depth and fury it had torn them apart.

So, no, she didn't know this man. Not then. Not now.

And kissing him wasn't going to make it one whit better.

He'd said he still loved her. Ten years ago he'd said that, too, and yet he'd walked away, telling her to move on. Telling her to find someone else who could fit in with her dreams.

'Em, I'd like to—'

'Have your fish before it gets cold or gets snaffled by another bird?' She spoke too fast, rushing in before he could say anything serious, anything that matched the look on his face that said his emotions were all over the place. That said the kiss had done something for him that matched the emotions she was feeling. That said their marriage wasn't over?

But it was over, she told herself fiercely. She'd gone through the pain of separation once and there was no way she was going down that path again. Love? The word itself was cheap, she thought. Their love had been tested, and found wanting. 'That's what I need to do,' she added, still too fast, and took a chip and ate it, even though hunger was the last thing on her mind right now. 'I need to eat fast and get back to the kids. Oliver, that kiss was an aberration. We need to forget it and move on.'

'Really?'

'Really. Have a chip before we lose the lot.'

The kids were asleep when she got home, and so was Adrianna. The house was in darkness. Oliver swung out of the driver's seat as if he meant to accompany her to the door, but she practically ran.

'I need my bed, Oliver. Goodnight.'

He was still watching her as she closed the front door. She'd been rude, she admitted as she headed for the children's bedroom. He'd given her a day out, a day off. If he'd been a stranger she would have spent time thanking him.

She should still thank him.

Except…he'd kissed her. He'd said he loved her.

She stood in the kids' bedroom, between the two cots, watching them sleeping in the dim light cast by a Humpty Dumpty figure that glowed a soft pink to blue and then back again.

She had to work with him, she reminded herself. She needed to get things back to a formal footing, fast.

Resolute, she grabbed her phone and texted.

Thank you for today. It was really generous. The kiss was a mistake but I dare say the gulls are grateful. And Mum and I are grateful, too.

That's what was needed, she thought. Make it light. Put the gratitude back to the plural—herself and her mother—and the seagulls? She was thanking someone she'd once known for a generous gesture.

Only…was it more than that? Surely.

He'd kissed her. Her fingers crept involuntarily to her mouth. She could still feel him, she thought. She could still taste him.

After five years, her body hadn't forgotten him.

Her body still wanted him.

He'd said he still loved her.

Had she been crazy to walk away from him all those years ago? Her body said yes, but here in this silent house, listening to the breathing of two children who'd become her own, knowing clearly and bleakly where they'd be if she hadn't taken them in, she could have no regrets. Her mind didn't.

It was only her heart and her body that said something else entirely.

* * *

What he wanted to do was stand outside and watch the house for a while. Why? Because it felt like his family was in there.

That was a dumb thought. He'd laid down his ultimatum five years ago and he'd moved on. He'd had five professionally satisfying years getting the skills he needed to be one of the world's top in-utero surgeons. Babies lived now because of him. He'd never have had that chance if he'd stayed here—if he'd become part of Em's menagerie.

He couldn't stay standing outside the house, like a stalker, like someone creepy. What he'd like was to take his little Morgan for a long drive along the coast. The car was like his balm, his escape.

Em had smashed his car. She'd also smashed…something else.

She'd destroyed the equilibrium he'd built around himself over the last few years. She'd destroyed the fallacy that said he was a loner; that said he didn't need anyone.

He wanted her. Fiercely, he wanted her. He'd kissed her tonight and it would have been worth all the fish.

It had felt right.

It had felt like he'd been coming home.

His phone pinged and he flipped it open. Em's polite thank-you note greeted him, and he snapped it shut.

She was making light of the kiss. Maybe that was wise.

Dammit, he couldn't keep standing here. Any moment now she'd look out the window and see him. Ex-husband loitering…

He headed back to the hire car. He had an apartment at the hospital but he wasn't ready for sleep yet. Instead, he headed back to the beach. He parked, got rid of his shoes and walked along the sand.

The night was still and warm. This evening the beach had been filled with families, kids whooping it up, soaking up the last of Melbourne's summer, but now the beach seemed to be the domain of couples. Couples walking hand in hand in the shallows. Couples lying on rugs on the sand, holding each other.

Young loves?

He walked on and passed a couple who looked to be in their seventies, maybe even older. They were walking slowly. The guy had a limp, a gammy hip? The woman was holding his hand as if she was supporting him.

But the hold wasn't one of pure physical support, he thought. Their body language said they'd been holding each other for fifty years.

He wanted it still. So badly...

Could he take on the kids? Could he take that risk?

Was it a risk? He'd held Gretta today and what he'd felt...

She had Down's syndrome with complications. Tristan said her life expectancy could be measured in months. It was stupid—impossible even—to give your heart to such a kid.

He could still hear his adoptive mother...

'It's not like he's really ours. If we hadn't had Brett then we wouldn't have known what love really is. And now...we're stuck with him. It's like we have a cuckoo in the nest...'

If he ever felt like that...

It was too hard. He didn't know how to feel.

But Em had made the decision for him. She'd moved on, saying he was free to find someone and have kids of his own. Kids who he could truly love.

Hell. He raked his hair and stared out at the moonlit water.

Melbourne's bay was protected. The waves were small, even when the weather was wild, but on a night like this they were practically non-existent. The windsurfers had completely run out of wind. The moonlight was a silver shimmer over the sea and the night seemingly an endless reflection of the starlit sky.

He wanted Em with him.

He wanted her to be…free?

It wasn't going to happen. She had encumbrances. No, he thought, she has people she loves. Kids. Her mother.

Not him.

It's for the best, he thought, shoving his hands deep into his pockets and practically glaring at the moon. I should never have come to the Victoria. I wouldn't have if I'd known Em would be here.

So leave?

Maybe he would, he thought. He'd agreed with Charles Delamere on a three-month trial.

Twelve weeks to go?

CHAPTER TEN

ON MONDAY OLIVER hit the wards early. He'd been in the day before, not because he'd been on duty but because he'd wanted to check on Ruby. But Ruby was doing all the right things and so was her baby, so he didn't check her first. He worked on the things he needed for his embryonic research lab, then decided to check the midwives' roster and choose a time to visit Ruby when he knew Em wouldn't be around.

So he headed—surreptitiously, he thought—to the nurses' station in the birthing centre—just as Isla Delamere came flying down the corridor, looking, for Isla, very harassed indeed.

When she saw Oliver she practically sagged in relief.

'Dr Evans. Oliver. I know your specialty's in-utero stuff and I know Charles has said you can spend the rest of your time on your research but you're an obstetrician first and foremost, yes?'

'Yes.' Of course he was.

'I have four births happening and we're stretched. Two are problems. Emily's coping with one, I have the other. Mine's a bit of a spoilt socialite—she was booked at a private hospital but had hysterics at the first labour pain so her husband's brought her here because we're closer. I can deal with that. But Em's looking after a surrogate mum.

She's carrying her sister's child—her sister's egg, her sister's husband's sperm, all very organised—but the emotion in there seems off the planet. Maggie's a multigravida, four kids of her own, no trouble with any, but now she's slowed right down and her sister's practically hysterical. But we can't kick her out. Oliver, Em needs support. Our registrar's off sick, Darcie's at a conference, Sean's coping with a Caesar so that leaves you. Can you help?'

'Of course.'

'Excellent. Here are the case notes. Suite Four.'

'You're okay with yours?'

'My one wants pethidine, morphine, spinal blocks, amputation at the waist, an immediate airlift to Hawaii and her body back,' Isla said grimly. 'And she's only two centimetres dilated. Heaven help us when it's time to push. But I've coped with worse than this in my time. What Em's coping with seems harder. She needs you, Dr Evans. Go.'

The last time he'd seen her he'd kissed her. Now...

Em seemed to be preparing to do a vaginal examination. She was scrubbed, dressed in theatre gear, looking every inch a midwife. Every inch a professional. And the look she gave him as he slipped into the room had nothing to do with the kiss, nothing to do with what was between them. It was pure, professional relief.

'Here's Dr Evans,' she said briskly to the room in general. 'He's one of our best obstetricians. You're in good hands now, Maggie.'

'She doesn't need to be in good hands.' A woman who looked almost the mirror image of the woman in the bed—except that she was smartly dressed, not a hair out of place, looking like she was about to step into a boardroom—was edging round the end of the bed to see what Em was doing. She ignored Oliver. 'Maggie, you just need to push. Thirty-six hours... You can do this. It's taking too long. Just push.'

Em cast him a beseeching look—and he got it in one. The whole set-up.

A guy who was presumably Maggie's husband was sitting beside her, holding her hand. He looked almost as stressed as his labouring wife.

The other woman had a guy with her, as well, presumably her husband, too? He was dressed in casual chinos and a cashmere sweater. Expensive. Smooth.

Both he and his wife seemed focused on where the action should be taking place. Where their child would be born. Even though the woman had been talking to Maggie, she'd been looking at the wrong end of the bed.

Surrogate parenthood… Oliver had been present for a couple of those before, and he'd found the emotion involved was unbelievable. Surrogacy for payment was illegal in this country. It had to be a gift, and what a gift! To carry a child for your sister…

But Maggie wasn't looking as if she was thinking of gifts. She was looking beyond exhaustion.

Thirty-six hours…

'Can't you push?' Maggie's sister said again, fretfully. 'Come on, Maggie, with all of yours it was over in less than twelve hours. The book says it should be faster for later pregnancies. You can do it. You have to try.'

'Maggie needs to go at her own pace,' Em said, in a tone that told him she'd said it before, possibly a lot more than once. 'This baby will come when she's ready.'

'But all she needs to do is push…'

He'd seen enough. He'd heard enough. Oliver looked at Maggie's face, and that of her husband. He looked at Em and saw sheer frustration and he moved.

'Tell me your names,' he said, firmly, cutting off the woman who looked about to issue another order. 'Maggie, I already know yours. Who are the rest of you?'

'I'm Rob,' said the man holding Maggie's hand, sounding weary to the bone. 'I'm Maggie's husband. And this is Leonie, Maggie's sister, and her husband, Connor. This is Leonie and Connor's baby.'

'Maybe we need to get something straight,' Oliver said, gently but still firmly. He was focusing on Maggie, talking to the room in general but holding the exhausted woman's gaze with his. 'This baby may well be Leonie and Connor's when it's born, but right now it has to be Maggie's. Maggie needs to own this baby if she's going to give birth successfully. And I'm looking at Maggie's exhaustion level and I'm thinking we need to clear the room. She needs some space.'

'But it's our baby.' Leonie looked horrified. 'Maggie's agreed—'

'To bear a baby for you,' he finished for her. Em was watching him, warily now, waiting to see where he was going. 'But right now Maggie's body's saying it's hers and her body needs that belief if she's to have a strong labour. I'm sorry, Leonie and Connor, but unless you want your sister to have a Caesarean, I need you to leave.'

'We can't leave,' Leonie gasped. 'We need to see her born.'

'You may well—if it's okay with Maggie.' They were in one of the teaching suites, geared to help train students. It had a mirror to one side. 'Maggie, that's an observation window, with one-way glass. Is it okay if your sister and her husband move into there?'

'No.' Leonie frowned at Oliver but the look on both Maggie and Rob's faces was one of relief.

'I just...need...to go at my own pace,' Maggie whispered.

'But I want to be the first one to hold our baby,' Leonie snapped, and Oliver bit his tongue to stop himself snapping back. This situation was fraught. He could understand that sisterly love was being put on the back burner in the face of the enormity of their baby's birth, but his responsibility was for Maggie and her baby's health. Anything else had to come second.

'What Maggie is doing for you is one of the most generous gifts one woman can ever give another,' he said, forcing himself to stay gentle. 'She's bearing your baby, but for now every single hormone, every ounce of energy she has, needs to believe it's her baby. You need to get things into perspective. Maggie will bear this baby in her own time. Her body will dictate that, and there's nothing you or Connor can say or do to alter it. If Maggie wants to, she'll hold her when she's born. That's her right. Then and only then, when she's ready and not before, she'll make the decision to let her baby go. Emily, do you agree?'

'I agree,' she said.

Em had been silent, watching not him but Maggie. She was a wonderful midwife, Oliver thought. There was no midwife he'd rather have on his team, and by the look on her face what he was suggesting was exactly what she wanted. The problem, though, was that the biological parents exuded authority. He wouldn't mind betting Leonie was older than Maggie and that both she and her husband held positions of corporate power. Here they looked like they'd been using their authority to push Maggie, and they wouldn't have listened to Em.

Isla had sent him in for a reason. If this had been a normal delivery then Em could have coped alone, but with the level of Maggie's exhaustion it was getting less likely to be a normal delivery.

Sometimes there were advantages to having the word *Doctor* in front of his name. Sometimes there were advantages to being a surgeon, to having given lectures to some of the most competent doctors in the world, to have the gravitas of professional clout behind him.

Sometimes it behoved a doctor to invoke his power, too.

'Maggie, would you like to have a break from too many people?' he asked now.

And Maggie looked up at him, her eyes brimming with gratitude. 'I... Yes. I mean, I always said that Leonie could be here but—'

'But your body needs peace,' Oliver said. He walked to the door and pulled it wide. 'Leonie, Connor, please take seats in the observation room. If it's okay with Maggie you can stay watching. However, the mirror is actually an electric screen. Emily's about to do a pelvic examination so we'll shut the screen for that so you can't see, but we'll turn it back on again as soon as Maggie says it's okay. Is that what you want, Maggie?'

'Y-yes.'

'But she promised...' Leonie gasped.

'Your sister promised you a baby,' Oliver told her, still gently but with steel in every word. 'To my mind, that gift needs something in return. If Maggie needs privacy in this last stage of her labour, then surely you can grant it to her.'

And Leonie's face crumpled. 'It's just... It's just... Maggie, I'm sorry...'

She'd just forgotten, Oliver thought, watching as Leonie swiped away tears. This was a decent woman who was totally focused on the fact that she was about to become a mother. She'd simply forgotten her sister. Like every other mother in the world, all she wanted was her baby.

She'd have to wait.

He held the door open. Leonie cast a wild, beseeching look at Maggie but Em moved fast, cutting off Maggie's view of her sister's distress. Maggie didn't need anyone else's emotion. She couldn't handle it—all her body needed to focus on was this baby.

'We'll call you in when Maggie's ready to receive you,' Oliver said cheerfully, as if this was something that happened every day. 'There's a coffee machine down the hall.

Go make yourself comfortable while Maggie lets us help her bring your baby into the world.'

And he stood at the door, calm but undeniably authoritative. This was his world, his body language said, and he knew it. Not theirs.

They had no choice.

They left.

Em felt so grateful she could have thrown herself on his chest and wept.

The last couple of hours had been a nightmare, with every suggestion she made being overridden or simply talked over by Leonie, who knew everything. But Maggie had made a promise and Maggie hadn't been standing up to her. Em had had to respect that promise, but now Oliver had taken control and turned the situation around.

Now there were only four of them in the birthing suite. Oliver flicked the two switches at the window.

'I've turned off sight and sound for the moment,' he told Maggie. 'If you want, we'll turn on sight when you're ready, but I suggest we don't turn on sound. That way you can say whatever you want, yell whatever you want, and only we will hear you.'

'She wants to be here...' Maggie whispered, holding her husband's hand like she was drowning.

'She does, but right now this is all about you and your baby.' He put the emphasis on the *your*. 'Emily, you were about to do an examination. Maggie, would you like me to leave while she does?'

Em blinked. An obstetrician, offering to leave while the midwife did the pelvic exam? Talk about trust...

'But you're a doctor,' Maggie whispered.

'Yes,'

'Then stay. I sort of...I mean...I need...'

'You need Oliver's clout with your sister,' Em finished

for her. 'You need a guy who can boss people round with the best of them. You've got the right doctor for that here. Oliver knows what he wants and he knows how to get it. Right now Oliver wants a safe delivery for your baby and there's no one more likely than Oliver to help you achieve it.'

He stayed. Maggie's labour had eased right off. She lay back exhausted and Em offered to give her a gentle massage.

He watched as Em's hands did magical things to Maggie's body, easing pain, easing stress.

Once upon a time she'd massaged him. He'd loved...

He loved...

Peace descended on the little room. At Maggie's request Oliver flicked the window switch again so Leonie and Connor could watch, but she agreed with Oliver about the sound.

As far as Leonie and Connor were concerned, there was no audio link. Any noise Maggie made, anything they said, stayed in the room.

Maggie's relief was almost palpable, and as Em's gentle fingers worked their magic, as Maggie relaxed, the contractions started again. Good and strong. Stage two was on them almost before they knew it.

'She's coming,' Maggie gasped. 'Oh, I want to see.'

And Oliver supported her on one side and Rob supported her on the other, while Em gently encouraged.

'She's almost here. One more push... One more push, Maggie, and you'll have a daughter.'

And finally, finally, a tiny scrap of humanity slithered into the world. And Em did as she did with every delivery. She slid the baby up onto Maggie's tummy, so Maggie could touch, could feel, could savour the knowledge that she'd safely delivered a daughter.

The look on Maggie's face…

Oliver watched her hand touch her tiny baby, he watched her face crumple—and he made a fast decision. He deliberately glanced at the end of the bed and carefully frowned—as if he was seeing something that could be a problem—and then he flicked the window to black again.

He put his head out the door as he did.

'It's great,' he told Leonie and Connor, whose noses were hard against the glass, who turned as he opened the door as if to rush in, but his body blocked them. 'You can see we have a lovely, healthy baby girl, but there's been a small bleed. We need to do a bit of patching before you come in.'

'Can we take her? Can we hold her?'

'Maggie needs to hold her. The sensation of holding her, maybe letting her suckle, will help the delivery of the placenta; it'll keep things normal. Maggie's needs come first right now. I assume you agree?'

'I… Yes,' Leonie whispered. 'But we agreed she wouldn't feed her. I just so want to hold her.'

'I suspect you'll have all the time in the world to hold her,' Oliver told her. 'But the feeding is part of the birthing process and it's important. I'm sorry but, promises or not, right now my focus is on Maggie.'

Em's focus was also on Maggie. She watched while Maggie savoured the sight of her little daughter, while she watched, awed, as the little girl found her breast and suckled fiercely.

Her husband sat beside her, silent, his hand on her arm. He, too, was watching the baby.

Without words Em and Oliver had changed places—Oliver was coping with the delivery of the placenta, checking everything was intact, doing the medical stuff. This was a normal delivery—there was no need for him to be here—but still there was pressure from outside the room and he knew that once he left Leonie and Connor would be in here.

'You know,' he said mildly, to the room in general, 'there's never been a law that says a surrogate mother has to give away her baby. No matter how this baby was conceived, Maggie, you're still legally her birth mother. If you want to pull back now...'

But Maggie was smiling. She was cradling her little one with love and with awe, and tears were slipping down her face, but the smile stayed there.

'This little one's Leonie's,' she whispered. 'You've seen Leonie at her worst—she's been frantic about her baby and it was no wonder she was over the top at the end. But I can't tell you how grateful I am that you've given us space to say goodbye. To send her on with love.'

How could she do this? Oliver wondered, stunned. She'd gently changed sides now so the baby was sucking from the other breast. The bonding seemed complete; perfect.

'It's not like we're losing her,' Rob ventured, touching the little one's cheek. 'She'll be our niece and our god-daughter.'

'And probably a bit more than that,' Maggie said, still smiling. 'Our kids will have a cousin. My sister will have a baby. To be able to do this... She's not ours, you can see. She has Connor's hair. None of ours ever looked like this. But, oh, it's been good to have this time.' She looked up at them and smiled, her eyes misty with tears. 'Em, would you like to ask them to come in now?'

'You're sure?' Em asked, with all the gentleness in the world. 'Maggie, this is your decision. As Oliver says, it's not too late to change your mind.'

'My mind never changed,' Maggie said, serene now, seemingly at peace. 'While I was having her she felt all mine and that was how I wanted to feel. Thank you for realising that. But now...now it's time for my sister to meet her baby.'

'How could she do that?'

With medical necessities out of the way, Oliver and Em were able to back out of the room. Leonie was holding her daughter now, her face crumpled, tears tracking unchecked. Connor, too, seemed awed.

Rob was still holding Maggie but the two of them were watching Leonie and Connor with quiet satisfaction.

'Love,' Em said softly, as they headed to the sinks. 'I don't know how surrogacy can work without it.'

'Do you seriously think Leonie can make a good mother?'

'I do. I've seen her lots of times during Maggie's pregnancy—she's been with her all the way. Yeah, she's a corporate bigwig, but her life has been prescribed because she and Connor couldn't have children. Maggie seems the ultimate earth mother—and she is—but she and Leonie love each other to bits. I suspect the over-the-top reaction we saw from Leonie in there—and which you saved us from—was simply too much emotion. It felt like her baby was being born. She wanted what was best for her baby and everything else got ignored. Mums are like that,' she said simply. 'And thank God for it.'

'You really think she can look after the baby as well as Maggie could?'

'I have no idea. I do know, though, that this baby will be loved to bits, and that's all that counts.'

'She can love it as much as Maggie?'

'That's right, you don't think it's possible.' She lowered her voice to almost a whisper. 'It's a bleak belief, Ollie, caused by your own grief. Have you ever thought about counselling?'

'Counselling?' In the quiet corridor it was almost a shout. He stood back and looked at her as if she was out of her mind.

'Counselling,' she said, serenely. 'It's available here. We have the best people...'

'I don't need counselling.'

'I think you do. You have so much unresolved anger from your childhood.'

'I'm over it.'

'It destroyed our marriage,' she said simply. 'And you haven't moved on. I expected you to have a wife and a couple of your own kids by now. You were scared of adoption—are you worried about your reaction to any child?'

'This is nuts.'

'Yeah, it is,' she said amiably, tossing her stained robes into the waiting bins. 'And it's none of my business. It's just... I've got on with my life, Oliver. You kissed me on Saturday and I found myself wondering how many women you'd kissed since our split. And part of me thinks...not many? Why not?'

Silence.

She was watching him like a pert sparrow, he thought, as the rest of his brain headed off on tangents he didn't understand. She was interested. Clinically interested. She was a fine nurse, a midwife, a woman used to dealing with babies and new parents all the time. Maybe she had insights...

Maybe she didn't have any insights. Maybe she was just Em, his ex-wife.

Maybe that kiss had been a huge mistake.

Step away, he told himself. He didn't need her or anyone else's analysis. But...

'Em, I would like to see Gretta and Toby again.'

Where had that come from? His mouth? He hadn't meant to say it, surely he hadn't.

But…but…

On Saturday he'd sat on the beach and he'd held Gretta, a little girl who had very little life left to her. He should have felt…what? Professional detachment? No, never that, for once an obstetrician felt removed from the joy of children he might as well hand in his ticket and become an accountant. Grief, then, for a life so short?

Not that, either.

He'd felt peace. He acknowledged it now. He'd sat in the waves and he'd felt Gretta's joy as the water had washed her feet. And he'd also felt Em's love.

Em made Gretta smile. He was under no illusions—with Gretta's myriad medical problems and her rejection by her birth mother, she'd faced spending her short life in institutions.

And watching Em now, as she looked at him in astonishment, he thought, what a gift she's given her children.

It was his cowardice that had made that possible. He'd walked away from Em, so Em had turned to fostering.

If he'd stayed with her maybe they could have adopted a newborn, a child with no medical baggage, a child Em could love with all her heart. Only he'd thought it wasn't possible, to love a child who wasn't his own. He'd walked away because such a love wasn't possible, and yet here was Em, loving with all her heart when Gretta's life would be so short…

Had he been mistaken? Suddenly, fiercely, he wanted that to be true. For he wanted to be part of this—part of Em's loving?

Part of her hotchpotch family.

'Oliver, there's no need—'

'I'd love to spend more time with Gretta.' He was wise enough to know that pushing things further at this stage would drive her away. The way he felt about Em…it was so complicated. So fraught. He'd hurt her so much… Make it about her children, he thought, and even that thought hurt.

Her children.

'What time do you finish tonight?' he asked.

'Six.'

'I'm still reasonably quiet and I started early.' He glanced at his watch. 'I should be finished by five. What say I head over there and give Adrianna a break for an hour?'

'Mum'd love that.' She hesitated. 'You could…stay for tea?'

'I won't do that.' And it was too much. He couldn't stop his finger coming up and tracing the fine lines of her cheek. She looked exhausted. She looked like she wasn't eating enough. He wanted to pick her up, take her somewhere great, Hawaii maybe, put her in a resort, make her eat, make her sleep…

Take her to his bed…

Right. In his dreams. She was looking at him now, confused, and there was no way he was pushing that confusion.

'I have a meeting back here at the hospital at seven,' he lied. 'So I'll be leaving as you get home.'

'You're sure you want to?'

'I want to. And if I can…for what time Gretta has left, if you'll allow me, it would be my privilege to share.'

'I don't—'

'This is nothing to do with you and me,' he said, urgently now. 'It's simply that I have time on my hands— and I've fallen for your daughter.'

CHAPTER ELEVEN

SHE SHOULD HAVE said no. The thought of Oliver being with the kids when she wasn't there was disconcerting, to say the least. She rang Adrianna and warned her and Adrianna's pleasure disconcerted her even more.

'I always said he was a lovely man. I was so sorry when you two split. It was just that awful time—it would have split up any couple.'

'We're incompatible, Mum,' she said, and she heard Adrianna smile down the phone.

'You had differences. Maybe those differences aren't as great as they once seemed.'

'Mum…'

'I'm just saying. But, okay, sweetheart, I won't interfere. I'll say nothing.'

Which didn't mean she was thinking nothing, Em decided as she headed to her next case. Luckily, it was a lovely, normal delivery, a little girl born to an Italian couple. Their fourth baby—and their fourth daughter—was greeted like the miracle all babies were.

She left them professing huge gratitude, and Em thought: How come the cases where all I do is catch are the ones where I get the most thanks? But it cheered her immeasurably and by the time she went to see Ruby, her complications with Oliver seemed almost trifling.

Ruby was about to bring those complications front and centre. The teenager was lying propped up on pillows, surrounded by glossy magazines. She had the television on, but she looked bored. And fretful. She lightened up when Em came in, and before Em could even ask her how she was, she put in a question of her own.

'Emily, I've been thinking. You and Dr Evans split because you couldn't have a baby. That's what I guessed, but it's true, I know it is.'

Whoa! Hospital grapevine? Surely not. Sophia was the only one she'd told. Surely Sophia wouldn't break a confidence and even if she had, surely no member of staff would tell a patient things that were personal.

'How—'

'I'm sure I heard it.' Ruby's eyes were alight with interest, a detective tracking vital clues. 'When I was asleep. After Theatre. You and that other nurse were talking.'

Sophia. Em did a frantic rethink of what they'd talked about. Uh-oh.

'So I've been thinking. I've got a baby I don't want,' Ruby said, and suddenly the detective Ruby had given way to a scared kid. 'Maybe you could have mine.'

There was an offer. It took her breath away.

She plonked down on the bed and gazed at Ruby in stupefaction. 'Ruby,' she said at last. 'How can you think such a thing?'

'I can't keep it,' she said fretfully. 'Dr Evans says I have to stay in bed so I don't go into labour and it's driving me nuts, but it's giving me time to think. Ever since I got pregnant…first Jason said he didn't want anything to do with it, or me. Then Mum said she'd kick me out if I kept it. And I was pig stubborn—it just seemed so wrong. I thought I was in love with Jason, and when I realised I was pregnant I was happy. I wasn't even scared. I even

thought I might make a good mum. It was only after that…
the complications came in.'

'Most of those complications are over,' Em said gently.
'Your daughter has every chance of being born healthy.'

'Yeah, but I've been couch-surfing since Mum found
out,' she said fretfully. 'I had to leave school because I had
nowhere to stay, and how can I couch-surf with a kid—no
one's going to want me.'

'Then this isn't about adoption,' Em told her, forcing
herself to sound upbeat and cheerful. 'This is all about
plans for the future. We have a couple of excellent social
workers. I'll get one of them to pop in and talk to you. She
can help you sort things out.'

'But there are so many things…and if the baby's prem,
which Dr Evans says is even probable, how can I cope with
a baby? If she had a good home…if you and Dr Evans
could look after her…'

'Ruby, leave this.' The girl's eyes had filled with tears
and Em moved to hug her. 'Things will work out. You
won't have to give away your baby, I promise.'

'But you need her. It could save your marriage.'

'My marriage was over a long time ago,' she said, still
hugging. 'It doesn't need your daughter to try and mend it.
Ruby, I want you to stop worrying about me and my love
life. I want you to only think about yourself.'

Oliver arrived at Em's house right on five. Adrianna
greeted him with unalloyed pleasure—and promptly declared her intention of taking a nap.

'When Em rang, that's what I decided I'd do,' she told
him. 'The tea hour's the hell hour. If I can have a nap first
it'll take the pressure off both of us when Em comes home.'
She smiled and suddenly he found himself being hugged.
'It's great to have you back, Oliver,' she told him. 'And
it's great that you arrived just when we need you most.'

He was left with the kids.

He carried them out into the soft autumn evening, stupidly grateful that Mike from next door was nowhere to be seen. Both kids seemed a bit subdued, pleased to see him, relaxed but tired.

The end of a long day? He touched Toby's forehead and worried that he might have a slight fever.

Katy next door had a cold. Had she or her kids spread it?

Maybe he was imagining things. He was like a worried parent, he thought, mocking himself.

He wasn't a parent. Not even close.

He had these kids for an hour.

He set them on the grass under the tree. Fuzzy the dog came out and loped herself over Gretta's legs. Gretta's oxygen cylinder sat beside her, a harsh reminder of reality, but for now there was no threat. A balmy evening. Warm, soft grass.

'Look up through the trees and tell me what you see,' he said, and both kids looked up obediently.

'Tree,' Gretta said.

'Tree,' Toby agreed, and he found himself smiling. Gretta and her parrot.

Together they were family, he thought. They were a fragile family at best, but for today, well, for today this was okay.

'I'm seeing a bear,' he said, and both kids looked at him in alarm.

'Up there,' he reassured them. 'See that big cloud? It has a nose on the side. See its mouth? It's smiling.'

Neither kid seemed capable of seeing what he was seeing but they looked at each other and seemed to decide mutually to humour him.

'Bear,' Gretta said.

'Bear,' Toby agreed.

'He must live up there in the clouds,' Oliver decreed.

'I think he might be the bear from "Goldilocks". Do you guys know that story?'

Toby was two, a tiny African toddler suffering the effects of early malnutrition as well as the scoliosis and scarring on his face from infection. Gretta was a damaged kid with Down's. 'Goldilocks' was way out of their sphere.

'Well,' Oliver said serenely, settling himself down. The kids edged nearer, sensing a story. 'Once upon a time there were three bears and they lived up in the clouds. Baby Bear had a lovely soft little cloud because he was the smallest. Mumma Bear had a middly sort of cloud, a bit squishy but with a nice high back because sometimes her back hurt, what with carrying Baby Bear all the time.'

'Back,' said Toby.

'Back,' Gretta agreed, obviously deeply satisfied with the way this story was progressing.

'But Papa Bear had the biggest cloud of all. It was a ginormous cloud. It had great big footprints all over it because Papa Bear wore great big boots and, no matter what Mumma Bear said, he never took them off before he climbed onto his cloud. Mumma Bear should have said no porridge for Papa Bear but Mumma Bear is really kind...'

'My Emmy,' Gretta murmured, and he wondered how much this kid knew. How much did she understand?

My Emmy...

It had been a soft murmur, a statement that Gretta had her own Mumma Bear and all was right with that arrangement.

'Porridge,' Toby said, and Oliver had to force his thoughts away from Em, away from the little girl who was pressed into his side, and onto a story where porridge was made in the clouds.

And life was fantasy.

And the real world could be kept at bay.

* * *

Em arrived home soon after six, walked in and Adrianna was in the kitchen, starting dinner. She was singing.

Oliver's hire car was parked out the front.

'Where's Oliver?' she asked cautiously, and then gazed around. 'Where are the kids?' Had he taken them out? It was late. They'd be tired. Maybe they'd gone next door. But Katy had passed her cold on to her youngest. She didn't want them there, not with Gretta's breathing so fragile.

'Hey, don't look so worried.' Her mum was beaming and signalling out the window. 'Look.'

She looked.

The two kids were lying under the spreading oak in the backyard. Oliver was sandwiched between them. He had an arm round each of them and they were snuggled against him.

Fuzzy was draped over his stomach.

'You can hardly see him,' Adrianna said with satisfaction. 'It's an Oliver sandwich. He's been telling them stories. I went for a nap but I left my window open. He's an excellent storyteller. He makes them giggle.'

'They can't understand.'

'They can understand enough to know when to giggle. Cloud Bears. Porridge stealing. High drama. Lots of pouncing, with Fuzzy being the pouncee.'

'You're kidding.'

'He's adorable,' Adrianna said. 'He always was. He always is.'

'Mum…'

'I know.' Her mother held up her hands as if in surrender. 'It's none of my business and I understand the grief that drove you apart.'

'It wasn't the grief. It was…'

'Irreconcilable differences,' Adrianna said sagely. She looked out the window again. 'But from this angle they don't look so irreconcilable to me. You want to go tell him dinner is ready?'

'I... No.'

'Don't be a coward.'

'Mum, don't.' She swiped a stray curl from her tired eyes and thought she should have had more cut off. She needed to be practical. She wanted...

She didn't want.

'I don't want to fall in love with him again,' she whispered. 'Mum...'

And her mother turned and hugged her.

'It's okay, baby,' she told her as she held her close. 'There's no fear of that, because you've never stopped loving him anyway.'

She came out to tell the kids dinner was ready. She was looking tired and worried. She stood back a bit and called, as if she was afraid of coming further.

Fuzzy raced across to her, barking. The kids looked round and saw her and Toby started beetling across the lawn to her. The scoliosis meant he couldn't walk yet, but he could crawl, and crawl he did, a power crawl, his stiff legs making him look like a weird little bug. He was a bug who squealed with joy as Em swung him up in her arms.

Gretta couldn't crawl. She lay and smiled, waiting for Em to come and fetch her, and Oliver thought that, combined, these kids weighed heaps and Em was slight and...

And it was the life she'd chosen. The life she'd wanted as an alternative to staying married to him.

He rose, lifted Gretta and her oxygen cylinder and carried her across to Em. Gretta reached out her arms to be hugged. Oliver tried for a kid swap in midair and suddenly they were all squeezed together. Kids in the middle. Him on one side, Em on the other, Fuzzy bouncing around in the middle of all their feet.

It was a sandwich squeeze, he thought, a group hug, but he was holding Em. They were the wagons circling the kids. Keeping them safe?

Nothing could keep Gretta safe.

And then Toby coughed and Em tugged away with quick concern. 'Oh, no,' she whispered as she took in Toby's flushed face. 'Katy's bug…'

'I've had them lying on either side of me, and that's the first cough. In the fresh air it should be okay. Should we try and isolate them?'

'It'll be too late, if indeed it's Katy's cold. And besides…' Her voice fell away.

'Besides?'

'We made a decision, Mum and I. The first couple of years of Gretta's life were practically all spent in hospital. She was growing so institutionalised she was starting to not respond at all. Tristan's been her doctor from the beginning. After the last bout of surgery—it was a huge gamble but it didn't pay off—he told us to take her home and love her. And that's what we're doing. We'll be a family until the end.'

Her voice broke a little as she finished but her eyes were still resolute. 'She's Toby's sister,' she said. 'We know there are risks, but the fact that she's family overrides everything.'

'So you'll let her catch—'

'I'll do as much as I can to not let her catch whatever this is,' she said. 'Toby can sleep with Mum and I'll sleep with Gretta so they're not sharing a room. We'll wash and we'll disinfect. But that's all we'll do.'

'That alone will take a power of work.'

'So what's the alternative?' she demanded, lifting her chin. 'Gretta's my daughter, Oliver. The decision is mine.'

Toby's cold was minor, a sniffle and a cough, no big deal. He was quieter than usual, but that was okay because it meant he was supremely happy to lie under the oak tree every evening and listen to Oliver's stories.

Because Oliver kept coming every evening.

'Why?' Em demanded on the third evening. 'Oliver, you don't need to. You owe me nothing.'

'This is little to do with you,' he said, and was surprised into acknowledging that he spoke the truth. For at first these kids had seemed like Em's kids, the kids he'd refused her, a part of Em. And at first he'd agreed to take care of them because of Em. It had been a way to get to know her again—and there was a hefty dose of guilt thrown in for good measure.

But now... He lay under the oak and the bears became tortoises or heffalumps or antigowobblers—that one took a bit of explaining—and he found he was taking as much pleasure as he was giving. And as much quiet satisfaction.

The last five years had been hectic, frantic, building up a career to the point where he knew he was one of the best in-utero surgeons in the world. It hadn't been easy. He'd had little time for anything else, and in truth he hadn't wanted time.

If he'd had free time he'd have thought about Em.

But now, with his career back in Australia yet to build up, he did have that time. And he wasn't thinking about Em—or not all the time, he conceded. He was thinking of two kids.

Of what story he could tell them tonight to make them laugh.

Of how to lessen the burden on Em's shoulders while acknowledging her right to love these two.

How had he ever thought she couldn't love an adopted child?

And as time went on, he thought…How could he have thought that of himself? These kids were somehow wrapping themselves around his heart like two tiny worms. They were two brave, damaged kids who, without Em's big heart, would be institutionalised and isolated.

These were kids who could well break her heart. Gretta's prognosis was grim. Once Toby's medical condition improved, the paperwork to keep him in the country would be mind-blowing.

It didn't seem to matter. Em just…loved. Her courage took his breath away.

Her love made him rethink his life.

What sort of dumb, cruel mistake have I made? he demanded of himself after his first week of childminding. What have I thrown away?

For he had thrown it. Em was always happy to see him, always grateful for the help he gave, always bubbly with the kids when he was around. But as soon as possible she withdrew. What would she say if he asked her to reconsider their relationship? He had no right to ask, he thought. And besides… How could he cope with the pain she was opening herself up to? To adopt these kids…

Except he didn't seem to have a choice. He might not be able to adopt them but, lying under the tree evening after evening, he knew he was beginning to love them.

As he'd always loved their mother?

Every night Em got home from work and he was there. Unbidden, Adrianna pushed mealtime back a little. So instead of coming home to chaos, sometimes Em had time to lie under the tree with them.

It became a routine—they greeted her with quiet pleasure, shifted a little to make room for her on the lushest part of the lawn, Fuzzy stretching so he managed to drape over everyone.

Oliver never tried to talk to her. There was no 'How was your day, dear?' He simply kept on with his stories, but he included her in them.

He found an Emily-shaped cloud and demanded the kids acknowledge it had the same shaped nose, and the same smile. And then he made up a story about Emily and the beanstalk.

It was better than any massage, Em conceded, lying back, looking up through the trees, listening to Oliver making her kids happy.

For he did make them happy. They adored this story time. Gretta probably understood little, but she knew this was story time. Lying on the grass, she was totally relaxed. Her breathing wasn't under pressure, she wriggled closer to Oliver and Em felt her heart twist with the pleasure she was so obviously feeling.

And Toby... The scarring on his face had left the side of his mouth twisted. He had trouble forming words, but with Oliver's gentle stories he was trying more and more.

'And here comes the giant...' Oliver intoned, and Toby's scarred little face contorted with delight.

'S-stomp...stomp...stomp...' he managed.

And Em thought, How smart is my little son? And she watched Oliver give the toddler a high five and then they all said, 'Stomp, stomp, stomp,' and they all convulsed into giggles.

And Em thought...Em thought...

Maybe she'd better not think, she decided. Maybe it was dangerous to think.

What had her mum said? She'd never stopped loving him?

She had, she told herself fiercely. She'd thrown all her love into her children. She had none left over for Oliver.

But she lay and listened to giants stomping, she lay and listened to her children chuckling, and she knew that she was lying.

And she couldn't get away from him. The next morning she walked into Ruby's room and Oliver was there. Of course he was.

It seemed the man had slipped back into her world and was there to stay. He was an obstetrician, and a good one, so of course he was on the wards. He'd offered to help with Gretta and Toby, so of course he was at her house every night when she got home. He was the doctor in charge of making sure Ruby's baby stayed exactly where she was, so of course he was in Ruby's room.

It was just… Why did he take her breath away? Every time she saw him she lost her breath all over again.

She couldn't still love him, she told herself, more and more fiercely as time went on. Her marriage was five years past. She'd moved on. Oliver was now a colleague and a friend, so she should be able to treat him as such.

There was no reason for her heart to beat hard against her ribs every time she saw him.

There was no reason for her fingers to move automatically to her lips, remembering a kiss by the bay…

'Hey,' she managed now as she saw Ruby and Oliver together. She was hauling her professional cheer around her like a cloak. 'I hope Dr Evans is telling you how fantastic you've been,' she told Ruby. 'Because she has been fantastic, Dr Evans. She's been so still, she's healing beautifully and she's giving her baby every chance and more. I can't believe your courage, Ruby, love. I can't believe your strength.'

'She'll be okay,' Ruby said in quiet satisfaction, and her hand curved around her belly.

'We're going to let you go home,' Oliver told her. He'd

been examining her, and now he was tucking her bed-clothes around her again. 'As long as you keep behaving. Do you have somewhere to go?'

And Em blinked again. This was a surgeon—*a surgeon*—tucking in bedclothes and worrying about where his patient would go after hospital.

'Wendy, the social worker, has organised me a place at a hostel near here,' she told them. 'Mum won't let me home but Wendy's organised welfare payments. She's given me the name of a place that'll give me free furniture and stuff for the baby. It's all good.'

'You'll be alone.' Oliver was frowning. 'I'm not sure—'

'Wendy says the lady who runs the hostel has had other pregnant girls there. If I'm in trouble she'll bring me to the hospital. It sounds okay.' She hesitated. 'But there is something I wanted to talk to you about.'

She was speaking to Oliver. Em backed away a little. 'You want me to come back later?'

'No,' Ruby said, firmly now, looking from one to the other. 'I wanted you both here. I've been thinking and thinking and I've decided. I want you to adopt my baby.'

For Em, who'd heard this proposition before, it wasn't a complete shock. For Oliver, though... He looked like he'd been slapped in the face by a wet fish. How many times in his professional career had he been offered a baby? Em wondered. Possibly never.

Probably never.

'What are you talking about?' he asked at last. 'Ruby, I'm sorry, but your baby has nothing to do with us.'

'But she could have everything to do with you.' Ruby pushed herself up on her pillows and looked at them with eagerness. More, with determination. 'I've been think-ing and thinking, and the more I think about it the more

I know I can't care for her. Not like she should be cared for. I didn't even finish school. All my friends are doing uni entrance exams this year and I can't even get my Year Twelve. I don't have anyone to care for my baby. I don't have any money. I'll be stuck on welfare and I can't see me getting off it for years and years. I can't give my baby… what she needs.'

'She needs you,' Em said gently. 'She needs her mum.'

'Yes, but she needs more. What if she wants to be a doctor—how could someone like me ever afford that sort of education? And there'll be operations for the spina bifida—Dr Zigler's already told me there'll be more operations. She'll need special things and now I don't even have enough to buy her nappies. And the choice is adoption but how will I know someone will love her as much as I do? But I know you will. I heard…when I was asleep… It was like it was a dream but I know it's true. You two need a baby to love. You split up because you couldn't have one. What if you have my baby? I could…I dunno…visit her… You'd let me do that, wouldn't you? Mum probably still won't let me go home but I could go back to school. I'd find a way. And I could make something of myself, have enough to buy her presents, maybe even be someone she can be proud of.'

'Ruby…' Doctors didn't sit on patients' beds. That was Medical Training 101, instilled in each and every trainee nurse and doctor. Oliver sat on Ruby's bed and he took her shoulders in his hands. 'Ruby, you don't want to give away your baby.'

Em could hardly hear him. Look up, she told herself fiercely. If you look up you can't cry.

What sort of stupid edict was that? Tears were slipping down her face regardless.

'I want my baby to be loved.' Ruby was crying, too, and

her tears were fierce. 'And you two could love her. I know you could. And you love each other. Anyone can see that. And I know Em's got two already, but Sophia says you're round there every night, helping, and Em's mum helps, too, and she has a great big house…'

'Where did you hear all this?' Em managed.

'I asked,' she said simply. 'There are so many nurses in this hospital and they all know you, Em. They all say you're a fantastic mum. And you should be married again. And it'd be awesome for my baby. I'd let you adopt her properly. She'd be yours.' She took another breath, and it seemed to hurt. She pulled back from Oliver and held her tummy again, then looked from Oliver to Em and back again.

'I'd even let you choose her name,' she managed. 'She'd be your daughter. I know you'd love her. You could be Mum and Dad to her. You could be married again. You could be a family.'

There was a long silence in the room. So many elephants… So much baggage.

Oliver was still sitting on the bed. He didn't move, but he put a hand out to Em. She took a step forward and sat beside him. Midwife and doctor on patient's bed… No matter. Rules were made to be broken.

Some rules. Not others. Other rules were made to protect patients. Ethics were inviolate. No matter what happened between Em and himself, the ethics here were clear-cut and absolute.

But somehow he needed to hold Em's hand while he said it. Somehow it seemed important to say it as a couple.

'Ruby, we can't,' he said gently, and Em swiped a handful of tissues from the bedside table and handed them to Ruby, and then swiped a handful for herself.

The way Oliver was feeling he wouldn't mind a handful for himself, too.

Get a grip, he told himself fiercely, and imperceptibly his grip on Em's hand tightened.

Say it together. Think it together.

'Ruby, what you've just offered us,' he said gently but firmly—he had to be firm even if he was feeling like jelly inside—'it's the greatest compliment anyone has ever given me, and I'm sure that goes for Em, too. You'd trust us with your baby. It takes our breath away. It's the most awesome gift a woman could ever give.'

He thought back to the birth he'd attended less than a week ago, a sister, a surrogate mother. A gift.

And he thought suddenly of his own birth mother. He'd never tried to find her. He'd always felt anger that she'd handed him over to parents who didn't know what it was to love. But he looked at Ruby now and he knew that there was no black and white. Ruby was trying her best to hand her daughter to people she knew would love her, but they couldn't accept.

Would it be Ruby's fault if the adoptive parents turned out…not to love?

His world was twisting. So many assumptions were being turned on their heads.

He saw Em glance at him and he was pathetically grateful that she spoke. He was almost past it.

'Ruby, we're your treating midwife and obstetrician,' she said, gently, as well, but just as firmly. 'That puts us in a position of power. It's like a teacher dating a student—there's no way the student can divorce herself from the authority of the teacher. That authority might well be what attracted the student to the teacher in the first place.'

'I don't know what you mean.'

'I mean we're caring for you,' Em went on. 'And you're seeing that we're caring. It's influencing you, whether you know it or not. Ruby, we couldn't adopt your baby, even if we wanted to. It's just not right.'

'But you need a baby. You said…it'll heal your marriage.'

'I'm not sure what you heard,' Em told her. 'But no baby heals a marriage. We don't need a baby. Your offer is awesome, gorgeous, loving, but, Ruby, whatever decision you make, you need to take us out of it. We're your midwife and your obstetrician. We look after you while your baby's born and then you go back to the real world.'

'But I don't want to go back to the real world,' Ruby wailed. 'I'm scared. And I don't want to give my baby to someone I don't know.'

'Do you want to give your baby to anyone?' Oliver asked, recovering a little now. Em had put this back on a professional basis. Surely he could follow.

'No!' And it was a wail from the heart, a deep, gut-wrenching howl of loss.

And Em moved, gathering the girl into her arms, letting her sob and sob and sob.

He should leave, Oliver thought. He wasn't needed. He was this girl's obstetrician, nothing else.

But the offer had been made to him and to Em. Ruby had treated them as a couple.

Ruby had offered them her baby to bind them together, and even though the offer couldn't be accepted, he felt… bound.

So he sat while Ruby sobbed and Em held her—and somehow, some way, he felt more deeply in love with his wife than he'd ever felt.

His wife. Em…

They'd been apart for almost five years.

She still felt…like part of him.

Em was pulling back a bit now, mopping Ruby's eyes, smiling down at her, pushing her to respond.

'Hey,' she said softly. 'Hey... You want to hear an alternative plan?'

An alternative? What was this? Surely alternatives should be left to the social workers?

If Em was offering to foster on her own he'd have to step in. Ethics again, but they had to be considered, no matter how big Em's heart was.

But she wasn't offering to foster. She had something bigger...

'My mum and I have been talking about you,' she told Ruby, tilting her chin so she could mop some more. 'I know that's not the thing to do, to talk about a patient at home, but I did anyway. My mum lives with me, she helps care for my two kids and she's awesome. She also has a huge house.'

What...what?

'Not that we're offering to share,' Em said, diffidently now, as if she was treading on shifting sand. 'But we have a wee bungalow at the bottom of the garden. It's a studio, a bed/sitting room with its own bathroom. It has a little veranda that looks out over the garden. It's self-contained and it's neat.'

Ruby's tears had stopped. She looked at Em, caught, fascinated.

As was Oliver. He knew that bungalow. He and Em had stayed in it in the past when they'd visited Adrianna for some family celebration and hadn't wanted to drive home.

Josh had been conceived in that bungalow.

'Anyway, Mum and I have been talking,' Em repeated. 'And we're throwing you an option. It's just one option, mind, Ruby, so you can take it or leave it and we won't be the least offended. But if you wanted to take it...you could have it for a peppercorn rent, something you could well afford on your welfare payments. You'd have to put up with our kids whooping round the backyard and I can't promise they'd give you privacy. But in return we could help you.

'The school down the road is one of the few in the state that has child care attached—mostly for staff but they take students' children at need. They have two young mums doing Year Twelve now, so if you wanted to, you could go back. Mum and I could help out, too. It would be hard, Ruby, because your daughter would be your responsibility. But you decided against all pressure not to have an abortion. You've faced everything that's been thrown at you with courage and with determination. Mum and I think you can make it, Ruby, so we'd like to help. It's an option. Think about it.'

What the...?

But they couldn't take it further.

Heinz Zigler arrived then, with an entourage of medical students, ostensibly to talk through the success of the operation with Ruby but in reality to do a spot of teaching to his trainees.

They left Ruby surrounded by young doctors, smiling again, actually lapping up the attention. Turning again into a seventeen-year-old?

They emerged into the corridor and Oliver took Em's arm.

'What the hell...'

The words had been running through his head, over and over, and finally he found space to say them out loud.

'Problem?' Em turned and faced him.

'You'd take them on?'

'Mum and I talked about it. It won't be "taking them on". Ruby's lovely. She'll be a great little mum, but she's a kid herself. She made the bravest decision when she chose not to terminate. It's becoming increasingly obvious that she loves this baby to bits and this way...we could maybe help her be a kid again. Occasionally. Go back to school. Have a bit of fun but have her baby, as well.'

'She offered it to you.' He hesitated. 'To us. I know that's not possible.' He was struggling with what he was feeling; what he was thinking. 'But if it was possible… would you want that?'

'To take Ruby's baby? No!'

'I was watching your face. It's not possible to accept her offer but if it was it'd be your own baby. A baby you could love without complications. Is this offer to Ruby a second-best option?'

'Is that what you think?' She was leaning back against the wall, her hands behind her back, watching him. And what he saw suddenly in her gaze…*was it sympathy?*

'You still don't get it, do you?' she said, gently now. This was a busy hospital corridor. Isla and Sophia were at the nurses' station. They were glancing at Em and Oliver, and Oliver thought how much of what had just gone on would spin around the hospital. How much of what he said now?

He should leave. He should walk away now, but Em was tilting her chin, in the way he knew so well, her lecture mode, her 'Let's tell Oliver what we really think of him'. Uh-oh.

'You scale it, don't you?' Her voice was still soft but there was a note that spoke of years of experience, years of pain. 'You scale love.'

'I don't know what you mean.'

'You think you couldn't love a baby because it's not yours. That's your scale—all or nothing. Your scale reads ten or zero. But me…you've got it figured that my scale has a few more numbers. You're thinking maybe ten for my own baby, but I can't have that. So then—and this is how I think your mind is working—you've conceded that I can love a little bit, so I've taken in Gretta and Toby.

'But according to your logic I can't love them at ten.

Maybe it's a six for Toby because he'll live, but he's damaged and I might not be able to keep him anyway so maybe we'd better make it a five. And Gretta? Well, she's going to die so make that a four or a three, or maybe she'll die really soon so I'd better back off and even make it a two or a one.

'But Ruby's baby…now, if she could give her to me then she'd be a gorgeous newborn and I'd have her from the start and she'll only be a little bit imperfect so maybe she'd score an eight. Only of course, I can't adopt her at all, so you're thinking now why am I bothering to care when according to you she's right off the bottom of the caring scale? Baby I can't even foster—zero? So why are we offering her the bungalow? Is that what you don't understand?'

He stared at her, dumbfounded. 'This is nonsense. That's not what I meant.'

'But it's what you think.' She was angry now, and she'd forgotten or maybe she just didn't care that they were in a hospital corridor and half the world could hear. 'Yes, your adoptive parents were awful but it's them that should be tossed off the scale, Oliver, not every child who comes after that. I work on no scale. I love my kids to bits, really love them, and there's no way I could love them more even if I'd given birth to them. And I'll love Ruby's baby, and Mum and I will love Ruby, too, because she's a kid herself.

'And it won't kill us to do it—it'll make us live. The heart expands to fit all comers—it does, Oliver. You can love and you can love and you can love, and you know what? All that loving means is that you can love some more.'

'Em—'

'Let me finish.' She put up her hands as if to ward off his protests. 'I almost have. All I want to say is that you've put yourself in some harsh, protective cage and you're staying there because of this stupid, stupid scale. You can't have what you deem worthy of ten, so you'll stick to zero. And I'm sorry.'

She took a deep breath, closed her eyes, regrouped. When she opened them again she looked resolute. Only someone who knew her well—as well as he did—could see the pain.

'I loved you, Oliver,' she said, gently again. 'You were my ten, no, more than ten, you were my life. But that love doesn't mean there can't be others. There are tens all over the place if you open yourself to them. If you got out of your cage you'd see, but you won't and that has to be okay with me.' She pushed herself off the wall and turned to go. She had work to do and so did he.

'That's all I wanted to say,' she managed, and she headed off down the corridor, fast, throwing her last words back over her shoulder as she went.

'That's all,' she said again as she went. 'We agreed five years ago and nothing's changed. You keep inside your nice safe cage, and I'll just keep on loving without you.'

CHAPTER TWELVE

SHE SPENT THE rest of the day feeling shaken. Feeling ill. She should never have spoken like she had, especially in such a public place. She was aware of silences, of odd looks, and she knew the grapevine was going nuts behind her back.

Let it, she thought, but as the day wore on she started feeling bad for the guy she'd yelled at.

Oliver kept himself to himself. He was a loner. His one foray out of his loner state had been to marry her. Now he'd withdrawn again.

But now she'd put private information into the public domain. He might quit, she thought. He could move on. He hadn't expected her to be here when he'd taken the job. Would the emotional baggage be enough to make him leave?

She'd lose him again.

She'd told him it didn't matter. She'd told him she had plenty of love to make up for it.

She'd lied.

That was problem with tens, she thought as the long day continued. If you had a heap of tens it shouldn't matter if one dropped off.

It did matter. It mattered especially when the one she was losing was the man who still felt a part of her.

Her mother was right.

She still loved Oliver Evans.

He was kept busy for the rest of the day, but her words stayed with him. Of course they did. Tens and zeroes. It shouldn't make sense.

Only it did.

Luckily, he had no complex procedures or consultations during the day—or maybe unluckily, because his mind was free to mull over what Em had said. Every expectant mum he saw during the day's consultations…he'd look at them and think ten.

He wasn't so sure about a couple of the fathers, he decided. He saw ambivalence. He also saw nerves. Six, he thought, or seven. But in the afternoon he helped with a delivery. In the early stages the father looked terrified to be there, totally out of his comfort zone, swearing as he went in… 'This wasn't my idea, babe. I dunno why you want me here…'

But 'Babe' clung and clung and the father hung in there with her and when finally a tiny, crumpled little boy slipped seamlessly into the world the man's face changed.

What had looked like a three on Em's scale became a fourteen, just like that.

Because the baby really was his? Maybe, yes, Oliver thought, watching them, but now…with Emily's words ringing in his ears he conceded, not necessarily.

Afterwards he scrubbed and made his way back to the nursery. There was a premmie he'd helped deliver. He wanted to check…

He didn't make it.

A baby was lying under the lights used to treat jaundice. Two women were there, seated on either side. Maggie and Leonie. Surrogate mum and biological mum.

They didn't see him, and he paused at the door and let himself watch.

Leonie's hand was on her baby's cheek, stroking it with a tenderness that took his breath away. Where was the tough, commanding woman of the birth scene? Gone.

Maggie had been expressing milk, the staff had told him. Leonie had paid to stay in with the baby, as his mum.

She looked a bit dishevelled. Sleep-deprived? He'd seen this look on the faces of so many new mums, a combination of awe, love and exhaustion.

Maggie, though, looked different. She'd gone home to her family, he knew, just popping back in to bring her expressed milk, and to see her sister—and her daughter?

Not her daughter. Her sister's daughter.

Because while Leonie was watching her baby, with every ounce of concentration focused on this scrap of an infant, Maggie was watching her. She was watching her sister, and the look on her face...

Here it was again, Oliver thought. Love off the Richter Scale.

Love.

Zero or ten? Em was right, it came in all shapes and sizes, in little bits, in humungous chunks, unasked for, involuntarily given, just there.

And he thought again of his adoptive parents, of the tiny amount of affection they'd grudgingly given. He thought of Em and her Gretta and her Toby. He thought of Adrianna, quietly behind the scenes, loving and loving and loving.

He stood at the door and it was like a series of hammer blows, powering down at his brain. Stupid, stupid, stupid... He'd been judging the world by two people who were incapable of love outside their own rigid parameters.

He'd walked away from Em because he'd feared he'd be like them.

His thoughts were flying everywhere. Em was there,

front and foremost, but suddenly he found himself thinking of the woman who'd given him up for adoption all those years ago. He'd never wanted to find her—he'd blamed her.

There were no black and whites. Maybe he could… Maybe Em could help…

'Can I help you?' It was Isla, bustling in, wheeling a humidicrib. 'If you have nothing to do I could use some help. I'm a man short and Patrick James needs a feed. Can you handle an orogastric tube?'

Patrick James was the baby he'd come to see. He'd been delivered by emergency Caesarean the day before when his mother had shown signs of pre-eclampsia. Dianne wasn't out of the woods yet, her young and scared husband was spending most of his time with her, and their baby son was left to the care of the nursery staff.

He was a thirty-four-weeker. He'd do okay.

It wasn't an obstetrician's job to feed a newborn. He had things to do.

None of them were urgent.

So somehow he found himself accepting. He settled by the humidicrib, he monitored the orogastric tube, he noted with satisfaction all the signs that said Patrick James would be feeding by himself any day now. For a thirty-four-weeker, he was amazing.

All babies were amazing.

Involuntarily, he found himself stroking the tiny, fuzz-covered cheek. Smiling. Thinking that given half a chance, he could love…

Love. Once upon a time he'd thought he'd had it with Emily. He'd walked away.

If he walked back now, that love would need to embrace so much more.

Black and white. Zero or ten. Em was right, there were no boundaries.

He watched Patrick James feed. He watched Leonie love her baby and he watched Maggie love her sister.

He thought about love, and its infinite variations, and every moment he did, he fell deeper and deeper in love with his wife.

She arrived home that night and Oliver's car was parked out the front. His proper car. His gorgeous Morgan. Gleaming, immaculate, all fixed. It made her smile to see it. And it made her feel even more like smiling that she'd yelled at Oliver this morning and here he was again. Gretta and Toby would miss his visits if they ended.

When they ended?

The thought made her smile fade. She walked into the kitchen. The smell of baking filled the house—fresh bread! Oliver's nightly visits were spurring Adrianna on to culinary quests. Her mum was loving him coming.

She was loving him coming.

'Mumma,' Toby crowed in satisfaction, and she scooped him out of his highchair and hugged him. Then, finally, she let herself look at Oliver.

He was sitting by the stove, holding Gretta in his arms. Gretta wasn't smiling at her. She looked intent, a bit distressed.

Her breathing…

The world stood still for a moment. Still hugging Toby, she walked forward to see.

'It's probably nothing,' Adrianna faltered. 'It's probably—'

'It's probably Katy's cold,' Oliver finished for her. 'It's not urgent but I was waiting… Now you're here, maybe we should pop her back to the Victoria so Tristan can check.'

Congestive heart failure. Of course. She'd been expecting it—Tristan had warned her it would happen.

'You won't have her for very long,' he'd told Em, gently but firmly. 'Love her while you can.'

One cold... She should never...

'You can't protect her from everything,' Oliver murmured during that long night when Gretta's breathing grew more and more labored. 'You've given her a home, you've given her love. You know that. It was your decision and it was the right one. If she'd stayed in a protective isolette then maybe she'd survive longer, but not lived.'

'Oh, but—'

'I know,' he said gently, as Gretta's breathing faltered, faltered again and then resumed, even weaker. 'You love, and love doesn't let go.' And then he said...

'Em, I'm so sorry I let you go,' he said softly into the ominous stillness of the night. 'I was dumb beyond belief. Em, if you'll have me back...'

'Ollie...'

'No, now's not the time to say it,' he said grimly. 'But I love you, Em, and for what it's worth, I love Gretta, too. Thank you for letting me be here now. Thank you for letting me love.'

She was past exhaustion. She held and she held, but her body was betraying her.

Gretta was in her arms, seemingly asleep, but imperceptibly slipping closer to that invisible, appalling edge.

'You need to sleep yourself,' Oliver said at last. 'Em, curl up on the bed with her. I promise I'll watch her and love her, and I'll wake you the moment she wakes, the moment she's conscious.'

They both knew such a moment might not happen. The end was so near...

But, then, define *near*. Who could predict how long these last precious hours would take? Death had its own way of deciding where and when, and sometimes, Oliver thought, death was decided because of absence rather than presence.

Even at the time of death, loved ones were to be protected. How many times had a child slipped away as a parent had turned from a bed—as if solitude gave permission for release? Who knew? Who understood? All he knew was that Em was past deciding.

'I'll take your chair,' he told her, laying his hand on her shoulder, holding. 'Snuggle onto the bed.'

'How can I sleep?'

'How can you not?' He kissed her softly on her hair and held her, letting his body touch hers, willing his strength into her. This woman… She gave and she gave and she gave…

How could he possibly have thought her love could be conditional? How could he possibly have thought adoption for Em could be anything but the real thing?

And how could he ever have walked away from this woman, his Em, who was capable of so much love and who'd loved him?

Who still loved him, and who'd shown him that he, too, was capable of such love.

'I'll wake you if there's any change. I promise.'

'You do…love her?'

'Ten,' he said, and he smiled at her and then looked down at the little girl they were watching over. 'Maybe even more.'

She nodded, settled Gretta on the bed, then rose and stumbled a little. He rose, too, and caught her. He could feel her warmth, her strength, the beating of her heart against his. The love he felt for this woman was threatening to overwhelm him, and yet for this moment another love was stronger.

Together they looked down at this tiny child, slipping away, each breath one breath closer…

Em choked back an involuntary sob, just the one, and then she had herself under control again. There would be no deathbed wailing, not with this woman. But, oh, it didn't mean she didn't care.

'Slip in beside her,' he said, and numbly she allowed him to tug off her windcheater, help her off with her jeans.

She slid down beside Gretta in her knickers and bra, then carefully, with all the tenderness in the world, she held Gretta, so the little girl's body was spooned against hers.

Gretta stirred, ever so slightly, her small frame seeming to relax into that of her mother's.

Her mother. Em.

Somewhere out there was a birth mother, the woman who'd given Gretta up because it had all been too hard. Down's syndrome and an inoperable heart condition that would kill her had seemed insurmountable. But Em hadn't seen any of that when she'd decided to foster her, Oliver thought. She'd only seen Gretta.

She'd only loved Gretta.

'Sleep,' he ordered as he pulled up the covers, and she gave him a wondering look in the shadows of the pale nightlight.

'You'll watch?'

'I swear.'

She smiled, a faint, tremulous smile, and closed her eyes.

She was asleep in moments.

The quiet of the night was almost absolute. The only sound was the faint in-drawing of breath through the oxygen tube. Gretta's tiny body was almost insignificant on the pillows. Em's arms were holding her, mother and child ensconced in their private world of love.

Mother and child... That's what these two were, Oliver thought as he kept his long night-time vigil. Mother and child.

In the next room, Adrianna had Toby in bed with her. Whether Toby needed comfort—who knew what the little boy sensed?—or Adrianna herself needed comfort and was taking it as parents and grandparents had taken and given comfort since the beginning of time—who knew?

Adrianna's love for Toby was almost as strong as Em's.

Grandmother, mother, child.

He wanted to be in that equation, and sitting there in the stillness of the night, he knew he wanted it more than anything else in the world. What a gift he'd had. What a gift he'd thrown away.

But Em had let him into her life again. She'd allowed him to love...

Gretta shifted, a tiny movement that he might not have noticed if all his senses weren't tuned to her breathing, to her chest rising and falling. There was a fraction of a grimace across her face? Pain? He touched her face, and she moved again, just slightly, responding to his touch as he'd seen newborns do.

On impulse he slid his hands under her body and gathered her to him. Em stirred, as well, but momentarily. Her need for sleep was absolute.

'I'm cuddling her for a bit,' he whispered to Em. 'Do you mind?'

She gave a half-asleep nod, the vestige of a smile and slept again.

He gathered Gretta against his chest and held.

Just held.

The night enfolded them. This was a time of peace. A time of blessing?

Gretta was snuggled in his arms, against his heart, and she fitted there. Em slept on beside them.

His family.

Gretta's breathing was growing more shallow. There

was no longer any trace of movement. No pain. Her face was peaceful, her body totally relaxed against his.

He loved her.

He'd known this little girl for only weeks, and her courage, her strength, her own little self had wrapped her around his heart with chains of iron. She was slipping away and his chest felt as if it was being crushed.

Her breathing faltered. Dear God...

'Em?'

She was instantly awake, pushing her tumbled curls from her hair, swinging her legs over the side of the bed, her fingers touching her daughter's face almost instantly.

She just touched.

The breathing grew shallower still.

'Would you like to hold her?' How hard was it to say that? How hard, to hand her over to the woman who loved her?

But he loved her, too.

'I'm here,' Em whispered. 'Keep holding her. She loves you, Oliver. You've lit up our lives in these last weeks.'

'Do you want to call Adrianna?'

'She says she couldn't bear it. If it's okay with you... just us.'

Her fingers stayed on her daughter's face as Gretta's breathing faltered and faltered again. Gretta's frail body was insubstantial, almost transient, but Oliver thought there was nothing insubstantial about the power around them.

A man and a woman and their child.

'I wish I'd been here,' he said fiercely, though he still whispered. 'I wish I'd had the whole four years of her.'

'You're here now,' Em whispered as her daughter's breathing faltered yet again. 'That's all that matters.'

And then the breathing stopped.

They didn't move. It was like a tableau set in stone.

'*Stop all the clocks...*' Who had said that? Auden, Oliver thought, remembering the power of the poem, and somehow, some way it helped. That others had been here. That others had felt this grief.

Grief for parents, for lovers, for children. Grief for those who were loved.

Gretta had been loved, absolutely. That his own parents had doled out their love according to some weird formula of their own making—this much love for an adopted child; this much love for a child of their own making—it was nothing to do with now, or what he and Em decided to do in the future.

Their loving was so strong it would hold this little girl in their hearts for ever.

It would let them go on.

And Em was moving on. She was removing Gretta's oxygen cannula. She was adjusting Gretta's pink, beribboned pyjamas. She was wiping Gretta's face.

And finally she was gathering her daughter's body into her own arms, holding her, hugging her, loving her. And then, finally, finally the tears came.

'Go call Mum,' she managed, as Oliver stood, helpless in his grief as well as hers. 'She needs to be here now. And Toby... You need to bring him in, Oliver. For now, for this moment, we need to be together. Our family.'

They buried Gretta with a private service three days later. It was a tiny service. Only those who loved Gretta most were there to share.

Gretta's birth mother, contacted with difficulty, chose not to come. 'I don't want to get upset. You take care of her.'

'We will,' Em promised, and they did, the best they could. They stood by the tiny graveside, Oliver at one side of Em, Adrianna at the other, and they said goodbye to a part of themselves.

Such a little time, Oliver thought. How could you love someone so deeply after such a little time?

But he did. Years couldn't have made this love deeper.

He gathered Em into his arms afterwards and there were no words needed for the promises that were being made.

She knew and he knew. Here was where they belonged.

Katy had looked after Toby during the service—there were some things a two-year-old could never remember and couldn't hope to understand—but afterwards she brought him to them. 'Let's go to the Children's Garden,' Mike had suggested. 'The Botanic Gardens is a great place to play. That's where I think we all need to be.'

And it wasn't just Katy and Mike and the kids who arrived at the Gardens. Their hospital friends met them there, appearing unbidden, as if they sensed that now was the time they were needed. Isla and Alessi, Sophia, Charles, Tristan, even the obnoxious Noah—so many people who loved Em and knew the depths of Em's grief.

Heaven knew who was looking after midwifery and neonates at the Victoria, for at two o'clock on this beautiful autumn afternoon it seemed half the staff were here.

And suddenly, as if by magic, pink balloons were everywhere. They wafted upwards through the treetops and spread out. It seemed that each balloon contained a tiny packet of seeds—kangaroo paws, Gretta's favourite—with instructions for planting. Who knew who'd organised it, and who knew how many kangaroo paws would spring up over Melbourne because of Gretta? It didn't matter. All that mattered was that the love was spreading outwards, onwards. Gretta's life would go on.

There were blessings here, Oliver thought as he gazed around at the friends he'd made in such a short time, the friends that had been Em's supports while he'd been away, the friends who'd stand by them for ever.

For ever sounded okay to him.

Their friends drifted away, one by one, hugging and leaving, knowing that while friends were needed, alone was okay, as well. Sophia and Isla took Adrianna by an arm apiece. 'Rooftop Bar?' they queried, and Adrianna cast an apologetic glance at her daughter.

'If it's okay...I'd kill for a brandy.'

'If anyone deserves a brandy or three, it's you. I... We'll meet you there,' Em said, holding back, watching Oliver hugging Toby.

'Do you want me to take Toby?' her mum asked.

'I need Toby right now,' Oliver said, and Em blinked. Of all the admissions...

But no more was said. She stood silent until Sophia and Isla and Adrianna disappeared through the trees and they were alone. With her son. With...*their* son?

Then Oliver tugged her down so they were in their favourite place in the world, lying under a massive tree, staring up through the branches.

Toby, who'd submitted manfully to being hugged all afternoon, took off like a clockwork beetle, crawling round and round the tree, gathering leaves, giggling to himself. Death held no lasting impression for a two-year-old and Em was grateful for it.

'I think that's Gretta's nose,' Oliver said, pointing upwards at a cloud. 'I think she's up there, deciding whose porridge is hers.'

And to her amazement Em heard herself chuckle. She rolled over so her head lay on his chest, and his lovely fingers raked her hair.

'I love you, Em,' he said, softly into the stillness. 'I

love you more than life itself. Will you let me be part of your family?'

She didn't speak. She couldn't.

She could feel his heart beneath her. His fingers were drifting through her hair, over and over. Toby crawled around them once and then again before she found her voice. Before she trusted herself to speak.

'You've always been my family, Oliver,' she said, slowly, hardly trusting herself to speak. 'Five years ago I was too shocked, too bereft, too gutted to see your needs. So many times since, I've rerun that time in my head, trying to see it as you saw it. I put a gun to your head, Ollie. Black or white. Adoption or nothing. It wasn't fair.'

'Even if your way was right? Even if your way *is* right?'

She could feel his heart but she could no longer feel hers. There'd been so many emotions this day... Her world was spinning...

No, she thought. Her world had settled on its right axis. It had found its true north.

'I'm so glad I came back in time to meet Gretta,' Oliver said softly, still stroking her hair. 'I'm so glad I was able to be a tiny part of her life. If I hadn't... She's a part of you, now, Em, and, believe it or not, she's a part of me. A part of us. Like Toby is. Like Adrianna. Like everyone is who released a pink balloon today. You're right, there is no scale. Loving is just loving. But most of all, Em, I love you. Will you take me on again, you and all your fantastic menagerie? Toby and Adrianna and Fuzzy and Mike and Katy and the kids, and Ruby and her baby when she's born? Will you let me love them with you? Will you let me love you?'

Enough. Tears had been sliding down her cheeks all day and it was time to stop. She swiped them away and tugged herself up so she was looking into his face. She gazed into his eyes and what she saw made her heart twist with love. She saw grief. She saw love.

She saw hope.

And hope was all they needed, she thought. Heaven knew how their family would end up. Heaven knew what crazy complications life would send them.

All she knew for now was that somehow, some way, this man had been miraculously restored to her.

Her husband. Her life.

'I can't stop you loving me,' she managed, swiping yet more tears away. 'And why would I want to? Oh, Oliver, I'd never want to. I love you with all my heart and that it's returned…well, Gretta's up there making miracles for us; I know she is.'

There was a crow of laughter from right beside them. They turned and Toby had a handful of leaves. He threw them at both their faces and then giggled with delight.

Oliver tugged Em to lie hard by his side, and then picked Toby up and swung him up so he was chortling down at them.

'You're a scamp,' he told him. 'We love you.'

And Toby beamed down at both of them. God was in his heaven, all was right in Toby's world.

He had his Em and now he had his Oliver. His Gretta would stay with him in the love they shared, in the love they carried forward.

Toby was with his family.

And two weeks later they went back to the gardens, for a ceremony they both decreed was important. For the things they had to say needed to be said before witnesses. Their friends who'd been with them in the tough times now deserved to see their joy, and they were all here. Even Ruby was here this time, carefully cosseted by Isla and Sophia but increasingly sure of herself, increasingly confident of what lay ahead.

Oliver had asked Charles Delamere to conduct this unconventional ceremony—Charles, the man who'd recruited him—Charles, the reason Oliver had finally come home.

Charles, the head of the Victoria Hospital. The man who seemed aloof, a powerful business tycoon but who'd released balloons for Gretta two weeks before. Who'd promised all his support, whatever they needed. Who'd also promised to move heaven and earth to cut bureaucratic red tape, so Toby could stay with them for ever.

But the successful bureaucratic wrangling was for later. This day was not official, it was just for love.

They chose a beautiful part of the garden, wild, free, a part they both loved. They stood under a tangled arch, surrounded by greenery. They held hands and faced Charles together, knowing this was right.

'Welcome,' Charles said, smiling, because what he was to do now was all about joy. 'Today Em and Oliver have asked me if I'll help them do something they need to do, and they wish to do it before all those who love them. Ten years ago, Emily and Oliver made their wedding vows. Circumstances, grief, life, drove them apart but when the time was right fate brought them together again. They've decided to renew their vows, and they've also decided that here, the gardens that are—and have been—loved by the whole family, are the place they'd like to do it. So if I could ask for your attention...'

He had it in spades. There was laughter and applause as their friends watched them stand before Charles, like two young lovers with their lives ahead of them.

'Emily,' Charles said seriously. 'What would you like to say?'

They'd rehearsed this, but privately and separately.

Oliver stood before Emily and he didn't know what she'd say but he didn't care. He loved her so much.

But then the words came, and they were perfect.

'Just that I love him,' Em said, mistily, lovingly. 'That I married Oliver ten years ago with all my heart and he has my heart still. What drove us apart five years ago was a grief that's still raw, but it's a part of us. It'll always be a part of us, but I don't want to face life's griefs and life's joys without him.'

She turned and faced Oliver full on. 'Oliver, I love you,' she told him, her voice clear and true. 'I love you, I love you, I love you, and I always will. For better and for worse. In sickness and in health. In joy and in sorrow, but mostly in joy. I take you, Oliver Evans, back to be my husband, and I promise to love you now and for evermore.'

He'd thought he had it together. He hadn't, quite. When he tried to speak it came out as a croak and he had to stop and try again.

But when he did, he got it right.

'I love you, too, Em,' he told her, taking her hands in his, holding her gaze, caressing her with his eyes. 'Those missing years are gone. We can't get them back, but for now this is all about the future. We have Toby, our little son, and with the help of our friends we'll fight heaven and earth to keep him. As well as that, we have the memory of a baby we once lost, our Josh, and we have so many wonderful memories of our beloved Gretta. And we have all our friends, and especially we have Adrianna, to love us and support us.'

He turned and glanced at Adrianna, who was smiling and smiling, and he smiled back, with all the love in his heart. And then he turned back to his wife.

'But for now...' he said softly but surely. 'For now I'm holding your hands and I'm loving you. I love you, Emily Louise, as surely as night follows day. I love you deeply, strongly, surely, and I swear I'll never let you down again. From this day forth I'll be your husband. You hold my heart in the palm of your hand. For richer, for poorer, in sickness and in health, we're a family. But maybe…not a complete family. I'm hoping there'll be more children. More friends, more dogs, more chaos. I'm hoping we can move forward with love and with hope. Emily Louise, will you marry me again?'

'Of course I will,' Em breathed, as Toby wriggled down from Adrianna's arms and beetled his way between legs to join them. Oliver scooped him up and held and they stood, mother, father and son, a family portrait as every camera in Melbourne seemed to be trained on them.

'Of course I will,' Em whispered again, and the cameras seemed to disappear, as their surroundings seemed to disappear. There was only this moment. There was only each other.

'Of course I will,' Em whispered for the third time, as they held each other and they knew these vows were true and would hold for all time. 'I'm marrying you again right now, my Oliver. I'm marrying you for ever.'

* * * * *

THE CHILD
WHO RESCUED
CHRISTMAS

JESSICA MATTHEWS

To my family, especially my husband,
whose support never wavers

PROLOGUE

This day just kept getting better, Sara Wittman thought wryly as one of the morning headlines caught her eye.

Three people killed in medical helicopter crash.

She hated reading news like that—it was a horrible way to start her day—but morbid curiosity and a healthy dread drove her to read the few facts listed in the article.

En route from the University of Oklahoma Medical Center in Oklahoma City to Enid, the A-Star 350 helicopter went down in an open field thirty miles outside its destination for unknown reasons. The three people on board, pilot James Anderson of Dallas, Texas, Nurse Ruth Warren of Tulsa, Oklahoma, and Nurse Lilian Gomez of Norman, Oklahoma, died at the scene.

According to statements released by AirMed, the company that operates this flying medical service, the circumstances of the crash are still uncertain. The incident is under investigation by the Federal Aviation Administration and the National Transportation Safety Board.

As a nurse assigned to the medical-surgical floor of Nolan Heights Hospital, she occasionally cared for a patient who had to be flown to a tertiary care center for treatment and consequently had met the dedicated staff who flew those missions. Although Nolan Heights used a different company for their flying ambulance service, the men and women who specialized in providing that type of medicine were a special breed who'd garnered her respect. These people would be missed, not only by their families but also by the medical community as a whole.

"You're looking rather glum this morning." Cole, her husband of nearly three years, breezed into the kitchen wearing dark slacks and a rust-colored shirt—his usual attire for another busy day in his medical practice. He bussed her on the cheek before heading for the coffeemaker where she'd already poured a cup of the French roast she'd made strong enough to keep him running all morning.

She savored his husbandly peck before rattling the newspaper. "I was just reading about a medical helicopter crash in Oklahoma. Two nurses and the pilot were killed on the way to collect a patient."

"That's too bad," he remarked as he sipped from his mug and slipped a slice of bread into the toaster. "No one we know, I hope."

"No," she said, "although one of the nurses is from your old stomping grounds."

"Tulsa?"

"For being gone most of the night because of a patient, you're remarkably sharp this morning," she teased.

"It's all done with smoke and mirrors," he answered with a grin that after one year of dating, two years of living together and three years of marriage still jump-started her pulse every time. "But in answer to your question, Tulsa is a relatively large city. I didn't know every kid in my grade, much less my entire school."

"I suppose it would be surprising if you knew Ruth Warren."

He visibly froze. "Ruth Warren?"

"Yeah," she confirmed. "It doesn't give her age, though."

Then, because the news had obviously startled him, she asked, "Did you know a Ruth Warren?"

"The one I knew was a schoolteacher," he said slowly, his gaze speculative. "High school biology. Now that I think about it, she'd always talked about going into nursing. Maybe she finally did."

"Then it could have been your friend."

"I doubt it. Even if she did make a career change, the Ruth I knew was scared of heights. She'd always joked about how she'd never get on an airplane."

"There must be two Ruth Warrens," she guessed. "Both names are common enough and her surname could be her married name."

"It's possible," he murmured thoughtfully.

"Regardless, I'm sure her family, and everyone else's, is devastated."

"Hmm."

"And when a tragedy like this happens close to Christmas, it has to be even more difficult to handle," she commented, imagining how the season would never again be the same for those left behind. In the blink of an eye for these families, the holiday had lost its inherent excitement.

"Hmm."

Sara recognized his preoccupied tone. Certain his mind was already racing ahead to concentrate on the day's hectic schedule, she said offhandedly, "It's nice that we're closing the hospital at noon today."

"Yeah."

He was definitely not paying attention. "And Administration is doubling everyone's salaries."

"That's nice." Suddenly, his gaze landed on her. "What?"

"You weren't listening to me, were you?" she teased.

A sheepish expression appeared on his face. "Apparently not. Sorry."

"You're forgiven," she said lightly. "As long as you won't forget our annual anniversary getaway."

"I haven't," he assured her. "We have reservations for the weekend at the hotel in Bisbee, just as we decided, and we fly to Arizona on Thursday morning. It amazes me that you wanted to stay at that elevation and see snow when we'll be seeing plenty of it soon enough," he added in a mock grumble. "A sunny beach would have made more sense."

"We did the sunny beach last year," she pointed out. "This is different. Besides…" she gave him a sultry smile "…if we run into any of the resident ghosts that our hotel claims to have, we can bar ourselves in our room."

He grinned. "I vote we do that anyway."

As if on cue, Sara's watch beeped with her five-minute warning. Without looking at the time, she drained her mug and placed it in the sink. "Gotta run or I'll be late," she said as she stopped to give him a goodbye kiss.

He threaded an arm around her waist and pulled her close, his solid warmth comforting. "Do we have plans for this evening?"

She thought a minute. "No, why?"

The playful expression she recognized appeared on his face. "I predict I'm going to need a nap when I get home."

Ordinarily, the prospect would have thrilled her, but not today.

"Maybe we'll get lucky and make a baby tonight," he murmured with a feral smile and a seductive voice.

If only that were possible…

"We won't," she said flatly. "As of a few days ago, I'm not pregnant. It's the wrong time."

Her husband's appreciative gaze turned sympathetic. "Oh, honey. I'm sorry. Maybe next month."

Next month. It always came down to next month. For the last year and a half, those words had become her mantra.

"Yeah, maybe." Avoiding his gaze, she tried to pull out of his embrace, but he'd obviously heard the disappointment in her voice because he didn't let her go.

"Hey." His hand against the side of her face was gently reassuring. "It'll happen. Just be patient."

After all this time, her account holding that particular virtue was overdrawn. "I'm tired of being patient, Cole. We should see a different specialist." She finally voiced what she'd been contemplating off and on for the last month. "Dr. Eller could refer us to—"

"Sara," he chided, "Josh Eller is the best ob-gyn man in this part of the country. You know that."

"Yes, but another doctor might have a different opinion. He might take a more aggressive approach."

"A different doctor might," he agreed, "but Josh hasn't steered us wrong so far. You've gotten pregnant once. It's only been nine months."

Sadly, she'd miscarried within days after she'd learned she'd been expecting. Had she not been concerned about what she'd thought was a lingering stomach flu virus, she'd never have gone to the doctor, and when she'd miscarried, she would have attributed it to just another horrible period.

"But nothing's happened since," she protested. We should—"

"Be patient. Your body needs time to heal."

"Yes, but—"

"Josh said we should allow ourselves a year and we're close to that," he reminded her. "Life hasn't been so bad with just the two of us, has it?"

While their relationship hadn't sailed along on completely smooth seas—there'd been a brief ten days when they'd gone their separate ways because she'd despaired of him ever proposing and giving her the family and home life she wanted—

she couldn't complain. "No, but a baby is like the icing on the cake when two people love each other. It—"

He stopped her in midsentence. "A baby will come if and when he's supposed to. You have to trust that Josh knows what he's doing. If he says not to worry, then don't."

She'd wanted Cole to be as eager to grow their family as she was, and his attitude grated on her. Didn't he understand how much she wanted this? Didn't he see that each passing month chipped away at her confidence and self-esteem?

And yet she understood Cole's propensity to maintain the status quo when it came to his personal life. Although he never said, she guessed that losing his parents at such an early age and the subsequent turmoil in his life had made him reluctant to modify an established routine. She didn't necessarily like his behavior, but it was a part of his character and she accepted it.

"Look," she began, "I know how difficult it is for you to change course when you're happy with the path you're on. After all, between dating and living together, it took you almost three years before you finally proposed, but you should be as excited about a baby as I am."

"I am."

"You don't act like it," she mumbled.

He raised an eyebrow. "Would wringing my hands and calling Josh every week, pestering him for information and advice, change things?"

He had a point. "No," she conceded. "But I want you to want this as much as I do and I'm not getting that impression from you." While she knew Cole was more reserved than most, she wanted to see a more enthusiastic response. "Sometimes I think you only agreed to have a baby to humor me."

"Oh, Sara." He patted her back as he hugged her. "I'll admit that I'm not eager for our lives to change because I'm happy with just the two of us. But I'd be happy if you got pregnant, too. A little girl with your pixie nose would be cute. So, you see, I'm basically a happy kind of guy." He winked.

His teasing tone defused her aggravation. "Oh, you." She poked him playfully. "Pixie nose, indeed."

"Seriously, Sara…" his gaze grew intent "…stressing out about the situation won't help matters. Josh won't steer us wrong."

Her husband's confidence soothed her frazzled nerves. Slowly, she nodded. "You're right, he won't."

"Good girl." He cupped her face with both hands and kissed her. "There's no doubt in my mind that it'll happen, so stop worrying. Before long, you'll be complaining about morning sickness, swollen ankles and not being able to see your own feet."

She offered a wan smile. "I guess. Now, I'd better run or I really will be late."

After she'd left, bundled against the cold, Cole noticed how quiet the house seemed without his bubbly wife's presence. He'd hated seeing her so downcast for those few minutes and he wished Sara would focus on what she had rather than what she didn't have. She'd always made it plain that she wanted a large family—two boys and two girls—like the one she'd had growing up, and while the thought of being responsible for four children—*four*—was enough to scare him spitless, he'd been willing to patiently *and thoroughly* do his part to fulfill her dream. He grinned as he remembered the last time they'd made love. They'd started in the kitchen then detoured to their oversize soaker tub before ending up in bed.

He enjoyed nights like those—craved them, in fact—and he wasn't in any particular hurry to lose them. Truth was, he liked having his wife to himself. The idea that he someday would have even fewer private moments with her than he did now only made him cherish those times all the more.

While he looked upon their inability to conceive as one of the temporary mountains of life some people had to face—and was, in fact, a little relieved because he'd had so little experience with a loving family—she saw it as a personal failure. She shouldn't, of course, because they were only in the early stages of the process. She'd gotten pregnant within six months of when they'd stopped using any birth control and although she'd lost the baby, only another nine months had passed. Consequently, they'd never thought they'd needed fertility testing, although if nothing happened soon, they would.

And yet he truly did believe what he'd told her. Mother Nature simply needed time to work and Josh would decide on the proper time for medical science to intervene.

Content to leave the situation in his colleague's capable hands, he sat down to polish off his toast and coffee. As he munched, he idly glanced at the newspaper his wife had discarded and the trepidation he'd felt when Sara had first mentioned the helicopter crash came back, full force.

Ruth Warren.

Surely the woman wasn't the same Ruth Warren from his youth—the same Ruth Warren he'd spent time with a few years ago at his fifteen-year class reunion. The same class reunion when he'd drowned his sorrows with far too many margaritas because Sara had left him.

In spite of his reluctance to take the step she'd wanted—marriage—he'd come to his senses quickly. Accepting that his life would stretch ahead interminably without her, he'd proposed a week later. Sara had never pressed for details about his change of heart and he'd never offered them, except to say that he'd been miserable without her. Six months later, after Sara had planned her dream wedding, they had been married. Now, in a few more weeks, they'd celebrate their three-year anniversary.

Three years of the happiness and contentment he hadn't felt since he was eight.

Suddenly, he had to know if the Ruth Warren mentioned in the article was the girl who'd often sat beside him at school because their names fell so close alphabetically. Now that he thought about it, hadn't she mentioned during their reunion weekend that she'd turned her teaching certificate into a nurse's diploma? To be honest, there was a lot about those two days he didn't remember...

Determined to find an answer, he abandoned his coffee on his way to his office and powered up his computer. Minutes later, he'd found the online obituary at the *Tulsa World* website and scanned the details. Most, he already knew.

Age 33, preceded in death by her parents, attended the University of Oklahoma, earned a degree in secondary education and later in nursing before taking a position as a flight nurse.

Reading the facts suddenly made them seem familiar, as if she'd told him of her career change and he'd simply forgotten. He read on...

Survivors include a son, as well as many friends and former students.

She'd had a son? She hadn't mentioned a child, but she'd never been one to share the details of her personal life. He was certain he'd asked about her life—it had been a reunion, after all—but he'd been too focused on his own misery to remember the things she'd told him. Idly, he wondered if the boy's father was still in the picture. Probably not, if the man hadn't received mention.

A graveside service will be held at 10:00 a.m. Wednesday at the Oaklawn Cemetery.

Cole leaned back in his chair and stared blankly at the screen. The description of Ruth's life had been rather succinct, and certainly didn't do justice to the young woman he remembered. She'd lived through a horrible childhood, carried enough baggage to fill a plane's cargo hold and had a gift for defusing tense moments with a wisecrack, but she'd always been a great listener.

And now Ruth was gone. Of course, he hadn't talked to her since that weekend, but now he wished he'd contacted her and told her that he'd taken her advice. He'd faced his demons and followed his heart. Now it was too late.

Then again, Ruth had probably known…

It was hard to believe that someone Cole's own age, someone who should have lived another fifty years or so, someone with whom Cole had grown up with, was gone. Her death gave him a glimpse of his own mortality, and suddenly he wished he'd taken off the entire week to spend with Sara instead of just two days.

For an instant, he toyed with the idea of attending Ruth's funeral, then decided against it. Depending on how old her son was, offering condolences would either be overwhelming or wouldn't mean anything at this point. It would be better if he wrote a letter for the boy to read when he was ready— a letter telling him what a wonderful friend his mother had been.

And although he knew Ruth would never have mentioned their one-night stand to anyone even in passing, in one tiny corner of his heart he was relieved that now it would remain a secret for all eternity.

CHAPTER ONE

"WHAT do you say you run away with me this weekend?" Sebastian Lancaster asked Sara two days later as she straightened his bedsheets during her last patient round before her shift-change report. "I know this great little place for dancing. I could show you a few steps that will make your head spin."

Sara smiled at her eighty-five-year-old patient who relied on a walker and wheezed with every breath, thanks to his years of habitual smoking. No doubt the only head that would spin with any sudden move would be his.

"No can do," she said cheerfully, already anticipating her upcoming weekend away from the daily grind of hospitals, patients and housework. "I already have plans."

"No problem." He coughed. "What is it they say? Plans are made to be broken."

"I think you're referring to rules, not plans," she corrected.

He waved a wrinkled, age-spotted hand. "Same difference. It's been ages since I've tangoed and if I'm not mistaken, you'd be good at it. Got the legs for it."

Knowing the elderly gentleman couldn't see past his elbow, she let his comment about her legs slide. "I'll bet you were quite the Fred Astaire in your day," she commented, giving the top blanket a final pat.

"Oh, I was. My wife and I could have outshone these young whippersnappers on those celebrity dance shows. So whaddya say? Wanna spring me from this joint so we can take a spin?"

She laughed at his suitably hopeful expression, although they both knew she couldn't fulfill his request. Between his emphysema and current bout of pneumonia, he was struggling to handle basic activities, much less add a strenuous activity like dancing. However, his physical limitations didn't stop this perpetual flirt from practicing his pickup lines. Sara guessed his wife must have been adept at keeping his behavior in check, or else she'd turned a blind eye to his Romeo attitude.

"Sorry, but I'm already running away this weekend," she told him, glancing at the drip rate of his IV. "With my husband, who just happens to be your doctor."

He nodded matter-of-factly, as if not particularly disappointed by his failure. "Shoulda known. The pretty ones are always taken. Must say, though…" he stopped to cough "…that if Doc had the good sense to pick you out of the eligible women, then he's got a good head on his shoulders."

"I like to think so," she said lightly, aware that her relationship with Cole had endured some dark days. However, in spite of the usual differences of opinion between people of diverse backgrounds and ideas, in spite of his initial reluctance to commit and in spite of her miscarriage nine months ago, life had been good.

"You two just going away for nothing better to do or for something special?"

"It's our three-year anniversary," she replied. "Actually, we still have a few weeks before the actual date, but this was the only weekend we could both get away."

"Ah, then you're still newlyweds. I'll bet you're eager to have your second honeymoon, even if it wasn't that long ago since your first, eh?" He cackled at his joke before ending on a cough.

Sara smiled. "It's always great to get away, honeymoon or not."

She'd been looking forward to this weekend for a month now and could hardly wait. Cole, on the other hand, had been preoccupied the last few days, which had been somewhat surprising because he'd been as eager to stay in the haunted historic hotel as she was.

"Too much to do before I can leave with an easy conscience," he'd said when she'd asked.

While that was probably true—as a hospitalist, he'd put in long hours to ensure the doctors covering his patients would find everything in order while he was gone—she had to wonder if something else wasn't on his mind. Still, she was confident that once they shook the dust of Nolan Heights off their feet, he'd leave those worries behind. And if distance didn't help, then the skimpy black lace negligee in her suitcase would.

"Well, go and have a good time," Sebastian said. "If he takes you dancing, dance a slow one for me." He winked one rheumy brown eye.

"I will," she promised. "When I come back to work on Monday, if you're still here, I'll tell you all about it."

"Do that," he said before he closed his eyes, clearly spent from their short conversation.

Sara strode out of the room, her soft soles silent on the linoleum. She'd begun to chart her final notes for her patients when another nurse, Millie Brennan, joined her.

"How's Mr. Lancaster this afternoon?"

Sara smiled at the twenty-six-year-old, somewhat jealous of her strawberry blond tresses when her own short hair was unremarkably brown. The only plus was that Sara's curls were natural whereas Millie's came from a bottle.

"As sassy as ever. Given his medical condition, it's amazing how he can still flirt with us."

"Wait until he feels better," Millie said darkly. "Then he'll grab and pinch. When he does, it's a sign he's ready to go back to his assisted living home."

"I'll keep it in mind," Sara said.

"So," Millie said in an obvious prelude to a change of subject, "are you packed and ready to go tomorrow?"

Sara smiled. "Almost. I just have to throw a few last-minute things into my bag and I'm ready. Cole, on the other hand, hasn't started. I'm going to work on his suitcase as soon as I get home."

Millie grinned. "Don't forget to pack a swimsuit. And that teddy we bought a few weeks ago."

"Those were the first things in the case," Sara answered, already looking forward to modeling the lacy negligee under her husband's admiring gaze. While most people thought they were going to enjoy ski slopes and mountain hikes, Sara had planned a far more private itinerary—an itinerary that focused only on the two of them.

"When are you leaving?" Millie asked.

"Our flight leaves early tomorrow morning. We'd thought about staying the night at one of the airport hotels, but it depends on Cole. You know how he is." Sara added, "He can't leave if he doesn't have every *i* dotted when it comes to his patients." She was convinced that was why everyone thought so highly of her husband—he didn't cut corners for convenience's sake.

She sighed. "Sometimes, his attention to detail is rather frustrating, especially when it interferes with our plans."

"Yeah, but you love him anyway."

Sara had half fallen in love with him the first day she'd met him, when he'd waltzed onto her floor as a first-year family medicine resident. She'd been suffering her own new-job jitters and he'd taken pity on her when she'd knocked a suture tray off the counter in obvious nervousness. The cup of coffee he'd subsequently bought her and the pep talk he'd delivered had marked the beginning of their professional and personal relationship.

"Yeah, I do," she said, returning Millie's grin with one of her own. "The only problem I have right now is knowing what to get him for Christmas. It's still two months away, but it'll be here before we know it."

"Has he mentioned anything that he wants?"

"Lots of things, but afterward he goes out and buys them for himself. I've told him not to do that, but so far it hasn't made an impression."

"It will when he wakes up on Christmas morning and there's nothing to open under the tree," Millie predicted. "Or you could just fill a box with socks and underwear."

"I could," Sara agreed, "but I couldn't be that cruel. I'm sure I'll get an idea this weekend."

"Well, good luck. As my mother always says, what do you get a man who has everything?"

What indeed? Sara thought. The one thing she'd wanted to give him—news that he'd be a father—wasn't something she could accomplish on her own, no matter how hard she wished for her dream to come true. Having grown up with a sister and two brothers, she wanted her house to ring with the same pitter-patter of footsteps as her parents' house had.

Be patient, Cole had reminded her. She'd try, she told herself. So what if it took them a little longer for their family to grow than she'd like? As long as it happened, as long as they loved each other, it would be worth the wait.

Fortunately, for the rest of her shift, she had little time to dwell on her personal plans, but the minute she left the hospital shortly after six o'clock, her thoughts raced ahead to her upcoming weekend.

Her excitement only grew when she found the lights blazing in their home and Cole's SUV parked in the garage.

Pleased that Cole had finished earlier than she'd expected, she dashed through the cold garage and into her cozy house.

"This is a pleasant surprise," she called out to Cole from the mud room as she tugged off her gloves and hung her parka on a coat hook. "I honestly didn't think you'd make it home before eight."

He rose from his place at the table as she entered the kitchen and kissed her on the cheek. "Things turned out differently than we'd both anticipated," he answered with a tight smile that, with his strained expression, set off her mental radar. "How about some coffee?"

He turned away to dump several sweetener packets into his own mug. "You never drink caffeine at this time of night," she said as she watched his movements with a knot forming in her stomach. "What's wrong?"

"It's cold outside. How about hot tea instead?"

He was trying to distract her, which only meant that something was wrong. *Horribly* wrong. The knot tightened.

"Cole," she warned. "I know it's cold, but I'm not thirsty or hungry. Something is obviously on your mind. What is it?" As a thought occurred to her, she gasped. "Oh, no. We can't go on our trip, can we? Something happened and Chris can't cover for you at the hospital. Oh, Cole," she finished on a wail. "Not *again!*"

"Sara," he interrupted. "Stop jumping to conclusions. This isn't about my schedule. Just. Sit. Down."

She sat. With her hands clasped together in her lap, she waited. He sank onto the chair beside hers and carefully set his mug on the table. "An attorney spoke with me today."

Dread skittered down her spine. A lawyer never visited a physician with good news. "Is someone suing the hospital? And you?"

"No, nothing like that. Mr. Maitland is a partner in a law firm based in Tulsa."

"Tulsa?" Knowing he'd grown up in that area of Oklahoma, she asked, "Does this involve your relatives?"

"No."

"Then what did he want with you?"

"Do you remember reading the newspaper article about the medical helicopter crash the other day?"

"Yes. We'd talked about one of the nurses. I can't remember her name…"

"Ruth Warren," he supplied.

"Yeah. What about the crash?"

"As it turns out, I *did* know this particular Ruth Warren. Quite well, in fact."

His shock was understandable. She reached out to grab his hand, somewhat surprised by his cold fingers. "I'm sorry."

"In high school, we were good friends, although I've only seen her once since then. At our class reunion a few years ago."

She furrowed her brow in thought. "You never mentioned a class reunion. When was this?"

"Remember those ten days in July, after you and I had broken up?"

"Yes," she said cautiously.

"During that time, I went to my class reunion. It was over the Fourth of July weekend, and I didn't have anything else to do, so I went."

"Really? Knowing how you've avoided going back to the area so you can't accidentally run into your relatives, I'm surprised."

"Yeah, well, it was a spur-of-the-moment decision," he said wryly. "Anyway, during that weekend, I met up with Ruth."

She touched his hand. "I'm glad you had a chance to reconnect with her after high school. Had you heard from her since then?"

"No. Not a word."

Sara had assumed as much because Cole had never mentioned her, but he was a closemouthed individual and often didn't mention those things he considered insignificant.

"Then what did the lawyer want?"

"He represents Ruth's estate. She named me, *us,* in her will."

Sara sat back in her chair, surprised. "She did? What did she do? Leave you her box of high school memorabilia?"

She'd expected her joke to make him smile, but it fell flat, which struck her as odd.

"She left us something more valuable than a box of dried corsages and school programs," he said evenly. "She entrusted the most important thing she had to us. Her son."

"Her son?" Of all the things he might have said, nothing was as shocking as this. "How old is he?"

"He's two and a half. His birthday was in April. April 2."

Surprise and shock gave way to excitement. "Oh, Cole," she said, reaching across the table to once again take his hand, her heart twisting at the thought of that motherless little boy. "He's practically a baby."

As she pondered the situation, she began to wonder why this woman had chosen them out of all the people she possibly could have known.

"Exactly why *did* she appoint us as his guardians? She never met me and you said yourself that you hadn't kept in contact with her. What about the boy's dad? Or her family? Didn't she have friends who were closer to her than you are? I'm not complaining, mind you. I'm only trying to understand why she gave him to people who are, for all intents and purposes, relative strangers, instead of choosing substitute parents who were within her current circle of friends."

"She had no family to speak of," he told her. "Ruth grew up in foster care and as soon as she graduated, she was on her own."

"If you hadn't seen her for three years, it's especially odd she'd ask us to take care of him. There has to be a connection—"

"There is," he said, clutching his mug with both hands. "But to explain it, I have something to confess."

Once again, warning bells clanged. "Okay," she said slowly.

"Ruth and I—that weekend we were together at the reunion…" he drew a deep breath as if bracing himself "…I did a stupid thing. Several stupid things, in fact. I was angry that you weren't satisfied with our relationship as it was—"

"Just living together," she interjected for clarification.

He nodded. "I was hurt that after all those years of being a couple, you wouldn't be satisfied or happy until I put a ring on your finger."

"Oh, Cole," she said, disappointed that he hadn't fully understood why she'd pressed him to take their relationship to the next level. "It wasn't about flashing a gold band or a huge diamond. It was what the ring *represented*—a commitment to spend the rest of our lives together."

"I realized that. Later. But during that first week we were apart, while I was angry and hurt and feeling everything in between, I went to my reunion and…" he took another deep breath "…drank a few too many margaritas. A *lot* too many." He paused.

She was surprised to learn that Cole—a man who couldn't even be classified as a moderate drinker—had over-imbibed. While she wasn't condoning his action, she figured most people had done so at one time or another. His actions weren't smart or ideal, but drinking too much on one occasion wasn't an unforgivable offense, in her opinion, even if at the time he'd been old enough to know better.

"And?" she coaxed.

"When I saw Ruth again—we confided a lot in each other

during our teen years—we talked. We both unloaded on each other and she helped me admit a few hard truths—"

"Do you mean to say that your friend *Ruth* convinced you to propose?" She'd always believed that he'd come to that conclusion on his own. It was disappointing to imagine that he'd been persuaded to marry her not because he loved her but because of a relative stranger's advice.

"Ruth didn't convince me to do anything," he insisted. "She pointed out what I already knew but couldn't quite admit—that I loved you and couldn't imagine my life without you—which was why I was so angry and hurt and miserable. And if I loved you, then I had to face my fears and propose."

Fears? He'd been afraid?

"Wait a minute." She held up her hands to forestall him so she could sort through his confession. "You'd always said that you wouldn't marry until you were ready, but now I learn that you were *scared?* Why didn't you explain? We could have discussed this."

"If you'll recall, we'd tried, but the conversation deteriorated and you walked out."

She wanted to protest that he could have stopped her, or that he could have called, or he could have done any number of things, but placing blame at this date was silly.

"Okay," she said evenly, "both of us could have done things differently, but truly, Cole, what were you afraid of?"

"That I couldn't be the husband you wanted or needed. That our relationship would change. We were doing great just living together and I had this…this *fear*…that marriage might ruin what we had."

"How was that possible?" she asked, incredulous. "We'd been living together for two years and dated for a year prior to that. How did you think marriage would ruin—?"

"You forget that the last functional family relationship I

was in ended when I was eight. What did *I* know about how a healthy marriage should be? By the time I started college, I didn't know if the happy home I remembered was real or make-believe. Do you really wonder why I might be afraid our relationship would change, and not for the better? And when it did, both of us would be stuck in an untenable situation."

She fell silent as she processed the information. "Okay, I can respect that, but you obviously faced your fears because you found me at my friend's house and proposed." It bothered her to think that he could discuss his fears with a woman he hadn't seen in years instead of with her, but there was little she could do about it now. She only hoped he wouldn't tell her that at the time asking her to marry him had simply been the lesser of two evils.

"Proposing—marrying you—was the best decision I ever made. Don't ever forget that."

His vehemence both surprised and alarmed her. "Okay," she said warily. "But meanwhile you had your heart-to-heart with Ruth and because you two drowned your sorrows together, she wanted you to raise her child if something happened to her."

He visibly winced and avoided her gaze. "Unfortunately, we did more than talk and drown our sorrows."

The bottom dropped out of her stomach. "Oh, Cole. Please don't tell me that you— That you and this high school friend…"

He nodded, his expression grave. "We slept together. We didn't plan it, I swear. I didn't even know she was going to *be* at the reunion. The combination of everything from my insecurities and alcohol level to Ruth needing her own listening ear all coalesced until events just…happened. I've never done anything like that before or since and I regretted it right away. You have to believe me."

A part of her brain heard his near-desperation, but she was still too numbed by his newest revelation to grant him absolution.

"You should have told me," she said as her whole body seemed to turn into ice. "We should have had this conversation as soon as you rolled back into town. About your doubts and your...and Ruth."

"I couldn't," he admitted. "I was too embarrassed and ashamed. I didn't go to my reunion intending to do anything but meet with old friends. After my lapse in judgment—" his voice was rueful "—I knew this news would be devastating and even though we technically weren't a couple at the time it happened, I couldn't risk my mistake potentially destroying our future."

Would she have refused to marry him if she'd known he'd slept with another woman? Knowing how devastated she'd been at the time he'd stormed out after their argument, hearing that would have probably convinced her to count her blessings that he'd walked away.

At this point, however, she didn't know for certain what she might have done. She might only have extended their engagement until she'd been fully persuaded that he hadn't entertained second thoughts about marriage, but one truth remained undeniable. He'd taken away her opportunity to choose.

"I can't begin to tell you how sorry I am," he added. "If I could turn back the clock and live that night over, I would."

His remorse seemed genuine, but it did little to ease her sense of betrayal. "Sorry that it happened or sorry that you told me?"

He didn't have to explain, her little voice pointed out. *He could have simply let the story stand that they were old friends who'd reconnected during a class reunion. You'd still never know...*

"There isn't a day that goes by that I don't feel regret for my actions," he said, meeting her gaze. "That's something I have to live with for the rest of my life."

The pain in his eyes wasn't feigned; she recognized that. Unfortunately, his revelation made her question so many things. Had he *really* wanted to marry her, or had he only asked her because he'd found his courage in the bottom of a bottle?

How many other secrets had he kept from her? He probably had many, because there were so many personal topics he refused to discuss.

And yet, technically, they *had* severed their relationship, which meant he hadn't been required to answer to her. No vows had been broken at the time he and Ruth…

But it still hurt to know that he'd fallen into bed with another woman so quickly. Granted, the alcohol and his own anger had contributed to his decision, but still…

Although the truth weighed heavily, she had to give credit where it was due. He'd been a faithful husband for the past three years and he'd been honest when he could have kept this secret forever and no one would have ever known. Yet he'd taken the risk and apologized profusely rather than simply brush off the incident.

Emotionally, she wanted to bristle and remain angry, but logically the incident was over and done with. Walking away from him because of one relatively *ancient* mistake committed when they'd been separated suggested her love must be terribly shallow if she couldn't forgive and forget.

"Sara?" he asked tentatively.

She exhaled a long, drawn-out sigh and offered a tremulous smile. "As disappointed as I am, as betrayed as I feel, even though some would say I shouldn't, I can't change the past. We'll leave it there, shall we?"

"Unfortunately, there's more," he said.

"More?" she asked, incredulous. "What more can there be? Isn't this *friendship* you had—" she chose that word instead of "affair" because she didn't know if a one-night stand fit the true definition "—the reason why she wanted you to look after her child?"

He didn't answer at first. "Sara," he said softly, "Brody is thirty months old. His second birthday came during the first part of April."

"Yes, you already told me."

He rubbed the back of his neck. "Do the math."

She did. Then, with a sinking heart, she knew. The apology on his face confirmed it.

"Oh. My. God. He's your son, too."

If Sara's face had revealed her shock before, now Cole only saw horror. From her sudden intake of breath, the oxygen in the room had vanished with the news, just as it had when Parker Maitland had delivered the same bombshell to him a few hours ago. This news had knocked his world off its axis, just as it had for his wife.

Eternity had only lasted forty-eight hours.

An unholy dread had filled him from that moment on because he would have to explain the inexplicable to Sara. His confession had crushed her, just as he'd suspected it would, and, just as he'd feared, the light in her eyes had faded. Already she stared at him as if he'd become someone she didn't know.

How ironic to be in this position. After spending his entire life always weighing his options and plotting his course carefully to avoid potential pitfalls, *the one time* he'd acted impulsively would haunt him for ever.

Oh, he could have ended this earlier without Sara ever being the wiser. He could have told the lawyer that he didn't want to raise Ruth's son—and his—and all this would have vanished like morning mist on a hot summer day. Yet he couldn't build one lie upon another, no matter how enticing the idea was. Untruths always had a tendency to be revealed.

"You had a baby with this Ruth person."

She sounded dazed, much as he had when he'd heard the news. "Apparently so."

"Are you certain? I mean, if she slept with you at your reunion, she might have spent time with someone else, too."

Her faith in him was bittersweet and only made him feel worse than he already did. He, too, had posed the question, hoping there'd been some misunderstanding, but the possibility had died an instant death after Maitland had presented him with undeniable proof.

"She didn't," he assured her, hating to destroy her hopes but understanding how the possibility was a lifeline for her to grab—a lifeline that their life wouldn't be turned upside down so easily. "Maitland gave me a picture of the boy. There's a strong...family resemblance."

It was more than a resemblance. The phrase "chip off the old block" came to mind. If he compared photos of himself at that age, he'd think his image had been cut and pasted into a scene from today.

"And she wants you to look after her—your—child."

From past experience, Cole knew that Sara's reserved tone was merely a smoke screen, especially given the words she'd chosen. *Her. Your child.* Underneath her deadly calm was a churning cauldron of emotions held in check by sheer force of will. Cole would have rather seen her yell, scream or throw things, instead of seeing her so controlled.

"She wants *us* to look after him," he corrected. "She wanted Brody to have two parents, not one."

As she sat frozen, Cole hastened to continue. "Apparently, Ruth knew the situation would be...difficult...which was why she left a letter for you to read."

He dug in the manila envelope Maitland had given him and placed the small sealed white envelope that bore Sara's name in front of her. Next to it, he positioned Brody's photograph so that those impish dark brown eyes were facing her.

Sara didn't move to accept the envelope or glance at the picture.

"Ruth rightly believed you would play an important role in Brody's upbringing, which is why she stipulated that you also had to agree to take him."

"And if I don't?"

He paused, torn between wanting her to refuse and hoping she'd accept the challenge ahead of them. "Then the search will begin for different parents," he said evenly. "According to Maitland, Ruth hoped that wouldn't happen. He and his wife, Eloise, were Ruth's neighbors and they knew how much she worried about Brody going into the same foster-care system she had."

"If they knew Ruth so well, why didn't she appoint them as his substitute parents?"

"Parker is sixty-nine and Eloise is sixty-seven. As much as they love Brody, it isn't feasible for them to parent a child at their age." Parker had told him that he and Ruth had discussed this scenario and they'd both agreed that Brody needed younger parents who would conceivably give him siblings as well as live long enough to see him through high school and college.

"Where is he now?"

"He's with Maitland and his wife at a hotel." He paused. "Parker invited us to stop by at our convenience tonight. However, he did mention that Brody usually goes to bed at eight and with all the commotion of the past few days, he's been a little cranky if he stays up later than that."

The silence in the room became deafening and Cole watched helplessly as Sara rubbed her forehead with a shaky and. "I don't know what to say," she murmured. "I'm tempted to believe I'm dreaming, that this is just an elaborate hoax or a misunderstanding."

"I know how you feel, but this…" he fingered the photo "…proves otherwise."

He stared at the snapshot lying on the table, picking out the facial features that seemed to be carbon copies of his own—coal-black hair, dimples, a straight nose and lopsided grin. Yet, even with the proof before him, he was still hardly able to accept that he had a son.

A *son*.

While he'd been willing to add to their family—*someday* in the future—knowing he had a son *now* was mind-boggling. It was one thing to feel guilty about his one-night stand, but quite another to know a child had resulted. He didn't know if he felt happy or sad, disappointed or excited, but he'd sort through those emotions later. At this moment, the reality had to be addressed, which was, namely, would they accept Brody into their home, or would Brody enter the same state-run children's services that Ruth had loathed?

He simply couldn't go against Ruth's wishes, but her way was filled with pitfalls. Having grown up in a situation where he hadn't been wanted, he'd always vowed to keep some sort of "escape clause" in his relationships, which was why he'd had so much trouble making a commitment to Sara. But now, if he accepted Ruth's child, *his* son, there would be no escape. If he intended to do this, he had to do so with the intent of being in it for the long haul.

This, at least, was the same decision he'd made before he'd proposed. And that had worked out, hadn't it? he told himself.

Or, it had, until he'd lost all common sense on that long-ago night.

He wanted to scream at the fates for putting him in this po-

sition, but what was done was done. There was only one way
to escape this time, but as he glanced at Brody's photo, the
idea didn't appeal as much as it might have. After all, if he'd
been willing to face his fears and have a baby with Sara, how
was this any different?

There was a big difference, he thought tiredly. Sara was his
wife and she'd stand beside him, helping him, guiding him
along the right path, correcting his mistakes. Now the question was, would she stay with him or not? Would he lose his
son *and* his wife?

He studied her, wishing she'd say or do something rather
than remain locked in icy calm. If only they had time to come
to terms with the situation and what it meant to them as a
couple, but time was a luxury they didn't have.

"Sara?" he asked tentatively. "We have to make a decision."

"Right *now?*" She sounded horrified.

"Maybe not this instant," he conceded, "but definitely
within the next twenty-four hours. Brody's future has to be
settled, one way or another. Keeping him in limbo isn't in
his best interests."

He'd wondered if the prospect of having the baby she'd
wanted would overshadow its origins, but she clearly hadn't
reached that level of acceptance yet. He understood. He was
still stunned and he'd felt the bombshell several hours earlier.

She nodded, almost absentmindedly.

Thinking that Sara would benefit from seeing Ruth's
wishes in black and white, he pulled a copy of the will out of
the manila envelope and flipped to the pages in question.

"Ruth had arranged for all of her assets to be placed into
a trust fund for Brody and she named us as the trustees. She
didn't want finances to factor in to our decision, so she left
a modest nest egg for his care."

Not that he intended to tap into it if they chose to raise him. After all, Brody was *his* son, and his responsibility.

"There are a few personal things she asked that we keep for him, heirlooms if you will. Everything else will be sold."

"I see."

"She also asked that we legally adopt him so he carries our surname rather than hers."

"She thought of everything, didn't she?" she said wryly.

"I'm sure she and her legal counsel tried to cover every contingency."

"Did she have a plan if we decided not to raise her child?"

Cole's cautious optimism fell as Sara asked this same question for a second time, as if she wanted to be sure she had other options.

"As I said earlier, Ruth had hoped you wouldn't make that choice."

"Did she make a plan B?" Sara pressed on, as if through gritted teeth.

Cole sighed. "She did. Brody will become a ward of the state and will be eligible for adoption by another couple."

In that instant, he knew he was facing an untenable situation. Ruth had guessed correctly that he wouldn't be able to easily give up his son, but if Sara wasn't in favor of keeping him, he'd be forced to choose between his wife and a boy he'd just learned was his. Neither was a palatable option.

Still, he wanted to think positive...

She frowned. "Wouldn't you have to relinquish your rights if you're his father?"

He'd wondered if she would have realized that. While everything within him fought that idea, the letter Ruth had left for his eyes only had requested him to do just that if Sara wouldn't agree to her terms.

I know how difficult this would be for you, Ruth had written, *but you know far better than I how much harder Brody's*

*life would be to live in a home where one parental figure
didn't want him...*

He might not want to sign those documents, and his decision would haunt him if he did, but he'd do it, for Brody's sake. "Yes," he said simply, hating the mere notion of it. "I would."

And he'd regret it for the rest of his life.

She paused. The wrinkle between her eyebrows suggested she was weighing her options. "And if we take him?" she finally asked. "What then?"

A spark of optimism flared. "Then, starting tomorrow, he'll spend time with us. The Maitlands will stay in town for a few days to ease his transition but they can't stay longer because they have family commitments of their own."

"That's it? He just moves in?"

"More or less. There are several legal details to take care of during the next few days and weeks but, to be honest, I can't remember what Maitland told me they were. As soon as we come to an agreement, they'll arrange for the personal belongings to be shipped here."

"But all of this hinges on our decision."

As far as he was concerned, there wasn't a decision to make. The thought of committing himself to the responsibility of another human being who would depend upon him for years to come might send a cold shiver down his spine— a fact that Ruth had known full well—but he couldn't deny her request, not just because Brody was his own son but because it was time to face his fears.

Unfortunately, the decision wasn't completely his to make.

It was ironic to think that Sara would have jumped for joy at taking in Brody had someone else fathered him. Unfortunately, Brody's presence would not only be a visual and constant reminder of his error in judgment but also that she'd lost her own child. The only question was, could she look past those reminders or not?

"Yes," he answered simply, threading his fingers together in a white-knuckled grip. "Keep in mind he has nowhere else to go."

She met his gaze. "That's not fair, Cole. Don't play on my sympathies to get what you obviously want."

"I'm only stating a fact."

Slowly, she rose, leaving the photo on the table. "I won't apologize for needing time."

"Okay," he conceded, "but—"

She held up her hands. "I can't rush into a decision without thinking this through. The thing is, whatever we—I—decide to do about your son, our lives will never be the same."

As if he needed to be reminded… He was damned if he did, and damned if he didn't. Sara must have come to the same realization, too.

Suddenly, holding a person's life in his hands, medically speaking, seemed like less of a minefield than the situation looming ahead of him. Although he'd mentioned a twenty-four-hour deadline, somehow he sensed that announcing the Maitlands were expecting a decision by tomorrow morning wouldn't be well received.

He watched helplessly as she walked out of the room.

As he sat alone, he thought about how he'd enjoyed almost three years of blissful ignorance. Ruth should have told him and the fact she hadn't angered him. He had deserved to know, damn it!

Like Sara deserved to know? his little voice asked. *You wanted to protect your relationship with Sara, so maybe Ruth was doing the same for you…*

He sighed as he recognized the truth. Ruth's silence *had* provided a simpler solution to their dilemma. She'd known how crazily in love he'd been with Sara and breaking the news would have driven a wedge into his new marriage. Not only that, Ruth would have had to share Brody with him because as unprepared as he felt about fatherhood, he would have insisted on knowing his own son, even if he'd been a long-distance parent.

The idea that he might never have known about Brody if Ruth hadn't died didn't set well and was too close to his own situation for comfort. His only aunt and uncle hadn't bothered to make contact with him until he was eight, when circumstances had forced them to do so. While Brody's fate was still undecided, he certainly wouldn't ignore the boy in the meantime.

Idly, he wondered if this one subtle difference proved that his fears of repeating his relatives' dysfunctional behavior were unfounded. Of course, wanting to meet Brody was hardly enough evidence to make a case, but it was a difference that he could think about and consider. In the meantime, he had more pressing concerns...

The clock on the microwave showed six-thirty. Had only thirty minutes passed since he'd broken the news to Sara? Thirty minutes since he'd shattered his wife's faith in him?

He glanced at the sealed envelope on the table before focusing on the photo of his son. *His son.* A living, breathing product of his own DNA, a continuation of the Wittman family tree.

The same awed thoughts had bombarded him after Sara had announced her pregnancy but this time the feelings were a little different. Now he had a name and face whereas before the only tangible evidence of his child had been a number on her lab report. Before he'd had time to dream big dreams, to imagine a little boy or girl with Sara's beautiful eyes and his crooked smile, or to work through his reservations about being a parent, Sara had miscarried.

Brody, however, was here. In the flesh. Already walking and talking with a personality of his own.

Suddenly, the past two-plus years of ignorant bliss were far too long. He wanted to meet his son *tonight,* regardless of the hour or how cranky he might be. Waiting until tomorrow seemed like an eternity.

As he heard a loud thump coming from the direction of their bedroom, however, his eagerness faded. Meeting a child he might never be able to claim as his own could easily be a prelude to heartache.

CHAPTER TWO

SARA stared at the suitcase she'd dumped unceremoniously on the floor and sat on the edge of the bed. Whether she unpacked or not, their trip was over. Done. Finished. If they took in Brody, they wouldn't go. And if they didn't, they still wouldn't go because these events had killed her romantic-weekend mood.

Oh, who was she kidding? Tonight's revelation had ruined more than the weekend. It had completely cracked the foundation of their marriage. Complete collapse was only a nudge away.

The question was, did she want to give their marriage that nudge, or not? Half of her was tempted beyond belief. The other half encouraged her to weather the storm.

She had to think. She had to decide what was the best option, which was the better course, but her emotions were far too raw to make a logical decision. Leaving meant the end of every hope and dream she'd nurtured.

Staying meant…meant what? That she'd already forgiven Cole? She hadn't. That she loved him? At the moment, it was questionable.

Whatever her choice, she had to make it for the right reasons. Right now, she felt as if she were balanced precariously on a wet log, struggling to maintain her footing while knowing it wouldn't take much for her to fall in either direc-

ion. With a decision this monumental looming over her, she
needed time.

Not making a decision was making a decision.

Not true, she argued with herself. She wasn't choosing to
stay or go. She was simply choosing to give herself time to
come to terms with the fact that Cole had a son.

He had a son.

Without her.

Once again, much as it had when she'd first connected the
dots, hurt and anger crashed over her in debilitating waves.
She kicked the luggage defiantly, well aware it was a poor
substitute for the man who deserved her wrath, but she still
hoped that small act would ease her pain.

It didn't.

She hoisted the case back on the bed and unzipped the top.
In spite of her rough treatment, the clothes inside were just as
neat as when she'd placed them there. Once again, she was
racked with indecision.

"Are you okay, Sara?" Cole asked from the doorway, a
worried wrinkle on his forehead.

"I'm just peachy," she answered waspishly. "How do you
think I am?"

He didn't answer, as if he knew the answer. "May I come
in?"

"Suit yourself." She spied the edge of the black silk teddy
she'd purchased specifically for this weekend and poked it
underneath her jeans and sweatshirts to keep it out of sight.

"Are you unpacking?" he asked.

"Yes." She eyed the case and suddenly didn't feel inclined
to empty it, especially when the urge to grab it and run away
was far too strong. "No. I'm not sure."

"Maybe this will help. Packing means you're leaving. To
stay, you have to *unpack*."

He sounded calm, as if he were simply helping her de-

cide between wearing a pair of blue or green scrubs. "I real
ize that," she answered sharply. Then, realizing she sounded
shrewish, she softened her tone. "I'm trying to decide.
Unfortunately, I can't decide what is the right thing to do."
She rubbed at the crease on her forehead.

"I know you're upset," he began as he crossed the threshold.

"Wow. Whatever gave you that idea? Why would I possibly
be upset to hear that my husband…" Her voice cracked. "My
husband had a child with another woman while we were separated? My God, Cole. It was only a week. *One lousy week.*"

"Actually, it was ten days," he corrected, "but, yes, those
were lousy days on so many levels."

She brushed aside his comment. "One week, ten days, it's
practically the same thing. All I know is that I didn't fall into
bed with anyone during that time, even if I *technically…*" she
made imaginary quotation marks in the air "…could have."

"It was a one-night error in judgment. It didn't mean a
thing."

"Oh, that's wonderful, Cole. I'm sure Brody will be happy
to hear his dad say that he was a mistake. An error in judgment."

"I only meant—"

"The point is," she continued, "I haven't forgotten why we
split up or why we got back together."

"I haven't either," he said evenly.

She rubbed the back of her neck. "But now you're asking
me to ignore what you did and welcome your son with open
arms."

His expression grew grave. "I'm only trying to explain
what happened. While I know it's too soon to ask for forgiveness, I'd like you to understand—"

"I'm having trouble with that," she said flatly. "The Cole
Wittman I knew prided himself on his control and for you to

do something so obviously *out* of control...well, it makes me look at our life together in a different light, which is why I can't decide...about this." She motioned toward her suitcase.

"I knew the situation would be...tough to handle," he admitted. "If it's any consolation, I've dreaded telling you from the moment Maitland showed me Ruth's will. I expected the news would be hard for you to swallow."

At least he was cognizant enough of her feelings to guess at her reaction. "You were right."

"I'm sorry to have landed us in this predicament."

Predicament was such an insipid term for the situation they were in, she decided.

"Would you rather I'd kept this from you and told Maitland then and there that we weren't interested in taking Brody?"

It would have been so much easier, she thought with irritation, but she also knew that "easy" didn't always mean "better." Successful marriages were built on honesty, not secrets, and if Cole had kept this from her—even if part of her wished he had—they could be setting a dangerous precedent for their future relationship. What would stop him from withholding information from her again, especially if he deemed it was information she'd find uncomfortable?

"Why didn't you?" she asked, curious.

He shrugged. "The truth eventually comes out. Maybe not today or next month or next year, but sometime down the road it would surface again. Fate has a way of doing the unexpected," he said wryly, "and I figured that learning about Brody would be easier to handle now rather than in ten or twenty years.

"And," he continued tentatively, "knowing how badly you wanted a baby, I'd hoped..." His voice faded.

"That I'd overlook Brody's origins because he would satisfy my own need?" she asked icily.

He had the grace to wince. "Something like that."

"You were wrong. Yes, I want us to have a baby, but only because a child is a logical extension of our love for each other. While I'd be happy to adopt a child, too, the fact that Brody is yours and not a stranger's makes this situation unique. There's another layer of emotional baggage that has to be dealt with."

He nodded, his face lined with a combination of resignation and misery. "I know."

"You're placing me in a no-win situation," she pointed out. "You realize that, don't you?"

"It isn't a no-win," he insisted. "If we can't agree on Brody's future, then that's the end of it."

His even tone wasn't reassuring because in her gut she knew this wouldn't be the end. For the rest of their lives together, if she denied Ruth's request, the what-ifs would plague them.

On the other hand, if she walked away from Cole and the situation, she'd lose as much if not more.

"You want to bring him home, don't you?" That observation was irritating in itself. While she'd been eager to start the process of fertility testing, Cole had been content to bide their time, claiming he was happy with or without a baby. Now, though, he was almost falling over his own feet to welcome his secret child into their household.

In a distant corner of her heart she knew she was being unfair, but at this moment she was still too crushed by a multitude of emotions to be rational.

"I do, but not if we aren't in agreement. We're a team, Sara. We have to function like one. Besides, you're the one with the strong family background. Without your support, I can't be his father, or anyone else's," he said flatly.

The idea that he needed *her* to do this job mollified her to some degree. It also helped to hear that her husband—a brilliant, meticulous, caring physician who'd graduated in the top ten percent of his medical school class—suffered from a few feelings of inadequacy, too. Unfortunately, could she trust him again? She didn't realize she'd voiced her thought until he answered.

"We've had nearly three wonderful years together," he said simply. "And three before that. Have I given you any reason to doubt me during the time we've been together?"

"I presume 'together' is the operative word?"

Her barb had struck home because he fell silent. "I deserve that, I suppose, but I'm the same man I was yesterday, the day before, last week and last year. I love you more now than ever and I don't ever want to hurt you. Every decision I make is tested against that standard. Yes, on that one occasion, I let my fear overrule my good sense. Yes, I drank more than I should have and, yes, I made a bad choice that I'll regret for the rest of my days, but I don't want to lose you over this, Sara. I…I *can't*."

The solution to this utterly devastating change in their circumstances was simple. Leave the past in the past and focus on the future. Unfortunately, that was easier said than done, especially when she would face the proof of his poor choice every day for the rest of her life.

Could she do it? Could she ignore how his son had been conceived? Could she let go of her anger and her sense of betrayal even if Cole had been a free agent at the time?

She had to, otherwise she might as well walk out now with her packed suitcase. As her mother had always cautioned her, "Don't do anything in the heat of the moment. You'll always live with your regrets." At this moment, her emotions were too raw to think rationally, so she cautioned herself to bide her time until she could approach the situation sensibly.

On the other hand, the difficulty she had went much deeper than the notion of having Cole's child underfoot. It was the reminder that Ruth had succeeded in one night with what she had failed to achieve for months. If that wasn't enough to howl at life's unfairness, she didn't know what would be.

"I'd do anything if I could turn back the clock," he said quietly, "but I can't."

He sounded sincere. She wanted to believe that he'd never done anything like this before or since, and part of her *did* believe, but her heart was still too bruised to forgive. Given enough time, she hoped she would, but at this moment she couldn't.

"I know you want me to smile and say everything's okay. That I'll unpack so we can bring Brody home and be one big happy family, but I can't say those things." She met his gaze. "I *can't*. Not yet."

He fell silent. "I can respect that, but while you're mulling over the situation, we need to meet him, Sara. I *need* to see him. Not just a photo, but *him*. Brody didn't arrive under ideal conditions, but he's my son."

She'd half anticipated his request. What man wouldn't be curious about his own flesh and blood? She, on the other hand, wasn't eager to meet the little person that he and another woman had produced so easily.

"If you're asking for permission, feel free to do whatever you want."

"I'd like you to go with me," he said.

She shook her head. "I can't. Not yet. Not tonight."

Expecting him to protest, she was surprised when he simply paused. "Okay," he said, weariness evident in those two syllables. "If you can't handle seeing him so soon, you can't. I'll call Maitland and decline his invitation."

As he rose and strolled toward the door, his usually squared shoulders slumped in defeat, she regretted being so petty. The thing was, she already guessed at how this situation would play out and she was simply trying to hold it at bay as long as she could, hoping another solution would present itself or, better yet, she'd wake up soon and discover this was only a nightmare.

As Cole had said, the boy's future had to be decided. How could she possibly make the right choice if she didn't face her demons? He was, after all, Cole's son no matter how, why or when he had been conceived. Being with Brody would be a painful experience whether she met him tonight, tomorrow or next week, so she had to handle it like one handled any adhesive bandage. Rip off the tape in one swift motion rather than by degrees. Besides, she'd always faced her problems head-on. Ignoring them, pretending they didn't exist, wasn't her way, even if she wanted to indulge herself.

"Cole, wait," she said as he reached the threshold.

He stopped and turned. "Yeah?"

"Would you really cancel and stay home tonight?"

"If that's what you wanted," he said simply. "I may not be the most sensitive fellow in the world, but I'm well aware that seeing the boy won't be easy for you. If giving you more time to adjust will help, then that's what we'll do."

It would have been so much easier if he'd been less thoughtful, less understanding, but he was being all those things and more, which meant she had to respond in kind.

"Unfortunately, I'm not sure there's enough time in the world to do that," she said wryly. "So…" she drew a shaky breath "…we should put this first meeting behind us."

His gaze narrowed. "Are you sure?"

"No." Her smile wobbled. "But it won't be any easier tomorrow."

"Probably not.

"But after we visit, what happens if I decide I can't be his mother?" *Or your wife?* she mentally added.

He hesitated, his expression uncertain. "Let's take this one step at a time, shall we? When we come home, we'll talk. All I ask is for you to consider the possibilities."

She only hoped she could.

Sara walked with Cole toward the Maitlands' hotel room, lost in her thoughts. Cole had explained and apologized both profusely and sincerely, but until she came to terms with what had happened, talking about those long-ago events seemed futile. She'd never imagined their future would become as muddled as it was at this moment, but muddled it was. Now she steeled herself for what would come next.

"Come in, come in," a tall, white-haired Parker Maitland welcomed them far more warmly than Sara felt inside. "Eloise and I were just reading Brody a bedtime story."

Without looking at Cole—she still found it difficult to meet his gaze because if she did, she'd break down and now wasn't the time to fall apart—she crossed the threshold.

Inside, she found Eloise, a petite woman with salt-and-pepper hair, sitting against the pillows with a small, dark-headed boy wearing racecar flannel pajamas plastered against her.

Eloise smiled at her as she continued reading from her book about the exploits of a puppy. While she read, Sara watched the youngster's bright eyes follow the pictures, indicating how intent he was on the story. When Eloise said clearly, "The end," the youngster smiled, giggled, then flipped the book to the beginning and said plainly, "Again!"

"Not again," Eloise said firmly. "We have guests who want to say hello to you."

Taking their presence in obvious stride, Brody took the book, climbed off the bed and ran toward her. "Owie," he said, presenting his thumb to Sara.

She dutifully examined the nearly invisible scratch across

the knuckle. "I see," she said as she crouched down for a better view. "Does it hurt?"

"Kiss?" he asked.

"Will that make your finger feel better?" she asked as the ice in her chest began to crack under his innocent friendliness.

He bobbed his head, so she kissed the spot, feeling his tiny bones in her hand as she smelled his bath-scented little-boy smell. His was a request guaranteed to enchant, and in spite of her reservations she was touched by his trust in an apparent stranger. It would have been so much easier if he'd run away from her and hid...but, no, he'd approached her with the assurance that, although she was a new face, she wouldn't reject him.

She wanted to, she really did. She wanted to walk out of the room and pretend the past few hours had never happened, but it was impossible. She held this child's future in her hands.

No, she held all three of their futures in her hands.

As sympathetic as she was to Brody's situation, she still had one question she couldn't answer. Was she strong enough to welcome Cole's son by another woman into her home when up until a few hours ago she'd always imagined it would be *her* son or daughter she carried across the threshold?

Happy with the attention his finger had received, Brody turned to Cole and presented him with his book. "Again," he repeated, this time with a lopsided grin resembling Cole's so closely that it was painful to see.

Master Brody was his father's son, from the cowlick in his dark hair to the cute dimple in his right cheek.

She'd secretly feared that once Cole met his son, he wouldn't be able to let him go. If the awe in his eyes, the benevolent smile on his face and the shaky hand as he gently stroked Brody's baby-fine hair were any indication, she was right.

Perhaps it might have been easier to watch the two together if she hadn't studied Brody closely enough to decide that his pointy chin and eyes were visible reminders of his mother.

Reminders that Cole had poured out his troubles to a woman he hadn't seen in years. Reminders that this same woman, after one night, had given Cole what she could not after all this time. Obviously, *she,* Sara Jean Wittman, was at fault for everything from her miscarriage to her failure to get pregnant.

She wanted to weep with frustration and disappointment, and when she was finished, she wanted to hate the faceless Ruth for being so fertile while she was not. Shouldn't the love she felt for her husband carry some weight with cosmic fates? Obviously not.

As she watched Cole and Brody together, saw Brody's curiosity about this new man who was willing to read his story again, two choices lay before her in stark black and white.

She could be the bad guy and stop everything pertaining to Brody's guardianship, but if she did, Cole would never forgive her. Oh, he said he'd accept her decision, but that had been before he'd seen Brody and been exposed to his winsome ways. There would always be a hole inside him that she would never be able to fill.

On the other hand, could she be Brody's mother? Could she handle the constantly visible reminder of her failure to give him a child of *their* own—a child who represented *their* love and devotion? The little boy needed and deserved a mom who would nurture him as much as his had. Would she shortchange *him* if she wasn't completely sold on the idea?

Answers eluded her.

While Cole read the story one more time, Sara visited with the Maitlands, although admittedly she couldn't remember any part of their conversation afterward because she'd focused most of her attention on her husband and his son.

This time, when the end was declared and the book closed, Brody yawned and his eyelids drooped, but he simply snuggled against Cole as if he intended to fall asleep in his lap.

Sara was certain Cole would be more than happy to let him.

"We probably should go," Cole said, his tone wistful as he stared down at the little boy.

"We should," Sara agreed, more than ready for a chance to distance herself from the situation—and her impending decision. "Brody needs his rest."

"We're really glad you came by," Eloise told Sara with a smile. "I know you and your husband have a lot to discuss."

Sara glanced at Cole. His longing expression only sent her spirits into a deeper nosedive, but she pasted a smile on her face. "Yes, we do."

Her heart, however, insisted otherwise. They didn't have anything to discuss. Not one simple point had to be debated because in that instant she was reminded of her marriage vows... *For better, for worse...*

This definitely fell in the "for worse" category.

Regardless of how she classified their new circumstances, those vows made her path clear—the same path that was uneven and strewn with boulders of varying sizes, the same path that it would be easier *not* to travel on. In spite of her reluctance, in spite of her reservations, in spite of the small vindictive streak that demanded retribution, she couldn't deny Cole the opportunity to parent his own son. Neither could she deny Brody the opportunity to know his father.

Oh, she could, of course, but it would be the beginning of the end of their marriage and deep down she didn't believe she wanted that.

She simply *had* to welcome Brody into their home and learn how to deal with her jumbled emotions.

* * *

Normally, Sara snuggled against Cole when they climbed into bed but not tonight. For the first time ever, she remained on her side of the mattress, curled into a ball with her back toward him.

He sighed, wishing he knew the right words to break the silence as frigid as the great outdoors. He'd already apologized, but repeating himself wasn't breaking through the barrier between them.

He deserved her wrath, he supposed, but didn't six years of being together—minus one week—mean anything? He also knew he was asking a lot of her to raise his son when she so desperately wanted her own, but what else could he have done? Turning Brody over to someone else would rip open the scars on his heart that Sara hadn't realized she'd healed.

As the silence grew to unbearable proportions, he knew from her steady breathing and the occasional sniffly hiccup that she wasn't asleep. He wanted to reach out and draw her next to him in order to give as well as receive comfort but, given her mood, he might end up with a black eye. Still, the possibility was worth the risk.

He reached out and hauled her against him.

"What are you doing?" she asked, her body tense.

"Holding you."

"I don't want to be held," she said, although she didn't attempt to move away.

"Too bad."

"I'm not making love with you."

"I wasn't offering," he said with equanimity.

"In fact, if our second bedroom was furnished for guests, I'd be sleeping in there."

He didn't doubt it. From the moment he'd silently followed her into the house, he'd mentally prepared himself to watch her grab her still-packed suitcase and leave. As the evening had worn on and they'd gone through the motions of their normal routine of watching the ten o'clock news and weather broadcast before going to bed, he'd slowly grown more optimistic.

At the moment, though, he was grateful that the only other available room in their house was being used as their home office.

"So just because I'm sharing this bed with you doesn't mean you're off the proverbial hook," she added. "As far as I'm concerned, our relationship is on indefinite probation."

He had suspected as much when she hadn't unpacked her clothes. Instead, she'd simply set the case near the wall, ready to grab at a moment's notice.

All he could do was take heart that she wasn't calling it quits. Probation, not to mention the suitcase standing in their bedroom rather than at the front door, meant he still had a chance…

"Indefinite?" he asked. "Seems like a long time, but we can debate that topic another day."

"I assume you have a different subject in mind?" she asked coolly. "Your son, perhaps?"

She knew him too well, he thought ruefully. He hated to press her for a decision about Brody, but as he'd told her before they'd left the house, they'd talk after they met the boy. Ever since they'd left the hotel, she hadn't said more than a few words. Now was as good a time as any for conversation. "Yeah. We should discuss—"

"Was she pretty?"

In spite of the conversational detour, he instinctively knew she was asking about Ruth. He paused, trying to remember the woman who'd only slightly resembled the same mousy, unassuming girl she'd once been. "She was nice-looking, yes. I never really noticed." He winced, realizing how horrible that made him sound, especially since they'd created a child together.

"Tell me about her."

"Don't do this," he begged.

"I need to know, Cole. If I'm going to make sense out of this—"

"You can't," he interrupted harshly. "You can't rationalize an irrational decision. God knows I've tried."

"Maybe I can't, but I need to know who she was, what she was like. Why she could help you sort out your problems but I couldn't."

Her quiet, almost defeated tone convinced him to dredge up his memories in order to reassure her. "She didn't compare to you, in looks or temperament. She was…different from the other girls."

She flopped onto her back. "Different how?"

He sighed, sensing she wouldn't rest until he told her what she wanted to know—whatever that was. "She tended to be a spectator, a bystander if you will, rather than a participant, which meant she'd faded into the background. Ruth got shuffled from foster home to foster home, so she didn't trust many people. Only a few of us got to see the real Ruth—the Ruth who could crack jokes with a straight face, the Ruth who'd do anything for a friend if it was within her power. She'd helped me with my senior English project—we had to create a papier-mâché character from *Beowulf*—and I was all thumbs when it came to art. To repay her, I took her to the senior prom because I knew she was dying to go but no one had asked her."

Sara turned to face him, which was promising, in his opinion. "I didn't know you ever went to your prom."

"Yeah, well, it wasn't important enough to mention." Suddenly aware that he'd recited that same excuse throughout his entire life when anyone asked about his past, he winced.

"So what did you wear?"

She clearly wanted to know every detail. "After four months

of saving my money, I rented a tux," he admitted. "Ruth found a bright pink dress that made her look like a bottle of stomach medicine, but it had all this glittery stuff on it and crinkled when she walked. She said that even though it came from a secondhand shop, she felt like a fairy-tale princess."

"What happened to her parents?"

"I'm not really sure," he said. "She'd mentioned living with a grandmother and after she died, Ruth went into foster care."

"No aunts or uncles or siblings?"

"I don't think so, at least none that she ever talked about. I'm sure if there'd been a relative, social services would have located them."

She fell silent for a minute. "What happened after high school?"

"Our paths didn't cross. Occasionally, I'd hear what she was doing, but Ruth didn't stay in touch and I didn't expect her to. She'd wanted to forget her childhood and everything associated with it. I didn't blame her. We were both biding our time until we finished school and could leave and be on our own."

"Yet she came to your reunion."

"Yeah, it was the first one she'd ever attended. As I said before, I was surprised when I saw her."

For the longest time, he waited for her to speak again. When she didn't, even though he hated to break their uneasy truce, he had to.

"What did you think of Brody?" he asked.

She sighed. "He's a cute kid and obviously very intelligent, too. He looks a lot like you."

He pictured his son's face and felt an odd sense of male pride, which was quite amazing when he considered how a few short years ago he hadn't planned to get married, much less have a family. "Do you think so?"

"Oh, yes. Definitely. Were you as busy a fellow as he was?"

"I don't remember," he said honestly. Sadly enough, he had no one to ask, either. "I imagine I was, though."

He felt her nod. "That's how I pictured you, too. Speaking of pictures, do you have any of you as a child?"

Cole thought of the shoebox tucked away on the top shelf of his closet, buried behind an odd collection of off-season clothing and Sara's handbags. "A few," he said.

"Will you show them to me?"

Somehow, it had always seemed safer to keep those photos—and the memories—locked away, but if Sara had her way, he'd eventually bring them into the open.

"Yeah, sure. Sometime," he said, because refusing wouldn't help his cause and if fate was kind, she'd forget she'd asked. Then, because the suspense was killing him, he asked, "Have you thought about Ruth's request?"

"Yes."

He allowed the pause to last for a full minute before he prompted her to continue. "And?"

"I saw the way you looked at him," she said simply. "You want him, don't you?"

He'd tried to hide his feelings—and his potential disappointment—but Sara clearly knew him too well. Although he felt completely inadequate to be a parent and hated the emotional cost she would pay for his past actions, he couldn't deny that he wanted the privilege of raising Brody.

"Did you think I wouldn't?" he asked instead.

She sighed. "No. I would have been worried if you didn't."

It occurred to him that his reaction could represent another difference between him and his relatives… Somehow, he felt as if he'd passed a test that he hadn't realized he'd been taking.

"And yet," she continued, "when we talked about having a baby of our own, you didn't seem as eager."

How could he explain that while he wanted to have a baby with Sara because he loved her, in the back of his mind his less-than-admirable role models had made him reluctant to embrace the idea with Sara's degree of enthusiasm?

"Just because I was happy to take things slow didn't mean I wasn't eager," he pointed out. "Besides, you can't compare us having our own baby to present circumstances. What we're facing now isn't the ideal way to start our family, but it's the situation we have to deal with."

Slowly, she nodded. For a few seconds they both lay in silence until she finally spoke with resignation in her voice.

"We don't have a choice, do we? He *is* your son, and as you said, he doesn't have anyone else."

"Yes, he's mine, but our decision can't be based on *obligation.* If that's how you feel, then this won't work," he finished flatly. As a child, he'd learned quickly how uncomfortable it was being treated as an "obligation" rather than a member of a family.

Her eyebrows drew together. "I don't feel obligated, but as your wife I suppose I feel a sense of responsibility, even if I'm not completely sold on the idea. At least not yet," she tacked on. "So if you're expecting me to jump up and down with excitement about bringing him into our home, you'll be sorely disappointed. However, I know that we're both too softhearted to live with the idea of giving him up."

He suspected as much and, in fact, her admission was more than he'd allowed himself to hope for. Somehow he sensed a smile wouldn't be appreciated, so he simply nodded to acknowledge her decision.

"Softhearted or not, I appreciate your willingness to welcome him here. I can't imagine trying to raise him without you."

For a man who'd learned to hide weakness and hated to reveal an insecurity, he was almost surprised he had. Sara, however, didn't seem to take his comment as a confession. Instead, it was as if she suspected he was only paying her a compliment to make this bitter pill more palatable to swallow.

"With or without me, I think you can do whatever you put your mind to doing," she told him evenly.

"Oh, Sara..." He leaned over and kissed her, noticing how she held herself stiffly under his caress.

"I know how difficult this is for you," he began contritely, "but everything will work out."

"I hope so, Cole."

Her packed suitcase and his probationary status indicated as much. The truth was, he wasn't confident at all. Brody's presence would remind her of the baby they'd lost and of the baby she was trying so hard to create, so she'd need time—and love—to recover.

"I'll do my best to convince you," he promised. "You won't regret doing this for Brody or for us, Sara."

She sighed. "I just don't want to compound one mistake with another."

He couldn't agree more. "As long as we pull together, we'll make it work."

CHAPTER THREE

WHEN Sara padded into the kitchen at seven-thirty the next morning, wearing her nightgown and robe, she found the coffee ready and Cole seated at the table. His mug was half-empty and the top page of a legal pad full of nearly illegible handwriting lay in front of him.

"Good morning," he said cautiously, as if he suspected from the way she'd tossed and turned all night that she wasn't disposed to doling out forgiveness just yet.

"Morning," she mumbled as she poured a mug for herself. "How long have you been awake?"

"A couple of hours," he admitted. "I couldn't sleep, thinking of everything we have to do today. So I got up and made a list."

She hadn't been able to sleep, either, although she couldn't claim the same excuse. Her thoughts had lingered along the lines of trying to work out how she was going to be the mother that Brody so obviously needed when the idea of inflicting a few medieval tortures on his father held immense appeal.

By 2:00 a.m., though, she'd gotten past her thirst for bodily harm and she'd started to look at her situation with a little more objectivity. The hurt was still there, as well as the disappointment over his one-night stand—even if it had occurred while they'd been separated—but, as Cole had said,

their time together over the past six years had been good. He
deserved credit for that.

A little credit, anyway.

And maybe, someday, she would be able to trust him again.
At the moment, the man she'd thought she'd known seemed
like a stranger.

As for Brody and the task she'd accepted, she simply had
to think of him as a motherless little boy with no one to take
him in. A motherless little boy who needed someone, namely
her, to assume his mother's role.

Unfortunately, it wouldn't be easy because he resembled
Cole in such a painfully obvious manner. She'd have to train
her thoughts to not go down that fruitless path, just as she'd
have to train herself not to wonder if he was still unable to
share his fears with her and if he had any other secrets that
would eventually haunt them.

Idly, she wondered how long it would take before those
thoughts of Brody became second nature because right now
they were not. In any case, Cole was studying her with cautious optimism as if hoping she'd already forgiven and forgotten, which meant it was time to begin that painful process.

She forced herself to sit beside him at the table when she'd
rather take her coffee into the other room to drink in peace.
"What's on your to-do list?"

"First was to cancel our plane tickets and our hotel reser-
vation, which I've already done."

Although she'd known it had been inevitable, a fresh pang
of disappointment struck. "That was fast," she commented
before she, without thinking, sipped on her hot coffee and
burned the roof of her mouth in the process.

"I'm sorry about this weekend, but I promise we'll go another time."

But it won't be the same, she wanted to cry, before she realized that given these events and her shattered feelings, cele-

brating their anniversary as if their lives hadn't taken a right turn seemed hypocritical.

"Yeah, sure. Another time," she echoed, wondering if another anniversary was actually *in* their future.

"I mean it," he insisted, as if he sensed her doubts. "I'll make it up to you."

"Fine." Then, because she wanted to push that subject aside before she embarrassed herself with tears, she asked, "What else is on the list?"

He shoved the pad closer to her. "Childproof the house, which means we have to put away all the things he might destroy, like your figurines. Then we need to install latches on the drawers and cupboard doors that we don't want him to open, which means a trip to the hardware store. The unused electrical outlets need plugs, too, which is something else we have to buy."

She perused the list, impressed by his thoroughness. Then again, he'd been at this for hours. "You've given this a lot of thought."

He shrugged. "I tried, but I'm hoping you'll notice something I've missed."

"It looks rather complete to me."

He glanced at the clock. "It's nearly eight. I thought I'd call the Maitlands while you're getting dressed and then we'll run to the store before they arrive."

"Slow down a minute," she said. "I know how eager you are, but they might be sleeping in. Absolutely do *not* call them before nine."

He frowned, then his expression turned sheepish. "You're right. Nine o'clock is early enough. Do you think we can drive to the hardware store and back before then?"

"Is that a hint I should hurry and get dressed?" she asked wryly.

He chuckled. "It is."

While she showered and dressed, hurrying because his impatience was so obvious, she reminded herself not to look on the situation with dread but with anticipation. Even though the child she'd been hoping, praying and waiting for wasn't coming in the way she'd envisioned, one was coming nonetheless. The only way they could make this work was to pull together, as Cole had said last night.

As it turned out, Cole didn't phone the Maitlands until almost nine-thirty. After that, they worked feverishly to accomplish as many projects on Cole's list as possible before their guests arrived at eleven.

After Cole had dropped a screw several times while he was trying to install a latch on a cabinet door, Sara smiled at her husband's uncharacteristic clumsiness, wishing for an instant that the anxiety—and suppressed excitement—she'd seen all morning had been for *her* child, and not Ruth's. Unfortunately, it didn't accomplish anything for her thoughts to dwell there, so she pushed them aside.

It was a sad day when every thought had to be discarded...

"Nervous?" she asked.

He looked up at her and grinned sheepishly. "Does it show?"

"A little," she admitted.

He sat back on his heels. "This all seems so surreal. As a physician, I'm used to juggling responsibilities for my patients, from making a diagnosis to choosing the best treatment option, and yet the idea of being responsible for one little boy is..." He shrugged, as if unable to find the right word.

"Overwhelming? Daunting? Frightening?" she supplied.

"All that and more," he answered. "None of that hit me until I started looking at all the possible ways a child could hurt himself around here." He glanced around the kitchen, his expression rueful. "I'd always preached safety to parents and felt rather smug about it, but now that *I'm* standing on the other side, knowing *I'm* the one who has to have eyes in the back of my head and practice what I've always preached, it's a different story."

"We'll definitely have a steep learning curve," she said.

He studied her for a moment. "What about you? Are you nervous?"

She paused to consider. "A little," she finally answered. "As you said, this is a huge responsibility. Normally we'd have nine months to get used to the idea of being parents and to physically prepare. Instead, we've gotten twenty-four hours. Less than that, actually."

He nodded, then met her gaze. "Have you told your parents?"

"Heavens, no. Not yet." She'd thought about phoning them, but hadn't arrived at a way to explain the situation without making Cole look bad. Another wife facing these circumstances might not care, but for reasons she couldn't pinpoint, *she* did. Suggesting to her parents that she hadn't known Cole as well as she'd thought she had didn't slide down well at all.

"If you don't mind, when you're ready, *I'll* break the news to them," he declared.

His offer took her by surprise before she realized it required both guts and a strong dose of humility to face his in-laws and admit to actions that didn't show him in the best light.

Silently, she added several points into his plus column. If he could brave the wrath of her mother and father, then he was obviously willing to accept whatever penance they doled out.

But penance or not, the fact remained that he'd kept so much of his life hidden, even from her, and she begged to know why. It wasn't for lack of asking, because she had. The most he'd told her was that he'd moved in with his aunt and uncle after his parents had died, and that those times had not been happy ones. Because he'd treated those questions with easy nonchalance, she'd assumed his life had been filled with the usual teenage problems and angst with nothing remarkable to note.

Now she suspected otherwise. Now she suspected that those days had been so traumatic that he refused to revisit them. It would certainly explain why she'd never met any of his relatives, even at their wedding.

But, she vowed to herself, the time for secrets was over. She wanted to know *precisely* what experiences had shaped Cole into the man he was. Dredging up bad memories wouldn't be pleasant, but it was necessary. While this particular minute wasn't the appropriate time to ask those questions, those days would be discussed.

Soon.

She shook her head. "We'll tell my parents together. Knowing my mother, she'll be thrilled to have a grandbaby, especially this close to Christmas. My dad will be happy, too, *after* he delivers his famous right hook. And after my brothers throw a few punches of their own."

A ghost of a smile appeared on his face. "I figured as much." He met her gaze. "What about you? How are you holding up?"

Like I'm being held together with a wad of used-up chewing gum, she wanted to say. Instead, she answered, "Fine."

His gaze landed on her arms crossed protectively over her chest and she dropped them to her sides. "Really?" he asked.

"Yes," she said more firmly than she felt. It was pointless to belabor how her biggest problem came when she thought of how Brody was more Cole's than hers. While Cole only saw Brody's arrival as the beginning of a wonderful future with his own flesh and blood, she saw it as the beginning of an extremely difficult emotional journey.

"If I could relive that weekend, I would. I wish I'd never gone," he added fiercely.

"Don't apologize again, Cole. I know you're sorry and, as you said, technically we were both free to…see…other people during that time."

She wished she hadn't been so delighted to see him when he'd appeared on her doorstep after their ten-day separation. In fact, she'd been so thrilled by his declaration that he'd been miserable without her that she hadn't bothered to ask questions. Instead, she'd assumed he'd been sitting at home every night, alone and lonely, just as she had been.

That was the problem with assuming.

However, she couldn't correct that mistake now.

"I'm still trying to sort out everything," she continued honestly. "One day, I hope I'll be as thrilled with Brody as you are, but it won't be today."

He nodded, as if he accepted her terms. "I don't want him to pay for my mistake."

"Regardless of what you've done, I wouldn't make a child become your scapegoat," she chided, suddenly realizing that Cole had his own trust issues to work on.

He shrugged. "One never knows how another person will react when the chips are down."

Part of her wondered what had happened during his childhood and the other part was irritated that after a six-year relationship, he still questioned her character.

She poked him in the chest. "You can take what I said to the bank," she said fervently. "I haven't broken a vow to you yet, have I?"

"No," he said slowly.

"Then consider what I just said to be a new vow. I won't hold Brody accountable for your actions. He's an innocent little boy and it isn't his fault how he came to exist."

He nodded, as if satisfied she meant what she'd said. "Okay."

The doorbell chimes sounded and she exchanged a glance with him. "They're here," she said inanely, feeling her heart skip a beat.

As she met Cole's gaze in that instant, the realization of what she'd agreed to came crashing down. A combination of dread and excitement caused her to take Cole's hand. They still had a lot of personal issues to deal with, but they were in this new venture of raising Brody together.

Cole squeezed Sara's hand, grateful that in spite of the problems in their relationship, she had reached out to him in this moment.

That alone gave him hope that they'd eventually be able to repair the damage. Working on that restoration, however, would have to wait for another time. Right now, they had the more immediate task of welcoming the Maitlands inside.

"Brr, it's gotten cold early this year," Parker said, stamping his feet. "I'm thinking we'll have a white Christmas."

While he and Cole discussed Parker's prediction and a long-term weather forecast, Cole's gaze never left his son. He watched as young Brody ripped his stocking hat off his head and his mittens off his hands. His coat was closed with snaps and in a flash he ripped them apart and his royal-blue parka had landed on the floor.

Eloise stared at him fondly as she handed her own knee-length leather coat to Sara. "That boy," she said with a trace of exasperation. "Before you know it, his shoes will be off, too."

She'd hardly finished speaking when Brody plopped onto the floor, twisted off his shoes and stared at the grown-ups, looking pleased at his accomplishment.

Eloise shook her head. "Just like his mother."

Like a sudden, noxious fume, her words hung in the air and

Cole hated seeing Sara's response. For an instant, a stricken expression crossed her features, which made Cole wish he had the ability to erase Eloise's thoughtless remark. Fortunately, Eloise took matters into her own hands.

"I'm sorry, dear," the woman said softly, her face pink with obvious embarrassment. "My observation just slipped out. It's just that Ruth was like our own daughter. I still can't believe she's gone."

"Don't give it another thought," Sara said magnanimously, but Cole saw her brittle smile, knew how much her gesture cost and felt a now-familiar ache of regret and sorrow lodge in his chest.

"Naturally, he'll have some of her traits," Sara continued. "Ignoring them doesn't change the facts. I'm sure you have a lot of things to tell us, so please sit down."

"Yes, please do," Cole echoed, once again mentally telegraphing his apologies to his wife.

"Brody?" Eloise chided as she did. "Please pick up your coat and give it to your daddy."

Daddy. The sound of his new title came as a blow to his solar plexus. Was this how his own father had felt when *he* had been born? Had he been as overwhelmed by the responsibility as *he* now was? But as the little boy shyly glanced at Cole, that panicky feeling slowly transformed into a firm resolve to handle the job to the best of his ability.

Brody clearly didn't have the same conflicting emotions to sort through because he simply smiled before he thrust his coat into Cole's hands. Without hesitation and clearly without dwelling on the ramifications that having a father would mean for him, Brody brushed past Sara and grabbed the oversize bag that Eloise had carried inside. With a herculean effort on his part, he hauled the sack to Cole and dumped it at his feet. "Toys."

Realizing his son had taken the news in his stride, Cole

laughed with some relief that the little boy didn't sense his new father's insecurities. "Are you asking me to play?"

Immediately Brody bobbed his head and began pulling out cars and trucks, a container of blocks and an assortment of other colorful items.

"We brought his favorites," Parker said as he sat on the sofa beside his wife.

"Including his teddy bear," Eloise said. "A word of warning—do not lose that bear. It's his bedtime buddy."

"That's good to know."

Suddenly, Brody tugged on Cole's fingers. "Daddy, play," he demanded. "Box."

As the child grabbed the drawstring bag containing his blocks, Cole sat on the floor beside him, overjoyed to hear that one word coming from his son's mouth. "Okay," he said agreeably, "we'll stack blocks."

As Sara watched the two build a tower that eventually leaned, then crashed to Brody's delight, the sight of the two dark heads together was a bittersweet moment.

He should have been their *son.*

The fact that he wasn't bothered her more than anything else. She still wasn't happy about so many things but being around his child only emphasized how after a miscarriage and subsequent months of trying to get pregnant again, nothing had happened on that front. Although Cole had suggested waiting for Josh's recommended year to pass before going ahead for fertility tests, she had suddenly become too impatient. If there was truly a problem of some sort, she wanted to know now, rather than later. After all, what difference would a few months make?

Of course, to get pregnant, she couldn't keep to her side of the bed every night and she wasn't ready to cross the center line. Her emotions were too raw and her faith too crushed to entertain the idea, which meant her wish for a special

Christmas present wouldn't happen. She wanted to howl out her grief for that setback, too, but now wasn't the time or the place.

For the next ten minutes, Cole played with his son while Sara stoically listened to the information that Eloise and Parker freely shared. She really should write their tips down, she decided, because at the moment, her brain felt like a sieve.

Finally, the youngster rose from his kneeling position and hurried over to Eloise.

"Dwink," he demanded.

"Ask your Mama Sara," Eloise encouraged.

He cocked his head and his face grew thoughtful. "Mama?"

Eloise pointed to Sara. "Sara is your new mama," she told him. "Ask her. Ask Mama Sara."

He stared at Sara, the wrinkle between his little eyebrows revealing that he didn't understand how this was possible. "No." He shook his head before glancing around the room. "Want *my* mama."

As he looked back at Sara, his face wrinkled with unhappiness and he burst into tears. "Mama," he cried, crawling into Eloise's lap.

Although Sara hadn't expected Brody to accept her easily, his rejection bothered her more than she'd thought it might. "Please don't push the issue," she said.

"I'm so sorry, dear," Eloise apologized as she cuddled Brody. "I'm not doing a very good job with this transition, am I? It was thoughtless of me and I should have known... I've been trying to tell him that you're his new mother, and I thought that by tacking on your name, he'd accept the change, but he doesn't seem to understand."

"I'm sure he doesn't," Sara said, feeling sorry for the child who was faithfully waiting for the most important person in his young life to reappear. The ironic thing was that she'd been worried about how *she'd* accept being his mother when she should have been more concerned about Brody accepting *her*.

"He knows what he called his mother," she pointed out, "and adding another name is probably confusing him. All things considered, he should probably think of me as Sara for now. It'll be less stressful."

"You're probably right, dear," Eloise said as she kissed Brody's forehead and smoothed his hair.

Wondering how long it would take for Brody to turn to *her* for comfort instead of seeing her as the enemy, Sara rose. Perhaps if she left the room, Brody would calm down. "I'll get him a cup of juice," she mentioned to no one in particular. "And coffee for the rest of us."

As Brody's wails increased in volume, she fled to the kitchen and began preparing a tray.

"Need help?" Cole asked a few minutes later.

She brushed past him to remove the creamer from the refrigerator, refusing to meet his gaze and see the pity in his eyes. "No, thanks. I can manage."

He grabbed her arm and tethered her in place. "He doesn't understand, Sara."

She wasn't ready to accept his comfort and she stiffened. "Don't you think I know that?" she asked.

To her surprise, as if he'd decided he wouldn't be rejected so easily, he didn't release his grip. "He'll come around."

"Sure he will," she dutifully agreed. *Maybe when he's eighteen.*

"He will," he insisted. "He'll soon learn what I've known for a long time...that you're a kind and loving person who has a heart big enough to let him in, no matter what."

"Stop trying to flatter me."

"This isn't flattery. It's the truth. I may not be a psychiatrist, but this isn't a rejection of you. He's frustrated because his life has crumbled around him and he doesn't understand why or know how to repair it."

Boy, could she relate to that!

She sighed. Young Brody had to learn how to make the best of an uncomfortable situation just as she did. She might not share a blood bond with the child, but they certainly shared this emotional one.

"I know," she agreed. "As Parker told us last night, the adjustment won't happen overnight."

Slowly, Cole's hold became more of a caress than a leash, making her realize how much she'd missed the closeness of their physical contact and she'd only done without for less than twenty-four hours. Yet, she wasn't quite ready to forgive him, even if he was being thoughtful and supportive.

"Dwink," she heard a plaintive voice demand loudly in the other room.

Brody's request broke the mood of the moment and she tugged free of Cole's hand. "Would you mind carrying in Brody's juice? I'll bring the coffee in a minute."

He nodded, then left with the plastic cup she'd poured.

As Sara lifted the tray and prepared to follow him, the incident painfully reminded her that she wasn't Brody's mother. She knew it and the sad thing was that little Brody knew it, too.

CHAPTER FOUR

THE time with the Maitlands went all too quickly and before Cole knew it, he and Sara were on their own. Fortunately, both of them had received short-term compassionate leave so Brody wouldn't have to attend day care just yet, but Cole knew those two weeks would flash by.

After only three days of being a parent, Cole had decided that a hectic day at the hospital was less exhausting than following this little whirlwind of energy. At the same time, though, these new experiences were energizing. They also reminded him of all the usual milestones he'd missed—first steps, first smiles, first words. He hated that those were memories he could never recover, but he was also grateful that he'd stand nearby for the subsequent ones.

At the moment, though, the tense moments were balancing out the good ones. He'd caught himself on several occasions thoughtlessly commenting on Brody's habits that were so characteristic of his mother, like kicking off his shoes whenever he could.

As if Sara had needed a reminder that Brody wasn't hers, he'd scolded himself. Although she had nodded and gone about her business, Cole had seen the bleakness in her eyes in spite of the smile she'd pasted on her face. Gut-wrenching guilt had swept over him for his insensitivity and the urge to fall back into old habits and look for a means of escape sounded more and more attractive. He'd been tempted to call the Maitlands on more than one occasion and announce that they'd changed their minds—that having Brody around was as painful as probing an open wound, that he simply couldn't subject his wife to such misery—but he never acted on those thoughts. For one thing, it was cowardly to use Sara as his excuse when she hadn't uttered one word of complaint.

Neither was he the ten-year-old boy who'd clung to the only hope he'd had—the hope that one day his life would no longer be subject to the whims of others. He'd grown up with one goal in mind—to endure as best he could, while vowing to never be placed in a similar situation.

Sadly, that mindset had nearly cost him Sara. It seemed as if his present circumstances were another test that the fates had decided to give in order to see if he was willing to face a few more of his deep-seated fears. While escape seemed attractive at times, it really wasn't an option—not if he wanted to keep any measure of self-respect.

Then there were the moments when Brody's mannerisms mirrored his and he saw himself in the youngster's features. How could he possibly give up the privilege of raising his own son?

Those feelings were reinforced whenever Brody came to him without hesitation or fear. Without any muss or fuss, Brody had accepted him as his father and their relationship was already growing by leaps and bounds, probably because he was still trying to sort out what role a father played in his young life when he'd never had one before.

Unfortunately, Sara wasn't faring as well. Although she'd said several times that she wasn't taking Brody's rejection to heart, Cole suspected the little boy's wariness troubled her. Normally, children gravitated to her, but ever since Eloise had referred to her as "Mama," Brody had stared at her with suspicion and only went to her when no one else was available.

Cole had tried to stand in the gap, but he suspected he wasn't doing a stellar job. While he told the youngster that Sara hadn't been responsible for his mother's disappearance, he wasn't sure that Brody understood. Somehow, he had to figure out a way to persuade the little boy that Sara hadn't created this sudden gaping hole in his short life, but so far he'd drawn a blank.

It wasn't the only blank he was drawing, either. Their anniversary was coming up soon and he still didn't know how they could celebrate the occasion. Dinner at the fanciest restaurant in town ranked high on his list, but he couldn't figure out the logistics. He might still be finding his way when it came to juggling the roles of parent and husband, but he instinctively knew that bringing Brody with them defeated the purpose of giving his wife his full and undivided attention. One of his colleagues had mentioned how he and his wife had kept a date night to keep their romance fresh after the kids had started to arrive, and he couldn't think of a better time to start the habit than with their anniversary. Unfortunately, hiring a sitter for the evening was out of the question. Brody didn't need another stranger introduced into his life so soon after moving in with a couple he'd only known a few weeks.

Of course they could always postpone their celebration until their life with Brody settled into a routine, but that could take months. Sara would probably understand if their special day passed without their usual fanfare, but Cole didn't *want* her to have to understand. He wanted her to know that she was still number one in his life. He simply needed to be creative. Luckily, he still had about ten days to dream up the perfect celebration.

As he mentally considered his options and scanned the newspaper's business ads, Brody climbed onto his lap as he clutched one of his cars. "Daddy, wet."

"That's nice," Cole murmured idly, his thoughts still focused on creating the perfect anniversary celebration.

Brody babbled something that Cole couldn't understand, but as he dropped the newspaper to listen, he suddenly became aware of a dampness seeping into his jeans.

"Are you wet, Brody?" he asked.

"Wet," the little boy echoed as he enthusiastically bobbed his head.

Suddenly, Cole realized that he'd never dealt with Brody's basic needs since he'd come to live with them. While he was willing to do his share, he also realized that he'd never changed a diaper before in his life. He didn't have the first idea of how to go about it.

"Okay, bud," he said as he rose and took Brody's hand. "Shall we see if Sara will help us out this time?"

He led Brody to the kitchen, where Sara was drying dishes. She paused, tea towel in hand. "If you're here to beg for more cookies, the answer is no. We just had lunch."

He grinned. "As wonderful as another cookie sounds, we're not here for that. Brody needs his britches changed."

Sara met his gaze. "Then change him. You can take off his clothes and put on a fresh diaper as well as I can."

"But I've never diapered before," he protested.

"There's no time like the present to learn," she said smartly.

"I've never even *seen* it done." He hoped that would sway the argument in his favor. "Can you show me? For Brody's sake?"

For a minute, she looked as if she might refuse, but then her shoulders slumped in an obvious sign of capitulation. She tossed the towel onto the counter and shooed them ahead of her to Brody's bedroom where she proceeded to stand back and supervise while Cole pulled off Brody's pants.

"All you have to do is pay attention when you remove the

wet one," she said as he ripped off the tapes holding the soggy diaper around Brody's waist. "Then put the new one on."

Cole followed her instructions as she watched, feeling as clumsy as the first time he'd sutured a gash under the critical eye of his professor.

"Shouldn't he be toilet trained by now?" he asked, desperately hoping this stage would soon fall behind them.

"Eloise said that Ruth had started to work with him, but she hadn't gotten very far."

"Then maybe we should make that a priority."

"You're welcome to try," she answered cheerfully, "but until he adjusts to his new circumstances, I think it best if we wait awhile. Even if we started immediately, it won't fix Brody's immediate problem. So resign yourself to changing a few diapers. Just be glad he's only wet."

Now, *that* was a scenario Cole hoped he'd never have to face by himself.

In the end, the entire process was far less stressful than Cole had expected.

"Will you two be okay by yourselves while I run a few errands this afternoon?" she asked.

It would be the first time Cole had been completely alone with Brody without Sara for backup. While he knew that day had to come, he wasn't ready to face it just yet, which was an odd thing for a man who'd gone through medical school and an internal medicine residency to fear, he thought wryly.

"Why don't we go with you?" he asked instead.

Sara paused. "It's really cold to be taking him outside unnecessarily," she began.

"We're driving, not walking," he pointed out. "And we'll warm the car before we go. He'll be fine. Besides, it'll be fun."

"Fun?" She stared at him as if he'd grown another nose. "You clearly haven't shopped with a toddler before."

"I haven't," he admitted, "but how hard can it be with both of us?"

An hour later, Cole's words of *how hard can it be?* came back to haunt him. He could explain in vivid detail of how difficult it was to keep one active, curious toddler occupied while taking care of the business of shopping.

Fortunately, Sara didn't say "I told you so." Instead, she simply smiled and suggested that he concentrate on his son while she filled the cart with the essentials.

So Cole obliged. At first it wasn't too difficult to entertain the little boy as he sat in the cart, but that soon grew boring.

"At the risk of making a huge mistake," Cole said as Brody kicked his legs and arched his back to try and escape his seat, "maybe he'd be less noisy if I let him walk."

"Do you really think you can hold on to him?" Sara asked. "If he darts away…"

"I'll hold his hand," he said as he lifted the youngster out of the cart.

"You'd better," she said darkly.

Freed from his constraints, Brody clung to Cole's hand until he suddenly jumped up and down with obvious delight. "Toys!" he squealed, before slipping out of Cole's grasp and racing toward every child's favorite section of a store.

Fear struck Cole's gut. Although he was never more than two steps behind his son, the idea that his little boy was quicker than he was gave him new sympathy for parents whose children darted into harm's way while under their watchful eye. By the time he'd toyed with the idea of tethering Brody to him until he was at least sixteen, he'd caught up to him.

Brody, with reflexes as quick as any pickpocket's, had snatched a stuffed lion off the shelf and wrapped both arms around it. He talked to the lion as if it were his long-lost pal.

"What did you find, Brody?" Cole asked.

"Grr," Brody said. "Wions grr."

Like all parents, Cole was impressed with his son's obvious knowledge. "Yes, lions growl."

The little boy nodded. "Grr."

Cole glanced at Sara, who'd finally caught up with them. "Smart kid," he said proudly. "Who would have thought a stuffed lion would catch his eye?"

"Who would have thought," she echoed, looking both relieved and exasperated. "Unfortunately, as much fun as it is to stay and play, I have everything on my list."

Cole spoke to Brody. "Okay, son. Put down the lion. It's time to leave."

Brody shook his head and clutched the toy to his chest. "No."

"Yes," he said firmly.

"No-o-o-o," the toddler yelled as Cole reached for the toy. "Mine."

"It's not yours," Cole said patiently.

Brody frowned. "Mine."

"Brody," Cole said sternly. "We have to leave the lion."

Brody's lower lip quivered and a huge tear slid down his cheek as he continued to hug the lion. "Mine," he sniffled. "My wion."

Although Cole knew that giving in to tears didn't bode well for the future, Brody's obvious distress tugged at his sympathies. Unsure of what to do, he glanced at Sara and shrugged helplessly, hoping she'd give him some direction on how to handle Brody's tantrum.

Sara saw Cole's indecisiveness and knew he wanted her to intervene. The resentful, still hurting side of her insisted that she let him deal with the situation on his own—after all, he'd wanted to be a parent and she was struggling with her own feelings of inadequacy, so why shouldn't he?—but one thought after another popped into her head and made her repent.

I can't do this without you, Sara.

Brody is yours, too.

She'd stepped into Ruth's shoes, albeit reluctantly, but an agreement was an agreement. She needed to fulfill her part of this bargain and if the truth were known, she wasn't immune to Brody's obvious distress, either. However, before she could offer a suggestion, Cole crouched beside the youngster, held out his hand and spoke softly, yet firmly.

"Brody, give me the toy."

"Daddy, *mine,*" Brody wailed. "Warry is my wion."

"This lion isn't yours," Cole explained with surprising patience.

Suddenly, Sara understood what was happening. She placed a hand on Cole's shoulder. "You don't suppose he has a stuffed lion like this one, do you? It would explain why he thinks this is his."

Cole stared up at her. "He could just be throwing the usual two-year-old temper tantrum."

Sara glanced at Brody and watched as he buried his nose in the lion's neck. "He might," she admitted, "but I don't think he is. He called the lion Larry. What child his age names a toy in less than five minutes?"

Cole hesitated as he obviously mulled over Sara's comment.

"Even if he is acting like a normal toddler who wants what catches his eye," Sara continued, "after all the adjustments he's been forced to cope with lately, do you really want to deny him this one small thing just to prove a point or establish that you're the boss?"

The little boy's soulful gaze would have melted Sara's heart even if she hadn't connected the dots about the lion and it obviously had the same effect on Cole because a look of relief spread across his face, which suggested that he hadn't wanted to disappoint the little boy but had thought he'd had to.

He rose, plucking Brody and his lion off the floor in one smooth motion. "Okay, sprout. Let's take Larry the lion home."

This time, Brody didn't fuss as Cole settled him back in the cart. Instead, he bestowed such a huge smile on his father—a smile of gratefulness that was only more powerful because of the tears glimmering in his eyes—that Sara sensed she'd read the situation correctly.

Over the next few hours, Sara watched Brody shower attention on his lion. She'd obviously done something right for the boy, which made her rethink her ability to act as his mother. Granted, what she'd done was minor in the grand scheme of things, but it pleased her to know that she'd been able to put her personal issues aside—for a short time, at least—to focus on Brody. Maybe, given enough time, she *could* be the mother he needed her to be.

Now she had to focus on trying to be the wife that she still was… It wasn't easy. The hurt was still there and it showed in their stilted conversations—conversations that centered around Brody to the exclusion of all else.

It would take more time than had passed so far for her to return to their former easiness but, strained relations or not, she was still observant. And she'd observed that her husband, who wasn't a talkative man on any given day, seemed more introspective than usual.

She sensed it had to do with their trip to the store—maybe he was still fighting the same heart-stopping fear that she had when Brody bolted out of reach—but she waited for him to speak.

As the late-afternoon shadows began to lengthen, she decided enough was enough. While there were still many topics that she considered off-limits, they had to start communicating about *something*. Discussing Cole's current feelings seemed like a good place to start.

As she watched Brody drive his lion across the living room floor in his largest dump truck, she was certain the right moment had arrived when Cole finally joined them.

"I just phoned the Maitlands," he said offhandedly before she could broach the subject on her mind.

"What for?"

"To satisfy my curiosity. It seems Brody *does* have a stuffed lion but Eloise said he didn't play with it very often, so she didn't bring it with him. It's boxed with the rest of his things that should arrive any day now."

Sara smiled, inordinately pleased by his announcement. "I wonder what he'll say when he realizes he now has *two* Larrys."

"Yeah, I wonder." He fell silent for a few seconds. "How did you know it was so important to him?" he asked.

She shrugged. "I didn't. I watched, listened and had a hunch. That's all."

"Yeah, well, your hunch seems fairly accurate. Obviously the conclusion I drew was way off base."

She heard the disgust in his voice. From personal experience, she recognized his suffering as a bout of perceived failure and while part of her wanted him to stew over it, she simply couldn't let it happen. Not because she was feeling particularly benevolent but because he was her husband, and she still hated to see him hurting.

"Don't be so hard on yourself," she told him. "You were only trying to do what any parent would do under the circumstances."

"Maybe, but you were obviously more attuned to the situation than I was. I didn't hear him call the toy by name, but you did."

"Only because I was the objective bystander and you weren't."

"Maybe, but what happens next time, especially if I'm by myself and don't have your powers of observation? This is exactly—"

He stopped short and Sara waited for him to continue. "Exactly what?" she prompted.

He hesitated.

"This is exactly *what*, Cole?" she repeated.

"It's what I was afraid of," he burst out. "Being inadequate. Maybe I'm not cut out to be a father."

"You aren't the only one who suffers from doubts," she pointed out. "My dad always said that anyone who isn't daunted by the responsibility of parenthood has an overinflated view of himself. The question is, do you still *want* to be a father?"

He nodded.

"Then stop worrying about making a mistake. If there's a repeat of today's incident at the store, you'll make the best decision based on the circumstances at the time," she said simply. "Sometimes we'll get it right, like we did today, and sometimes we won't. Parenthood isn't a perfect science."

His chuckle was weak. "No kidding."

"The point is, the more we get to know Brody, the easier it'll be to tell the difference between a tantrum and when he's truly upset about something."

He nodded slowly before his gaze grew speculative. "Thanks for the pep talk."

Given that their relationship was still broken and that she hadn't been able to dole out any forgiveness yet, his gratitude made her a little uncomfortable. "It was nothing," she said, dismissing him with a breezy wave of her hands.

"Thanks also for not saying 'I told you so.' Shopping with a toddler isn't as easy as it sounds," he added ruefully.

"It isn't," she agreed. Then, because she was curious, she asked, "Would you have felt better if I had?"

"No, but you would have had the satisfaction. It was a perfect opportunity for you to point out how inexperienced and unqualified I am."

"It would have been," she admitted, "but all first-time parents are inexperienced until time solves that problem. Besides, what purpose would it have served?"

"You'd have felt vindicated."

"Maybe, but, again, how would that have helped either of us?" she asked, fully aware that the urge to do just that hadn't completely left her. She'd simply been able to take the moral high ground today but who knew what she'd do tomorrow? "As attractive as the idea is, being resentful and throwing recriminations at each other won't make life easier. As you've already pointed out, we're in this together."

As soon as she finished speaking, she felt his gaze grow intent. "Did I say something wrong?" she asked, uncomfortable under his piercing stare.

He shook his head. "You said everything right. I was just thinking how lucky I am to have you," he said soberly.

His kind words, coupled with her roller-coaster emotions of the past few days, threatened to bring on tears that she couldn't explain. Intent on holding them at bay, she swallowed hard and forced a smile.

"Hold that thought for when you have to change Brody's pants again," she said lightly.

The next two weeks passed quickly and they settled into a routine of sorts, although the day came when the responsibilities of their respective jobs couldn't be ignored. On Monday, because Cole didn't report to work until eight and Sara's shift began at six, he was automatically elected to take Brody to the hospital's day care. Not that he'd minded, of course. Knowing

Sara was still struggling with the situation to varying degrees depending on the day, he was doing everything possible to make life easier on her. It was the least he could do because they wouldn't be in this situation if not for him.

While he would have preferred that Sara quit her job to look after Brody, her decision to cut her hours from full-time to part-time came as a relief.

In a way, he felt guilty over Sara being the one to disrupt her schedule and career for Brody, but she'd suggested it herself as being the logical solution. Another woman might not have been as accommodating, but he wasn't fooling himself. Her willingness to act as Brody's mother wasn't a guarantee that their marriage would return to its same open and unguarded status. He had a lot of bridges to build and instinctively he knew that if he didn't construct them properly, he and Brody could easily end up on their own.

Fortunately, as soon as he'd dropped Brody off to join the rest of the children, a toy fire truck had caught his son's eye and their parting had occurred without incident. If Cole's schedule permitted, he hoped to sneak away throughout the day so Brody could see his dad's familiar face and know he hadn't been deserted.

Now he only hoped the events he had planned for their anniversary celebration tonight would help Sara realize that she hadn't been deserted, either...

Sara's first day back at the hospital was stressful, not only because she had to add Brody to her early-morning routine but also because she'd been running at full speed ever since she'd clocked in to work. As of this morning, nearly every patient bed was filled because of a sudden influx of influenza cases. The poor respiratory-therapy staff looked frazzled as they struggled to keep pace with the demand for their services. According to the charge nurse for Sara's medical unit, the new patient she would soon receive would add to that workload.

She was on her way back to the nurses' station after silencing another IV fluid alarm when the ward clerk waved to her. "What's up, Georgia?" she asked.

"Delivery for you."

"What?"

Georgia, a forty-year-old black woman who wore a perpetual smile on her face, handed her a large mug emblazoned with the local coffeehouse logo. "This is for you."

Sara recognized the aroma wafting out of the cup and knew it was her favorite espresso flavor, skinny caramel macchiato. "Who brought this?" she asked.

Georgia shrugged. "Some kid. Didn't leave his name or ask for a tip. I asked who'd sent him and he just said you'd know."

Which meant Cole had done it. Her favorite coffee shop had been across the street from the hospital where they'd first met and Cole would often bring espressos or lattes to share when they'd had a free minute. For him to do so now, when the nearest coffee bar was across town, showed he'd put some thought into today's surprise.

Our relationship is on indefinite probation.

As she held the still-warm cup in one hand, she understood what the drink represented. He was trying to court her again.

Suddenly, her friend Millie fell beside her. "You lucky dog," she breathed. "Where did you get that?"

"A secret admirer," Georgia supplied.

"Cole sent it," Sara explained.

"Ooh," Millie gushed in obvious envy. "Must mean you had a fantastic trip." Millie turned to Georgia. "We're taking five so she can drink that while it's still warm."

Before Sara could protest, Millie herded her to the ward kitchenette. "I've been dying to hear about your weekend for the past two weeks. Imagining the fun you two were having was the only thing that kept me going when I was at home, dealing with kids and a husband with stomach flu." She shook her head. "Why is it that none of them could come down with it at the same time? Anyway, I want to know if you did any sightseeing, or if Cole didn't let you out of your hotel room."

"We didn't go."

"Didn't go?" Millie's mouth formed a surprised O. "What happened?"

"A family emergency."

"Oh, my gosh. What happened?"

She sipped her drink, reveling in the familiar flavor. She didn't want Cole's thoughtfulness to soften her attitude toward him, but it was working quite successfully. "We became parents instead."

Millie's smile instantly spread across her face. "You're parents? Wow, Sara. I had no idea you were trying to adopt. I knew you wanted a baby for the longest time—"

As if she suddenly realized that Sara's response wasn't typical of a new mother, she cut herself off. Her smile faded and her gaze became intent. "You don't seem as excited as I would have guessed. This is a good thing, isn't it?"

"It is," she agreed obediently.

"So how old is he? What's his name? Is it a boy or a girl? Did you get a phone call or wake up one morning and find him on your doorstep? *What?*"

Sara smiled at Millie's rapid-fire questions. "Brody James is his name and we learned about him when I got home from work on the Wednesday night before we were going to leave. The lawyer representing the mother of Cole's son broke the news to us."

Millie's eyes widened. "Whoa, back up a minute. Cole has a son?"

"Yes." She paused. "We were just as surprised as you are."

"Oh, Sara." Her expression became sympathetic. "No wonder you look stressed. He must be fairly old by now, though. You've known Cole for a long time."

"Brody is almost three."

Millie's eyes widened. "Almost three?" she echoed. "But you and Cole have been a couple for..."

Sara filled in the blank. "Six years."

Millie's eyes narrowed. "Do you mean to tell me that he *cheated* on you?"

Sara closed the door. "Could you please lower your voice?" she muttered. "I'd really rather this doesn't end up as fodder for the hospital grapevine." The rumors would begin soon enough, especially after people saw father and son together.

"But, Sara, people can add two and two. When they do, they'll come up with four."

"Cole didn't cheat on me," she defended. "Not really. Not technically."

Her defense sounded lame to her own ears because the situation involved more than a mere technicality.

Millie looked skeptical. "Sorry, but according to my math, he had to have something going on the side if he has a two-year-old and you've been together for six."

"You may not remember, but before Cole proposed, we'd had a huge argument and we broke up. It wasn't for long, but we'd gone our separate ways. During that time, Cole met a high school friend and...Brody is the result."

"Oh, Sara." Millie's face registered distress, or perhaps it was concern, but Sara didn't bother to classify it.

"All they need to know," Sara said firmly, "is that the boy's mother was an old friend of Cole's and when she was killed, she'd granted custody to us."

"Killed?"

"Did you read about a medical helicopter crash a few weeks ago? One of the nurses on the flight was Brody's mother."

"Oh, Sara. How awful."

Millie's pitying expression was more than Sara could handle, although she knew she'd see it often in the coming days. People would speculate all they liked but, as far as she was concerned, Brody's parentage was none of their business.

"I'd appreciate it if you give the edited version to anyone who asks," she said.

Millie nodded. "Of course. But, Sara, how are you handling this? It can't be easy for you."

Not being easy was an understatement. "We're managing," she said instead. "Brody seems to have accepted Cole as his daddy and I do okay with him as long as no one refers to me in his hearing as 'mama.'"

Millie shook her head. "You're a good woman, Sara Wittman. I don't think I could be as gracious as you are under the circumstances."

"I don't always feel gracious," she admitted. "I have my days, but on the whole it's getting better." Seeing Brody's and Cole's similarities was a bittersweet reminder of so many things that had gone wrong, beginning with the secrets she'd allowed Cole to keep and ending with her failure to conceive. Some days she wanted to scream with frustration and throw things, like Brody did when life seemed to be too much to handle, but she didn't. Flying out of control would only cause Cole to suggest either a counseling visit or a prescription for an antidepressant. She didn't need or want either.

However, all things considered, as much as she wanted a baby of her own, getting pregnant right now wasn't a good idea. Bringing another child into the mix while she and Cole were sorting out their trust issues wouldn't be a wise move.

"Then why are you here at work?" Millie asked bluntly. "You should be taking maternity leave."

"I've had the past two weeks as compassionate leave," she replied. "Now I'm on part-time status for a few months. After

hat, we'll see how things are working out both here and at
ome before we decide what to do next."

Sara had been happy to accept a temporary option of part-
ime work because going to the hospital, even two or three
lays a week, allowed her to feel as if her life hadn't totally
pun out of control.

A brisk knock interrupted. "Your new patient is on her
vay, Sara," the ward clerk announced before she disappeared
gain.

"Thanks, Georgia." Sara took another long swallow of her
lrink, savoring the taste before she set the mug in an out-of-
he-way spot on the counter. "Catch you later, Mil."

Interruptions were commonplace, so she didn't worry that
ler friend and colleague would take offense at their abrupt
arting. She reached the nurses' station in time to greet the
mergency nurse who was delivering a woman in her sixties,
)orothy VanMeter, courtesy of a wheelchair.

"Caught flu?" she commiserated as she guided the pair to
n empty room.

Dorothy's answer was a deep, harsh and productive cough.
ara handed her a box of tissues and set the trash can nearby
or her use. When Dorothy's episode had ended, her facial
olor held a bluish tinge and she was holding her ribs. "I
aught something," she rasped. "If this is flu, then it's some-
hing I've never had in my life. I'm so exhausted, sometimes
wonder if I can draw my next breath."

"We'll do everything we can to make you feel better," Sara
aid kindly. "First, though, we'll make you comfortable so
ou can rest."

The next twenty minutes passed quickly as Sara listened
o the nurse's update, helped Dorothy into bed and brought
wo blankets from the warmer to cover her. As she started
er IV, Sara asked about her family.

"I have three children," Dorothy rasped. "Stepchildren actually, but they don't...we aren't close."

Sara had heard similar stories before. Estrangement in families were more common than one might imagine. "Sometimes people react differently when an illness is involved," she offered. "I'll be happy to call them for you, to let them know you're in the hospital."

"Won't matter," the older woman said tiredly. "They have their own lives now." She closed her eyes and Sara took it as a signal that she either couldn't or wouldn't continue this particular conversation thread.

Fortunately, the IV fluid was dripping steadily as Cole arrived.

Her pulse jumped as it always did when she saw him looking so handsome and authoritative in his white coat, and she wondered how she could respond to him as easily as she always had. Events of the past few days should have doused the sparks quite effectively, but clearly they had not.

Sara lingered in the room while he introduced himself to Dorothy and discussed his treatment plan for her while she took mental notes. As soon as he'd finished, she washed her hands and followed him into the hallway.

"Do you really suspect whooping cough?" she asked.

"I do," he said. "According to the E.R. docs, there have been two confirmed cases in town over the weekend and her symptoms fit."

"But that's a childhood disease. We vaccinate everyone for it."

"We try," he corrected, "but the incidence has been increasing among children who haven't completed the full course and among adolescents and adults whose immunity has faded. Before you ask, though, pertussis *is* included with the tetanus booster that's recommended every ten years, but not everyone stays on top of their immunization schedules."

"I suppose not. To be honest, I'm not certain when I got my last booster shot," she confessed.

"We'd better find out," he advised, "especially with a toddler in the house."

The thought of carrying the germ home to Brody horrified her. "You're right. I'll look into it."

"Good. Meanwhile, we'll give Mrs. VanMeter supportive care and start her on an IV antibiotic. Be sure everyone uses their personal protective equipment, including a mask, when they go into her room. Hand-washing is a must, but I don't have to tell you that."

"I'll take care of it," she said, already planning to place a cart outside the room with the necessary items and post the appropriate signs on the door.

"Check with the lab. If they haven't received a sputum specimen for a *Bordetella* culture, then collect one."

"I will," she promised. "Anything else?"

"No. Er, wait, there is one more thing," he said.

While she waited expectantly, he met her gaze. "I've made plans for this evening, so don't fix dinner."

"Plans? What for?"

His dark eyes suddenly sparkled. "Tsk, tsk, Sara. Don't tell me you've forgotten what day this is?"

"It's Monday."

"Monday. Our anniversary," he reminded her.

Her face instantly warmed. "I guess I did forget."

"Well, I didn't and so I've planned our evening."

"You planned…? But what about Brody? We can't leave him with a sitter after he's been with one all day."

"We aren't leaving him," he announced.

"Then how—?"

"I have everything under control, at least if the timing works out," he said ruefully. "I would have surprised you, but I was afraid you'd throw a tuna casserole in the oven before I got home."

Clearly, he knew her well enough to know that when she was irked at him, she served tuna casserole—his least favorite meal. No doubt with today being their anniversary, he'd been afraid she'd make him pay for their lost weekend.

"It's your lucky day," she said lightly, "because I'm out of canned tuna. I had hamburger in mind."

"Tonight calls for something a bit more special than ground beef, don't you think?"

She really didn't feel like celebrating, anniversary or not. Physical exhaustion after working a full day aside, she was still struggling to keep her emotions in check. It was ironic to realize she'd been worried at one time that he'd forget their anniversary date and yet she was the one who'd forgotten. More than likely, she'd blocked it out of her mind, she thought wryly.

"Why are you going to this much effort?" she asked bluntly. "It isn't as if you have to worry I'll send Brody back, like a refused package."

"This is about us, not Brody," he said. "You put me on probation, remember? I planned this because I know how much our anniversary weekends mean to you. Although what I arranged doesn't compare to the trip we would have taken, the occasion deserves to be marked, don't you think?"

"Oh." For the past few weeks their entire lives had revolved around one small boy to the exclusion of all else, but apparently Cole had taken time to look at the calendar. "I don't know what to say."

"Then it's a date?"

Why not? she asked herself. A quiet evening wouldn't make her feel less lacking as his wife, but it might give her an opportunity to finally establish why Cole hadn't ever been able to share his deepest secrets with her. Maybe their anniversary wasn't the best night for a soul-baring conversation, but emotionally, she hadn't been up to tackling that touchy subject before now. The shock had finally worn off and they were trying to give their relationship a solid footing again, so dinner might be the perfect opportunity to ask those hard questions.

She nodded slowly. "Yeah. Dinner sounds nice. But I don't see how—"

"Leave the details to me," he said with a smile. "Just feed Brody like usual."

"Okay. By the way, thanks for the espresso. It was really good, at least what I drank of it."

His smile lit up his face. "I'm glad."

"It must have cost you a fortune to have it delivered."

He shrugged. "Worth every penny." Immediately, he leaned down and kissed her before he strode away.

For a moment, she simply stared at his retreating back, still feeling the impression of his lips against hers. For the first time in weeks, she actually found herself anticipating an evening alone with her husband.

Brody had been eager to leave the day-care facility and his little face had brightened as soon as he saw her—which had made Sara hope she'd turned the corner and he no longer thought of her as "the lady who wasn't his mother no matter what everyone called her"—but as soon as they were back at home, he alternated between throwing his toys and yelling "No" to whatever she suggested.

Frustration became the emotion of the day but that faded to sympathy when she saw him crawl onto the sofa, scrunch the sheer curtain in his hand and peer out the window, clearly watching for someone. Occasionally, she'd hear him babble, but one word was always recognizable. Mama.

He was waiting for someone who would never come.

She'd studied enough grief counseling to know that Brody was caught between the denial and anger stages of loss. She recognized the signs and could certainly relate.

Oddly enough, though, she'd assumed she'd dealt with the psychological issues of losing their baby, but Brody's presence seemed to prove otherwise. Her grief wasn't far beneath the surface and it reared its head more often than she'd like.

However, while she couldn't sit at the window and wait for her baby to return, analyzing every abdominal ache and pain each month and hoping she'd miss her period was very similar to his faithful action of standing lookout for his mother. Like Brody, each day of unrealized hopes only made her feel the loss again and again.

In essence, they were both waiting for a miracle. Sadly, Brody didn't have a chance at getting his, but she did, provided that she and Cole repaired their trust issues. The possibility was the only thing that kept her going.

CHAPTER FIVE

BEING late had definitely tightened Cole's schedule for the evening considerably, but as he walked into the kitchen and saw his son with macaroni and cheese woven through his hair and ground into his clothes, those concerns faded.

"Brody!" he exclaimed with a hearty chuckle. "Are you eating dinner or wearing it?"

"What he isn't wearing, I am," Sara muttered.

"Daddy," Brody yelled as he held out his arms and offered a gamin smile.

Cole tickled a spot under Brody's chin as he leaned over to kiss Sara's cheek. Her stiffness bothered him, but she clearly wasn't in a loving mood, considering how frazzled she looked and how he was an hour late. He hoped she'd feel a little more charitable as the night wore on.

"So I see," he said. "Mmm, cheese."

"Among other things," she said darkly.

He pulled a strand of macaroni out of Sara's hair. "Does this mean he hated your cooking or loved it?"

"Who knows?" She reached for the wet washrag and began scrubbing Brody's face and hands. "Okay, bud. Dinner is officially over."

Brody ran off to the living room and a few minutes later Cole heard the distinctive sound of toys being thrown against the wall.

Cole moved to the doorway to check on the youngster, aware that Sara had followed him. No blood and nothing broken was a good state of affairs.

Sara sighed. "I'm not sure if watching his anger is better than having him stand on the sofa and stare out the window, looking for Ruth."

Cole watched Brody grab a plastic car and begin driving it in circles. He hated the thought of the little boy struggling to understand how and why his life had changed so drastically because he'd *been* that child at one time in his life, too. Granted, he'd been older—eight—but age didn't insulate one from grief and loss.

"I did the same thing," he murmured.

"Throw things or stare out the window?"

"Both. How did he handle day care?"

"According to the staff, he definitely wasn't a model child."

"Oh?"

"He had a hard time sharing the toys and got into a couple of tugging matches. Eloise had said he's such a happy-go-lucky fellow so I'm hoping he's simply expressing his frustration rather than revealing his true personality."

"He's feeling insecure and will settle down when he realizes this is his new life."

"Let's hope so," she answered fervently. "How long did it take you to adjust?"

"A while," he answered. "For me, it wasn't so much acceptance as tolerance. Then again, my situation was different."

"How so?" she asked.

He brushed aside her question. "It's too long to explain now. We have an anniversary to celebrate."

She pointedly glanced at his hands. "Celebrate with what? I didn't cook and it's obvious you didn't bring dinner."

"Nope," he said cheerfully. "I thought you deserved something more classy than food in a take-out bag."

"Ah," she said in a knowing voice. "You're having something delivered, I assume. What kind of pizza did you order this time?"

He wasn't surprised by her guess. "It's better than pizza."

"Better than pizza?" Another crash sounded in the other room and she visibly winced. "I can't imagine."

"Pizza isn't special enough for our anniversary," he insisted.

She slowly shook her head. "Whatever it is, we should save your plans for another day. The kitchen is a mess. Brody needs his bath, I'm bushed and—"

"And I have our evening all arranged," he informed her. "I'll take care of Brody and get him ready for bed while you work your magic in here." He motioned around the room. "And when everything is spick-and-span, like it always is, I want you to enjoy a nice long, relaxing soak."

"In the tub?"

He grinned. "Where else?"

Longing flared in her eyes. "I shouldn't. We have stories to read and—"

"You can have the honors tomorrow night," he said. "Tonight, I'm letting you off the hook so you can pamper yourself. I only have two requests, though."

"Only two?"

He nodded. "Wear your little black dress and no matter what you might hear in the rest of the house, don't leave the bedroom until I call you."

Her smile slowly spread. "Sounds interesting. Okay, I'll stay put, but if you find me asleep in the tub, don't be surprised."

"If I do, I'll wake you," he promised.

Brody's bath became a challenging endeavor, but Cole learned that his son responded quite well to the authority in his deep voice. Soon Brody was wearing his pajamas and

ready for his bedtime story, which Cole happily supplied
By the time Cole turned the last page, the little boy's eyelid
were drooping. Clearly he'd worn himself out from his stress
ful day.

Although timing was of the essence this evening, he al
lowed himself a few minutes to simply hold his son and enjoy
the feeling of closeness and trust between them. He'd neve
experienced this depth of emotion before and it filled him
with awe.

The idea of potentially losing this precious little boy
pierced his chest with an intensity so powerful he could hardly
breathe.

This, he realized, was what Sara had felt after her miscar
riage.

She'd lost a future little person she could love, cherish an
raise to adulthood.

Intellectually, he'd understood that the child within her
was gone. Without close family ties, without the experience
of seeing baby brothers and sisters, nieces and nephews, he'
treated the incident as a minor event in the grand scheme o
life and moved on.

However, holding Brody in his lap with his head resting
against his chest, he finally realized the full depth of thei
loss. *Their* son would never sit on his lap, listen to a story o
drool on his shoulder. It was *their* loss, not just Sara's.

While he'd known Brody would be a difficult reminder
this moment was the first time he actually felt the same pain
He truly *hadn't* known what he was asking of her and now
he could only hope that Brody's presence would eventually
soften the blow.

Carefully, Cole placed him in his bed, then tiptoed from the
nursery. From the delicious smells coming from the kitchen
his catering company had obviously come in through the ga
rage door Cole had left open and made themselves at home

He found two of the Chefs-to-Go catering staff hard at work. The owner, a woman in her mid-forties, was busy with the food while her assistant was in charge of creating the ambience. After receiving last-minute instructions from both, he went to the master bedroom.

"No peeking into the other room while I take a quick shower," he ordered as he watched her put on the finishing touches to her makeup.

"You know the suspense is killing me." Her good-natured complaint sounded so much like the old Sara—the one before Brody had arrived—that he felt as if he'd stepped back in time.

"Suffer through a few more minutes," he told her. "I promise I won't be long."

He wasn't. He showered, shaved and put on the tux he'd lug out of a dusty garment bag. Satisfied with his appearance, he approached Sara, looking beautiful in the black dress he'd requested her to wear. The fabric clung to her curves and made him wish they were walking *into* the bedroom instead of walking *out* of it.

"You look fantastic," he said, regretting that he couldn't show her off at a fancy restaurant, although having her to himself came with its own benefits.

She smiled. "Thanks. You clean up nicely, too, although I hadn't expected a tux."

"As I said, it's a special night." At least, he hoped the evening would be a success. "And you're wearing my favorite perfume."

She shrugged. "It goes with the dress."

He didn't follow the logic, so he chose to believe she'd fallen into the spirit of things, which was a promising sign.

He crooked his arm. "May I escort you to dinner?"

"I'd like that very much."

As he led her into the hallway, she inhaled sharply and

froze in her tracks. "Something smells fabulous. What did you do, Cole Wittman?"

"I arranged for an intimate dinner," he said, guiding her through the house toward the cozy breakfast nook where the round table had been covered with a white linen tablecloth and set for two. A single red rose floated in a rose bowl beside a white tapered candle, which flickered in the subdued light. A freestanding silver ice bucket stood beside the table, the bottle of wine he'd requested chilling inside. He flicked a switch and a romantic soundtrack began playing softly.

Sara stopped short, her jaw slack from her surprise. "Oh, my," she said, sounding surprised and a little dazed.

"Have a seat." He pulled out a chair and seated her. "I chose a special menu for tonight. I hope you'll like it."

"I'm sure I will."

"Relax while I serve the first course."

Cole quickly referred to the sheet of paper left on the counter and served the tossed salad with Italian dressing.

"This is…phenomenal," she praised as she placed her linen napkin on her lap. "I'm totally impressed."

"I'm glad," he said. "But before you dig in, I have one rule about this evening."

"Which is?"

"This night is for us and us alone."

"But what if Brody—?"

"If he wakes up, we'll deal with him, but unless he does it's just you and me—like it would have been if we'd flown to Arizona."

She blinked in surprise and, darn it, he thought he saw her eyes shimmer. "Okay," she whispered before she repeated herself with a stronger voice. "Okay."

He pulled the bottle out of the ice and deftly removed the cork with the tool lying on the table. "Would you like some?"

"Please."

After pouring two glasses, he held his aloft. "To us and many more anniversaries."

At first, she hesitated, which gave him a moment of concern, but then she smiled and chinked her glass against his. "To us," she echoed, before she took a sip.

Relieved and feeling as if he'd done something right with this dinner, he began to enjoy the meal, noting how Sara appeared to do the same.

"How was your day?" he asked.

"At the hospital, it was busy, but you already know that," she said. "I heard two peds patients were admitted with a preliminary diagnosis of whooping cough."

He nodded. "A six-month-old and an eighteen-month-old."

"From the same family?"

"The same day care."

"Then the disease is spreading."

"Afraid so," he said ruefully. "I hope we can nip this before the town ends up in a full-blown epidemic. Did the infection control team come to your floor?"

"Right before I left. Of course, they didn't tell us anything we didn't already know, but it never hurts to be reminded. By the way, I got my new work schedule. I'm off duty until Thursday."

"How does your weekend look?" he asked.

"It's free. Why?"

"Your parents want to visit on Sunday."

"Sunday?" Her chocolate-brown eyes widened. "Did you tell them about Brody?"

"I did."

She sat back in her chair. "Oh, dear."

"We can't keep him a secret forever," he pointed out. "Unless you don't want to see your folks for the next twenty years or so, someone had to tell them they're grandparents."

She sighed. "I know, but what…what did they say?"

"After her initial shock, your mom squealed in my ear until I thought I'd go deaf," he said wryly.

"And Dad?"

"He had a few choice words, which I won't repeat, but after he got those out of his system, he sounded excited, too."

"Did they wonder why we waited to mention Brody?"

"They did, but I told them we didn't want to raise anyone's hopes until we had squared away all the legal issues." He'd been half-surprised she hadn't called them with their announcement several weeks ago, but she'd obviously needed time to accept the situation. As much as he liked his in-laws, he had been glad of the reprieve because it had allowed the two of them to settle into the situation without well-meant outside interference.

"Good idea."

"They wanted to call you right away," he added, "but I convinced them to wait until you were at home tomorrow. So be prepared."

"I will. If they're coming on Sunday, I'll plan dinner. Did they say when they were coming?"

"As excited as they sounded, I suspect they'll arrive early and stay all day," he said, "but you'll have to ask them yourself. In any case, because Sunday will be busy with family, we should pick up our Christmas tree on Saturday."

"We don't have to get a live one," she began. "An artificial might be more practical."

"We've always had a real tree. I don't want to break our tradition, do you?"

"No, but…" Her gaze grew speculative. "I didn't realize this until now, but we've always incorporated my family traditions into our holiday celebrations, never yours. What kind of tree did your family have?"

Without thinking, he gave his standard answer. "I don't remember."

She leaned back and stroked the stem of her glass. "I don't believe you. You were eight when your parents died. That's old enough to recall your Christmases. Unless, of course, you don't trust me enough to share those stories."

He couldn't believe what he was hearing. "You think *I* have trust issues?" he asked in a tone he reserved for staff members who hadn't done their jobs to his satisfaction.

She met his gaze without flinching. "Don't you?"

"Of course I don't," he snapped.

She raised an eyebrow in response. "If you didn't have trust issues, you would have come to me with your fears instead of going to Ruth."

Back to that again! He clenched his jaw, frustrated that everything circled around to those two fateful days. "I didn't *go* to Ruth. She just happened to be in the same place that I was. And for the record, any trust issues that I had I'd resolved before we got married, remember?"

"I believe you," she said softly, "but I'm only using her as the most obvious example. Whenever I've asked about your growing-up years, you've always brushed off my questions. If not for Brody showing up on our doorstep, I would never have learned that she had been a close friend."

"Is that what this is about? You want a play-by-play account of my childhood friends?" He was incredulous. "Fine. If you'd like a list, I'll go through my yearbook and give you one."

She shook her head. "You're missing the point, Cole. There's a whole side of you I've never learned about. A side that these people knew, but I don't."

"If you're accusing me of keeping more secrets from you—"

"It isn't about secrets, as such. I want to know what makes you tick."

"We've been together for six years and you still don't know?" he asked wryly.

He'd expected her to back down, but she didn't. "You've never been open about your past. Yes, you've told me the basics, but I want more than the bare minimum facts."

He knew what she wanted—for him to spill his guts and talk about his feelings—but he couldn't give it to her. "Why do you need to hear every little detail about my youth? None of it matters. Events can't be changed."

"No, but all I'm asking is for you to share some of those stories with me. Whether they were good or bad, I really don't care. I just want to hear them so I can see how they shaped the man you are."

He'd tried to block out most of those experiences because the memories had left a bad taste in his mouth. He'd done remarkably well, too. His life had become what he'd made of it. Now Sara was asking him to reminisce about the days he'd rather forget.

Damn, but he *knew* going to his reunion had been a mistake. He should have stayed home and guzzled those margaritas in the privacy of his apartment. When the twenty-year reunion invitation arrived in two years, he'd toss it in the trash, unopened, and save himself a ton of grief.

"You said tonight was about us," she reminded him. "Which to me, translates to a date night. And like anyone on a date, the idea is to discover new things about each other. I want to learn things about my husband that I never knew."

This wasn't how he'd planned his evening. Somehow he'd lost control and they were only on the first course.

"What I'm asking won't be easy for you," she said kindly. "I suspect you never shared those things for a reason—"

"What was the point?" he asked wearily.

"But," she continued, "we can use them to help Brody adjust to his life-changing loss in a healthy manner. You don't want him to suffer through what you did."

Could she be onto something? Would baring his soul help Brody in any way? Because the idea of his son experiencing what he did turned him cold.

"He won't," Cole said fiercely. "I won't allow it."

"Can you be sure?"

"Of course I can," he snapped. "You and my aunt are as different as night and day."

"I hope so, but unless I know what she did, what happened to you, I can't avoid her same mistakes, can I?"

While he knew in his heart that Sara's loving nature would never allow her to do the things his aunt had done—even in her hurt and anger the past few weeks, she hadn't come close to his aunt's vindictiveness. However, Sara obviously had her own fears in that regard—fears that wouldn't disappear just because he'd discounted them.

"Whatever you say won't make me think less of you," she added softly.

Logically, he supposed that was right. No one knew him as well as she did, except perhaps for Ruth, and she'd only known because she'd lived in foster care and they'd compared experiences quite often. After he'd graduated, he'd started a new life for himself—a life that had come with a carefully edited past because he hadn't wanted anyone's pity or scorn.

He definitely didn't want his own wife's, so he'd avoided the risk completely.

She reached out and touched his hand. "Let's start with your Christmases. I really want to know what they were like."

Drawing a deep, resigned breath, he forced himself to remember. "The Wittman family tradition included a real tree, but after the fire, my aunt and uncle always used artificial."

"Fire? There was a fire?"

He nodded. "It was my second Christmas in their home.

Apparently no one filled the stand with water and the tree dried out, although no one knew it. I was told to light the scented candle in the living room and my older cousin, who took pride in making my life miserable, started playing with the lighter. The next thing I knew, the tree was blazing." After twenty-five years, he still hadn't forgotten the scene, or the horror he'd felt.

"I'll bet his parents were furious at him."

"No," he said calmly. "He said I did it and, of course, they believed his story, not mine. The fire chief gave us both a severe lecture on fire safety, although I think he knew from my cousin's actions and cocky attitude that I was telling the truth. Anyway, after that my aunt and uncle always used an artificial tree." They'd never let him forget the incident, either.

"And your parents?" she asked softly. "What did you do when they were alive?"

He eyed his glass with its token splash of wine, reluctant to share the few precious memories he had. He'd only allowed himself to replay them when he felt strong enough to deal with his loss, but if Sara could face her demons, then he could do no less.

"We went to a nearby tree farm to cut our own. It was always so much fun, traipsing through the rows in search of the perfect pine. After we sawed down ours, we drank hot apple cider and ate sugar cookies my mom had baked for the occasion while we listened to Christmas carols. It was the one time of year when she added red and green sprinkles to the frosting." Amazingly enough, he hadn't recalled that detail until just now...

"Sounds like fun," she said.

"It was. I always thought a day couldn't be more perfect."

"Did you have a similar tradition with your aunt and uncle's artificial tree?"

If he hadn't sworn off alcohol two years ago, he might have refilled his glass and drained it dry. Instead, he simply rotated the glass and watched the liquid swirl around inside.

"I really can't say. I usually wasn't around when everyone decorated it."

"You weren't? Where were you?"

"At a friend's house. Or the movies. Or the library. In high school, they usually chose a Saturday when I was out of town at a swim meet."

Sara's face registered her confusion. "Why would they exclude you?"

He watched the wine swirl faster, hardly aware that he was causing it to slosh like storm-tossed seas. "My aunt insisted on creating traditions with her own kids," he said evenly, relying on the nonchalant tone he'd perfected over the years. "I wasn't part of that group."

"How awful." Her face registered dismay. "Did they go to your school events?"

"Only if one of my cousins was also involved, which wasn't often. They weren't in the same classes or didn't have the same interests I had."

"Cole, that's terrible!" she protested.

He shrugged. "It was the way things were."

She leaned across the table and placed her hand over his. "I'm sorry."

"Why?" he asked bluntly. "It wasn't your fault."

"No, but your story explains a lot. Thank you for sharing," she said softly.

A response didn't seem indicated, so he nodded. Then, eager to change the topic, especially to one on a lighter note, he eyed her empty salad plate. "Are you ready for the main course? It's stuffed chicken breast with a sun-dried tomato pesto. And be sure to save room for dessert. Red velvet cheesecake."

That had been the menu on the night he'd proposed and he'd chosen it again for tonight to make a statement. Honestly, he couldn't say why he'd remembered those details, but he had…probably because the meal had been a prelude to a future he'd wanted but had always considered out of his reach

Her gaze flew to meet his and she blinked in obvious surprise. "You remembered," she said, clearly awed.

"It was the most important night of my life," he said simply. "How could I forget?"

Even in the dim light, he could tell her eyes grew misty. Although he knew he wouldn't redeem himself with one special meal, it obviously wasn't hurting his cause. "Sit tight. I'll be right back."

He left the table and thanks to the instructions he'd been given, he soon returned with two steaming plates of gourmet-quality food—even if his presentation didn't quite look like the photo—and a basket of garlic-Parmesan bread.

"You… I… This is more than I'd ever imagined," she managed to say. "What a wonderful surprise."

"I'm glad you think so."

She began eating. "Did you plan all this or did you talk some poor ward clerk into organizing it for you?"

"This might come as a surprise, but I even dialed the phone number myself."

She chuckled. "Now I really am impressed."

"And you should be," he teased. "So dig in before it gets cold."

As the dinner progressed, Cole noticed how Sara's wariness of late seemed to fade. He hoped that what he'd planned next would banish it for good.

CHAPTER SIX

SARA carefully placed her silverware across her dessert plate and leaned back, feeling remarkably mellow after two glasses of wine and a melt-in-your-mouth meal. "That was wonderful," she told him.

"I'm glad you liked it."

"The wine was delicious, too." As he attempted to fill her glass again, she covered it with her hand and shook her head. "No more or I'll be snoozing under the table." Then, because she'd noticed he'd never emptied or refilled his own glass, she asked, "Aren't you going to finish yours?"

"The hospital might call me."

"You aren't on call, are you?"

"No, but I had a couple of dicey patients today. One never knows what will happen."

Her theory suddenly seemed less like conjecture and more like fact. "You don't drink alcohol of any kind anymore, do you?"

He blinked, clearly startled by her remark. "Not really, no."

"You stopped after that weekend," she guessed.

He shrugged. "It seemed the right thing to do."

Although she'd suspected she was right, having it confirmed stunned her. "You really *did* regret your actions that evening."

"I told you I did."

She warmed under his gentle rebuke. "Hearing someone say so doesn't mean as much as when he actually modifies his behavior as a result," she defended.

"Then you believe me now?"

"I think I always did," she said slowly, "but it helps knowing you weren't merely paying lip service." Then, because she didn't know what else to say, she changed the subject.

"Thanks again for the great meal and the wonderful evening," she told him. "I'll help with the dishes—"

He rose and pulled her to her feet. "Oh, but the evening isn't over yet."

"It isn't?"

"No." Using the remote control, he selected a different playlist and music suitable for slow dancing drifted out of the speakers. He pulled her against him and because she could either follow his lead or lose her footing, she fell into step.

"What are we doing?" she asked as they moved to the song's rhythm.

"Isn't it obvious?" His breath brushed against her temple "We're dancing."

"Yes, but—"

"Shh. You're ruining the mood," he teased.

Suddenly, being in his arms seemed like the best place to be. "Can't have that," she murmured as she allowed him to draw her close enough that she could feel his heart beat.

His hand engulfed hers and being in his embrace gave her the sense of being both protected and cherished.

For several minutes, she didn't say a word. After the stress of the last few days, it was far too easy to pretend that someone had turned back the clock and everything was as wonderful as it once had been.

"Now I know how Cinderella felt," she mused aloud.

"How so?"

"At the moment, everything is perfect, but at midnight everything changes. The coach and six white horses will become a pumpkin and a few mice. Her gown disappears into rags and—"

"And the prince eventually finds her because of the glass slipper," he said. "Did you ever wonder why her shoe didn't disappear, like everything else?"

She looked up at him. "Honestly? No. Have you?"

"Oddly enough, I have, because it didn't make sense."

Spoken like a man who looked for logic in everything. "Of course not. It's a fairy tale. You have, though, so what did you decide?"

"Well," he began slowly, "other than the author took liberties with the plot to create a happy ending, I like to think it meant that those two created enough magic during their time together that it *couldn't* disappear completely, even after they were separated at midnight. Granted, the magic was only strong enough to affect her shoes, but that small amount was able to bring them back together again."

She'd never thought of the story in those terms before and the parallel to her present circumstances didn't escape her notice. "Since when did you become a philosopher and literary critic?"

"Hey, you're the one who mentioned Cinderella."

She had. She simply hadn't expected him to draw this lesson out of it.

"It's these magical moments that make life bearable when troubles come," he continued. "They give us something to hold on to—they bring hope for happier times. That's why we have to enjoy them when they come along."

She thought of his stories about his childhood and suddenly understood her husband a little better. Granted, he'd only shared a minuscule amount, but it was a very good start.

His determination to steer clear of his few remaining family members had never made sense until now. While he'd only shared one small Christmas experience, if his aunt could treat him so poorly during the most generous, happy season of the year, what must she have done throughout the other eleven months?

Was it any wonder why he was worried about how she'd accept Brody into their lives? He'd clearly wanted to include Brody in their family, but he obviously didn't want his son to endure the constant rejection he'd had. Given his stories, she certainly couldn't blame him.

She imagined a younger Cole trying to please his aunt in order to win her approval and her love, and getting rebuffed time and again. It nearly broke her heart to imagine his disappointment and hurt until he'd finally walled off any and all expectations. At one time, he'd used the word "tolerance" instead of "acceptance" when he'd mentioned his only relatives and she understood why.

She also understood why he'd been so introspective after the lion incident. "Are you afraid of following in your aunt and uncle's footsteps? Of perpetuating their mistakes?"

"Would you blame me if I were?" he asked instead.

"No, but I don't think you have anything to worry about. You've always shown a remarkable amount of patience with Brody—far more than it sounds as if you'd received."

"I appreciate the vote of confidence."

She smiled. "You're welcome."

A distinctive wail interrupted the moment.

Sara bit back her sigh. "Our midnight has arrived," she murmured, more to herself than to Cole.

"Sooner than I'd thought, too." His voice held the same disappointed note that hers did.

"I'd better check on him," she said, but Cole didn't let go. "I want to have more nights like this, Sara."

Considering how she'd learned a lot about her husband, it

ad been quite productive, not to mention thought-provoking.
he'd been so certain they'd been ready to have a baby, but
ow she wasn't so sure. In fact, in light of Cole's personal
sues, she wondered if they were truly ready to be Brody's
arents, but if not for Brody's untimely arrival, she'd still be
perating under her old assumptions that everything was fine.
ll things happened for a reason, she supposed, and helping
ole deal with his past was clearly long overdue.

Regardless, thanks to the magical evening, she felt less
ke she was lacking and more like a woman who could con-
uer any challenge, including the ones facing her.

"Yes," she said. "I'd like that, too."

ole had just finished making his rounds on Sara's floor when
e saw her approach the nurses' station. He tapped his patient
otes into the computer as she sat beside him and began en-
ring her own information.

"How's it going today?" he asked.

"Busy, as usual. Any change to Mr. Harvey's orders?"

George Harvey was a spry fellow in his seventies who'd
ist had a hip replaced and now seemed to be suffering an
fection in the joint.

"Not really. Continue the gentamicin and send an order
the lab for an ASAP creatinine level. And page me if the
sults are abnormal," he said.

"Will do."

"One more thing." He logged off the computer, aware that
e'd paused to listen. "Do you mind if we buy our tree to-
ight instead of this weekend?"

"Tonight? It'll be dark."

"So? The tree lot has lights."

"You can't wait until Saturday?"

He shrugged and grinned. "No."

"I don't know, Cole. I hate to take Brody out when it's s
cold."

"It won't be any warmer this weekend," he told her
"Besides, we're painting his room, remember? That'll tak
most of the day by itself."

After weeks of waiting, his son's furniture had finally ar
rived yesterday and they'd spent all evening organizing hi
belongings, trying to create a space similar to that the bo
had enjoyed in his old home. Thanks to the pictures Elois
had emailed, they had been fairly successful, but until the
painted the walls sky blue and included the same woodland
creature wallpaper, they wouldn't achieve the result the
wanted—to make Brody feel as if he were at home.

To that end, Sara had spent last night poring over the sam
ple books from several home-decorating stores and they'
planned to begin the room's transformation bright and earl
on Saturday. With any luck, they'd finish before Sara's par
ents arrived and if not, he was sure they'd welcome the op
portunity to help.

"I'd almost forgotten. Weekends just don't seem to be lon
enough, do they?" she said wryly.

They didn't, and this particular weekend would seem eve
shorter to her if she knew of the plans Cole had tucked awa
in his proverbial lab coat. Sally Thompson, their neighbor
had agreed to slip over on Friday evening after Brody ha
gone to bed so he could take Sara on another date. Granted
it would be a short night out, two hours, max, and he stil
didn't know for certain what they'd do—Christmas shop
perhaps?—but it would be two hours spent together, withou
any interruptions.

With any luck, they'd come home and spend the rest o
the night setting the sheets on fire. The nights of loving eac
other hadn't yet resumed, but she'd stopped staring at hir
with those sad puppy-dog eyes and seemed more like the ol

Sara. Their anniversary had been a turning point of sorts and while their relationship wasn't completely back to normal, it had settled into an even—and amicable—keel.

His coffee deliveries on the days she worked hadn't hurt either.

"Two days go fast," he said. "And speaking of going fast, the day's half-over. Would you care to join me for lunch?"

His hopeful note reminded her that they hadn't coordinated their meal breaks since Brody had arrived. Granted, he'd only worked two shifts since then, but she'd purposely been too busy to join him.

"They're serving your favorite ham-and-cheese pockets in the cafeteria today," he added, as if trying to entice her. "If we don't go soon, there won't be any left."

Sara laughed at his warning, quite aware that even if the menu had included all the foods she disliked, being in Cole's company wasn't as difficult as it once had been. In fact, as much as she hated to admit it, during her days at home with Brody she missed sharing that half hour with her husband.

"Okay, I'll do my best to meet you, *after* I take care of Harvey's orders. His doctor is a real stickler for promptness, you know. In fact, it wouldn't surprise me if he calls and hounds me for the results in about thirty minutes." She grinned to soften her complaint.

He winked. "What can I say? Some physicians are real bears to work with."

"They are. Now go…" she gave him a gentle nudge "…so can tend to my patient."

Sara hefted Brody on her hip as she followed Cole around what once had been an empty lot but was now filled with every size, shape and color of Christmas tree. Lights were strung along the perimeter and throughout the enclosure to add a festive touch. The scent of freshly cut pine was strong

and intermingled with the wood smoke from the bonfire i
the center. Several tall patio heaters were strategically locate
so that shoppers didn't feel the cold while they selected thei
perfect holiday decoration.

In fact, it was warm enough that Sara struggled to kee
Brody's stocking cap on his head.

"Aren't the lights pretty?" she asked him, pointing over
head.

He clapped his hands and grinned.

"Which tree do you like?" Cole asked her, standing be
tween two blue spruce that dwarfed his six-foot frame. "Th
skinnier or the wider?"

"How about something smaller?" she suggested. "I don'
think either of yours will fit in our living room. What abou
those over there?" She pointed to a grouping on the left.

"Too small," Cole said. "Those are barely three feet tall."

"Too 'mall," Brody echoed. "Down."

He squirmed to the point Sara would drop him if she didn'
let go, so she lowered him to the ground and he raced over t
Cole. "Up," he demanded.

"You're supposed to let Sara hold you," he scolded lightly

Brody shook his head as he clung to Cole like a leech
"Daddy hold me. Not 'ara."

Cole glanced at Sara and she shrugged. "Be my guest. He'
starting to weigh more than I can handle."

Before long, Cole had perched Brody on his shoulders an
the three of them wandered around the lot. By the time they'
found a tree they could live with—a five-foot Douglas fir—
hauled it home and set it in the garage in a bucket of water
it was nearly Brody's bedtime.

Because Brody was so keyed up from their excursion, Sar
had expected a fight about his bath and she got one. Finally
he was dressed in his footed fleece pajamas and ran into th
living room with his puppy book in hand.

"Daddy, read me."

"Sara will read your story."

"No. Daddy read." The little boy's lip lowered into a pout.

"Brody," Cole warned. "You know this is how we do things. Sara reads this story."

From the beginning, they'd opted for Sara to read his puppy book because Ruth had always read it. The hope had been for him to subconsciously associate Sara with the things his mother had done, but after nearly a month it didn't seem as if they were making progress. Brody simply wasn't ready for Sara to take over the more precious routines in his memory. Tonight Sara was too exhausted to fight him.

"Read the story, Cole," she said, resigned. "He needs to go to bed."

"But—"

"Please, Cole. His bedtime should be a pleasant experience rather than a traumatic one and if listening to you will do the trick tonight, that's the price we'll pay."

He frowned and before he could protest again she sank onto her easy chair and opened the newspaper to signal an end to the discussion.

"Daddy!" came an insistent voice.

"Okay, but kiss Sara good-night," he instructed.

Obediently, Brody rushed over to her, bussed her on the cheek with an openmouthed kiss, then latched on to Cole's side.

"Only one story tonight, peewee," Cole said as he headed down the hall. "Then it's lights-out."

Sara lowered the newspaper and closed her eyes as she touched her face where Brody's sloppy kiss lingered. To Brody, this small nighttime ritual was probably a necessary evil, but to her, it was another bittersweet moment among many. If not for her miscarriage, she might have been feeling *her* child kiss her good-night, not because he'd been coaxed but because he loved her as his mother.

The rumble of her husband's deep voice and Brody's childish giggles carried down the hall. Wanting to be a part of their circle, even if only from the sidelines, she tiptoed to the bedroom door and watched.

Cole was sitting on the padded rocking chair with Brody on his lap as the two gazed intently at the colorful pages of his picture book. Her husband changed the tone of his voice to match the characters, which clearly tickled his son's funny bone. Occasionally, Cole would glance at his son and hug him. Brody smiled, clearly feeling secure in his father's love.

At one time, Cole had claimed he needed her help to be Brody's father, but ever since that day at the store and the incident with Larry the lion, as far as she could tell, he was doing just fine on his own. As for Brody, the little boy seemed to thrive under his dad's attention, which only confirmed that regardless of how difficult her decision had been, she'd made the right one for the two of them.

The ironic thing was that Cole had been afraid of being an inadequate father, but she was the one who felt completely inadequate for the task of raising *this* child. No matter what she did, Brody still hadn't warmed to her and she wondered if he had sensed her reservations about bringing him home from the very beginning. Then again, the dynamics of her relationship with Brody were different than what she'd have with her own child. Brody had to sort through his grief and his anger over being told that Sara was taking his mother's place. While a child inherently trusted his or her parents, she had to *earn* Brody's.

Just like she was trying to earn his father's.

Their heart-to-heart conversations so far had been great. She'd learned so much about her husband that she hadn't known before. His focus on excellence had begun long be

'ore he'd entered medical school, she'd discovered, in order
.o gain his family's approval. When he'd accepted that they
were ambivalent about his achievements, he'd worked even
harder because of the personal satisfaction. In some respects,
she felt as if they'd done things backward by sharing these
things after they'd married rather than before, but, regardless
of the timing, she wanted to believe the seeds of trust were
beginning to take root, in both of them.

If they were getting to know each other all over again,
wasn't it time she stopped keeping him at arm's length? She'd
declared their relationship on probation while waiting to reach
a nebulous milestone, but wasn't she, in essence, acting like
his aunt, who'd withheld her love and affection as a way to
control him?

It seemed ironic that Brody's presence had caused the
cracks in their armor to finally be revealed. It would be even
more ironic if Brody helped to repair them.

Cole left Brody's room and went in search of his wife. Although he was more than happy to read Brody his bedtime
stories, he refused to do so at Sara's expense. The boy would
never learn to depend on her if they catered to his every whim.

He found her in the kitchen. "We need to talk," he began
firmly.

Sara turned away from the stove and handed him a mug.
"I already know what you're going to say."

"You do?" He eyed the steaming cup in his hand and inhaled the spicy apple fragrance. "What's this?"

"Hot cider. If it wouldn't be so late, I'd whip up a batch
of sugar cookies so we could continue your Christmas tree
tradition, but I had to create a plan B. We're having the cider
now and I'll have the cookies ready for when we decorate on
Saturday."

He wouldn't have been more surprised if she'd handed him
an early Christmas present. Then again, perhaps she had...

"I can't believe you went to the trouble," he said.

"It's no trouble." She blew across the top of her drink
in an obvious effort to cool it to a drinkable temperature.
"Correction. It will be when I'm trying to make cookies tomorrow with Brody trying to help, but there's another generation of Wittmans, so it's time we reestablish the Wittman
family traditions, don't you think?"

He stared at her, taking in her tousled hair, her gentle smile
and the soft expression in her eyes. After working all day,
coming home to prepare dinner and then going on a shopping
excursion, she was the most beautiful thing he could possibly
hope to see.

Hope that she'd finally forgiven him flared. He wanted to
believe she had but didn't dare in case he was mistaken.

Maybe he was dreaming. The hot mug in his hand indicated otherwise.

"Yeah," he said, speechless. "Thank you."

"So let this be a lesson to you for next year," she scolded
without heat. "We have to plan our tree purchase in advance
so I'm not caught unprepared, like I am now."

She was talking about *next Christmas*.

"Then you're planning to stick around?" he asked, wanting confirmation.

For a second, she seemed taken aback by his question.
Then her expression became speculative as if she realized
she'd spoken of the future in a general way rather than with
any real plans. "Did you think I wouldn't?"

He shrugged. "Your suitcase is still packed."

"My suitcase?" She sounded as puzzled as she looked, but
in the next instant her expression became sheepish. "It is, isn't
it? I hadn't realized..."

He didn't see how she could overlook that detail. He saw

the bulging piece of luggage every time he walked in and out of their bedroom. Having lived his entire life with an escape plan in place, he recognized it for what it was. Oddly enough, now he understood how the concept had troubled Sara because it bothered him to see her do the same.

"I'll take care of it," she said.

He pressed on. "I've also seen the way you sometimes look at Brody."

"Oh? And what way is that?"

"Like you're sad and ready to cry. He reminds me of the baby we lost, too."

She stared at him, incredulous. "He does? You've never said."

"I should have," he said. "I should say a lot of things, but I don't."

"Because you don't want anyone to discover your weak spots."

He'd never considered his reticence in those terms. He'd learned to hold his feelings and thoughts close to his chest because some things were just too personal to share while others—his mind froze as he suddenly realized how accurate she was—made him vulnerable. If there was one thing he'd learned, it was to avoid being vulnerable.

But if he couldn't be open and honest with his wife, then who *could* he be open and honest with?

He nodded, surprised by her perception. "When I think about losing the baby," he began slowly, "*our* baby, it hurts."

"Really? You never acted as if you cared."

He thought back to those days and realized she was partially correct. "I didn't have time to get used to the idea before he…was gone."

"I really didn't either," she admitted. "And that almost makes losing him worse. Maybe if I'd suspected sooner, I

would have done something different. I'd have skipped my
aerobics class or wouldn't have helped lift a patient—"

"No, don't go there. Don't blame yourself. It was merely
nature's way."

She nodded. "Yeah. Survival of the fittest and all that."
Her smile seemed weak. "Unfortunately, when you want
something so badly you ache from the wanting, blaming it
on Mother Nature doesn't always help. And sometimes when
I'm around Brody…" Her voice died.

"It only emphasizes what we lost," he finished for her. "I
discovered that, too. It wasn't just a mass of tissue or a few
cells, but a little boy or girl who'd grind macaroni into his
hair, suck his thumb or bring a book and say, 'Daddy, read
me.'"

"Then you really do understand."

He met her surprised gaze and nodded. "Which is why I
wouldn't have been shocked if you'd decided to walk away,
although I hoped and prayed you wouldn't."

"The idea seemed attractive at times," she admitted, "but
we promised to stick together through good *and* bad times. As
I want our marriage to last and our family to grow, then—"

"After Brody's tantrum tonight, do you really want more
children?" he asked, incredulous.

"I do," she said with a soft smile. "Maybe not immediately
but soon. If you recall, we'd talked about having four."

He hadn't forgotten. Running after Brody kept him busy
enough; he couldn't imagine keeping tabs on four at once and
he said so.

She laughed. "It's a matter of organization. The important thing is that there will be four individuals who need us
to look after them and guide them into adulthood."

"It's the years between babyhood and adulthood that are
daunting," he said dryly. All that aside, though, the one thing

he wouldn't mind would be *creating* them. It seemed like such a long time since he'd made love with his wife...

"As you brought up his tantrum," she continued, "you're going to tell me to be more firm with him, aren't you?"

He leaned against the counter and cradled his mug in his hands when he'd rather cradle the woman a few feet away. "We can't cater to his whims, not if we ever want him to accept you as his mother."

"I'm beginning to doubt if we ever will," she murmured.

"What makes you say that?"

She paused, her expression downcast. "When Brody's with you, he acts as if the sun rises and sets in his daddy while I'm merely someone to tolerate. I feel like a third wheel—handy to have around in a pinch but useless the rest of the time."

"You're imagining things."

"I'm not, Cole. You might think he's more accepting of me when you aren't around, but he isn't. Rather than follow me around the house, he sits by the door like he's waiting for Ruth to walk in at any minute. It breaks my heart to know he's hurting and I want to minimize that as much as I can, but he won't let me."

Unable and unwilling to stop himself, he set his mug on the counter and drew her into his arms. "He will. It's only been a few weeks. Of course he's hurting, but he can't avoid the truth. One day, he'll wake up and the hole in his chest won't feel quite so big because we—*you*—will be filling up the space."

Having her against him had never felt so good. He ran a finger along her jawline, marveling at her soft skin. "Just like you filled my empty spaces."

He lowered his head and brushed his mouth against hers. As her lips parted in invitation, he continued his gentle assault, uncertain of where this might lead.

"I've missed this," he murmured between his kisses. "I've missed having you next to me."

"I have, too," she answered, "but—"

"No buts," he responded as he nuzzled the spot on her neck that had always made her melt. "I want to make love with my wife. Tonight. *Now*."

"Oh, my," she breathed. "I want it, too."

He ran his hand under her shirt. "Then what are we waiting for?"

"To finish our conversation?"

"Later," he promised. "Much later."

Eager to enjoy the comfort of his own bed, he pulled away and began flicking off the lights.

"What are you doing?" she asked.

"Being discreet. We have a two-year-old in the house."

She giggled, sounding like the girl he'd married. "I'd forgotten."

It gave him immense satisfaction to know that she had, because it meant he hadn't lost his ability to drive his rational-thinking wife into a mindless state. "I haven't."

He tugged her toward the door, but she stopped. "The stove," she reminded him.

"Oh, yeah."

After a two-second detour to turn off the burner, Sara found herself swept along to their bedroom where Cole closed the door with a quiet snick.

She stripped off her sweatshirt and stepped out of her jeans, aware of Cole doing the same, but before she could dive under the comforter, he stopped her.

"I want to see you," he said hoarsely. "Like the first time."

"The first time wasn't in the dead of winter," she returned.

His grin turned feral. "You won't be cold for long."

Under his heated gaze and reverent hands, the chill in the

air no longer affected her and she reached out to conduct her own exploration.

She'd seen him naked before and knew his body almost as well as she knew her own. His shoulders were broad, his muscles defined from the hours spent on his weight bench in the basement, and the crisp dark hair on his chest that arrowed down to below his waist was soft against her skin.

"Tell me you want this as much as I do," he said.

"I want this."

"Then far be it from me to withhold Cinderella's wish." His fingers found her nipples and toyed with them until she ached.

"Oh, Cole," she whimpered, and she whimpered again when his mouth took over and his hands ventured into other territory with such skill that she found herself standing on the brink.

She gripped his shoulders and whimpered again, this time more loudly.

"Shh," he said, his voice as soft as his caress. "We can't wake Brody."

"Mmm," she murmured as his hands drove her wild.

Lost in her sensation of fireworks, she only vaguely noticed when they landed against the sheets. "Oh, don't stop. Please."

"I love it when you beg," he teased, "but don't worry. I'm not stopping. Not now, not ever."

Impatient, she tugged him onto her and welcomed him into her body. Slowly, he moved, until she thought she'd die from impatience. His hands roamed again, locating the responsive areas he'd mapped earlier. Sensation after sensation rocked her, demanding release, but she forced herself to hold back until he was ready.

Finally, just when she couldn't bear it any longer, his shudders drove her off the edge. They soared together until the tremors stopped and she slowly drifted into the most peaceful state she'd ever experienced.

Sara snuggled against Cole's back, grateful for his warmth and remarkably content for the first time in weeks. She'd missed this closeness and was glad they'd finally found their way back to each other again.

She smiled, thinking of how intense their lovemaking had been. It was as if digging into Cole's past, encouraging him to face his fears, as well as forgiving and forgetting previous mistakes, made a powerful combination.

As she lay there, she decided her first order of business that morning would be to unpack her suitcase. For all she knew, Brody had picked up on her subconscious symbol of escape, which was why he still resisted her attempts to get close to him. With any luck, he'd sense the change in her attitude and respond accordingly.

Pleased with her decision, she slowly drifted off, but an odd sound startled her awake. She listened, but just as she dismissed it as nothing, she heard it again.

A child's whimper.

"Cole." She nudged him. "Brody's crying."

"Hmm," he mumbled, unmoving.

She touched his warm shoulder. "You have to see what's wrong."

"Okay," he murmured sleepily. "I'll go."

A subsequent soft snore indicated her request hadn't registered.

"Cole," she urged again.

"Uh-huh…going," he muttered.

When he didn't move, Sara knew she had to take matters into her own hands. After all, if she didn't sleep well tonight, she could nap tomorrow when Brody did. Cole didn't have that luxury. Still, uncertain of what she might do to console the boy, she slipped out of her warm cocoon, blindly slipped on her nightgown and fuzzy robe, then padded into Brody's room.

He wasn't there.

Panic-stricken into full wakefulness, she wondered what had happened to him. News stories of children abducted out of their beds flooded her mind. She was ready to throw on the lights and yell for Cole when she heard the whimper again.

She followed the sound and found Brody curled in a ball on the sofa, with his teddy bear and blanket. He was asleep, but the hall night-light was strong enough for her to see the wet glimmer on his cheeks.

"Oh, sweetheart," she said, sad that he was clearly acting out his dreams. "Let's go to bed."

She tried to pick him up, but he protested. "No-o-o."

"Brody, you'll sleep so much better in your own bed," she coaxed.

His eyes remained closed, but his objection was plain. "No."

Sara debated waking Cole, then decided she had to resolve this on her own. This time she picked him up and cradled his weight against her. And when he mumbled "No," she simply rocked him.

Eventually, he melted against her and she leisurely strolled back to his room where she changed his wet diaper and settled him in his bed. "Good night, sweet prince," she said as she kissed his chubby little cheek.

Minutes later, she'd just started to doze when she heard the same sound.

Once again, she found Brody on the sofa, crying softly in his sleep.

Certain they'd both spend the night traipsing back and forth, which meant no one would sleep well if at all, she pulled a spare comforter out of the linen closet and returned to the living room. Ignoring his weak protests, she tucked the blanket around them and settled down for the rest of the night with Brody cradled in her arms.

"Good night, young man," she murmured against his tear-dampened hair. "Sleep tight."

He let out a deep sigh and nestled against her, as if he'd either finally found the comfort he'd been searching for or he was too exhausted to fight her. Yet, as his shuddering sobs slowly evened into peaceful breathing, she felt satisfied to have been the person who'd seen him through his nightmare.

In his half-asleep state, he probably didn't realize she'd been the one providing comfort, but she didn't mind. He might reject her nurturing while he was awake, but he obviously was content with it while he was asleep.

This certainly wasn't the way she'd envisioned mother-hood would be, but for now it was better than nothing.

CHAPTER SEVEN

'OH, COLE, how could you?" Sara wailed on Sunday as soon as she walked into the kitchen where he and Brody were snacking on her homemade chocolate-chip cookies.

"How could I what?" he asked, popping the last bit of evidence into his mouth.

"Eat cookies right before lunch. I was saving those for this afternoon."

"We only took two and, besides, please note." He pointed to the artfully arranged tray she'd prepared. "I moved the rest around so no one will ever notice a few are missing."

"I'm not worried about the numbers or how the platter looks," she groused. "Brody's the one with chocolate smeared from ear to ear."

He glanced at his son, who stared back at him with wide-eyed innocence as if to ask, What's wrong? As Sara had said, chocolate and cookie crumbs were all over his face and the hands clutching the cookie were grubby as well. To make matters worse, a dark smear ran across the appliqué of Rudolph on Brody's red pullover sweater.

"He'll wash."

"Yes, but my parents will be here any minute and I don't have time to change his clothes again. You were *supposed* to keep him clean while I got ready," she said sternly. "We're trying to make a good impression."

He smiled at her distress. "Your parents are going to be too excited to notice he's wearing a few crumbs and stained with chocolate. If they do, they'll understand. They had four kids of their own, remember?"

She shot him an exasperated glare. "That's not the point, Cole. I wanted everything to be perfect—"

The doorbell rang and her exasperation turned to shock. "Oh, dear. They're here." She glanced at the clock. "They're *early!*" she wailed.

For an instant he wanted to wail with her. In spite of his assurances that Sara's parents could arrive when they wished and stay as long as they liked, in spite of his easygoing manner and the smile on his face, his gut churned. He'd spent most of his childhood being on the receiving end of thinly veiled hostility and he braced himself for more of the same today. As a teen, he'd sworn he'd never allow himself to be put in the same situation, and yet here he was, about to endure it again.

The only difference was, as a kid, he hadn't deserved such treatment. Fortunately, he'd usually been able to escape to his room or a friend's house, or even his school books, but that luxury wouldn't be granted him today. Today, he *deserved* his in-laws' wrath and he'd bear it with grace because deep down he knew they were only acting out of love for their daughter.

He hoped she realized how lucky she was.

"Take a deep breath," he ordered with undisguised humor. As soon as she obeyed, he added, "Now, let your parents inside before they freeze on the front porch."

While Sara flew out of the room, Cole bent down to brush off the worst of the crumbs on his son's clothing. "Shall we meet your grandparents?" he asked.

Brody babbled something that Cole took to mean agreement.

As the sound of Greg and Marcia Adams's voices drifted in his direction, Cole hoisted Brody into his arms and held him like a talisman as he went to greet Sara's parents.

Greg was a few inches shorter than Cole, gray-haired and, thanks to his job as a mechanic and his weekend job as a woodcutter, extremely fit for a man his age. As he noticed Cole and Brody hanging in the background, his normal smile spread widely and his eyes softened.

"There's my grandson," he said, sounding like a proud grandfather. "He's a fine-looking boy, isn't he, Marcia?"

Marcia, an older version of Sara, nodded with her eyes suspiciously bright. "Oh, my, yes. I'm so glad our appointment for a family photo isn't for another two weeks. Now he'll be included. What do you think about everyone wearing red and—?"

"Enough about the annual photo," Greg chided his wife good-naturedly. "Brody and I have more serious things to discuss than what to wear. Like what's in my box of goodies."

He picked up the large box at the door and carried it to a draft-free spot in front of the Christmas tree. After a bit of coaxing, Brody joined him in the game of pulling out all sizes and shapes of brand-new cars and trucks.

Cole watched the two hard at work, pleased that his son had such a kind and forgiving grandfather. Yet how could he not? Sara was a reflection of those traits. As his gaze landed on her, he silently thanked the fates for bringing her into his life. As far as he was concerned, she was his saving grace.

Suddenly, Brody ran out of the room and returned with more toy cars in his arms.

"Goodness!" Marcia exclaimed. "I do believe he has as many vehicles to play with as you had dolls, Sara."

Cole's ears perked. "How many did you have? You never told me you had a *collection*," he teased his wife.

"Because I didn't *collect* them," she informed him grandly.

"Yes, you did," Marcia corrected her. "Maybe not in the sense of acquiring them just to look at, but somehow they always managed to come home with you." She addressed Cole. "Whenever we passed a thrift shop, we had to go in so she could see if anyone had dropped off a doll. If one was there, we had to buy it."

Cole eyed his wife, surprised to hear this story. And yet he wasn't. "Why haven't I heard this before?"

"Because I'd forgotten myself until now," Sara answered. "For the record, though, we didn't buy *every* doll we came across."

"Maybe not, but you came close," Greg added from his spot on the floor. "I built enough miniature bunk beds that I could make them in my sleep. Thank goodness we had enough bedrooms for her and her sister to each have their own, because no one could walk around in hers."

"You made seven beds," she defended. "I only kept fifteen dolls and one always slept with me."

"Fifteen?" Cole asked.

She shrugged. "It wasn't so many, really. I took the dolls that I didn't think anyone else would buy so I could give them a home."

"You *rescued* dolls?" Cole asked.

Sara grinned. "Sure, why not? Someone had to."

"But *dolls?* Why not cats or dogs?"

"We didn't have room for pets," she said. "The expense of feeding them would have been horrific and dolls didn't have to go to the vet."

"What made you start in the first place?" Cole asked.

"I can answer that," Marcia interjected. "Sara always complained that because she was the baby of the family, no one needed her for anything. So I told her to find something she could call her own. She always loved dolls and one day—"

Sara picked up the story. "One day, I was at a friend's

house and she had a doll that she didn't want anymore because its clothes were torn and her brother had cut off one pigtail. Because I knew my dad could fix anything..." she cast a benevolent glance at her father "...I brought her home and the rest, as they say, is history."

"And, boy, was she right," Greg added affectionately. "She dragged home dolls that had more problems than you can imagine. Missing eyes, hair, arms, legs, you name it. Her mother and I became good enough at repairing them that we could have opened a side business."

"Don't forget that once they were restored, I found them new homes," she pointed out.

"True," her father admitted. "She only *kept* fifteen, but I'll bet we had hundreds over the years."

Sara laughed. "Now, Dad, I'm sure you're exaggerating."

"Want to bet?" he retorted without heat. "So, Cole, be prepared for Brody to follow in her shoes. With all these cars and trucks, you could end up adding master mechanic skills to your medical degree."

"I'll keep it in mind," Cole answered. "But, Sara, with fifteen dolls, how did you ever play with them all?"

"I had a system," she began.

"I'll say," her mother interrupted. "I can't tell you how many times we had to wait on Sara because she was feeding or changing or bathing one of them."

Clearly, Sara's mothering gene had been activated early in her life. In light of the doll story, she probably felt she was limiting herself to her dream of four. No wonder she was so impatient to start their family.

Cole listened to their good-natured banter, knowing that this was the sort of home life he wanted Brody to experience. He wanted him to feel loved enough to say and do what he wanted without fear, secure in the support of his parents.

As the stories continued, oddly enough his own insecurities inched their way to the surface. Had Sara reconciled so quickly with him because she loved him, or because he was only a means to the end she wanted?

"Our ward is taking on the overflow from Peds," Beverly McCarter announced during an impromptu early-morning ward staff meeting on Monday. Beverly was the medical-surgical unit supervisor and the strain of handling the increased patient census with a shortage of staff showed on the forty-eight-year-old's face. However, she wasn't the only nurse who sported dark circles under her eyes. To varying degrees, everyone was working overtime.

Except for Sara, of course. When she considered her lack of progress with Brody, she'd glumly thought her time would be better served if she worked more hours to take care of people who really needed her, but, as her mother had reminded her yesterday during their visit, she and Brody would never form a bond if they didn't spend time together.

"We're getting peds patients?" someone asked. As glances were exchanged, plainly most of the nurses were feeling out of their element when it came to caring for the younger set.

"Don't panic," Bev ordered. "They're only sending us the older kids, ten and up. We decided it would be in everyone's best interests if the experienced peds nurses looked after the littlest."

"That's a relief," another nurse remarked.

"Age aside, we have six very sick kids with us now," Bev reported. "They range from age ten to fourteen and the doctors are warning we might get more."

"Do they all have whooping cough?" Sara asked.

"With complications," Bev told her. "Two have had seizures and four have secondary bacterial pneumonia. I might remind you that pneumonia is the most common cause of pertussis-related deaths, so don't take their conditions lightly. These are very sick children."

"Shouldn't they be in ICU?" Millie asked.

"ICU is also bursting at the seams," Bev said wearily. "Once again, I want to remind everyone that transmission of this disease is through direct contact with respiratory secretions. I don't want to see anyone without proper protective equipment, including a mask. Granted, once these kids have finished their five-day erythromycin regime, they aren't considered contagious, but in the meantime they are."

"So who's the doctor in charge?" another nurse asked. "Do we call Dr. Wittman, or one of the pediatricians?"

"Dr. Wittman is our first contact as usual, but he's working closely with the pediatricians and the family physicians. Unless he tells you otherwise, run everything you see, do or suspect by him. Any questions?"

The group dispersed with each outgoing nurse giving specifics about her patients to those who were relieving them. In addition to her other patients, Sara had been assigned siblings Mica and Mandy Berton, who had pneumonia.

Normally, pertussis patients were isolated but because these two came from the same household, they were allowed to share one of the larger rooms so their mother could stay with them.

After donning her protective gear, including a mask, Sara found the woman dozing in a recliner between the two beds. Knowing how exhausted she must be, Sara quietly began to replace Mica's bag of IV fluid.

Mrs. Berton stirred. "Is it morning already?" she murmured.

"Afraid so. Feel free to go back to sleep. I'm only going to check their vitals. After the night they had, I suspect they won't even know I'm here."

"They both had a rough time," Mrs. Berton admitted. "If

one wasn't coughing, the other was. In between that, the respiratory therapist was here giving breathing treatments. I was beginning to think we were at a bus stop from all the people coming and going."

Sara smiled as she noted blood pressures and pulse rates. "It seems that way at times, doesn't it?"

As she finished her tasks, their mother asked, "How are they?"

Sara wasn't inclined to speak as bluntly as the night nurse had to her. *No real improvement. Persistent mild fever with intermittent spikes. Coughing spells often result in cyanosis.*

"From what the night staff told me," she said instead, "no real change."

Mrs. Berton's sigh said it all. "I'd hoped we'd see some improvement by now."

Sara would have liked that, too.

"How much longer can they go like this?"

Another question Sara couldn't—and wouldn't—answer. "I wish I could give you an exact timetable, but so much depends on staying ahead of any secondary problems."

"Like their pneumonia."

"Like the pneumonia," Sara agreed. "We're doing everything we can to help them kick this. Unfortunately, recovery takes time."

Mrs. Berton nodded, but the bleakness in her eyes said that she wasn't particularly comforted by Sara's remark.

"I know this is rough on you," Sara added, "but sometimes a little thing like a break to run home and shower can change our perspective. Maybe you'd like to do that when the RT comes in?"

According to the nursing reports, the children's mother hadn't left the hospital since they'd arrived two days ago.

"My husband is coming in after he takes our youngest boy to school. Until then, I have to stay. I *need* to stay." She gave mirthless chuckle. "It sounds crazy, but I feel like as long as I'm here, they're going to be all right."

Sara understood what she meant. "A lot of parents have told me that," she said kindly.

"Mica always drove me crazy when he asked, 'What's to eat, Mom?' before I'd cleaned the kitchen from the last meal. Now it would be music to my ears." She glanced at Sara. "I won't ever complain again about that boy's bottomless stomach."

"When he's past the worst of this, he'll be hungry again. You'll see."

Mrs. Berton sighed. "I hope so. I'd be devastated if the worst happened…"

"Of course you would be," Sara murmured. "But, as I said earlier, they're holding their own." Her pager went off and she checked the display. Today would definitely be one of those days that would go down in the annals of nursing infamy… I have to go, but I'll be back as soon as I can. Meanwhile, you know where the call button is. Let me know if you sense a change of any kind."

Sara checked in another new patient—thankfully, this one was a thirty-year-old woman with a complicated leg fracture as a result of a car accident rather than another whooping-cough case—before continuing on her rounds. Then she had to make a quick trip to the blood bank to pick up a unit of blood for a severely anemic patient. On the way back, she stepped into the elevator to find Dr. Eller, her ob-gyn.

"Congratulations," the fifty-four-year-old specialist told her with a smile. "Cole told me your good news. You're looking well for being a new mother."

She smiled, tamping down the lingering disappointment that motherhood hadn't come in the manner she'd expected. While all of her energies were focused on Brody, she still had

unanswered questions about her own health—questions th
she hoped Dr. Eller could answer in order to ease her min

"Thanks," she answered politely. Then, because the e
evator was empty and there was no time like the presen
she pressed on. "I'd like to set up an appointment to see yo
though."

"Feeling tired, eh?" He grinned. "I haven't met a woma
yet who has a two-year-old and isn't tired."

"This isn't about feeling tired or stressed," she correcte
him carefully, hating to go into detail in an elevator, even
they were the only people on board. "While now probabl
isn't the best time for me to get pregnant, I'd like a reassu
ance that when we *are* ready, I *can* have a baby."

His bushy eyebrows drew together. "You miscarried abou
what, six months ago?"

"Nine," she corrected.

Dr. Eller stared thoughtfully at her before he spoke. "Ho
long has it been since you had a thorough physical?"

She shrugged. "I have no idea."

He nodded. "Then we'll start with that, just to rule out ar
of the obvious health issues."

"Perfect," she said, relieved he was willing to be proac
tive.

His gaze grew intent. "I talked to Cole the other day ar
he didn't mention you were concerned."

Not long ago, she *had* been concerned because not hav
ing a child made her feel as if an important part of her wa
missing. Brody's presence had helped, but while she coul
accept him as part of their family, Cole's son didn't fulfill he
personal dream of having a baby of her own. Granted, ge
ting pregnant had dropped its top-priority status in relatic
to the other events in her life but, regardless of those event
she still had questions that demanded answers.

"I'm more curious than concerned," she explained.

He smiled. "Understandable. In any case, a physical is always the best place to begin. Call my office for an appointment and meanwhile I'll have my nurse phone in lab orders."

Her knees shook with relief. "Thank you."

"After I see those results—it may take a week or so to get them—we'll talk. How does that sound?"

"Marvelous. You don't know what this means to me, Dr. ller."

The door slid open and he stepped out. "I haven't done anything yet," he said cheerfully, before he disappeared around the corner.

Sara leaned weakly against the rail as the door closed. erhaps she should have talked this over with Cole before he talked to Josh, but when the opportunity had presented self, she'd seized it. Cole surely couldn't fault her for that, ould he?

However, the answer to that question never came because s soon as she arrived at her floor, she immediately started er patient's blood transfusion. By the time she returned to he Bertons' room, where the respiratory therapy technician as finishing up the children's treatments, nearly an hour ad passed.

"What do you think?" she asked the woman after she followed her into the hall.

"To be honest, I'd expected them to be better by now. Has Dr. Wittman come by to see them this morning?"

"Not yet."

"See if he can come sooner rather than later," the therapist advised. "Mica's lung function seems to be dropping. I don't now if a different antibiotic might be helpful, but see what he thinks. Page me if he wants me to come more often."

"Will do."

She returned to find Mica coughing and clutching his abomen. "Hurts," he murmured.

"What's wrong now?" his mother asked, obviously worrie

"It could be something as simple as sore muscles." Sar frowned. "But I'll be sure to point it out to the doctor." Sh punched in a text message to Cole's phone. "He's running late than usual, but don't worry. He'll stop by soon, I'm sure."

Sara returned to her station to record her nursing note Then, hearing an alarm which seemed to originate in th Berton children's room, she gowned again and went inside

This time, the children's father was in the room, talkin in a loud whisper to his wife. A big, burly man wearing jean and a plaid flannel shirt under the paper hospital gown, h was the sort one didn't want to meet in a dark alley. The glar he shot her above his mask when she walked into the roor only reinforced her opinion.

"Tom," his wife said, "this is Sara, and she's their nurs today."

"I don't care who she is," he retorted hotly. "I want to tal to the doctor."

Sara identified the source of the alarm—kinked tubing— and silenced the offending noise, using those few second delay to modulate her tone in the face of the man's hostilit

"And you will," Sara promised once the only noise i the room was the whoosh of the humidifier. "I've page Dr. Wittman and he should be arriving shortly. He's alway happy to talk to family members."

"My kids aren't getting better."

"We're doing everything we can—"

"It isn't enough," the man insisted. "They should be i ICU or have constant nursing care or something."

"We're giving fluids and antibiotics, and the breathin treatments are delivering medicine into their lungs," she ex plained. "We simply have to wait for our measures to ge ahead of the infection."

He approached her, his face grim. "That's the best you ot? To tell me that we have to *wait?*"

"Tom," his wife chided. "Yelling at the nurse won't help. he's—"

"You aren't hearing me," he growled at Sara, ignoring his ife's plea. "My kids are not getting better." With each care- ully enunciated word he poked a finger into her shoulder ard enough to throw her off balance.

Sara had dealt with belligerent patients before but this guy ad caught her off guard. The call button seemed a million iiles away, but even if she reached it, she had no guarantee iat anyone would answer it soon enough to help her defuse ie situation.

"And I want to know what you're going to do about it," he ontinued grimly.

"I know you're concerned and upset," Sara said evenly in pite of her racing heart, "but getting angry won't help them r you."

"Tom," his wife urged again. "Calm down."

"I will *not* calm down," he rasped. "I want to know why iy kids aren't getting better and what you so-called medical *xperts* are doing about it."

This time, as he reached out to poke her again, Sara found erself being unceremoniously moved out of the way.

"I will tell you *exactly* what we're doing, Mr. Berton." `ole's eyes glittered with fury. "*We're* all going to take a eep breath while *you* put your hands in your pockets. And f I see you touching my wife or any of the staff again, *for iy reason,* I will ask Security to escort you from the build- ıg. Do I make myself clear?"

Although he spoke pleasantly, Sara heard the steel in his oice. Obviously Tom did, too, because he shuffled back a w steps.

"Didn't mean to push her," he mumbled as he avoide Sara's eyes. "I was just trying to get some answers."

"Answers come easier when the questions are asked in civil tone and the help isn't threatened," Cole answered cold! "Can we continue this conversation like adults or not?"

As Tom focused on a point near the ceiling, his eyes su piciously as red as his wife's, Sara took pity on them. "N harm done," she said softly. "Tom was just concerned abo his kids."

While Tom nodded, his eyes expressing his gratitude, Co frowned. He shot her a glance that promised the discussio was merely postponed and not over, but she simply smile at him.

"Tom, why don't you and your wife step outside while D Wittman examines Mica and Mandy?" she suggested. "Th waiting room at the end of the hall has a pot of coffee. Hav a cup and when we're finished, we'll find you."

Mrs. Berton nodded. "I think that's a wonderful idea. Ton shall we go and let the doctor work?"

Tom hesitated, as if he was uncertain about leaving, b between Sara's encouraging smile and his wife tugging o his arm, he strode from the room.

"What in the world were you doing?" Cole muttered. "Wh didn't you—?"

"Cole, please. Not now. We have two sick kids and tw worried parents." She immediately went into nurse mod repeating everything the respiratory therapy technician ha reported, as well as adding her own observations.

He examined Mica first. "Do we have his sputum cultur results?"

"They were posted an hour ago," she replied, pulling u the document on the computer screen.

He studied the report. "According to this, the drug we'r

sing is only marginally effective, so I'm going to switch to higher-powered antibiotic. Continue with everything else."

After noting his orders in the computer, she joined him at Mandy's bedside.

"Hi, hon," Cole said softly. "How're you doing today?"

"Not…not so good."

"I'm not surprised," he said. "But you'll be up and around oon."

The nine-year-old smiled. "Okay." After Cole finished listening to her lungs, she coughed. "I'm sorry about my dad. ometimes he can be scary, but he's not. Really."

Sara patted her arm. "I know. He was just worried about ou."

"You'll let him keep coming to see us, won't you?"

Sara raised her eyebrow at Cole and immediately saw resnation in his eyes. "As long as he behaves, no one will stop im from visiting," Cole answered, his gaze meeting Sara's.

"Promise?" Mandy asked.

"I promise."

"We're finished, so you can rest," Sara told her. "Meanhile, we'll send in your parents, okay?"

Mandy nodded as she closed her eyes. "Okay."

Outside the room, Cole stripped off his protective wear. Hell," he muttered.

"What's wrong?"

"I was looking forward to watching Security escort him om the premises."

Her husband wore a distinctly disgruntled expression, uch like a little boy who'd plotted some misdeed only to ave his plan thwarted at the last minute. "But now you n't," she reminded him. "If you do, you'll have one upset ne-year-old."

He ran a hand through his hair. "I know. Do you have any ea how worried I was?"

She smiled. "I think so, but I had the situation under control."

He snorted. "Yeah, right. Guys like that usually have trouble with their tempers, which means that I may get to see Security in action after all. His presence in the hospital contingent on good behavior."

"Cut him some slack, Cole. The man's worried about h kids. If you were in his shoes—if Brody were lying in th bed—wouldn't you take on the world for him?"

He frowned. "I guess so. When I saw him threaten you—"

"He didn't hurt me," she assured him.

"Well, I'd feel better if you didn't go into that room alon when he's there."

"Trust me, Cole. He'll be on his best behavior. His wi will see to it. Besides, he loves his kids and if he knows— which he does now—that if he steps out of line, he won't able to see them, he'll be motivated to stay calm."

"Let's hope so."

She grinned at him. "Now go and be nice to the Berton while I phone the pharmacy with your new drug orders."

"You don't want to join me to make sure *I* behave?"

"I could, but we want to show Tom that we're attackin Mica's medical condition aggressively. That means the soon we start the new antibiotic, the better."

"Okay, but just so you know, I plan to stick around th ward as much as I can. To keep an eye on things," he mu tered darkly.

She smiled at his protective streak, deciding this wasn a good time to point out she'd encountered far more antago nistic patients than Tom Berton and had lived to tell the tal "As much as I appreciate your coming to my rescue…" sl rested her hand on his arm and noticed the tension unde neath the layers of clothing "…we—I—will be fine, so dor do it on my account," she said.

He met her gaze and spoke in a serious tone. "Of course 'm doing it for you."

"Oh, Cole," she said, surprised by his blatant protective treak, "were you really worried?"

"Why wouldn't I be? A fellow twice the size of my wife vas pushing her around. I had no idea what he'd do next. For ll I knew, he intended to throw you through the window."

"He wasn't *that* far out of control."

He raised an eyebrow. "Are you sure?"

In spite of wanting to believe that her calm attitude would ave activated Tom's common sense, she wasn't sure.

"I'm sticking around as much as possible," he said in no ncertain terms, "and I'm doing it as much for me as I am or you. Now, we'd both better get to work before Tom gets o impatient and comes looking for us."

For the rest of the afternoon, Sara was certain she walked round her ward with a goofy expression of surprise, but it vasn't because Cole was true to his word and had a very vis-le presence so she'd feel safe. Neither was she surprised by is obvious concern. As he'd pointed out, Tom wasn't a feath-rweight and an angry male could be a dangerous force to be eckoned with.

No, what had surprised her the most was that he'd *admit-d* to being worried. Had this incident happened a few weeks go, he would have been just as protective, but he'd never have onfessed to needing peace of mind for himself.

There was hope for him yet.

CHAPTER EIGHT

IF COLE lived to be a hundred, he'd never forget Sara's ex
pression after he'd announced his reasons for not letting he
out of his proverbial sight. If he'd been thinking more clearl
at the time, he would have simply called Security and aske
them to patrol the ward, but he hadn't.

He also could have hung around under the guise of mon
itoring the Berton children, but he hadn't done that eithe
Instead, he'd blurted out what he'd really been feeling.

To his own surprise, the sky hadn't fallen, the earth hadn
trembled, his tongue hadn't snapped off its rollers and Sar
hadn't made fun of him. Instead, she had looked as happy a
she had on the day he'd finally proposed, and that happines
seemed to carry her for the next week.

Did he really hold that much of himself back, especiall
from his own wife? If so, he truly needed to make a few per
sonal changes, especially if the rewards would be so great.

However, a few days later, when Sara had tentatively an
nounced her upcoming doctor's appointment, his own re
sponse made it obvious that he'd been changing and hadn
realized it...

"I know we'd talked about waiting before we pursued fe
tility tests," she began, almost apologetically, "but the oppo
tunity presented itself and I just couldn't pass it up. And
isn't like we're going gangbusters on this. It's only a phys

al, Cole. When life with Brody has settled down and he's
djusted, we'll do something, but until then…please don't be
ngry—"

Cole interrupted her breathy explanation with a short kiss.
Vhile he was a little disappointed that she'd taken this step
n her own, he understood about seizing opportunities. And
ow that Brody had enriched their lives, he discovered he
vasn't as reluctant to eventually add to their household as
e once had been.

"It's okay," he told her. "You don't have to explain. I'm not
ngry."

"Truly?" she asked, the worry in her eyes lessening.

"Truly. If a physical will give you peace of mind, then
nat's what we should do," he said firmly, certain a doctor's
eport would chase away her doubts and restore some badly
eeded confidence in this area of her life. Considering every-
ning she'd done for him, this seemed like the least he could
o for her.

However, as they sat in Josh Eller's office a few days later,
he was anything but peaceful…

"Nervous?" Cole asked as she thumbed through her third
nagazine in less than five minutes.

She flashed him a half smile. "Silly of me, isn't it?"

"No, but worrying won't change anything."

"I know." Her chuckle was weak. "It's just that I'm torn
etween hoping he found something abnormal and hoping
nat he didn't."

"Don't look for trouble," he advised. "Chances are every-
ning is fine and you're worrying for nothing."

"Let's hope so."

"Mrs. Wittman?"

As soon as the nurse called her name, Sara exhaled once,
miled at him tremulously, then rose. "You're coming, aren't
ou?" she turned back to ask him.

His wife was obviously giving him permission to sit in o her exam, so he jumped to his feet. "Of course."

For the next thirty minutes, he chatted with Josh as th ob-gyn checked Sara from the top of her head to the soles c her feet. As soon as he'd finished, he ushered Cole into hi office where they talked of inconsequential things until San rejoined them.

"Your physical exam was unremarkable," Eller told then "I didn't expect it to be otherwise. Your basic lab results wei also within the established reference ranges."

"That's good, isn't it?" she asked.

"It is. However…" he shuffled a few papers on his des "…we also ran a few hormone assays and one result stoo out." He placed the page in front of them so they could bot review it.

The FSH result was in bold-faced print with an *H* besid it, indicating it was higher than normal.

"As you can see," Eller continued, "the level of FSH, c follicle-stimulating hormone, is elevated."

Sara glanced at Cole and he steeled his face into impassiv lines to hide his dismay. "Which means what?" she asked.

"As Cole can tell you, FSH does what its name implies– it stimulates the growth of immature ovarian follicles."

"But that's good, isn't it?"

"If the level is high in the first days of a woman's cycl yes. But then, as a follicle grows, other hormones kick in t stimulate maturation and then these in turn suppress the FSF Based on what Sara told me, high levels of FSH at this tim in her cycle indicate that this restricting feedback mechanisr is either absent or impaired."

"Are you saying that Sara is menopausal?" Cole asked.

Menopausal? Fear struck Sara's heart. That couldn't b It just couldn't…

"I'm not saying anything," Josh said. "While prematur

menopause is a possibility, at her age it could also indicate she has poor ovarian reserve, which is a fancy term to describe a woman's chance for conceiving. Because women are born with all the eggs they're going to have, we have to assess if the elevated FSH level is due to a decreased number of eggs or some other hormonal condition that is interfering with the normal feedback mechanism."

"Would IVF be a solution for us?" Cole asked.

"It might be," he admitted, "and it might not. So much depends on properly diagnosing the cause of your infertility. However, the fact that she'd been pregnant before suggests that structurally there isn't a problem. Because the FSH is elevated and is the most obvious issue, we'll focus our attention down that path."

Then she still had hope... "If in vitro fertilization is the answer, then how did I get pregnant the first time?"

Eller smiled. "What can I say? The conditions must have been just right. In any case, IVF would simply increase your chances of achieving pregnancy, but before we rush you to an IVF facility, we'll run a lot more tests, including a sperm count on you, Cole."

"More tests?" Sara asked, trying to remember what she'd learned during her nursing-school days.

"We'll start with the clomiphene citrate challenge test. This procedure will indicate how well you'll respond to induced ovulation and is the best predictor of ovarian reserve that we have at the moment."

"What's involved?" she asked.

"On day two or three of your next menstrual cycle, we'll draw a blood sample for another baseline FSH level and perform a transvaginal ultrasound. On day five, you'll begin taking the clomiphene citrate tablets and continue for five days through day nine. Then on day ten or eleven, we'll draw blood for another FSH level."

Sara glanced at Cole. "Sounds simple enough."

"And this will give us the answers we need," Cole stated as if asking for confirmation.

"Yes and no. This test is merely a predictor. If the results are abnormal, a very poor chance of pregnancy is predicted. Studies have shown that these women respond poorly to injectable fertility drugs, have fewer eggs retrieved for IVF, lower pregnancy and higher miscarriage rates, and an increased risk for chromosomally abnormal embryos. Which is why many fertility programs use this test to screen prospective IVF patients to eliminate those with odds against their success."

"And if the results are normal?" Sara asked, her tone hopeful.

"Unfortunately, normal FSH levels during this challenge test don't tell us anything. A normal result doesn't *prove* your ovaries are working well and therefore the test won't predict that you *will* get pregnant. This is confusing, I know."

"Then why run the test?"

"Because predicting what *won't* work saves a lot of stress and heartache on everyone, especially the couple, for the reasons I mentioned earlier. And if you can screen out those who don't have good odds, you can save them a huge financial burden as well."

"In other words, an abnormal result identifies patients with poor ovarian reserve," Cole clarified.

"Exactly. Then these couples can pursue other options. But before we debate the predictive value and your candidacy in an IVF program, let's see what the test reveals. No sense in getting ahead of ourselves."

Eller addressed Sara. "You're close to your next period, aren't you?" At her nod, he added, "Then we can either arrange to perform this test at your next cycle, or we can wa

ntil next month, after the holidays are over. Or we can wait
o continue until you're both ready to add to your family."

Sara exchanged a glance with Cole, uncertain about what
o do next.

"Can we have a few minutes to discuss this?" Cole asked
osh.

"Of course."

As soon as Josh closed the door behind him, Cole faced
Sara. "What do you want to do?"

Her smile was weak and she plucked at some imaginary
int on her pants. "Logically, we should wait. Brody is still
dapting and we've just recently ironed out our own differ-
nces. Maybe we should just be satisfied with the three of us
s a family."

"But you'd still like to know for certain."

She met his gaze. "Yes, I would."

"Then it's settled." As he rose to summon Josh into the
oom, she stopped him.

"I don't want you to feel pressured."

He bent down and kissed her forehead. "I don't. In fact,
he idea of giving Brody a brother or a sister isn't as fright-
ning as it once was, thanks to you."

She searched his face for the truth. "Really?"

He smiled. "Really."

Six months, even six weeks ago, Sara would have taken
is words at face value and blithely continued on, believing
Cole's reticence was because he was a man of few words.

Then Brody had come along and his presence had forced
er see her husband in a new light. While she'd demanded that
Cole change and bring more openness and honesty to their re-
ationship—and he was making progress—she had changed,
oo. She'd become more cognizant of when his mood didn't
uite match his remarks, and less inclined to take situations

and comments at face value. And right now his smile didn'
quite reach his eyes, which suggested he had a few worries

"But you have reservations," she continued.

He paused, brow furrowed, as if weighing his words. "
suppose I do," he finally admitted. "Not because we don'
love each other enough to handle another baby but becaus
couples can get so caught up with trying to get pregnant tha
it interferes with the rest of their family life."

His concern suddenly seemed so obvious she didn't knov
why she hadn't seen it before.

"This won't detract from our first Christmas with Brody,
she assured him. "He won't miss any of the usual holiday fes
tivities and I won't deprive him of any of our family tradi
tions. We'll do everything we'd normally do at this time o
year and more."

She made her promise with sincere determination, but a
the same time she hoped and prayed for a breakthrough wit
the little boy who didn't want her to be his mother.

Although Cole didn't mention it, he was relieved to see tha
Sara had followed through on her promise to make Brody'
first Christmas in their home special. He watched as sh
decorated the house, baked cookies and made candy. The
took him to ride the holiday train at the mall where a prett
young elf snapped his picture as he sat on Santa's lap. Whe
the first snowfall came, as the weatherman had predicted
Sara ushered Brody outside so he could catch snowflake
for the first time.

The little boy's wide eyes clearly showed his wondermen
as he took in these new sights and experiences but, in spit
of Sara's efforts, he still treated her with wariness.

"I know I should be patient," she revealed during on
particularly trying afternoon when Brody refused to let he
change his wet diaper. "He tolerates me doing things for hir

if he and I are alone, but if anyone else is here, especially you, then he won't have anything to do with me."

Cole studied his son, wishing the little boy would give Sara a chance to be the mother she so desperately wanted to be. If only he didn't feel so powerless. "Maybe he's just experiencing the normal terrible twos."

She shook her head. "I don't think so. It's more deep-seated than that. It's like he's focusing his anger at the world on me and I don't know how I can help him channel it in another direction. I think we need professional help."

"Okay," he said slowly, "if that's what you think, we can certainly pursue that idea. And maybe it's a matter of you expecting too much from him too soon."

"He doesn't have a problem with you," she pointed out.

"No, but in his mind I wasn't replacing his mother. You are."

She heaved a great sigh. "I guess. I only want..." Her voice died.

"Want what?" he coaxed.

"I want him to need me," she said simply.

He stared at her, incredulous. "Of course he needs you. He's only two, going on three."

"I'm not talking about caregiving. I'm talking about *emotionally* needing me. When he's upset or tired, he goes off by himself, even though I'm right *here*."

"He will. Give him time." He pulled her against him. "You'll see."

Her smile wobbled. "I suppose. It's just that I feel like I'm failing at the most important job I could ever have—the job that Ruth should have had. And if I can't do my job with Brody, what makes me think I could be a mother to anyone else, even my own baby? Maybe we should just forget the rest Josh suggested."

"It's my turn to give the pep talk," he told her kindly. "You aren't failing at anything. This is only a rough patch."

"Yeah, right. A rough patch."

He sensed she didn't believe him. "As for your lab test, you don't want to give up so soon, do you?"

She rubbed the back of her neck. "Not really, no."

"Then just be patient." Then, because she didn't seem to welcome his advice, he asked, "Have you ever read Ruth's letter?"

"No."

"Why not? You might gain an entirely new perspective on what makes Brody tick."

"Maybe," she said, her tone noncommittal.

"Then you'll read it?" he coaxed.

She nodded. "Someday. When I'm ready."

"Don't wait too long," he cautioned. "For all you know, she had a few tips to make his adjustment easier." Then, sensing he wouldn't help his cause by pushing too hard, he traced her mouth with his thumb. "You know what you need at this very moment?"

"A kiss?" she asked hopefully.

He grinned before he planted a long, lingering one on her mouth. "Besides that."

"I can't imagine."

"You," he said as he tugged her to the mud room directly off the kitchen, "need some fresh air."

She laughed, sounding like a schoolgirl. "It's freezing outside."

"It's thirty-one," he said, "which makes it perfect snowman-building weather."

"You've got to be kidding."

"I'm not. You can't build snowmen if it's warm enough for shirtsleeves. There won't be any of the white stuff."

"Yes, but—"

"No arguments. I'll get Brody while you find things to make their faces and accessorize."

"Faces?" she asked. "As in plural? I thought we were only making one snowman."

He shrugged. "One, three, who's counting? We'll see how many we can create before our noses and toes get cold."

"But I have so much to do—" she began.

"It can wait," he informed her. "Making the first Wittman now family can't."

"Is he asleep already?" Sara asked as Cole dropped onto his easy chair later that evening.

"Oh, yeah. After you finished his story and left the room, I only read as far as the third page of his second book before he closed his eyes. He had a busy day today."

"I'll say," she said. "Building a snow family is hard work." She thought of the trio they'd created. The biggest was Papa Snowman, as Cole had called him, and he sported a disreputable baseball cap on his round head. Mama Snowman was smaller, with a long strip of fabric around her neck to act as a muffler. Baby Snowman was Brody-size and without adornment until Brody had shaken his head and demanded a cap like Daddy's."

Fortunately, when Cole had named the family—Daddy, Mama and Baby—Brody hadn't objected. He'd posed happily beside *his* snowman for one of the many photos that Sara had taken.

To Sara's further delight, he'd joined her in making snow angels and had even gone so far as to grab her hand and tell her "More" when he wanted her to help him cover the yard with them.

Maybe she *was* making progress…

"Did you get any good pictures?" he asked.

"More than enough," she answered, mentally reviewing

the digital images of Brody giggling, his little cheeks rosy from the cold as he played in the snow. His red stocking hat drooped over his eyes and his matching mittens were caked with snow, but his smile stretched from ear to ear and his eyes sparkled with excitement.

And, of course, there was Cole, looking at his son with a benevolent air as he rolled a giant snowball and explained the finer points of his technique to a little boy who was more hindrance than help.

To think that Cole had been afraid he wasn't father material… As far as Sara was concerned, Brody could have none better.

An image of the one very special garment she hadn't ever worn popped into her head. Suddenly feeling rejuvenated, she dropped her magazine on the coffee table and rose.

"I'm going to take a shower," she said, "and go to bed."

Concern crossed his face. "This early?"

She smiled her best come-hither smile. "I didn't say anything about *sleeping,* did I? Unless, of course, you're too tired?" She raised an eyebrow.

His eyes sparkled with enthusiasm. "Me? Tired? Not a chance."

Sara tiptoed down the hall to their bedroom and after digging through a drawer and turning the contents into a jumbled mess she pulled out the teddy in a flurry of silk and lace. Then she hurried into the bathroom with her lingerie and her plans to make this an evening to remember.

When she came out of the bathroom twenty minutes later, Cole was lounging on top of the bed, obviously waiting for her.

A slow, feral grin spread across his face as he rose with the same grace as a jungle cat and approached her. "You look… fantastic."

"Thanks," she answered, pleased by his obvious delight, "but it seems to me you're overdressed."

"Not for long," he answered as he reached for her. "Not for long."

Cole woke up early the next morning blissfully content. As he reached instinctively for Sara, he was surprised to find her missing. Not only that, her side of the bed was cold, as if she'd been gone for hours. After the night of loving they'd had, he couldn't believe she'd left their cozy nest.

He was disappointed, too, because he would have loved to start their morning in a very special way...

Curious, he slipped on his bathrobe and padded out of the room to find her.

The last of his mental cobwebs disappeared as soon as he discovered Brody's empty room.

Thanks to the streetlight's glow streaming through the window, he found Sara on the sofa, spooned protectively around his son.

The sight made him smile.

Sara would wake up stiff and sore from her cramped position, he was certain. He debated the wisdom of carrying Brody to his own bed, but they seemed so comfortable together that he hated to disturb either of them. If he'd needed proof that Brody was on the verge of accepting Sara, this was it.

Seeing one of her feet had escaped the comforter, he tucked it around her toes and covered them with an extra afghan for good measure.

She stirred. "What time is it?" she whispered.

"Four-thirty," he told her. "Do you want me to put him in his own bed?"

"No," she murmured. "We'll end up back here anyway. He'll wake soon enough."

She talked as if this had happened often enough to establish a pattern. He was surprised he hadn't realized what had been happening under his own nose, but now that he did, he intended to grill her for details. At a decent hour, of course.

"Good night," she added sleepily.

Feeling oddly left out, he returned to his own cold bed. Although the sensation of being on the outside looking in wasn't new to him—his childhood had been full of those moments—this was the first time he'd experienced it with Brody.

As he lay there, he thought about the woman who'd wanted to be needed since she was a little girl. No wonder Sara struggled with the little boy's rejection, and no wonder she savored these nighttime moments when Brody's subconscious allowed him to accept her mothering. While he was glad their relationship was improving, even if only on such an elemental level, at this moment only one thought bounced around his head.

He was jealous of his own son.

"How long have you two been sleeping on the sofa?" Cole asked Sara the next morning over coffee.

Sara smiled as she liberally poured in sweetener and creamer. She'd anticipated this conversation from the moment she'd woken up and put Brody back in his own bed.

"I'm not sure. A week. Ten days, maybe," she answered. "It began one night when I heard him crying and found him in the living room. Every time I put him back in his bed, he'd eventually gravitate back to the sofa. I could have left him alone out there, but it didn't seem right." She sipped her coffee, hoping the warm drink would ease the familiar achy feeling in her abdomen.

"So you stayed with him."

"It seemed the only way either of us would get any sleep," she said simply.

"You could have brought him to bed with us."

"I could have," she admitted, "but he always gravitates to the sofa, so I thought it best to share it with him."

"We need to think of a different solution," he said. "Neither of you are getting a good night's sleep."

She flexed her arms and moved her head to ease the kinks in her neck. "Tell me about it," she said dryly. "But what choice do we have?"

"We should have retired his toddler bed and gotten a regular bed when he moved in," he said.

"If you recall, we wanted to surround him with as many familiar things as possible," she reminded him. "New furniture could wait, you said."

"That was before we had this problem. Now we're going to sell him on the idea of having a big-boy bed, like his mommy and daddy have."

"I'm not sure he's ready for that sort of change," she began slowly.

"We have to do something," he pointed out. "Continuing like this isn't an option."

He sounded so forceful that Sara smiled. "What happened? Did you miss me?"

"Always," he growled as he hugged her. "Then it's settled. We'll shop for a new bed and if he needs company because he's afraid or had a nightmare, we can join him there instead of on the sofa."

"A little behavior modification."

"Precisely." He smiled. "It's what you're already practicing on him so it should be easy to take matters a step further."

She stifled a yawn. "It's worth a try.

As it turned out, Brody began to wander into their room during his sleepwalking episodes. They took turns carrying him back to his room where they spent what remained of the night in his bed. Sometimes they simply allowed him to climb between them.

However, no matter what they did, he'd heave a sigh—of relief, perhaps, or maybe it was contentment—as she cuddled him close. Idly, she wondered if he'd ever climbed into bed with his mother, but that was something else she'd never know.

Immediately the letter Ruth had written came to mind, but she couldn't bring herself to read it. Not because she didn't want to potentially gain insights into Brody's first two years of life, but because she didn't want to risk reading that Ruth had been in love with her husband all this time or that his version of events wasn't quite as he'd explained. She was certain they had been—at least from Cole's point of view—but why dwell on the past and introduce unnecessary doubts?

So Sara continued to do what she always did and left the letter on top of their dresser, unopened.

A few days later, Sara began her clomiphene citrate challenge test with a combination of disappointment and relief—disappointment that she hadn't gotten pregnant on her own and relief that they were taking matters into their own hands. However, by the time the ten-day protocol ended, cautious optimism had taken hold. She also suffered from moments of dread, but she swiftly pushed those out of her head. Not knowing the truth was worse than knowing, she'd decided, and she was eager for answers.

"Are you ready for Christmas?" Eller's nurse asked her as she drew Sara's final blood sample during Sara's lunch hour.

"I think so," Sara answered. "Goodies are made, presents are under the tree and the house is ready for guests. The only problem I have now is keeping everyone healthy. Our son—" she still found it difficult to refer to Brody as such

—developed the sniffles and I'm hoping he'll fight off his cold before the holidays are upon us."

"At this time of year, it's tough," the nurse commiserated. Unfortunately, we seem to be passing our germs back and forth at my house and winter has only begun. Spring can't come soon enough for me." She taped a cotton ball over the puncture site on Sara's arm. "That's it for now. We'll see you in five days for your follow-up appointment."

Offering her thanks, Sara left, taking a detour to the hospital cafeteria for a carton of yogurt before returning to her ward.

Georgia, the ward clerk, immediately stopped her. "Your husband signed out the Berton kids while you were gone."

"He did? That's great." The two children had made remarkable progress over the past few days. The change she'd seen from the last shift she'd worked until today had been phenomenal, thanks to the miracle of antibiotics. "Did he say anything about Mrs. VanMeter?"

Dorothy had been off-color that morning, although Sara couldn't point to anything concrete that would account for it. Her vital signs were good, she wasn't having trouble breathing or had any unusual pain, but something wasn't quite right. She'd hoped Cole would see what she was missing.

Georgia shook her head. "Not to me. You might ask one of the other nurses, though."

"I will. First, though, I'll see about sending the Bertons home. As busy as this place is, it won't take long to fill an empty bed."

As expected, Mica and Mandy were delighted to be leaving the hospital. Although they weren't completely recovered, they were definitely on the road to recovery.

As soon as she took care of all the paperwork and discussed the list of dos and don'ts, she accompanied them to

their car and waved goodbye. Afterward, she went directl
to Dorothy's room.

"How are you feeling?" Noting that her patient's colorin
was still off, she automatically took her pulse.

"Oddly enough, not good," Dorothy admitted. "My che
and my back feel strange."

This was the first time the woman had mentioned a spe
cific symptom. "Did you tell Dr. Wittman about this?"

"No, because I just started feeling like this a few minute
ago."

Sara immediately dug her phone out of her pocket an
texted Cole, smiling all the while so as not to let Doroth
see her concern. "I'm sure it's nothing, but let's get the doc
tor back in here, shall we?"

Dorothy nodded. "Okay. By the way, I've been thinking
Would you mind calling my kids for me?"

Remembering how Dorothy had mentioned her kids wer
actually her stepchildren and her contact with them was min
imal, Sara was half-surprised by the request. "I'd be happ
to," she said. "Do we have their phone numbers?"

"I gave them to the lady when I checked in at the fron
desk."

"Then they're probably in your computer records. I'll loo
and if the numbers aren't there, I'll come back."

"Okay," Dorothy said. "My address book is in my han
bag if you need it."

"Is there anything specific you'd like me to tell them?
Sara asked kindly.

"No, just that I'm still in the hospital. And that I'r
sorry—" Suddenly, Dorothy clutched her chest and her hea
rolled limply to one side.

Sara immediately ran around the bed to grab the phon
and punch 0 for the operator. After a terse and well-rehearse
message, she hung up. Without hesitation and only a few se

nds later, she lowered the head of the bed and began cardiac compressions just as the disembodied voice came over the hospital loudspeaker.

"Code blue, room 412."

CHAPTER NINE

AFTER receiving his text summons to room 412, Cole was on his way when the announcement blared out of the speakers. Muttering a curse, he raced down the hall, up the stairs and burst into the room, not surprised that Sara and two other nurses were already at work.

"Status?" he barked.

Someone called out the most recent blood-pressure reading while another nurse was forcing air into Dorothy's lungs via an Ambu bag. Sara, meanwhile, was performing chest compressions with enough vigor to produce a sheen on her forehead.

"Still no pulse," a voice supplied.

"Okay, Sara," he said, "step aside. We'll defibrillate."

Another pair of hands slapped the paddles into his and as soon as he yelled "Clear," a jolt of electricity surged into Dorothy's body. The heart monitor, which had previously shown a flat line, now showed the characteristic blip they'd wanted to achieve.

"BP is one-ten over seventy and rising."

"Let's get labs and move her into CCU," he added. "Good job, everyone."

As soon as Dorothy was wheeled away, with an oxygen mask covering her face, Cole stopped Sara. "I presume you were here at the time of her MI?"

She nodded. "I'd come in to check on her because I didn't like the way she looked, which was why I'd texted you."

"I was on my way when the code blue was announced."

"Anyway, we were talking and she asked me to contact her kids. She's never asked me to do that before and as far as know, none of them have ever come to see her. Regardless, she'd asked me to give them a message and then she collapsed. immediately called the code and began chest compressions."

"You probably saved her life," he said. "If she was going to have a coronary, she had excellent timing to have one while you were in the room."

She smiled, clearly pleased by his praise. "Well, thanks. Let's hope her family feels the same way."

"Do you want me to call them?"

She thought a moment. "As tempting as it is, I'll do it. If they want more information, then you can call them later, after you see her settled in CCU."

"Okay." He hesitated. "How did the blood test go this morning?"

She rubbed the bend of her elbow and felt the wad of cotton underneath her long-sleeved shirt. "Like any blood test," she said. "One prick and it was over. All that's left now is the waiting."

He grinned. "Then that's what we'll do." Although he'd made light of it, he also knew that waiting was often the most difficult part.

Sara entered the house after work, exhausted from the day's hectic pace. She was pleased, however, to find Cole feeding Brody, although she wasn't happy with his choice.

"Fast food?" She raised an eyebrow. "I had our dinner in the refrigerator. All you had to do was heat it."

He chucked Brody under his chin as the little boy shoved our French fries into his mouth at once and grinned. "Ah, but this sounded so much better to our tummies, didn't it, my man?"

Brody wrinkled his nose and tried to shove another fry into his still-full mouth. His little cheeks resembled a chipmunk's from all the food he was trying to chew.

"Cole," she scolded. "He's going to choke. Brody, spit it out."

The little boy shook his head. "Umph."

"Spit it out," she said firmly.

Once again, he shook his head and tried to swallow. "No."

She heaved a deep sigh, but before she could say a word, Cole broke in, his voice stern. "You heard your mother. Empty your mouth before you eat any more."

Brody complied by spitting most of his food onto the floor.

It was a blatant act of defiance and Sara clenched her hands in her pockets, determined not to lose this battle of wills. "Brody," she said calmly, "you will not spit on the floor again or you will not get ice cream for dessert."

As it was his favorite, she expected him to comply. However, he pursed his lips as if he intended to spew more onto the floor, but before he could, Cole put a finger to Brody's mouth.

"No," he said firmly in a tone that meant business. "No spitting. Do you understand?"

Brody answered with a grin. "Okay," he said with good humor.

"Are you finished eating?" At the little boy's nod, Cole wiped his mouth and freed him from his booster seat.

"Play?" Brody asked.

"Yes, you can play," he answered.

As Brody ran off to do just that, suppressed fury made Sara's voice shake. "Did you see that?"

"Yeah. He definitely has an ornery streak."

"Yes, and you just rewarded him for it by letting him play."

He raised an eyebrow. "What would you have him do? Sit in the corner for an hour? Write 'I shall not spit' a hundred times?"

"Of course not," she snapped.

"This isn't like you to get upset over something this minor," he said evenly. "Have a seat and tell me what's *really* bothering you."

"That," she said, pointing to the booster seat, "is what is bothering me. Didn't you see what he did, *after* I told him not to?"

"He's testing you, that's all."

"That's all? That's *all?*" She raised her voice, irritated that Cole dismissed her concerns so easily.

"I've been doing some thinking about the situation and I came up with an idea that seems to fit. In his eyes, his mother left and never returned and now there's a new person in his life who's supposed to take her place. He's pushing you to see if you'll disappear, too."

"And why doesn't he treat you with the same mistrust?"

"Because he never had a dad before. I'm an extra, not a replacement."

"That's rather high-level thinking for a child his age, isn't it?"

He shrugged. "He may not consciously have plotted his actions, but kids sense more things than we might think. Two-year-olds normally begin testing the limits at their age, so why can't we assume he's expanded those limits to include you?"

Whether Cole was right or not, his theory sounded plausible. Could it be as simple as Cole described?

"Brody's actions aren't the real problem, are they?" he asked. "You normally don't freak out because we stopped at a burger place on our way home. What gives?"

Sara sat, chagrined that she'd overreacted. "I'm in a bad mood, I guess."

"Over what?"

"A lot of things." She paused. "No, mainly one. I phoned Dorothy's children. Stepchildren," she corrected.

"Your call didn't go well, I presume."

Sara shook her head. "One never answered the phone. The son was rude and told me not to bother him again. The third, a daughter, was more polite, but she basically told me that Dorothy wasn't a part of her family. Even when I shared…" Her voice cracked and she cleared her throat. "Dorothy asked me to tell them that she was sorry, but neither of the two I spoke to responded positively. The son laughed and suggested that she was only trying to appease her conscience before she went to meet her Maker."

"Any idea on what she was sorry for?"

She shook her head. "None. Oh, Cole. I feel so badly for that woman. To be her age, sick and nearly dying, and know that you're alone has to be depressing."

"You don't know the circumstances," he pointed out. "Blended families are hard to create. For all you know, she might have been the worst stepmother in the world."

"She might also have tried her best."

"That's true, but the point is you can't measure their experience against your frame of reference. Families like yours are more rare than you can imagine."

"I know. I keep telling myself that."

"As sweet as Dorothy seems now, she may have been a real shrew and those kids couldn't wait to leave. Abuse comes in many forms," he added soberly. "So don't judge them too harshly until you hear their side of the story."

"I've been telling myself that all afternoon, but you aren't going to be the one who tells Dorothy that her family doesn't care if she lives or dies."

"Don't take it personally," he told her. "You did what your patient asked and if her family doesn't respond, it isn't your fault. Your responsibility ended when you made contact. As they say, the ball is in their court."

"I know." She sighed as she met Cole's gaze. "It's just so *hard* not to try and fix what's broken."

"Yeah, but the trick is knowing what can be repaired and what can't."

She thought of his own family relationships. "What would you do if you got a call about your aunt? That she was sick and or dying and wanted to see you?"

"I'd like to think I'd be a bigger man and would meet her one last time," he mused, "but, honestly, I don't know what I'd do until I was faced with that situation. With all the bad feelings between us, I'd probably be just as disinterested as Dorothy's stepchildren are."

She'd suspected as much. Given the few stories he'd shared with her, she couldn't fault him for that decision. "I have to admit, the whole stepmother-stepchildren relationship is frightening."

"How so?"

"Of the three families I know with that sort of family dynamics—yours, Dorothy's and now ours with Brody—do you realize two of those situations turned out badly? Given those odds, what sort of chance do we have for success? Brody already thinks of me as the enemy. Will he eventually hate me, too? I don't want him to grow up so scarred that his future relationships suffer because of it."

There, she'd said it. She'd finally voiced the worry that had plagued her all afternoon. The idea of someday being alone to face a serious illness without family support sent a cold shudder down her spine.

"Sara," he chided gently, "you have nothing to fear. I can't speak for Dorothy, but you are not like my aunt by any stretch of the imagination."

"Yes, but maybe she'd tried to reach out to you, too, and you didn't realize—"

"I was old enough to see what my aunt was doing and I was also old enough to understand the vitriol she spewed at me for years as well as on the day I left. You, on the other hand, are as loving as any mother could possibly be."

"Brody might not agree with you," she said darkly.

"Of course he does. If he truly was afraid of you and hated you, he wouldn't try to push your buttons. He certainly wouldn't be happy sleeping beside you at night, but he is, so don't be so hard on yourself."

"It's hard not to," she admitted.

"Try," he ordered kindly. "My psychiatry skills are a little weak, but in my opinion he's only trying to decide if he can trust you to stick around. When he decides that you will, when he realizes that he can't push you away, he won't ever question your role in his life."

She wanted to believe him.

Cole threaded his arm around her waist. "You'll see I'm right. Just be patient."

Patience seemed to be the answer for everything. It was a word she was beginning to hate.

Two days later, Sara stopped by CCU during her lunch break to check on Dorothy. "Has any of her family come by or phoned to check on her?" she asked one of the nurses.

The other woman shook her head. "Not that I'm aware."

"Okay, thanks. How's she doing?"

"So-so. She's somewhat depressed, which isn't unusual in heart patients. The good news is that her tests don't show any residual damage. You may have her back on your floor in a day or two."

Pleased that Dorothy was doing well, physically at least, Sara wondered if her depression was partly due to her family's lack of interest. As Sara couldn't drag Dorothy's stepchildren to visit and she was certainly a poor substitute, she could at least pop in and let her know that someone cared.

"Thanks for stopping by, dearie," Dorothy said, looking far more frail than she had two days earlier. "I appreciate your concern."

"It's my pleasure," she said cheerfully. "I hear you're doing so well you might be back on our unit before long."

"So I hear," Dorothy said.

Sara talked of non-consequential things for a few more minutes, then, conscious of Dorothy's flagging energy, she left.

Back on her ward, she ran into Cole. "Where've you been?" he asked, sounding curious.

"I went to see Dorothy. Oh, Cole, it's so sad. I know she'd feel better if her children came to visit."

"You don't know that for certain," he countered.

"No, but it couldn't hurt," she insisted. "I wish there was something I could do…"

"Don't meddle in affairs you don't know anything about," he advised. "What if they came and were hateful toward her? Do you really think she needs that right now? Can you risk it?"

She hadn't considered they might be more of a hindrance than a help but, given their attitudes on the phone, it was entirely possible. As Cole had suggested, she couldn't risk upsetting Dorothy. "No, I can't."

Even so, there had to be something she could do…

The next afternoon, Sara was at home with a fussy Brody, trying to find ways to amuse him, when the phone rang.

"We had a cancellation for a three o'clock appointment,"

Eller's nurse told her. "Would you be interested in taking that spot instead of coming in on Friday?"

"You have the lab results already?" Sara asked, thrilled by the news.

"Yes, and Doctor would like to discuss them with you today, if you're free."

"We'll be there," she promised. Then, after disconnecting the call, she swung Brody around in her delight. "Did you hear that, buddy? They have my results. Oh, dear. We have to find a sitter, don't we? And I have to call your dad."

She dialed Cole's number, but he didn't answer, so she left a message. Then, knowing Millie was off duty today, she phoned her, and thankfully her friend agreed to watch Brody. With child care organized, she tried Cole's phone again. When he didn't answer this time, she called Georgia because he spent quite a bit of his time on her floor.

"He's really swamped today," the ward clerk told her, "but the next time I see him, I'll tell him you called."

Sara hated to go to her appointment without Cole, but what choice did she have? Waiting for an extra two days seemed like unnecessary punishment. Today patience wasn't a part of her vocabulary.

Cole read the text message on his phone and his heart sank. If only he'd read it earlier, but he'd been so busy that he hadn't heard the distinctive ring tone telling him he had a text.

Cancellation at Eller's office. Meet me there at three if you can.

It was four o'clock now, which meant that he'd missed the appointment. He hated knowing that Sara had gone with-out him because, whether she heard good news or bad, she'd have to deal with it alone when that was news best handled together.

He half expected her to come by the hospital, but she didn't.

When he tried to phone her, his call went straight to her voice mail.

He tried not to jump to conclusions, aware that not being able to reach her could mean anything, but he was quick to leave when his shift ended.

As he pulled into the driveway, the lights in the house were on and the Christmas lights hanging from the guttering twinkled as usual. He walked in, and found her sitting at the kitchen table, watching Brody chase his sliced hot dogs and macaroni across his plate.

"Sara," he said, "I'm so sorry I didn't get your message until it was too late. How did your appointment go?"

The minute she raised her head, he saw the red-rimmed eyes and he knew... "Tell me," he said.

"The test was abnormal," she said dully. "Not just a little abnormal, but a lot. My FSH was high."

"How high?"

"High enough that I won't ever have children of my own." She swiped at a single tear trailing down her cheek. "Gosh, I hate this. I've cried buckets all afternoon. You'd think I was cried out by now." She blew her nose for emphasis.

"Is he certain? Absolutely certain?"

"There isn't any doubt. I won't get pregnant on my own and I'm not even a candidate for IVF. According to Eller, my results are such that an IVF facility won't even consider me for the procedure. And if one would, chances are I'd have a low pregnancy success rate—about five percent. He also said that my poor egg quality may have been a factor in my miscarriage."

"Oh, Sara." He scooted a chair close enough so he could hug her. "I'm sorry. I know how much having a baby meant to you, but surely Josh suggested other options."

He had, but she'd been too numb to listen carefully. "He mentioned something about IVF with a donor egg."

"That's good news, isn't it?"

She stared at her husband. "But the baby wouldn't be *mine*."

"Then you won't consider the possibility? Is knowing Brody is my biological son and not yours that big a problem to you?"

"It's not a problem as such," she countered. "I wanted to give you something that no one else could, something that would be yours *and* mine. I wanted our kids to be *ours*."

"Then what are you saying?" he demanded. "If you can't have your own baby, you don't want to be *anyone's* mother?"

Was that what she wanted? "No," she said slowly. "It's just that I pinned my hopes on giving you a *part* of me, but I can't. Knowing that makes me feel so…" she searched for the right words "…inadequate. A failure."

"You are not inadequate *or* a failure." He spoke vehemently. "Absolutely do not say you are."

She met his gaze, her eyes wounded. "What would *you* call not being able to give you a son or a daughter? How would *you* describe it when I can't convince Brody to accept me as his mother? I couldn't even talk an old woman's step-children into visiting her after she suffered a heart attack. I those aren't failures, then I don't know what is.

"And to add insult to injury," she added, without giving him an opportunity to interrupt, "of all the health problems I could have had, mine is so elemental that it's part of being a female. And if I'm flawed in that area, then—"

"You are not flawed," he said fiercely. "So your body has a few issues. So Brody is slow at coming around and you couldn't break through three people's stubbornness. You're still a kind, thoughtful woman who has a heart bigger than she is.

"As for giving me something that no one else could, you already have," he said simply. "You've given me your love, your forgiveness and your understanding. Everything else is window dressing."

Touched by his comment, moisture trickled down her cheeks. "Thanks, but—"

"There's no buts about it," he said, moving in close to rest her forehead against his chin. "Those things mean more to me than you'll ever know or understand."

Cole sensed that he hadn't convinced her, probably because she was too mired in her own misery. She was grieving for her lost dreams and wouldn't hear what he had to say until she'd worked through the worst of her sorrow.

No matter. He'd repeat himself until she finally accepted his comments as truth.

The whole problem was that Sara needed to be needed. Even as a child, that had been evident, and recent events had raised those old doubts about her role in her family. It was up to him to convince her that the instances she'd named were simply rocky spots and not utter failures.

"Now," he said with mock consternation, "I want you to focus on all the things I told you—the positives and not the negatives—but the main thing I want you to dwell on is that I need you, Sara. You bring out the best in me. No one else can fill my empty places like you can."

"But, Brody—"

He cut her off. "A strand of thread is just that, a strand, and it's easily broken. However, two strands woven together make a cord that is stronger and more able to handle pressure. Together, we make that cord, Sara, the cord that's held together by mutual love and respect. Together, we'll be the best parents we can be to Brody, which means he needs *us*. Not us as individuals, but us as a team."

"You make it sound so simple."

"It is," he said. "Burdens shared are burdens halved."

For the next few hours, Sara moped. She tried to coun her blessings, to look at her situation through rose-colored glasses, but it was a constant battle.

As Brody became more recalcitrant and fussy, she won dered if she was only deluding herself that she had any moth ering genes in her at all. However, slowly, but surely, Cole' comments popped into her head periodically.

You are not inadequate or a failure.

You've already given me something that no one else has You've given me your love, your forgiveness and your under standing. Everything else is window dressing.

I need you, Sara... Together, we're whole.

Slowly, but surely, she accepted what she couldn't change What she had to do was focus on what she *did* have, and righ now she had a very crabby little boy on her hands.

By the next morning, Brody's cold hadn't improved. He' been running a mild fever and his nose was perpetually con gested in spite of her best efforts throughout the night to giv him relief. His dry cough had worsened, too, and the com bination had made him out of sorts, when he normally woke up bright-eyed and ready to greet the world. To make matter worse, he refused to eat or drink.

The thought of whooping cough occurred to her, but she didn't want to be one of those overreactive mothers who thought her child had caught every disease making the round at the time. After all, his records indicated that he only lacked the final booster which was given around age four, so the odd of that particular scenario were slim. Even so, she watched him carefully throughout the morning, monitoring each symptom and weighing it against the previous one.

Unfortunately, by midafternoon she still hadn't been abl

coax him to drink his favorite grape juice and he'd grown more listless than she'd ever seen him. After she checked his diaper and found it dry when it normally would have been soaked, she phoned his pediatrician.

"Bring him in," she was told. "We won't know if it's whooping cough without swabbing his nose and throat for culture."

So, with growing concern because he didn't fight the coat and hat routine as he normally did, Sara drove him to the doctor's office.

An hour later, after blood tests that revealed an elevated white blood count as well as dehydration, and an X-ray that—thank goodness—didn't show fluid in his lungs, she was on her way to the hospital, experiencing the inpatient process from the side of the consumer rather than the caregiver.

With a heavy heart, filled with remorse and self-recriminations, she carried Brody to the pediatric wing, accompanied by Amy, a forty-year-old pediatric nurse.

"Room 440 will be yours," Amy mentioned as she led her to the room in question. "There's a sofa that opens into a bed, as well as a rather comfortable recliner for you to use. If you'll have a seat, I'll get my supplies and we'll get the two of you organized."

As she left, Cole strode in, his face lined with worry. "I got your message. What's wrong?"

Relieved to see her husband, she sank onto the recliner with Brody in her arms. "Dr. Keller suspects whooping cough."

Cole stared at her. "You're kidding."

Sara shook her head. "I wish I was. She won't know for certain until the culture report comes back, but she's going to treat him as if that's the problem. The good news is that he doesn't have pneumonia. She would have sent us home with an antibiotic, but he's severely dehydrated and she wants him

on IV fluids. Oh, Cole…" Her eyes watered. "This is all m
fault."

"How so?"

"I've been so focused on me and my disappointments tha
I didn't notice how sick Brody had gotten. I should have—

"Stop berating yourself," he told her. "I saw him last nigh
too. If you're looking to blame someone, blame me. I'm th
physician in the house and I dismissed his symptoms, too."

Cole obviously considered himself as much at fault as sh
did. "Maybe we're both being too hard on ourselves," she ad
mitted. "I really didn't notice a change until this morning an
then he seemed to go downhill as the day progressed."

"Thank goodness you were alert," he said fervently. "I
he does have whooping cough, he'll get antibiotics before h
has a chance to develop a secondary infection."

Brody opened his eyes at the sound of Cole's voice, bu
didn't raise his head off Sara's shoulder. Cole stroked hi
son's baby-fine hair with a shaky hand. "Hey, big fella," h
crooned. "Aren't you feeling good today?"

Brody's smile was halfhearted and he closed his eyes a
if too exhausted to pay attention.

Cole's phone beeped. With movements suggesting frustra
tion, he checked the message and mumbled a curse. "I can'
stay," he said flatly. "There's a patient—"

Although she wanted Cole with her, his other obligation
came first. She offered a tremulous smile. "It's okay. There'
no point in both of us watching Brody sleep."

He frowned, then nodded, his expression resigned. "I'l
come back when I can."

"We'll be here."

"Call if anything changes," he ordered.

"I will." With Cole gone, Sara felt the need to do *some
thing,* so she helped Amy, the peds nurse, settle Brody int
bed. As he was already wearing his footed pajamas, they onl

had to remove his coat. The worst part came when it was time to start his IV.

"Some of the medical staff want to do the honors themselves when it comes to their own children, but I wouldn't recommend it," Amy said somewhat apologetically. "Right now, he needs to associate you with comfort, not pain."

Sara hadn't considered taking on that task at all and if she had, she would have dismissed the idea immediately. "That's okay. My hands aren't steady enough right now to hit anything smaller than the Alaskan pipeline."

It was a testament to both the nurse's skill and the severity of Brody's illness that he merely flinched when Amy inserted the needle. Afterward, he refused to lie in the strange crib with the tent over it.

"I'll hold him for a while," Sara offered.

"That might be best. Meanwhile, I'll start the vaporizer, which should help soothe his lungs and loosen the respiratory secretions. Although he's getting plenty of fluids now, try to convince him to drink on his own."

"I will."

For the rest of the afternoon Sara held Brody in her lap, mentally willing his health to improve. As she stroked the hair off his hot forehead and heard a couple of carolers in the background, she wondered when Brody had wiggled his way into her heart. As much as she'd resented his origins, now they no longer mattered. He was theirs to nurture and protect, much like another baby had needed nurturing and protecting some two thousand years ago—the same baby who'd eventually become responsible for the Christmas season.

She dozed herself, not realizing the late hour until Cole strode in after his shift had ended, minus his lab coat and tie.

"I'll take him," he said, reaching for Brody. "You need a break."

Although she knew he was right, she handed over the little boy reluctantly. She helped herself to the Popsicles in the ward's kitchenette and watched as Cole painstakingly urged him to eat. After Brody had nibbled away half of it, he closed his eyes and fell asleep again.

"Why don't you go home and rest?" Cole suggested. "I'll stay with him."

She started to protest, realizing she sounded like Mrs. Berton and so many other mothers whose children were in the hospital.

No, that wasn't right. She didn't just *sound* like a mother. She *felt* like one. And if she felt like one, she needed to *act* like one. Mothers did not leave their children.

"Just for a while," Cole coaxed, as if he understood the reason for her hesitation. "An hour or two is all."

An hour. She could do that, even though she really didn't want to go. "Okay."

"Good. Oh, and when you come back, bring something I can lounge in, will you?"

"You're staying, too?"

He nodded. "What would I do in an empty house by myself?"

What indeed? "Do you want dress clothes for tomorrow?" she asked.

He nodded. "I can shower and change in the doctors' lounge before I go on duty."

"I'll be back soon," she promised.

At home, she showered, changed clothes and threw Cole's things into a duffel bag. As she headed out of their bedroom, Ruth's letter caught her eye.

I'm sorry Brody got so ill, she silently murmured. *I should have been paying closer attention.*

But if you had, a little voice asked, *what would you have done?*

The question brought her up short. As a medical professional, she knew doctors didn't intervene just because a child developed a cough or a cold. Even if she'd taken Brody to the doctor yesterday, chances were they would have been sent home to try the home remedies she'd done on her own. Instead of blaming herself, she should do as Cole had suggested. She should be grateful she'd noticed a change when she had.

She would, she vowed. Then, as she took another step forward, her little voice spoke again.

Read the letter.

This isn't the right time, she told herself. She was on her way back to the hospital. Besides, with the disappointments and trials of the past few days, not to mention her struggle with feelings of inadequacy, did she really want to read a message from a dead woman now?

And yet would there *ever* be a good time to hear Ruth's last words?

CHAPTER TEN

UNDECIDED about the wisdom of her actions or her timing, Sara hefted the envelope in her hand. But as she debated, she realized she was tired of having the letter's contents hanging over her head like an ax about to fall. It was now or never.

She dropped the duffel bag onto the floor, sat on the edge of the bed and after a deep breath carefully slid one finger under the sealed flap.

Dear Sara,

If you're reading this, it means that I'm asking a favor of you that I never wanted or planned to ask. I know you must be devastated at the news that Cole is my son's father, but forgive me when I say our choices that night eventually led to the best thing that ever happened to me. I have nothing but the utmost respect for your husband and the few pleasant memories I have of my youth always included Cole.

For what it's worth, Cole could only talk about you during the time we were together. It won't be easy for you to forgive him or me, but for Cole's sake and the sake of his son, I hope you will. You see, the people we really needed weren't there that weekend and conse-

quently we turned to each other, not realizing we would hurt the very ones we loved.

If you're reading this letter, it means I'm not a part of my son's life, which saddens me a great deal. However, I won't regret that Cole could be Brody's father, should you allow him to fill that role. There are many people who would gladly take on this responsibility, but you and Cole are the only ones I'd choose. Cole is a special man—I knew he would be even when we were teenagers—and if he chose you to be his wife, then I know you are just as special. Because of that, and because I believe Brody will need both of you to help him become the kind, caring man I want him to be, I'm asking you to open your heart and let him inside. As wonderful and as strong as your husband is, he can't accomplish this job alone. You, Sara, are the one who has softened Cole's rough edges during the time you've been together and I trust you'll produce the same results with his son. From what Cole has said, I have utmost faith in you.

Time is so short and our lives so fleeting that I hope you'll not only tell Brody every day that I loved him, but that he'll experience a mother's love from you on my behalf. He's the best of both Cole and me, but he's more than that. He's a clean slate, waiting for you— Sara noted the word was underlined—*to write beautiful things on it.*

Someday, perhaps before too much time has passed, you'll have forgiven both of us for the pain we've caused and you'll think on me with fondness.

Sincerely,
Ruth

Sara brushed away the tears on her cheeks. At this moment, she certainly didn't feel like the right woman for the job Ruth had given her, but for all of her faults, flaws and failures, she was the one who was available.

Lost in her thoughts, she returned to the hospital, where she found Brody nestled against Cole as the two men in her life dozed. As she gazed at father and son, love welled up inside her until she thought she might burst. Brody might not share her genetic makeup, but love and acceptance had made him her son, too. Although she'd never implied otherwise, it was an earth-shattering revelation to her and she couldn't wait to share with her husband.

Cole didn't know what startled him awake, but he opened his eyes and saw Sara sitting on the sofa, paging through a magazine. Who would have thought that holding Brody would have made him stiff and sore?

"Have I been sleeping long?" he asked.

She chuckled. "Define long. I've been here for the past hour."

"That's long. What have you been doing?"

"Reading. Making phone calls."

"Phone calls? To your parents?" he guessed.

"And to Dorothy's stepchildren. This time I didn't hold back."

"Oh, my. They won't issue a complaint against you, will they?"

"No, because I didn't call as Dorothy's nurse. I called as her friend. I told them that this was Christmas and surely they could give Dorothy a chance to make amends."

"Will they?"

She shrugged. "Who knows? If my stirring speech doesn't soften their hearts, then she's better off without them."

"My wife, the crusader." He stirred, shifting Brody in his
p. "He's really a bag of bones, isn't he?"

"Want me to take him?" She dropped her magazine on the
at cushion and rose.

"Let's see how he does in his bed."

Carefully, they maneuvered him into the toddler-size crib.
'hen he didn't stir, merely let out a sigh, they breathed their
wn sighs of relief.

"Have you had dinner?"

"No." She shook her head. "I brought you a sandwich,
ough. Ham on rye with extra mustard, just the way you
ke it."

"Thanks."

As he dug into his food, he watched Sara gaze at Brody.
e couldn't define it, but something about her had changed.
he seemed more at peace than ever before.

"I am," she admitted when he remarked on it. "Sitting
ith Brody here in the hospital, worrying about him, made
e feel like his mother for the first time."

He grinned. "It took you long enough to figure it out."

"Afraid so. Anyway, I finally realized the biology doesn't
atter. Anyone can become a parent, but it's the *parenting*
at's most important."

"Wasn't that what I said all along?"

"Yeah, well, I had to figure that out for myself. Afterward,
read Ruth's letter."

"And?"

"She must have been a remarkable woman," she said sim-
y. "I want to help him become the son she'd be proud of."

For all of Sara's efforts, he'd sensed she'd been holding
ck a part of herself, but now it was as if she'd finally made
firm commitment to the task of raising Brody. He wanted
shout his happiness, but the noise would create a furor on

the ward and bring down everyone from code-blue teams
security personnel.

Instead, he abandoned his food and rose to take her into h
arms. "You are, without a doubt, the most fantastic woma
in the world. I love you."

She grinned. "You are the most fantastic man. And I lov
you, too, Cole Wittman."

As if on cue, Brody began to fuss. Cole went to the cr
and while Sara unlatched and lowered the rail, he reached
to pick him up. To his surprise, Brody shook his head. H
said one word as he held out his arms toward Sara.

"Mama."

His wife's eyes immediately filled with tears as she too
their son into her embrace. He couldn't imagine a better gi
he could have given her on this Christmas Eve.

Christmas Eve, four years later

"Mama," Brody bellowed at the top of his lungs as he e
tered the kitchen, where tins of Christmas cookies cover
the counter and the air smelled of apples, cranberries an
cinnamon. "We're home."

Sara smiled as she greeted him with a smile and a hug th
wasn't easy with her growing belly in the way. "I see that
she said softly. "But can you please use your inside voic
Alison is sleeping."

Alison was their two-year-old daughter, thanks to th
efforts of IVF and a donor egg. She had her daddy's brow
eyes and a cute little nose that obviously came from h
genetic mother, but she was what Cole affectionately call
"her mama's girl."

If all went well, their new son would arrive in Februar
also courtesy of the same medical technology that had broug
them Alison.

"Sorry," her son said, lowering his voice. "What time will Grandma and Grandpa get here?"

"Anytime now," Sara answered.

"I'm gonna watch for them." He raced off just as Cole walked in, his cheeks as rosy as his son's from the cold.

"Where's he going so fast?"

"To the living room and his lookout post. My folks should arrive any minute," she reminded him, "and you know Brody. He has to be the first one to spot them."

He snagged a celery stick from the vegetable tray on the counter. "Alison?"

"She's sleeping."

Cole grinned as he threaded his arms around what once had been her waist. "Then we're alone?"

"For the moment, yes."

"And Junior's behaving himself?"

She rubbed the bump in front of her. "He's quiet right now."

"Good, because I want to kiss my wife in private."

In the background, Sara heard Brody squeal with excitement. "You'd better hurry because we're about to get company," she warned.

"Now, Sara. Some things are simply not meant to be rushed."

Sara smiled at her husband. "I couldn't agree more."

* * * * *